PRAISE FOR THE NOVELS OF

JOEY W. HILL

"I can't tell you how impressed I am with Hill's books. Okay, hotter than hell, yes, but Hill manages to do more than that. She doesn't repeat herself even after such a big backlist, and somehow she manages to say something with her books . . . She loves her characters and treats them with respect. This is one hell of a writer."

—Angela Knight, *New York Times* bestselling author

"Joey W. Hill is one of the best authors of erotica for a reason—her exceptional ability to bring together complex characters along with gripping romances that revolve around the world of BDSM . . . When Ms. Hill writes a love scene she brings all of the senses to life."

—*Risqué Reviews*

"This is a scorcher! It's one of those books that keeps the sexual tension on superstrength and leave you squirming for a resolution."

—*The Forbidden Bookshelf*

"Joey W. Hill blends the erotic and emotional perfectly . . . providing readers with a gorgeous romance."

—*Joyfully Reviewed*

"Joey W. Hill's books are nigh on impossible to define as each has to be read for itself and each offers the reader something uniquely theirs to relate to. Not only are they great books, they also pick at your soul."

—*TwoLips Reviews*

continued . . .

UNRESTRAINED

JOEY W. HILL

HEAT | NEW YORK

HEAT

An imprint of Penguin Random House LLC
375 Hudson Street, New York, New York 10014

This book is an original publication of Penguin Random House LLC.

Library of Congress Cataloging-in-Publication Data

Hill, Joey W.
Unrestrained / Joey W. Hill. — Heat trade paperback edition.
pages cm
ISBN 978-0-425-26068-5
I. Title.
PS3608.I4343U57 2014
813'.6—dc23
2013016046

PUBLISHING HISTORY
Heat trade paperback edition / December 2013

PRINTED IN THE UNITED STATES OF AMERICA

11 10 9 8 7 6 5 4 3 2

Cover photograph: Getty.
Cover design by George Long.
Text design by Laura K. Corless.

Penguin
Random
House

ACKNOWLEDGMENTS

It's impossible to write a book where a SEAL is the hero without researching and attempting to understand the remarkable qualities these individuals have to possess to do what they do. Dale being a retired SEAL didn't change that a bit; if anything, my research made it clear that being a SEAL is a state of mind, more of a calling than an occupation.

So my great thanks to Lynn and Lauren for their contacts, guidance and research assistance on this part of the book. The military is a vast subculture, with so many details to get wrong when writing about them. I respect those in the armed forces greatly, and wanted to portray Dale accurately. I am grateful to Lynn and Lauren for helping me do that. Since Lauren indicated she "really, *really* loved it" when I inflicted the whole manuscript upon her for a beta read, I hope that reflects success (laughter).

Another vital part of the book was addressing the daily challenges of being an amputee. As a person fortunate enough to have two whole legs, I couldn't anticipate all the things this affects, like taking a shower, picking up someone to carry them—even the way a person takes off or puts on clothes (an important issue in an erotic romance—grin). So I extend my deepest gratitude to Sue for her personal insights on all these matters, large and small. She endured phone calls that were like mini-interrogation sessions and also beta read the whole thing for me to ensure I didn't miss anything. Thank you, Sue! (BTW: I put in the brownie comment just for you.) I also thank Lynn and Lauren for checking with their military/veteran contacts on this, particularly issues related to benefits, et cetera.

A final quick note: One of the research sources Lynn provided me was former Navy SEAL Marcus Luttrell's amazing book *Service*. Dale's "boat story" is a modified version of a true incident in Mr. Luttrell's book. Though that book and my other SEAL resources gave me so much information that developed Dale's overall personality, I wished to acknowledge my thanks for that specific example to demonstrate how they handle the difficult things they do.

As always, any errors I've made on any of the above or other details are entirely my fault, and I thank all of these folks and sources, as well as my usual beta readers and Berkley editing team, for helping to make this a far better book than it would be without them. If I've missed anyone, please forgive the oversight. An author never does it alone!

ONE

The first time she stepped into a BDSM club, it felt like home. *Surprised* wasn't the right word for her reaction. Surprise was what one felt toward a party thrown in one's honor, planned on the sly by someone else. When she stepped into that dim environment, inhaled the intangible layers of want and need intertwined with the surface scents of tears and sweat, perfume and leather, her unconscious revealed the secret it had kept for so long. This was where she belonged. It rose up into her chest, an unexpected comfort and validation. Ironic, given that she hadn't been there for herself. Not essentially.

Roy had talked her into giving it a try. He wanted to take the play they did in the privacy of their home into a discreet but more populated world. It had mattered to him, so she'd prepared herself to accept it, no matter how sordid it might end up being.

Everyone knew New Orleans had a seedy side. No one bothered to call it an "underside," since it was broadly displayed in the French Quarter at all hours of the day, and it had worsened since Katrina, when more of the city's criminal element shifted into that section. But then she found there was an actual underworld, and the darkness there was heated, welcoming. Not seedy at all. The perspiration gleaming on marked skin, the cries of pleasure and pain, the glitter of eyes in the dim light, the energy that pulsed in Club Release like its own power source . . . it reminded her of what she'd felt in some of the old churches in the city.

That connection had come much later, when Roy got sick.

Occasionally there would be things at the company she had to handle in person, so she'd leave him with his nurse for the bare minimum time necessary. One day, on the way back home, she obeyed an impulse driven by simple weariness of spirit and allowed herself a fifteen-minute detour into a small Catholic church. It had a trio of archways beckoning the faithful, and the smell of stone and wood over a hundred years old. She'd sat in the sanctuary, stilling her mind, letting everything go for those precious few moments. She realized the ambiance that compelled hushed voices, a still soul, was like what she felt in the club. There was also euphoria, a contained joy, the best kind to feel. Things always felt more intense when restrained. She'd seen it in how Roy reacted to it, though she'd never experienced it firsthand.

Though she didn't share why she'd stopped at the church, not wanting him to worry about her, she'd shared that comparison with Roy. He smiled at her, nodded, his eyes still bright in the gaunt face. They remained bright until the last few days, when he slipped into that pre-death, morphine coma so common to cancer patients. At the end, she'd whispered in his ear, commanded him to let go. She told him that she'd be all right, that his Mistress would always love him. He would like her putting it in those terms, she knew. So his Mistress let him go, even as his wife sat at his bedside, clutching his hand, the loneliness closing around her when his breath stopped and he obeyed her.

"Want another one?"

She returned to the present and Jimmy, who ran the bar at Club Release. He'd drawn her back out of herself. Since it was a private club run as a nonprofit membership group, they didn't serve alcohol, but they had a good selection of drinks, everything from chili pepper cocoa to lemonade or O'Doul's. He gave her glass a significant glance. "I can top that to two-thirds, Lady Mistress, so you can slip in a little more of that vodka you don't think I'm seeing."

She gave him a faint smile. "My sleight of hand's out of practice."

"Naw. You just know that I already know. And you're sad tonight." He hesitated, put his hand on the bar next to hers, no contact, but the offer of connection was there. "You know, it's been over two years. Dillon and Seth are easygoing, gentle subs. Either one of them would help you break the dry spell. It's no different for us than it is for a vanilla person going on that first date. It might even be a little easier, because they saw you work with Roy and know how you operate. You can tell me 'shut up, bitch' if I'm way off base, but I can't help but feel you're looking for something."

"Maybe. I'll think about it." It wasn't the first time he'd suggested it, though he hadn't been as blunt in the past. It also wasn't the first time she'd given that noncommittal response.

When she started coming back here, a few months ago, they'd let her lack of participation pass without comment. They'd known her and Roy in a way no one else did, which meant Club Release offered a unique type of sanctuary. However, not only was she no longer playing, she was hardly watching when she showed up. She just closed her eyes and listened, using the club's sounds as the soundtrack to her own personal memory reel. It was bound to invite more pointed comments after a while. Sometimes it could be a pain in the ass, people knowing certain parts of you too well . . . and other parts not at all.

Yes, she'd felt at home here, with Roy. But it was as if she'd lost weight and the mirror showed a core version of herself that other layers had disguised. It made her think it was time to put down the whip and do something different. Be on the other side of the whip. Craving the lash, the pain . . . the release.

The first time that thought crystallized in her mind's eye, refusing to be shrouded, it had startled her. She wasn't used to analyzing and thinking about herself in a solitary way. It was always in relation to something else, someone else. Roy, first and foremost, and then a hundred others lined up after him. Family members, the community, business.

Though this was when she normally would pay her tab and go home, she didn't want Jimmy to pry further, so she would make an effort. She rose, picking up her drink, and wandered into the Fortress of Solitude. In this section of the club, no talking was allowed. A safe gesture replaced a safe word, and submissives were gagged. Their bodies, eyes, and faces broadcast what was happening to them. A Master or Mistress ordered them through touch: a hand on their shoulder to guide them to a restraint, a tug of the leash, a pressure to put them on their hands and knees. It was a good place to avoid conversation.

With it being Tuesday night, she'd hoped no one would be in there, that the few members in attendance had gravitated toward the more social rooms, which also had more popular equipment. Her hopes were short-lived.

At least it was only one couple, a Master and his female sub. She didn't recognize the Dom, but she hadn't been to the club in over a month, too busy with other things. He wore a black eyemask and bandanna knotted at his nape. Together, they hid all of his features except his mouth, the line of his jaw. He wore tight black gloves.

Practitioners of BDSM came from all walks of life, many of them average Janes and Joes whose unremarkable facets became polished gems when their true natures sparkled in these rooms. She'd seen it happen with lean Goths, bikers, comfortable middle-class types, military, and then those like her. Her infallibly ladylike demeanor, the old Southern money roots she couldn't and wouldn't try to conceal, had earned her the nickname Jimmy had spoken tonight. Lady Mistress.

Despite the diverse club population, she was fairly certain she'd never seen a Master quite like this one. Unless it was in one of the confusing, erotic dreams that had been teasing the edges of her sleep of late, dreams she didn't feel comfortable sharing even in this venue. Perhaps especially in this venue.

She'd handled fund-raising for the USO charity ball three years running. During that time, she'd become friendly with a variety of military wives. One night she and Roy had the pleasure of hosting a dinner party for them and their spouses. Several of the husbands were Navy SEALs. She'd noted a unique stamp to the way they carried themselves, the look in their eyes. On top of that, each had an impressive physique. It was understandable since, in the SEALs, the body was pushed to the max in terms of endurance, speed and strength. One of the wives told Athena that many of the men, even those who'd never been injured, ended up requiring some disability benefits by the end of their career, due to the punishing demands on joints, muscles, skeletal system.

"They never quit. They just go until the body is completely worn out." The wife had said it half jokingly, though her eyes had followed her husband with that combination of fierce love and quiet acceptance military wives had to possess for the marriage to last.

This Master had that unique stamp to him. If Athena was right and he was a SEAL, he definitely wasn't at that worn-out point. The black jeans and unmarked black T-shirt defined a body that said he was capable of pretty much any physical demand. She wondered at his age, his hair color. He wore silver-tipped cowboy boots. There was no other ornamentation on him. His concentration was on the woman dependent on his mercy.

If it wasn't a Tuesday, with such sparse attendance, she expected he would have had far more of an audience, but maybe that was why he preferred a quiet weeknight. Maybe he considered her as much of an intrusion as she'd initially considered him. But though Athena sensed his awareness of her presence, he didn't seem distracted by it.

Willow, his submissive, was a regular at the club, one who craved heavy punishment from a Master, hence the pseudonym. A willow bent under any punishment, but didn't break. She was tied spread eagle to an upright metal frame. This room had several frames like that, as well as a pegboard of whips, floggers, paddles, thumpers and uncomplicated restraint options. The Fortress of Solitude tended to attract those who preferred to use the basics and let psychological domination do the rest.

At the moment, this Master was utterly still. He held a cane in one large hand, the end resting in the half-curled palm of the other, while his gaze coursed over his captive's body. Willow was stripped to the skin, which would be a viewing pleasure for anyone watching, but his body language said that was irrelevant to him. Even more importantly, it told Willow she was stripped for his pleasure alone.

He stood with feet evenly braced, T-shirt pulling across his shoulders and chest, his ass and thigh muscles taut beneath the mold of the denim. The tilt of his head, as if he was listening to something no one else could hear, made the rule of silence not a guideline, but a mandate that would incur punishment if broken. Athena wet her lips.

His profile could have been etched from granite, his jaw looked that resilient. She wanted to see the rest of his face. She thought he'd be dark haired, because the scattering of hair on his arms was dark, and his five-o'clock shadow was a blue-black that made a woman think of pirates. Since the shadowing in the room made it impossible to determine his eye color, she imagined them as green, then brown or blue. A dark blue, like a cold ocean, hiding pleasures and dangers both.

He moved then, sweeping the cane across Willow's buttocks, a strike across the widest part. She jerked, biting down on the gag. He did it again, creating an X, and then kept doing it, focusing on her ass and upper thighs.

The girl was a pale-skinned, white-haired blonde with a soft, pretty body. She had the tattoo of a rose on the back of her shoulder, the thorny stem winding its way around her shoulder blade and to the front. When she twisted in pain, reacting to the cane, Athena glimpsed the rest of the tattoo. The stem ended at her left nipple, which was pierced with a barbed barbell.

He stopped. The girl panted behind her gag, her fingers opening and closing in the cuffs that held her to the frame. She wore a blindfold, but Athena saw the tears that had trickled down to the corners of her mouth. Her body was shuddering. Athena's stomach was quivering in response, a sympathetic tingle in her thighs and buttocks where she had them pressed against the wall. She could sit down on the couch in the corner, but she preferred to be here, part of the ungiving and cool cinder block wall.

The masked man planted a boot between Willow's spread feet. Caressing her biceps, he slid a gloved hand over the tender bend of her elbow before he dropped his touch to her hip. Willow's head turned toward him, the attitude of her body one of yearning, desire for his attention. Wanting to please him.

Was he a consistent sadist, or had he tailored his skill set to Willow's need for pain? He might be the type of Dom who chose a different sub on each visit, enjoying the challenge of exploring various techniques, anticipating the needs of different playmates. Even so, he'd have a personal preference; most Doms did. Athena wondered what it was, wondered what it would be like to be bound to him uniquely, such that he would reveal his own desires and let her be the willing recipient of serving them.

"Her" meaning a special sub, bound to this faceless Master. She didn't mean herself, of course, except in the comfort of her fantasies.

Subs had their own preferences as well. Roy had liked the psychology of being dominated and enjoyed some pain to reinforce it, but the restraints, the sense of helplessness, that was what he truly needed.

Willow shuddered in the man's grip. From the slackness of her mouth, the jerky movements of her body, as well as the flushed look of her swollen clitoris, she was soaring. Teetering on the edge of climax, caught in mindless submission, the state a Dom loved to see.

He put his mouth against her ear. Speaking was permitted if the Master or sub had a safety issue to clarify. He spoke so softly, however, that Athena couldn't hear him. Willow did, her trembling increasing. She shook her head, a whimper escaping her. Though the sound was muffled by the gag, he gave her marked ass a sharp smack, and she stilled, obeying the rules. His touch now became more gentle, though his tone increased enough that Athena caught the rumble. He had a deep voice. She found that pleasing, soothing. Apparently, so did Willow. The girl nodded at last, more tears leaking out from under the blindfold. *Anything for you*, her body language said. *I will give you anything. I will fly for you.*

Athena swallowed.

The man moved back, switching out the cane for a six-foot single tail. It took considerable skill to wield one well, but Athena had no doubt he had that skill. When he assumed the proper stance, it was as if the room bent inward toward him like one of the Matrix movies, responding to his focus. Athena was a peripheral, no different from the wall itself. Everything for him would be about Willow's reactions, monitoring them, making sure this went where Master and sub both desired, until it became organic, a spiral where intuition was guiding every action and reaction.

Willow cried out at the pop on her tender flesh. No help for that, and why the sub wore a gag, in case she couldn't hold back involuntary noises. Club Release allowed bloodplay, but Willow's unbroken yet abraded flesh said she preferred the pain but not the injury, and he gave her the former in good measure. As she yanked against the bonds, the pain overcame her control, and she was screaming against the gag with every stinging strike.

Athena closed her eyes, imagining being where Willow stood, feeling that lash. Could such pure agony purge deeper, more emotional pain, bring it all to the surface, let it bleed out, boil forth like a pus? The idea mesmerized her, held her paralyzed against the wall, caught up in the sounds, the tears, the miasma of Domination and surrender.

When Willow went silent, except for more whimpering, Athena

brought herself back, though it was like pulling herself out of a womb. The man put the whip aside, came back to Willow.

He gripped her hair, yanked her head back as he slid his hand down her front, covered her clit and labia and began to massage. Two of his fingers pushed inside her wet pussy as his thumb worked her outside. Willow struggled, wailed, and then she came. Athena shifted to the other wall so she could see the girl's climax spurt over his gloved fingers. Her gaze latched onto his forearm, pressed against Willow's abdomen, and she thought about the heat of that arm against her own flesh.

He didn't stop when Willow was done, continuing until she was squirming in discomfort. He gave her another disciplinary smack, forcing her to accept her Master's will in motionless agony, his manipulation of the oversensitized nerves. By the time he chose to stop, she would have been in a puddle on the floor, had her restraints and the arm he had around her waist not been holding her up. He removed his other glove by pulling at the fingers with his teeth, then shook it loose so it dropped to the floor. Stroking her hair with the bare hand, he bent to press a kiss to the crown of her head.

The glove had landed three feet away from Athena. She stared at it as he performed aftercare for his sub. It was a vital process that gave emotional reassurance to Willow, told her she'd done well, that she'd pleased her Master. It also physically grounded her, since a sub could be so disoriented right after an intense session like this that she couldn't even be trusted to walk unaided.

After she'd punished Roy over a spanking bench with a paddle or flogger until he climaxed, Athena would make him stretch out fully on the bench. She'd bring him back down to earth with a slow massage of his broad shoulders and back, his firm buttocks.

Setting her drink on a shelf, she bent to pick up the glove. She told herself she did it so it wouldn't be in the way, so that the Master wouldn't step on it, but as she held it, she couldn't resist slipping it over her hand. The glove had retained the heat of his body. She imagined how it had emanated through the thin outer layer, adding to the burn as he slapped Willow's ass.

The man straightened and looked over his shoulder at her. The SEALs at her dinner party had registered the slightest shift of the other guests in the same way, particularly at the entry and exit points, or if a guest made an unexpected movement, as she'd just done. Now his gaze fell on her hand, covered in his glove.

Her cheeks flushed, but rather than prompting her to pull it off, his look made her fingers curl over it. Vaguely, she thought she should apologize, because she might be disrupting his session, but speaking wasn't allowed. Plus, she wasn't sure if she'd offended him. His body language gave nothing away. The dim light obscured his gaze, but she wondered if she was right, if his eyes were dark blue. Or maybe hazel, that intriguing gray-gold-green color.

At some point, she wasn't simply meeting his gaze; she was caught in it. Wishes, inarticulate needs, things so contained she wasn't sure she could move for fear of eruption, seemed to rise up to a perilous level inside her. She wanted to tell him something, tell him everything, but she had no idea what. Or even how to start.

Some shocking part of her wanted to sink to her knees, wait until his other gloved hand touched her face, lifted her chin. He'd command her to take Willow's place on the frame and send her soaring as well.

Jimmy's jaw would drop at that, for sure.

Retrieving her drink, she turned away, leaving the room. Aftercare was personal, intimate. It had been her favorite part of the sessions with Roy. Even though this Master and Willow were in a public club environment, Athena didn't have a desire to intrude on that. It made too many things hurt.

It wasn't until she'd left the room that she realized she was still wearing the glove. She took it off, left it on a drink table next to the archway leading into the Fortress, where he'd be sure to find it.

She had to suppress a strong urge to keep it. She wanted to sleep with it on her pillow, her cheek against it. She wanted to put it back on her hand, rub it between her legs the way he'd massaged Willow, and imagine him whispering in her ear. *Come for me.*

When she put her cup on the bar, Jimmy gave her a knowing look. "The new guy's something, isn't he? He's been really popular with the lowercase ladies."

Athena offered a faint smile at his reference to female submissives. When submissives wrote their names on the guest logs, most of them, even those who used their actual first names, wrote them in lowercase. Willow would be *willow.* Only Masters and Mistresses had capitalized names.

"He won't play with men?"

"No. To the eternal disappointment of those of us with bi or queer tendencies." Jimmy winked. He was bisexual and a switch on top of that, though she knew his preference was submissive. "But I'm not sure I'd call what he does play. He goes at it with a singular intensity, like he's performing a religious rite. You hear about that happening, but rarely see it in action. Not to the level he does it. You should come in one night, see him do it from beginning to end. The way he prepares himself, lays out what he'll use. That's why we've taken to calling him Master Craftsman—MC. He said he thought we were comparing him to a Sears department store. Solid quality but something most folks sadly consider outdated. That part didn't seem to bother him. In fact, I think he took it as a compliment."

Jimmy flashed a grin. "Oh, and on the straight versus gay thing, he told me he doesn't mind watching some Mistress-girl action."

Athena made a wry face. "That's every straight man's fantasy, Jimmy. You know that."

"Yeah. Isn't it peculiar, how many religions get worked up over two guys going at it, but they don't say diddly about two women?"

"Just proves men wrote religious texts."

"No argument there." Jimmy chuckled. "I bet MC would have enjoyed the heck out of that thing you orchestrated for Roy's last birthday."

She'd put Roy on that same frame that Willow was on now. She'd wrapped his arms, legs and torso with multiple bindings so that he could barely move. Then she lay down on a divan several feet in front of him. Marsha, a submissive who liked being commanded to do oral on men or women, had lent Athena her services that night. She'd put her soft lips between Athena's legs, curled her pretty hands around her thighs and brought Athena to climax while Roy watched. When she was done, Athena ordered Marsha on her knees in front of Roy to service him the same way while Athena watched, standing behind her. After she'd given him permission to come, Roy had gushed into the cherry-chocolate flavored condom Marsha was sucking.

Marsha had been thanked and dismissed, and then Athena had shifted behind him, laid her cheek on Roy's back. Listening to his breath go in and out, absorbing the shudder of his body through her own, she'd been captivated by what she'd done to him. He'd been hers, but she'd been his, too. Had he realized that? She missed having a man look at her with pure ownership in his eyes. Very much.

"I'm calling it a night, Jimmy. Thanks for the drink."

"Sure thing. Don't stay away so long next time. And hey . . . I mean, if Dillon and Seth don't interest you, I'm another option. Just give me a heads-up and I'll make sure I'm not on shift here."

"Thanks, I appreciate that. You're a good friend." The sudden flash of male interest made her uncomfortable, however. Perhaps sensing it, he waved his hand dismissively. "I'm a guy, Lady Mistress. You know it's a selfish offer. A lot of us would love to experience what Roy did. You're an amazing Domme."

How would he react if he knew she wanted to go to her knees for a Dom she'd just seen for the first time? Jimmy's innocuous and honest proposal made her want to flee. Not wishing to hurt his feelings, she gave him a distant smile, shaking her head to deflect the compliment, then took her leave.

The club was on the second level of a warehouse in an industrial area, so she took a set of stairs down to the first level. They had a volunteer at a table just inside the entrance door. He served as an informal security guard, keeping an eye on the cars in the parking lot. She nodded to him, pushing open the door.

Her dark blue BMW was close to the entrance, and she unlocked it, slipped in behind the wheel, closed the door. Embracing that personal cocoon, a haven from questions and the outside world, she tried to shrug off her confusing emotions. Jimmy's suggestion had stabbed something down deep inside her. Something that rose up with astonishing firmness and proclaimed *never again*. She'd been a Mistress to Roy alone.

Yet she wasn't done with this, was she? The sense that she belonged in this world kept drawing her back. She just didn't know how to change her role in it, or if she really wanted to change, or if she was just confused. Sometimes the simplest thing was best. Perhaps it was time to cut it out of her life. Bury it as she had her husband. Metaphorically, since he was cremated.

When she keyed the ignition, she saw she had less than a quarter tank of gas left. Enough to get home, but tomorrow she'd be heading to the Garden Club meeting, so it would be more convenient to get gas tonight. She should have thought about it earlier, but lately she'd been more forgetful about those kinds of things. Suppressing a sigh, she glanced across the street. There was a twenty-four-hour, credit-card-only station there. Despite the late hour, since she was across from the club entrance, it should be safe enough to put in a few gallons.

She cut across the quiet street. After she processed her credit card and inserted the pump into the BMW to start fueling, an old Cadillac pulled into the aisle across from hers. The two men driving didn't look particularly reputable, but in New Orleans, that didn't necessarily signify danger.

She was merely annoyed, not alarmed, when the driver approached her. He was probably going to try and bum a few dollars off of her. As she unhooked the gas pump from her tank, put it back in its slot, the other man emerged from the Caddy, circled around to the other side of her car.

In hindsight, she knew she should have jumped in the car at the first sight of them, locked the doors and laid down on the horn. The club volunteer was at the proper angle to view the parking lot, but he wouldn't be looking toward the gas station unless something drew his attention there, like a blaring horn. It might have been an overreaction if they meant her no harm, but it would be better than what she was facing now.

Hindsight never really did anyone much good, did it? She should have filled up earlier. She needed to give herself a firm scolding for that. Unbidden, she imagined "MC" giving her that scolding, and received a shiver up her spine at the mere thought.

What was the matter with her? Two men had her hemmed in at her car, and yet she seemed caught in a fog, her natural adrenaline reaction clogged. Her response to their threat was perilously slow. Almost apathetic.

"Give me your credit card and whatever cash you're carrying. As well as that sparkly ring you're wearing." The driver seemed laid-back, almost conversational about it. Not even particularly aggressive, but then, he didn't need to be. The look in his eyes told her he'd done violence before, and wouldn't hesitate to do it again. "C'mon, bitch. Just give 'em to me and you can go back to your fancy life, order a couple hundred more credit cards."

Of course. Because like all rich people, I simply pull money out of my ass by magic, not hard work. She was smart enough not to say it, but she met his gaze squarely. "No."

The punch in the face was unexpected, jarring. As the world

reeled, she thought of the masked man smacking Willow's ass. It had been intended to provoke pleasure as much as pain. This was simple violence, the companion to hate and resentment and all the things that made a person not care what they were doing to another. As a result, a matching response boiled up inside her.

She might have screamed in rage, she wasn't sure. All she knew was she flew at the young man with nails and teeth. She was a small woman in her forties with no fighting skills, so it would be nothing for him to beat her into the ground, but she didn't stop pummeling at him, no matter how ineffectually. His second blow caught her on the temple and she staggered. She was vaguely aware of the other one opening her car door to yank out her purse. She lunged at him and the driver shoved her against the gas pump, the handles jamming into her lower back.

"Stop fighting," he snapped impatiently.

He'd caught her hand, was wrenching at her rings. The engagement ring Roy had given her at a soiree with her family and friends. The twenty-year anniversary band. The plain gold wedding band. His mistake was he was trying to work all three off together, and her knuckles were not the same as they'd been at twenty-one, when Roy had placed two of them there. She screamed in rage, for help, to be noticed, to stop him. She also kicked at him, dropping to the ground so he had to follow her, practically roll with her as she curled around the rings like she was protecting a child.

He grabbed hold of her hair. Again she was struck with the contrast, the way the Master had seized Willow's hair to drag her head back. This man was going to smash her face against the raised concrete dais. She'd be another NOLA crime statistic.

Instead, he was yanked off her and slung back over her car. He hit the hood with a resounding thump, fell off. The BMW might need body work. A flurry of violent activity ensued, punctuated by male swearing. A cry followed a sound like breadsticks being snapped. Then there was a scramble, the two men running back to their car, one limping and the other holding his arm against himself. The Caddy sped away, the driver shouting obscenities out the window, his eyes wild, spooked.

She was trying to get up, but a large hand closed over her shoulder, keeping her down. "Easy, let's take this slow. See what's what." When he tried to uncurl her hands from her chest, she was too disoriented. She made a noise between angry protest and pleading. "It's all right. I'm not going to hurt you or take anything from you, I promise."

It was his rumbling tone that brought things into focus. The man in the Caddy had tried to take her rings, not this man. This man was trying to help her.

He gently manacled her wrist, using his hold on it and the arm he slid behind her shoulders to help her sit up on the concrete island. He unfolded her legs so they were stretched out in front of her. She blinked, bemused when he guided her calf so one ankle was crossed over the other. A ladylike pose, rather than sprawled ignominy. It helped.

"You okay?"

She focused. "Your eyes aren't dark blue."

Maybe it was because she was still fuzzy, but she had an impression of several colors. Green at the bottom of the iris, melding into blue at the top. A center ring of gold around the pupil. She knew it was him, not just because of the black T-shirt and jeans and his build, but because of that unique stamp to him. He barely seemed winded after dispatching the two men.

Her gaze shifted to his hair. It was charcoal colored, with a handsome peppering of gray. She suspected he was a little older than her, maybe late forties. She really had wanted to see his face, and now that she'd been granted her wish, she was having trouble focusing on it. She locked her attention on that granite jaw. That, and his touch, made good anchor points to help her steady. The heat of his palms on her arms was so much better than what she'd felt when she'd slipped her fingers into his glove. She wanted him to keep them there.

"Answer my question, Athena. Are you okay?"

"Yes. Just bumps and bruises." Her vision had only blurred when she was hit, so she didn't think she had a concussion. Her cheek had hit the cement, not her skull. She'd have quite a story to tell at the Garden Club luncheon. She'd make them laugh by telling them it was due to an unfortunate run-in with her rebellious rosebushes. She didn't think they'd laugh if she told them it was because of an attempted mugging outside her favorite BDSM club. "It was just a shock to be hit that way."

"Yeah. That's usually the first hurdle in combat training. Understanding you're going to get hit in hand-to-hand, and you can't flinch from it. You didn't flinch at all."

"I'd like to say it was bravery, but I simply didn't expect it."

"Most people don't expect someone to do that to them. Not if it's never happened before. If you had some training, I think you'd have kicked that bastard's ass."

"Thank you. A nice way of saying I fight like a girl. Would you mind helping me up?"

He rested his hand on her knee, drawing her attention to the fact that one was knocking against the other. Until he touched it, and then it stilled, with an uncertain quiver. "Let's sit here for another minute or two."

He was sitting next to her, which would ordinarily be pleasant, but the location wasn't.

"I'd like to at least move to my car," she said. "This isn't a very comfortable or aromatic position. The gas smell's a little overpowering."

"Aromatic?" His lips quirked, and they were handsome and firm. "No wonder they call you Lady Mistress. All right, then. Point taken. You're going to lean on me, though. No arguments."

It wasn't the only reason they called her that. She was Athena

Francesca Summers, born of old Southern money, married to Roy "Rocket" Summers. She'd been at his side for over twenty years as the two of them expanded and increased the success of the company he started, Summers Industries, which was now a multinational corporation that also employed thousands domestically. On top of that, she was practically a professional volunteer fund-raiser for various high-profile New Orleans charities.

Though most at Club Release hadn't known her true identity in the beginning, it wasn't hard to figure out as time went on, since photographs of her and Roy regularly showed up in the business and social columns. Club Release was known for its exclusive membership and small size, which was one of the reasons Roy had chosen it, despite more upscale fetish club choices in the New Orleans area, like the nearby Club Progeny.

There was no shame in a Southern lady leaning on a handsome male rescuer, but even if there had been, she would have had little choice. Despite the odd calmness of her mind, her legs couldn't support her weight. However, he did more than let her lean. When she expected him to open her driver's side door, instead he bent, slid his arms beneath her and lifted her off her feet. He walked around to the passenger side, letting her down there before he opened the door.

Roy hadn't been a weakling, but she could count on one hand the times he'd carried her. Worried he might throw out his back, she'd insist he put her down, even though she'd hold on to his neck as she fussed. When he did put her down, she'd compliment his show of manly strength, laughing at the mischief in his brown eyes. Lord, she missed that man's sense of humor.

She leaned against the frame of the door, swamped by the feeling. A near mugging could do that, remind a woman of the practicalities she faced when her husband was dead and no close family lived in the area. No one was directly involved in her day-to-day well-being. Had she even updated her emergency contact numbers in her purse or at the house? If she'd been seriously hurt, would the emergency room have tried to find Roy?

Oh, for heaven's sake. She wasn't going to fall into this self-pitying drivel. She'd update it tomorrow, choose one of her many friends to be primary contact. None of those friends knew about this part of her life, though. They'd have no clue why she was pumping gas in the middle of the night in a part of town none of them frequented. It didn't really matter, did it? If she needed an emergency contact, she expected discretion wouldn't be high on her list of priorities.

She noticed her purse was on the edge of the seat, straps dangling to the floorboards, her lipstick a glittering tube of silver on the carpet. It suggested the other man had gotten no further than that in pulling her bag from the car. The one responsible for thwarting him stood at her back, close enough for her to feel his heat. His hand was just above hers on the frame as he waited her out.

She had a sudden desire to slide her hand up over his, hold on tight, feel that human contact. If he turned his hand to clasp hers, she'd experience firsthand the restrained strength he'd used when he brought that cane down on Willow's flanks, and then again when he'd slid his hand down her bare body, fingers decisively capturing her clit, pushing her over the edge. One more small step, and he'd be as close to Athena as he'd been to his bound submissive.

"I'd like to thank you properly," she said, staring at that hand. "May I ask your name? Or do you prefer Master Craftsman?" She knew Jimmy had meant it as a joke, a teasing nickname, but it was all she had.

"Hardly. Do you feel Lady Mistress is a good fit for you?"

"It was, once." She spoke before she thought about the wisdom of saying so, but watching him had brought such thoughts to the surface, hadn't it? Her legs were trembling again, and her grip slipped on the door frame. "Damn it."

"Ease in there." He moved the purse to the floor and folded her firmly into the passenger seat. She'd lost her shoes during the scuffle, but he had them. He placed them neatly by her feet. Her toes curled into the rug, the rougher fibers a contrast with the silk of her nylons.

He shut the door, then came around to the driver's side. He reached beneath the seat to slide it back and accommodate his larger frame before he took the spot. Her purse was still on the console, her keys in the ignition, so he turned the engine over, adjusting the air so a low heat began to fill the car. Though it was a warm enough night in New Orleans, she was shivering. Shock, she supposed, and watched him press the seat warmer for the passenger side. It warmed both the back and backside, and she couldn't help a small sigh of comfort when it responded quickly. German luxury cars were a gift of the gods.

Her dashboard GPS came up, and he glanced at it, pressing the icon programmed for home. Just like that, he had her address. She wasn't that concerned about it, because he didn't feel like a threat. Not that way. Her gaze fastened onto his forearm, that dark sprinkle of hair. Lifting her attention to the silver hair at his temples, she reached out, touched it.

Those intent eyes locked with hers in a way that made her close her hand, lower it with only a brief impression of the soft texture. He held her gaze, unsmiling, until she put the hand back in her lap. She could almost hear the click, the connection made, a mutual understanding of their behavior. His wasn't a surprise to her, not after having watched him in the club. But his reacting that way now told her he wasn't simply a bedroom Dom, one demanding those terms in the boundaries of a defined session, a sexual scenario. Few men had the confidence to pull it off believably outside a structured environment.

That intel, rather than suggesting she might act with more caution around him, gave her far more unwise thoughts and desires.

If her reaction had surprised him, given that she was classified as a Domme, he didn't show it. "I'm taking you home," he said, "and then I'll call a cab to get me back to my place. I came with a friend tonight, so I don't have my truck here. Take a hot shower tonight and a couple aspirin. It'll make you feel better tomorrow."

"Voice of experience?" Her tongue seemed to be too thick in her mouth. "That didn't seem like your first fis-fisticuffs."

His lips quirked again. "Fisticuffs? Really? Are you a librarian?"

"Do I look like one?"

"Depends." His gaze covered her, head to toe, and he took his time about it. "I've had some interesting fantasies about librarians. The kind where I bend them over a stack of books and discipline them with a nice flexible paperback for shushing me one too many times."

Was he trying to steady her with the teasing? Giving him a silly smile, she leaned forward and put her finger to her lips, trying to summon a suitably stern librarian expression. "Shh."

He closed his hand over hers and brought the one finger to his lips, brushing a kiss over the pad. They knew what type of animal they each were, and they'd met through a sexually focused club, so this type of flirtation was meaningless. Two Doms teasing one another with no intent to engage. Except as he continued to hold her wrist, his eyes became more serious, while her fingers loosened, becoming more pliant.

"The name doesn't fit anymore, does it?" he asked. "That's what you were saying."

She swallowed, sat back. As she did, he let her slide free. She looked out the window. She'd been maudlin earlier. Sad, Jimmy had called it, but still dangerously mawkish. Now was not a time to make impetuous decisions. "You don't need to take me home. Use the car to go back to your own place, and by that time I'll be steady enough to drive. No sense in inconveniencing you by trying to get a cab out to my place this time of night."

When he said nothing, she settled deeper into the seat, closed her eyes, and crossed her arms over herself. "All right?"

"You're no inconvenience. And I'll see how you're doing when we get to my place. My name is Dale. Dale Rousseau."

"Rousseau." She smiled, eyes still closed. The warmth of the car was making her drowsy. Her trembling had stopped. Things were slowing down again, the fog returning. " 'Nothing is less in our power than the heart, and far from commanding, we are forced to obey it.' "

"Intriguing choice. 'To live is not merely to breathe; it is to act; it is to make use of our organs, senses, faculties—of all those parts of ourselves which give us the feeling of existence.' "

"A Master who knows his Rousseau. Thank you, Dale."

She wasn't sure if she was thanking him for knowing Rousseau, for driving her home or for rescuing her from the two thugs, but it didn't matter. A lady always offered her thanks for a kindness, and so far he'd been nothing but kind.

It just showed the depths of her capricious mood that she yearned for the part of him she'd seen earlier in the evening—when he'd been far less kind.

TWO

Athena opened her eyes. She didn't recognize her surroundings. The room was small, probably the size of her walk-in closet, though in all fairness, her walk-in closet was the size of a small bedroom. The quilt over her was clean, the mellow ivory of the white fields suggesting advanced age. It had a blue and brown wedding ring pattern. There was a braided rug on the floor with the same colors. The nightstand, the only other furniture in the room, held an old-fashioned alarm clock, the round kind with hands showing the time. Instead of a.m. or p.m., there was a dial just above the fulcrum of the arms, showing a sunrise for morning. She expected it would slowly shift into a full sun afternoon view, then a moon and starry sky picture for night. She remembered having one of those when she was younger.

The carafe by the bed held cold water, the ice partially melted and condensation collected on the glass sides, absorbed by the folded cloth on which the carafe sat. She saw a note next to the clock, propped up so she could see it in her current position.

Sit up slow. That's an order. Take the aspirin. Do you remember your name? My name?

She saw the two pills by the note. Dale . . . that was his name. Dale Rousseau. She certainly remembered her own. He'd woken her up a few times in the night, made her say it, made her tell him the name of the club, her favorite New Orleans restaurant, what color the sky was.

Slowly, things started coming back. She'd dozed off in the car.

She hadn't woken until he opened her passenger door. At that point, she thought she'd merely nodded off at the gas station, and still expected to find herself there. Instead, she'd blinked blearily at the chain-link gate in front of the car. Three strands of barbed wire ran along the top. From the silhouettes of old cars piled up behind it, it appeared to be the entrance to a junkyard. However, the forbidding appearance was meliorated by a wisteria-covered arbor, which graced a separate gate onto the property for foot traffic. A wooden sign stood next to that, telling her in cheerful yellow letters she was at Eddie's Junkyard and Temporary Home for Good Dogs. A whimsically animated car and puppy had been painted side by side beneath the lettering, both grinning at her.

"Is there anyone waiting for you at home, Athena? Someone I can call? Answer me."

His hand was on her face, commanding her attention the same way his words were. How did he know her name? She must have told him. Or maybe Jimmy had. "No. No one knows I'm out tonight. No one to call."

Her domestic staff left at five p.m., so her nights were her own. If she wasn't there when they arrived tomorrow, they wouldn't think anything of it. They'd assume she'd left early for the office, or to handle her never-ending list of errands and social engagements. Technically, no one would miss her for a couple of days. It was a stupid thing to tell a stranger, but when he told her to answer him, she did, without thought. She was usually mature enough to make the distinction between erotic fantasy and intelligent reality. Maybe she'd take a nap outside this nice junkyard before heading home.

He returned to the car, drove it through the now-open gate. The next thing she remembered was him sliding his arms under her legs and back, lifting her out of the car with the same ease he'd lifted her at the gas station.

"So strong," she mumbled. "But don't hurt your back. I can walk."

"You'll stay at my place tonight," he said shortly, ignoring that. "You're in no shape to drive, let alone be at home by yourself."

Well, he'd obviously been right about that. Coming back to the present and what must be his guest bedroom, she sat up slowly, feeling every ache. Looking in the mirror was probably going to be a bad decision, intensifying the mortification she was starting to feel. Good God. She stayed on top of every detail of her life. She was a problem solver. She didn't throw good judgment to the wind and trust a stranger to care for her the way a child would. But that was exactly what she'd done. How much vodka had she had in that Diet Coke? Not enough to impede her judgment to that extent. She was very prudent about that type of thing. If she'd overindulged, she never would have driven. She would have called a cab. Which in turn would have made all of this a moot point.

She cut herself some slack on the whole mugging scenario. She had made the wrong choice there, but it had been a calculated one, thinking she was close enough to the club to be safe. But then there was her behavior in the car with him, touching his hair . . . the things they'd said to one another, the subtle clues she'd given with her responses, or lack thereof. He had very nice hair, thick and soft. Those silver strands tempted a woman's fingers.

Looking down, she realized she was in a man's T-shirt and her panties, and that was it. Her clothes had been hung up and left on the hinge of a closet door. Her bra and stockings were folded into a neat pile on her shoes. They sat on an old wooden rocker. At the foot of the bed was a trunk. Her purse was there.

He'd changed her clothes. She was wearing his shirt, because it smelled like him. English Leather, mixed with a mint-based soap. When he'd carried her, she'd also detected cinnamon, perhaps his toothpaste, or maybe he was a fan of Big Red gum. It brought to mind the macho, cowboy-styled commercials for it. He was a good fit for that. English Leather and Big Red. One hundred percent testosterone, all the way.

Modesty wasn't a big issue in a BDSM club, given that submissives were often fully naked and even Dominants could wear provocative outfits. Environment dictated comfort zone, however, and realizing he'd undressed her in his home, in his guest bedroom, made her feel far more vulnerable than if he stripped her on Club Release's public floor and flogged her.

That image ran a new shiver up her spine. It wasn't so much what he'd done to Willow that titillated her. It was *how* he did it. He made all of the trappings—whip, cane, restraints, frame—seem unnecessary, as if he could have held Willow in place with a look alone, taken her to that state of mindless submission by the sheer force of his will.

She'd commanded Roy, tied him up, punished him, but she was always Athena, his wife, role-playing a Mistress to him. At least that was how it felt to her. Roy could get deep into it, but she didn't think he'd ever completely lost himself the way Willow had lost herself to Dale.

Could she have given that to Roy if she'd done something differently? Had she ever noticed him looking longingly at other scenarios, where things became more intense, where the Dommes were more fully in control? Where it was more natural to them?

Don't do this to yourself, Athena. He loved you and you loved him.

She touched the worn cloth of the dark blue T-shirt, and a memory surfaced. Dale's capable hands moving over her, removing the trim suit blazer she'd worn, the shell blouse, the bra beneath. Had his hands lingered, caressed her breasts, slid down her body, learning what he was going to claim? As she became more awake, her memory was fine-tuning, and that wasn't part of it, so the vision was apparently her fantasy addition to the scene. A good thing, too, since the line between that particular fantasy and its reality would be a clear demarcation between Good Samaritan and creepy predator.

She pressed her bare feet into the braided rug. While she waited for the world to stop spinning, she took the aspirin. She needed to go into the bathroom, clean up, put on her clothes—her armor—and go thank her host properly, then head for home. The Garden Club meeting was pretty much out of the question at this point, unfortunately, but she needed to make Junior League in the late afternoon. She was expected to present plans on their spring festival. Their goal was to raise fifty thousand for the local women's shelter, and she intended to surpass that by at least a fifteen percent margin.

Going into the bathroom, she took care of the necessities, and was pleasantly surprised by her face. She had a small scrape on one cheek from the concrete, and a red mark on the other one from being hit, but it wasn't as swollen and blotchy as she'd feared. Probably because of the ice pack.

It was amazing how the mind could do that, bring back hidden images like a dealer randomly tossing cards down on a green felt table. Now she remembered Dale holding the pack against her cheek, cupping the other side of her face. She'd rested the weight of her head in his hand, as trusting as an infant. He'd murmured to her in his deep voice, soothing as a lullaby.

She abandoned the idea of putting on the clothes. Instead, she wandered out of the room in the T-shirt. His living quarters were apparently the second level of the junkyard office, an efficiency apartment with a small kitchen and living area with TV. When she saw a neatly folded blanket and pillow at the end of the couch, she realized she'd taken his bed. For a man his size, the couch looked none too comfortable, and mortification spiked again. She owed him breakfast, at the very least.

Looking out the kitchen window, she saw an ocean of discarded cars and scrap metal covering several acres. Though it should have been an eyesore, the view possessed a creative energy. The cars' interesting shapes and colors hinted at the stories they could tell, the journeys they'd taken. Dale's presence only added to the interest factor.

He was standing in the gravel yard in front of the office, probably a staging area for customers bringing in cars or metal to sell. He was surrounded by over a dozen dogs of various breeds and sizes, from a trio of Jack Russell terriers that didn't reach his knee to a pair of Rottweiler mixes that pressed against his upper thigh. As she watched, all but two of the assembled dogs sat at his sharp, one-word command, reinforced by a gesture with his finger when one of the Jack Russells hovered a few inches short of sitting. The dog sat. Then Dale winged two tennis balls out over the cars, sending two mixed-breed Labradors charging off after them. The canines lithely dodged piles of metal or cleared them with dramatic leaps to pursue the projectiles.

When they brought them back, dropped them at his feet, he tossed each a treat, then he sent the Jack Russells off in the same manner. He performed the same miraculous feat with all the dogs in two- or three-dog groupings. The waiting ones quivered with excitement, but he didn't even have to glance at them after he told them to sit. They simply obeyed.

As he turned to survey them all at last, she was reminded of a drill sergeant inspecting the troops. His lips firm but eyes dancing, he barked another one word command. *"Free."*

They took off in all directions. Firing a dozen tennis balls after them, he watched them scramble about in happy chaos to salvage them from among the cars. They brought them back, encouraged by his praise and laughter, the affection he handed out in the form of ear rubs and fur stroking. While he was doing that, she quietly opened the door. There was a metal platform that served as a stoop and porch both, and she sat down on it, letting her legs dangle out from under the railings, crossing her arms on the one level with her chest.

With his manly voice, that laughter was exactly as she expected it to be. A rich sound, a mix of thunder and heady wine. When she settled, he glanced up, giving her the impression he'd been aware of her presence all along. Just like last night at the club.

"Good morning." His gaze coursed over her in the shirt. Though he didn't comment, she sensed he was pleased to see her still in it. Perhaps unexpectedly so. She liked having company in that emotion. All of this was unexpected to her. "There's some coffee on the stove," he said. "Help yourself to a cup and bring me one. I'll be in the potting shed." He pointed, drawing her gaze to it. Then he was moving that way, several of the dogs following him. Others, obviously realizing playtime was over, were wandering off to other pursuits. She hoped those pursuits didn't include lying in wait to eat visitors who'd not yet been properly introduced to them.

She lingered, watching the flex of his powerful body as he moved across the yard in his well-fitted T-shirt and jeans. Then, thinking she might get caught staring, she rose. She'd reached her embarrassment threshold for the morning. No need to let the cup overflow, though it might be worth it. She watched him an additional moment, her hand on the door latch. There was something about the way he moved . . . Yes, there. He had a very slight limp. She hoped he hadn't hurt himself coming to her aid.

She went back inside. When she fished her brush out of her purse, she discovered he'd left her a care package next to it. A new toothbrush, lavender face soap and new canvas sneakers in her size. When and how had he acquired all that? During any conscious memory she had of the night, she remembered him being there, but she supposed he could have slipped off for a little while, if there was a store close by.

She used the brush in her purse to fix her hair. Roy had always thought the light brown color was like the color of a winter forest. She'd added dark blond streaks at a certain point to mask the gray, and he'd teased her, saying she'd added birch to the forest. Finding a clip at the bottom of her purse, she pulled it into a tail at her nape and combed out her bangs, making herself as presentable as possible without a shower. She zipped herself into her sea green fitted skirt, keeping the T-shirt loose over it, and added the canvas sneakers, blessing his consideration. She wasn't yet steady enough to handle her three-inch heels.

She put her bra on under the T-shirt, then knotted the shirt at her waist. The blazer and blouse were far too formal for the situation. That was what she told herself, rather than the possible truth that the scent of his shirt, the indirect connection with his solid body, was another steadying influence she wasn't yet ready to relinquish.

Going back into the kitchen, she poured him a coffee. The pleasant smell had been part of what eased her mind when she woke. It didn't seem reasonable that a kidnapper would indulge in something as reassuring as a morning coffee ritual, right? She snorted at herself.

He'd told her to bring him coffee. Not "would you bring" but "bring me a cup." Was that simply his mode of communication, or something else? Still testing?

She was pouring it, wasn't she? Though it was the polite thing to do, that wasn't why she was doing it. She stopped, pressed her palms to the counter on either side of the cup. *Think about what you're doing, Athena. Don't be rash. Any more than you've already been.*

Since she didn't know if he used sugar and cream, she brought a sampling of both. A typical bachelor, he had a bowlful of single-sized condiments on the kitchen table from various restaurants. A jar served as a vase for cut wildflowers. She recognized the types from groupings that sprouted up among the cars. The wildflowers and the wedding ring quilt weren't exactly proof of a woman's touch, especially given the age of the quilt, but it showed his appreciation of things that could make a home more comfortable for him as well as guests. Roy had possessed that awareness. A man's man in every respect, he still enjoyed touches of color and would give his opinion on rugs or bedding, or help her decide where to hang a picture for best effect.

As she moved down the outside steps, she saw he hadn't used the term *potting shed* randomly. The man gardened. A vegetable plot was fenced off near the shed so the dogs couldn't trample or dig up the growing plants. To her personal delight, there was also an adjacent flower garden, landscaped in a crescent around the vegetables. It had a profusion of blooms native to the area, as well as some more exotic ones. He'd studied his English gardens, because it looked like one of their cottage styles, the heights of the plantings arranged so the taller flowers in back gave way to shorter plants that drew the eye in a slope toward the vegetables.

Former military, gardener, dog trainer and junkyard operator. As well as an extraordinary Dom. A man guaranteed to pique the interest of any intelligent, breathing woman, and she fit both those qualifications. If she was giving him his due, she might owe the latter state to him. She wasn't sure how last night might have turned out if he hadn't intervened, but in the rage of that moment, she knew her attacker would have had to render her unconscious or kill her to take her rings. It was extraordinary, what a person didn't know about herself until faced with such a situation. If he was still alive, she could well imagine Roy's concerned expression, his strong hands holding her. He would have given her a little shake, fussed at her. *Christ, Athena, it was just jewelry. Promise me you'll never do something that stupid again. You're more important to me than a bit of glass.*

Pushing back the sudden tears, she took a breath and moved onward toward the potting shed. The Rottweilers lay in the shade on the western side, tongues lolling. One of them rose to meet her, padding over to sniff at her legs, circle her. After that ritual, he allowed her to stroke his large head, his soulful eyes fixed on the coffee she was carrying.

"You've already had your caffeine fix this morning, Rom. Go lay down with Sheba."

The dog huffed, then moved back to the shade, collapsing into a ponderous pile of sleek furred muscle next to the other dog.

Dale probably had a great singing voice, but she suspected the gods who'd designed that riveting deep timbre had intended one primary use for it. Issuing commands. She stepped into the shed to find him at a workbench, up to his elbows in a bag of soil. When she placed the coffee on the edge of the bench, out of his way but within his reach, he glanced at it, then nodded to a stool. "You can sit there."

"Thank you. The first thing I should do is apologize for my abysmal behavior last night," she began. "I'm not usually that irresponsible around a total stranger."

"The first thing you should do is drink your coffee." He sent a pointed look toward the stool. "Sit."

She slid onto the stool. He had a sturdy wooden flat on the bench, and he'd arranged eight plastic inserts into it, with a half-dozen spaces in each. He divided the soil among them before he began to drop seeds into each opening. Though he had big hands, they handled the tiny seeds with gentle care. As he pressed the seeds below the blanket of dirt, the activity spread the smell of earth and growing things through the shed. Watching him kept her tranquil and quiet. She sipped her coffee.

He dusted off his hands over the soil bag and wiped them on a rag before he picked up his coffee. He didn't use the sugar or creamer she'd provided, so she assumed that was for the benefit of his guests. He preferred his black. She'd remember that. And ignore why she was making such mental notes.

"You weren't irresponsible," he said. "You were disoriented after a traumatic event. An event you handled well. You kept your cool, fought back. You looked pissed, not frightened. The only time you looked rattled was when you thought he was going to get your rings."

She gripped them in reaction, reminding herself they were there. "I need to take them off, put them in a safe at home. It's foolish to wear them, especially in that environment."

"It tells men you're still off-limits, that you haven't figured out what you want. Or if you want anything." Dale lifted a shoulder. "Under those conditions, it makes sense to wear them."

Athena took another sip of the coffee. Since she liked hers with some cream, a little sugar, it had a lighter texture than Dale's, like dark caramel. "So you know about my husband."

"Yes. I'm sorry."

No elaboration, but sincerely meant, which impacted her more than a hundred words. It made her throat ache, the coffee burn on the way down.

"I was looking for you in the parking lot. That's how I saw what was happening." He met her surprised gaze. "The way you looked at me in the club, I thought you wanted something from me. I came to find out what it was."

She nearly blushed, telling her she was desperately out of practice at this. At the club, blunt communication was typical and vital, no subtleties or beating around the bush. There might be flirtation, like what they'd briefly indulged in the car, but when clear information was needed, things were straightforward.

She should tell him he was mistaken. Compliment him on his work with Willow, make some polite chitchat, offer to take him to breakfast to thank him for his help, and that would be the end of it.

A refined woman to the bone, she was courteous to everyone, no matter what she felt. *I'm fine, how are you, how are your children?* Always doing the right thing. She didn't see that as a shortcoming, as so many seemed to feel it was these days, those who preferred to wear everything they were on the outside, like dirty underwear. She took pride in who and what she was, but this moment called for something different, a side of herself she hadn't explored . . . ever.

He was waiting for her answer. Since even in this different environment she was feeling the tug of that influence he'd had over her last night, it suggested it was more than a flight of fancy. But then she'd been thinking about this for a while, hadn't she? She'd just lacked the motivating agent. A hot and sexy Dom who rescued her from a mugging.

A wry thought, but it was more than that. Something about the way he handled himself, both as a Dom and a man, steadied her. He made her feel it was okay to say what she wanted to say. When she was ready to say it.

"Yes, I do want to ask you for something. But I need to think about it."

"Fair enough." He put down the coffee, settled back against the bench, crossing his arms over his chest, a relaxed pose that highlighted the easy power of his body. "So Jimmy says you were a pretty amazing Domme to your husband."

To your husband. It was a specific way to put it. She stilled beneath the penetrating look. She'd fantasized about him having dark blue eyes, but the reality was far more exceptional. A casual glance, like her dazed perception last night, would suggest they were hazel, maybe green. In another light, a pale blue. But the truth was his eyes contained all those colors, blues and greens like the ocean itself, touched by sunlight with that gold ring around the pupil.

"My buddies used to razz me by calling me 'Merman,'" he said. "They're distracting as hell, I know."

She smiled at the grumpiness. Only a straight man could get irritated about having beautiful eyes. Looking back down at her coffee, she traced the rim of the cup with her manicured nail.

"Have you been looking for a new sub since your husband?" he asked. "Is that why you were at the club?"

"Are you offering?" She tossed the smile his way, the tightness of it matching the feeling in her chest.

He chuckled. "Not hardly. But when you were watching last night, your focus seemed different . . . for a Domme. Technique interests me. Maybe you just need to talk it through with a fellow Dom, someone you know you're not intending to top. Removes the pressure. Like an actor going over his lines with a neighbor, rather than having to do it with his costar right off."

"Perhaps." She needed to move the conversation away from this direction. She hadn't denied she was looking for a new submissive, but in truth, such a thought hadn't crossed her mind since Roy's death. Not once in those two years, not once since she'd returned to the club, no matter how many unattached male subs had met her gaze briefly, extending the invitation. As Jimmy said, she'd been an amazing Domme. With Roy.

Never again. She'd had that thought last night, hadn't she?

He set aside the coffee. Before she could anticipate what he was doing, he removed his shirt in one fluid movement, set it aside. When he put his hand to the belt of his jeans, she wondered if he was going to strip it all off, but he was merely resting it there, shifting his weight to one hip. "Okay, no pressure. Take a look, evaluate me. Pretend I'm a sub. Let me feel it, the way you take control."

If her tongue was currently functioning, she'd say the same thing she would if he'd offered her a shot of Jack at nine in the morning. It was too early in the day for this. Of course, maybe the Jack would help her. She was in a different environment, with an unpredictable and overwhelming man. There was no way she could summon the focus, the control, for what he was suggesting.

However, she routinely handled herself in demanding board meetings, at the podium of fund-raisers attended by well over a thousand people. She knew how to genuinely smile for hours, remember a hundred different names and the key details about the people attached to them. She could coordinate or defuse complex situations, put people at ease, draw them to her with warmth and direct them toward her goals. She knew how to connect to them in ways that brought out their better sides. She took personal pride in figuring that out for each individual, so that they felt so good about signing a contract with her company, or writing a check to make the world a better place, they'd do it again.

But this wasn't like that. It wasn't even comparable to how she'd been a Mistress to Roy. Then she'd had his pleasure uppermost in her mind. Dale was asking her to treat this as an exercise, no one to please or understand but herself. She had no precedent for that.

From his demeanor, she was sure that any attempt to politely distance herself from the situation would be met with a frank response that left her as vulnerable as if she were sitting naked at the Garden Club. She heard the clank of the collar and tags of one of the dogs scratching outside.

She'd faced unexpected situations where she needed to adapt, evaluate and organize her response quickly. She could think on her feet. That, and the earlier feeling, the one that made her think she could tell Dale anything she was thinking, gave her the courage to test these waters, to see if she was right about what she was truly wanting.

She slid off the stool. The shed wasn't large, but she could circle him at close quarters. He was beautiful. Sculpted with hard muscle, as she anticipated. He had some scars. When she was behind him, she lifted her hand over one, but she didn't touch him. Her fingers hovered several inches from a mark that was likely caused by a bullet. She'd noted there was a similar one on his front side, somewhat lower. It had punched through him from a vantage point above, perhaps from a window. Or maybe from the ground, an enemy trying to deflect his charge. The thought of him facing that made her anxiety about this seem absurd.

Did he have scars below the denim as well? If he did, they hadn't hampered him last night when he threw her attacker onto her car hood.

With his shirt off, the jeans belted so they sat at his waist, his ass was molded nicely by the fit. She imagined catching her fingers in his belt loop, closing the area between them to dare one kiss between his shoulder blades. She'd press her body against his so the curve of the firm buttocks pressed against the tight coil happening in her abdomen.

"You can touch me, Athena."

His permission perversely made her draw her hand back to herself. She returned to his front. When she looked up into his face, he was regarding her with that unsmiling look. Her legs quivered, and she realized she was feeling a little lightheaded. She should move back to the stool. Instead, she sank down to her knees in front of him, wanting to study and absorb him from this angle. Feel.

As a girl, she'd gone to see *Saturday Night Fever* with her mother. She recalled the opening scene, where John Travolta was clad in nothing but a pair of snug dark briefs while styling his hair. The camera angle had been shot from the floor, practically from between his feet. The girls in the audience had squealed at the provocative angle. Her mother had laughed at their reaction.

To capture that view, the camera person had to be kneeling, looking up at him. What if, when the scene was over, the person on their knees stayed there, until he reached down and bade her to rise? Even at that tender age, the idea had captivated Athena. As it did now.

She put a light-as-a-feather hand on Dale's right leg, above his knee. Her gaze coursed up the terrain of his powerful thighs, to the curve of cock and testicles beneath the denim. He didn't wear his jeans tight, but they held to his shape and moved with his body as needed. Just right. She slid her attention to his belt and the layers of muscle above, then lifted her eyes to his chest. He had a mat of fine dark hair, not too thick, but not thin or nonexistent, either. She had friends who tittered over bare-chested twentysomethings, even as they laughed at themselves for ogling men so much younger than themselves. Such men were pretty of course, but a mature man that looked like this would steal her attention any day.

Roy had no patience for the idea of men going to stylists and fussing over their appearance, beyond making sure they wore a clean shirt and shaved. *Their faces*, he'd clarified to her with a mock scowl as her lips quivered with suppressed mirth, her gaze moving pointedly to his furred chest. She bet Dale would have liked him.

His thigh muscle flexed beneath her hand as he shifted his weight to his right hip. His buttock muscles would tighten from that change in position. She wouldn't mind having her hand there, feeling that transition.

He reached down, brushing a finger underneath the wisps of hair across her forehead. "It's interesting where you ended up, isn't it? On your knees?"

She tensed, but his tone made it a neutral observation. He wasn't mocking her. "Does that have anything to do with what you want to ask me?"

"Yes. Maybe."

He brought her chin up, holding it. As he did, her pulse rabbited, and he registered it, because he increased his grip. Her chin lifted further at the pressure, her neck elongating. She had to raise her haunches an inch or so off her heels. He kept her like that, fingers stroking her jaw. Her stomach quivered harder. With the subtle demand, the power had shifted. Now he was touching her for himself, to see what her skin felt like. To evaluate *her*.

She wanted to excel in that evaluation. Wanted to please him, with a fierce intensity that spooked her.

"I need to go." She disengaged her chin from his grasp. When she rose, she was still so close she had to brace herself on his hip. His hands went to her waist, steadying her. She stepped away, flustered even more. "I have some appointments this afternoon."

"All right."

She backed up to her stool, to the coffee. Picked up her cup. She'd put it in the sink, wash it out before she left. Then she remembered her intent to take him to breakfast. "I'd like to thank you for your help."

"Nothing to thank me for." He said it with frank honesty, not as a courteous brush-off. "Any man would have done the same."

"I don't know about that. Plenty would have dialed 911 and left it at that."

"I said a man. Just because you're born male doesn't mean you know how to be a man. Any more than being female makes you a woman. You seem like a remarkable woman, Athena."

She curled both hands around the coffee cup. "I'd still like to thank you. And . . . perhaps talk about what I want at that point. Would you come to my home for lunch on Friday? You already know the address from my GPS, but I can write it down if you don't remember it."

"No worries that I'm untrustworthy?"

She arched a brow. "If you had nefarious intentions toward me, you've had several prime opportunities to execute them."

"God, I love the way you talk. The whole librarian thing."

It was difficult not to give in to a smile with his eyes glinting like that. "If you're simply toying with me, and you do plan to murder me," she advised, "I have a domestic staff there until five. You'll have to cut up my body and bury it in the gardens after they leave."

"So a midafternoon lunch might be more convenient for my diabolical plans."

"Yes, precisely. How about three?"

Two hours to talk to him over a civilized lunch, and then the staff would be gone, leaving the two of them alone. Like now. Yet it was different, wasn't it? This moment had come about by necessity, and she expected he was still concerned about her mental state after the attack. When he came for lunch, that issue would no longer be restraining him. Especially if she behaved the way she'd behaved a few moments ago.

Whether or not he felt it necessary, she knew she had a responsibility to protect him as well. "You can ask Jimmy more about me; he's known me for some time, and of course he knows my husband, who is a member as well. Was a member."

She closed her eyes at the correction, pushed on. "I'd rather you not tell Jimmy you're coming to my home, but other than that, you can ask him whatever you like. I'll call him and tell him it's okay. If you change your mind and decide not to come to my home for lunch, I understand, but I hope you'll let me take you out to lunch or dinner one day. You might have been doing what your code of honor dictates, but my gratitude—and my own sense of honor—needs to be satisfied as well."

The blue color of his eyes intensified when he smiled, the green becoming more vibrant, the gold ring around the irises more rich. She could devote hours to studying his eyes, or watching him pot plants. She imagined him transplanting the young seedlings once they sprouted, handling them so tenderly. She thought about the way he'd touched Willow's arm, the gentle power to it. Despite his teasing, she had nothing to fear from him. Not like she had from those men last night. His danger to her was a far more personal thing.

She was a lamb, inviting the lion into her pasture while she lay down and waited to see what he would do. She liked the feeling. It made her anxious, too. Once she was back in her car, on her way home, would she doubt herself? Think she'd blown the whole situation out of control, misrepresented herself?

He tore a sheet off a notepad he had mounted on the wall, and plucked a pencil out of an old coffee mug on the bench. Scribbling down a phone number, he folded it over and extended it, holding it between two knuckles. "This is my cell, if you need to change the when and where."

Maybe he recognized her thought process. He'd just given her a tentative out. She could take him to a nice restaurant, order a good wine, and make sure she had commitments later in the afternoon to keep it a limited, one-time engagement. She'd see him at the club in a month or so. That would be a sufficient lapse to restore a proper perspective. Then, if she still felt the way she felt now . . .

"Three p.m. at my place on Friday," she confirmed. "I'll leave my cell number on your kitchen table, in case you have a change of plans."

He nodded. "I'll look forward to it. If the conversation you want to have with me goes the way I expect, I assume I'll be doing more of the telling from that point on."

His voice was a quiet rumble, but she'd been right about the cuffs on Willow's arms being unnecessary. His words and his gaze alone effectively pinioned her in place. The small room became exponentially smaller, cinching around her with that heated prom-ise. She was feeling too much, too fast.

He stepped forward. The T-shirt she was wearing had a pocket, and he slid the piece of paper she hadn't yet taken from him into the narrow space. Since the pocket lay over the crest of her breast, she shivered when the paper's edge teased her nipple, even beneath the thin cushion of her bra. As she drew in a breath, her right breast rose against the side of his hand. She hadn't intended that, but he tilted his head to look. His other hand touched her waist, sliding up to capture the left breast, weighing it in his palm. She had fairly sizeable breasts for her frame, something Roy had enjoyed immensely, and the pleasure that came into Dale's expression as he captured one in his strong grip made everything in her liquefy.

"Lovely," he said. "Keep the T-shirt. I like the way you look in it." Then he stepped back, fingers whispering away from the cotton. Her flesh yearned, but she managed not to totter toward him. Instead, she gave him what she hoped was a calm nod as she picked up the coffee once more, moved toward the door. Placing her hand on the screen, she glanced back at him.

"You know, I could be a serial killer myself. I might have all sorts of weapons. Guns, a grenade launcher."

"A grenade launcher? Cool. I'd accept the lunch invitation for that alone." He winked at her.

She shook her head at him. "I knew you'd been in the military. Which branch?"

"Anything with testosterone loves a grenade launcher," he corrected her. "What's not to like? But yes, I've served. Retired SEAL."

Hearing she'd guessed correctly restored some of her confidence. She was still steering the boat, her judgment engaged. It also terrified her a little, because if that was true, she might be headed toward whitewater rapids, too intrigued by the potential ride to turn back from the danger of her boat being overturned.

He'd effectively defused the moment, but she still felt like he'd spread heated wax over her exposed skin, especially when he met her gaze once more.

"I hope you won't cancel, but if you do, Athena, I don't require any explanations. Not at this stage of the game."

The lazy threat behind those last words was clear. Clear enough to give her another shiver.

THREE

"Roy, can you believe Mel Harper is still trying to get me to step down as board president?" Athena chuckled grimly as she pulled weeds from around the marble setting for his memorial statue. Watching Dale's efforts had inspired her to plant a few new flowers. Though she had a landscaping crew to maintain the estate grounds, this quiet corner with its small hobby garden and a bench for reflection was hers to manage. At least once a week, she came here to talk to Roy, do some weeding and thinking, and make sure the area remained interesting. Experimental groupings of shrubs and flowers alternated with seasonal plantings and decorations. At Christmas, she'd put a small lit tree near the statue, along with a group of garden gnomes to represent elves. That would have made him laugh.

She didn't believe the soul lingered with the body, but if Roy came by, she wanted him to see that she was thinking about him, remembering him with as much joy as sadness. The bronze had been fired with a handful of his ashes, the rest scattered in this section of the garden. In the statue, he was golfing, in midswing, his face crinkled with that good-humored look that said he expected a slice that would plunk the ball right into a sand trap. She'd never had any passion for the game, so it was one thing they rarely did together, but she'd clearly remembered that expression from the couple times she'd accompanied him. He was an abysmal golfer, so bad the club pro had given up on him. She'd wondered why he continued to play, when he succeeded at almost everything else he did. Roy had shrugged.

Ah well, life will knock you on your ass now and then. Gives you a reason to prove you can get up, right?

One night, she found a different use for his golf clubs he'd appreciated. She'd used one of the irons to tap his inner thighs while he was tied up, pressed the club end against his balls, lifted his chin with the shaft.

"You'd be proud of me. I met with Mel after the budget meeting and told him if he was so set on being president, he'd better plan my murder, because that would be far easier on both of us, versus all this wrangling in every meeting. I told him to let me know if he decided to go that route, so I could unleash my flying monkeys on him."

After a startled moment, Mel had chuckled, with charming self-deprecation. *You called my bluff, Athena. Roy told me not to underestimate you. I guess I've been testing you. My apologies.*

"Maybe we'll have a little less passive-aggressive dart throwing now, at least from him. Larry's still a pain in the ass, but that has more to do with his desire to get under my skirts than higher on the board. I wish he wasn't such a damn good financial manager. Now, don't get riled up." She waved her hand at the statue. "I can handle him. You know I can."

When it came to the advances of other men, Roy had been clearly protective. *My wife. My Mistress.* Jimmy had once told her that a lot of people new to the scene didn't realize that men who needed to experience submission could be just as possessive of their significant other as any male. *You don't turn in your man card just because you need to be tied up and spanked*, he'd declared.

"It looks like we'll be seeing an overall profit this year, despite the economy. I'm going to adjust the employee bonuses accordingly and bump up the healthcare contribution. Oh, Tessie Maddox in Shipping had twins. Can you believe it? That poor girl. Her husband's not worth the time of day, but I notice Jesse over in Receiving has been babysitting for her, running her errands. I'm not one to argue with the 'what God has brought together, let no man tear asunder,' but I tend to think that hormones brought Tessie and her husband together, not divine power. Jesse's a much better match for her. I guess we'll see if Tommy Lee becoming a father will make him a man."

She thought then of Dale, what he'd said about being a man. She was mature enough to know one heroic rescue at a gas station didn't guarantee he was a man a woman could count on a hundred percent—heroism in a relationship was sometimes as much about being there to help unload the dishwasher as to rescue her from a mugging—but it was an impressive start.

Of course, what she was considering with respect to him, was it the same thing as pursuing a serious relationship? If she went the way her mind was going on it, it was definitely safer to keep this a compartmentalized thing, restricted by a lot of boundaries that wouldn't cross into her daily life. Many club sessions fit into that mold. Two people coming together for a specific purpose, a mutual need, for a couple of hours once a week or even less often. Sometimes those people were married to other people, or, if the person they played with was their significant other, the club was the only place they exercised the Dom or sub tendencies.

No matter her thoughts on the long term, it was smart to approach it that way from the beginning. If it evolved beyond that, fine; she'd cross that bridge when it became necessary, but it was best to start with low expectations, one focused goal.

But what was her goal? With Dale, even during that brief moment in the potting shed, things tended to get off track, started to cycle around his indomitable will, not because he was imposing it on her, but because she slid under it like an umbrella in a rain storm.

"Mrs. Summers?" Her cell beeped, the speaker feature turned on. "Your guest is here."

"Thank you, Lynn. Show him to the gazebo and make sure he

has a drink. Bring out the hors d'oeuvres. I'll be right there, soon as I wash my hands."

Time had escaped her. Glancing at her slim gold watch, she realized he was right on time. "Well, here goes, Roy. I'm nervous as a girl on her first date. I bet you're laughing, old man."

She kissed her fingertips, pressed them to the foot of the statue. "I love you, baby." Then, pushing aside the familiar weight of sadness, she moved away from the area, headed for the guest house behind the pool area. She washed her hands, checked her hair and makeup. Removing the coveralls she'd been wearing to protect her blouse, she slipped on the skirt she'd hung up in there earlier, prepared for this eventuality.

With any other guest, she would have been waiting near the door to personally greet them. A twinge of hostess guilt struck her for not doing the same with Dale. However, she'd been jumpy as a cat since noon, so she'd needed to do something. She could lie to herself, say it was the residual tension she sometimes nursed after board meetings, mostly due to dealing with personalities like Mel's, but the truth was it was all about Dale.

She'd thought long and hard about the question she'd ask him. There was no requirement that she ask it, but she already knew she was going to do so. As a result, tiny manic frogs were jumping in her stomach.

Beyond that, for the first time in over two years, an attractive man she desired was coming to have lunch with her, and his parting words were practically branded in her mind—*at this stage of the game . . . I have a feeling I'll be the one doing the telling.* She wasn't even going to count how many times she'd thought about his firm caress of her breast. He'd touched her as if he already owned her.

She touched that same place, taking a deep breath as she did so. "I am forty-six years old," she told the mirror. "I am Athena Francesca Summers, a grown woman. If I simper, giggle, blush or do something equally ridiculous during this meal, I will stab myself with my own fork. So there."

He'd seemed to like the pencil skirt she'd been wearing, so today she wore one in purple, with a pale yellow blouse over it that had a sash that tied at her hip, the ends trailing down the side. The fabric gathered at the throat like a mock turtleneck, no decorative distraction between it and where it nipped in at her waist. As a result, it enhanced the size and shape of her breasts, drawing male attention to them. It was classy yet sensual. A message of *hands off* combined with *I am a woman and won't conceal it.* She slipped into a pair of two-inch heels and headed back up the garden walkway to the gazebo. She hadn't worn hose today, her legs excellent enough to get by without them in the informal venue of her home. Her hair was clipped loosely on her nape, a few tendrils loose and curling around her face.

She knew she was an attractive middle-aged woman. Even so, it was still gratifying to see him turn at the sound of her heels, watch his gaze latch onto her with obvious appreciation, coursing over her legs, the sway of her hips, the movement of her breasts. When he reached her face, the heat in his eyes made her body react as if he'd licked a trail right up her inner thighs. At the sight of him, she had to take a steadying breath of her own.

He wore black jeans and a forest green long-sleeved shirt. Her practiced eye knew it was a good quality Egyptian cotton, which defined his broad shoulders well. The sleeves were rolled up, revealing his forearms and the black watch he wore. She expected it was a military-grade or diver's watch. It had an outer dial that measured degrees and several smaller dials within the face. Given he'd been a SEAL, she was sure it was rated for underwater use. A man who wouldn't be lost, no matter where he was. The watch was probably a convenient trapping; he could likely make the same calculations in his head if needed. And wasn't she getting fanciful? In another moment she'd be imagining him in a cape and tights.

He was dressed appropriately for their lunch, but if he'd intended to maintain a sense of social distance, acquaintances getting to know one another better, he might have chosen slacks and a tucked-in dress shirt. The fact he'd selected a more informal outfit, a contrast to her more formal one, suggested something far different. It wasn't rudeness; it was anticipation of the roles they were both projecting. She wouldn't say playing, because it didn't feel that way at all. Her thoughts on the watch might be wrong, but she wasn't off base on this. There were no casual or unintended messages at this lunch. Whether unconscious or not, she'd chosen every aspect of her appearance carefully, and intuitively she knew he'd done the same.

His short dark hair lay smooth and gleaming against his head, and when those multicolored eyes reached her face, she was having a hard time not curling her fingers to hide their tremor. His dark lashes intensified the color, the matching brows giving his already strong face a more authoritative cast.

It's a pleasure to see you again. As she drew closer to the gazebo, she knew that was what she should say, initiate some polite chitchat. But she didn't. Anything like that died in her throat, the effort of forcing it out too much. It would be obvious how wrong it was.

She'd had Lynn set up their lunch in the large gazebo, because there was a good breeze today and it overlooked the man-made pond. A pair of ducks was swimming across it. Sometimes, in the early morning, deer came from the woods that backed her property, drank from it. Grazed on the lawn. The pear tree grove also screened the gazebo from the house, making their meeting private. Lynn and her assistant would bring the food or more drinks when Athena rang them, and not before.

The china gleamed, the silver was polished. The ironed tablecloth moved gently in the breeze coming off the water. The ceiling fan blades made a rhythmic hum.

She came to a stop a few steps away from the gazebo. He settled his hip on the rail, one long leg braced, the sole of his other boot sliding along the wood floor. They were the same boots he'd worn the other night, the ones with the silver tips.

"Come here, Athena. Stand in front of me."

A breath fluttered from her throat like a startled butterfly. She stood in place for another blink, teetering on indecision. Not a decision about what he wanted her to do, because the moment he said it, she wanted to go to him, but a decision about what it meant if she did. Dreams and fantasy were about to step over the line into nascent reality, and things could go wrong. Some things were better staying fantasy, letting dreams alone be the place where she let go of the reins.

Her gaze slid back up. Over his legs, the way his thighs outlined his groin area, though the loose shirttails hid most of that from view. Was he wearing the belt he'd worn the other day? He had a drink on the rail next to him. The dark amber liquid suggested Lynn had brought him a whiskey, or maybe a Coke mixed with something else. She didn't yet know his drinking habits, beyond black coffee.

She started to walk. It was nine steps to him. She made it five, and then she was at the table, her hand on the back of one of the chairs. She couldn't move further.

"Have you thought about what you want, Athena?" he asked. "Do you have an answer for yourself?"

He didn't ask if she had an answer for him, because he'd already understood that the question had never really been for him. He knew what she wanted, as much as he understood she had to accept her answer to make those last four steps.

"One more time, Athena. Come to me."

He wasn't coaxing. He was commanding. Those outside their world didn't understand that the command wasn't backed by a threat, but something far more powerful. Over here, by the chair, she was outside of herself, lost. Adrift in a world of beauty muted by a cloudy veneer she couldn't penetrate until she dropped her

shields, let herself accept the vulnerability that came with full awareness of who and what she was.

One and two. Three and four. Like hopscotch when she was a
little girl. She stood directly in front of the silver tip of his boot
now, her elegant pumps aligned with it as the center point.

She stared at his chest, dropped her gaze to his thighs again. His
arm rested on the right one, the side where his hip was half-cocked
onto the rail. His nails were clean, the potting soil that had collected
under them gone, but they were still rough hands, a workman's
hands. One of those hands lifted, cupped the side of her breast, just
as before. She pressed her lips together, that fluttering moving down
her sternum, spreading out beneath her rib cage as he curled his
fingers, stroked her with his knuckles. He didn't touch the nipple,
but it tightened beneath her bra, aching for him to do so. It was one
of her thinner ones, so she was sure her response became visible to
him, the breeze blowing the light fabric of her blouse against her.
But apparently it wasn't enough to suit his tastes.

"After five o'clock, when they're all gone, I want the bra off. You
understand?"

She nodded. Then she closed her eyes, shuddered hard. He shifted
off the rail, standing. Roy had been six feet. Dale was about the
same, perhaps a couple of inches taller. His shoulders were wide
enough to block her view of anything behind him, even if she'd
taken a step back. Now he put his hands on her upper arms, a brief
reinforcement of his words. He touched her hair.

Letting her go, he pulled out a chair, gestured. "Sit."

When she complied, he retrieved his drink from the rail and
took the chair next to hers. Though he leaned back, his knee stayed
close to hers. "So tell me what you want, Athena." His expression
wasn't hard or unkind, just unrelenting. She reveled in that inflex-
ibility, the decisiveness, and it gave her the courage to set a course.

"I'd like to try a few sessions here. With you."

"Not at the club?"

She shook her head. There were certain Dommes at the club who wouldn't understand this, an established Mistress deciding to switch. She didn't want to handle explanations, field veiled insults from people she liked to think of as friends. But beyond that, she was Roy's wife there. "I would pay you. A professional arrangement."

"No." His tone brooked no discussion on that point. "We do the sessions, see how it goes."

"Too personal. I need for it to stay professional."

"Then hire yourself a pro. That's not my deal. You connected with me, you want something from me. Same goes. You're not a timid woman, Athena, and I'm sure as hell not shy about what I want. I want to see where this leads. How about you?"

If she looked over her shoulder, she thought she'd see Jimmy's shocked face and the entire membership of the club behind him, judging.

"It's just you and me here," he said. "I know you worry about what others might think about this side of you. That's expected. But I'm interested in your husband. If he was alive, what would he think?"

"If he was alive, I wouldn't be considering it. He needed something different."

He studied her. "Athena, did he know you're a submissive?"

Just like that, a simple statement that shifted her world. She'd almost backed out of this meeting several times, embarrassed at her foray into an area she experientially knew nothing about. Yet every morning she'd woken from dreams where her subconscious embraced it. Flashes of her on her knees, Dale's hands on her, his mouth demanding things that went far beyond her body and deep into the core of who she was . . . of who she might be. She woke from such journeys aroused, uncertain but titillated, flushed by the rush of imaginings that pursued her outside of sleep.

During the daylight hours, she'd tried to contain and trivialize them. But when he acknowledged the truth now, all of that internal chatter died away. It simply . . . was. Like the breeze riffling his short hair, the intent focus of his blue-green eyes. It was as if he'd lifted a boulder off her chest, releasing the anxiety she'd been carrying, thinking about this moment.

"I'm not sure I even knew," she said. "Not until he died. It wasn't something I thought about. It wasn't onerous or awful, being his Mistress when he wanted that from me. I loved him, loved making him happy, and he made me happy. People don't understand that anymore. What honor and cherish, responsibility and love really mean."

"No. They don't." He spread his fingers out on the tablecloth. She'd said something that had surprised him, she could tell, but she wasn't sure in what way until he gave it to her. "A lot of people have a hard time understanding what drives a SEAL to do what we do. Honor and duty, responsibility . . . love of country . . . sacrifice. They don't understand, because so many of them no longer know what those words really mean. They're not monuments and medals."

"Just the way marriage isn't about flowers and diamonds on your anniversary." She met his gaze.

He nodded. "You're concerned what others at the club would think of you, but you don't seem to feel that way about your husband's memory. You don't think he'd judge or condemn you for it?"

"No. His form of submission was a deliberate decision to surrender. He had a need for it like a beer at the end of a hard workday. A more intense ritual than that, but still related." She offered a faint smile, and his lips curved in answer. "But he always understood I did this because he asked me to do it. Not because I had a driving desire to be a Mistress. I enjoyed the pleasure he took in my efforts, that others took in watching."

"Because that's what a true service sub does," Dale responded. "She takes pleasure in pleasing others. Her Master, all those in her life. A Master takes pleasure in holding power, a sub in surrendering to it. The way she surrenders may be mistaken for the flip side of the coin because of what you just described. You weren't a Domme to him. You were a Domme for him."

He was so straightforward, stating ideas she struggled to articulate because she couldn't see their shape from outside herself. She nodded, quietly amazed by the relief of claiming it as truth.

He leaned forward. "Put your hand on the table. Spread your fingers apart."

Curious, she did. He began to trace the outline of her hand with his forefinger. Because of the spread of her fingers and the size of his, he made contact with her skin, a light tease as he followed outside to inside, outside to inside. Then he stopped, his forefinger resting on top of one of her nails, a subtle gesture indicating she should leave the hand where it was. All her nerves were tingling, from that point of contact all the way up the inside of her arm.

"You have a pretty substantial Internet biography," he said casually. "You raised over a million dollars for Louisiana charities last year. Matched that from your own holdings. And you run the board of Summers Industries." He glanced around the grounds. "From what I saw of your staff, you also run an efficient household. You take care of your people. They look happy to have you as an employer, and they're protective. They all gave me the once-over, like if they were required to ID me to the police, they'd be ready. And willing. If they didn't take me out first."

It was an unexpected change of topic, but he left his fingertip on hers, holding her in that magnetic field he was projecting. She had to clear her throat first to respond.

"Lynn, my head housekeeper and cook, has been with us for more than ten years. Same with Hector, my groundskeeper. Lynn's assistant, Beth, has been here for five years, and most of the men who work with Hector are long-term employees or his family members. We've been through a lot of holidays, birthdays, family crises. It's perhaps made us a little more closely knit than most employer-employee relationships."

Lynn had helped her prepare Roy's body before the funeral home came to pick him up. She'd told the hospice nurse she'd do it, but she needed help to move him. Lynn had volunteered, but Roy was such a big man, the housekeeper called her son, Delray, who was also part of Hector's maintenance crew. They did it together, the three of them, putting Roy in one of his golf outfits, khaki slacks and a butter yellow placket shirt. On the left chest, there was an embroidered logo from one of his favored golf courses, an alligator with a golf ball sitting on his nose while a golfer put his foot on his snout to take a swing. It had always made her smile, the crocodile's aggravated expression, the golfer's intent concentration.

After she'd tied his loafers, she sat down in a chair. Delray sat on one side of her, Lynn the other, and then they held hands and cried together for a little bit.

"Are you ready for this, Athena?" Dale spoke in a low voice. Not interrupting her memories as much as stepping into the room and taking her hand. Prepared to lead her out of it, back to the present. "Or are you still grieving?"

"I don't think you ever stop grieving someone you loved for so many years," she said. "You learn how to make his memories part of your life, how to interweave them into your future, rather than letting them hold you down in the past. That's what I'm ready to do."

He nodded, his gaze telling her he approved of the answer. She knew SEALs were a small force, only a few thousand of them total, and they were assigned highly hazardous missions. As such, he would know the shape and feel of loss in a sharp, immediate way, one that would be empathic but not pitying. He'd likely faced some of the same lessons about grieving she had.

It might seem incongruous, that a New Orleans steel magnolia who'd lived in financial comfort and safety all her life could have things in common with a man who'd lived a large portion of his life in dangerous, difficult situations, but she'd learned emotions and loss were things all people faced, no matter what path they walked. People tended to celebrate their differences, make it their clarion call of accomplishment to the world; she'd learned it was discovering the similarities, the connections, that brought quiet joy and built lasting relationships. Such connections could sculpt happiness. And reassurance, especially in an uncertain moment like this.

"You're self-disciplined and selfless, and being both of those things takes a powerful will," he observed. "Anyone who doesn't really understand what a Dom and sub are about, would find it hard to believe you're not really a Domme. What we are deep inside is often the opposite side of what we show to others. Deciding to reveal that, explore it, brings balance. Are you seeking balance, Athena?"

"Yes." She looked down at his hand. He'd spread out his other fingers so they rested between hers. Just his fingertips, the curved digits above like a cage holding her hand there, a restraint she willingly accepted.

She moistened her lips. "How does what you feel . . . differ? As a Dominant, I mean." She'd often wondered, but of course had never been able to ask anyone without inviting curiosity about why she wouldn't know the answer herself.

He blinked. Crow's-feet from his age and exposure to the elements accentuated his eyes, adding to his rugged appeal. It balanced the beauty of his thick lashes, though she couldn't imagine anyone looking at this man and thinking him effeminate in any way. "I take pleasure in a sub's reaction, but my power over her gives me something, too. Like I said—two sides of a similar coin. It brings Master and sub together." He turned his gaze back to her hand. The sharpening of his attention drew her own like a rope cinching around her wrists, the slack end coiled around his strong hand.

"Close your eyes, Athena."

When she complied, he moved his index finger, but this time he traced her forefinger only, sliding down toward the V between it and her middle finger. When he reached it, he slid back up the inside of her middle finger, then returned to her forefinger again. "Part your legs, as much as you can in that snug skirt of yours. Are you wearing panties?"

"A thong. Yes." The skirt was tight enough panties caused unsightly lines, so she'd gone with the thong.

"After five, that comes off as well. You'll give it to me, so I can smell how wet you've gotten during our two hours together." His finger began to move again, sliding slowly, slowly down the inside of her forefinger. "Imagine this is my hand, moving over your ankle"—he passed over her first knuckle—"then past your knee." It quivered beneath the table, her legs instinctively pressing against the hold of the skirt, trying to widen for him. Her back arched against her chair.

"Now, deeper, deeper, until I reach your cunt." His fingertip caressed that tender juncture between index and middle finger. "It's hot and wet for me, isn't it?"

"Yes." She was breathless, lips parted, a flush climbing her cheeks, but not from embarrassment.

"Good. That's how I intend to keep it." He massaged that small V of skin, and she vividly imagined him rubbing her between her legs, such that she made infinitesimal lifts from the chair, her buttocks flexing. "Now, I'm moving from your cunt to your stomach, your sternum . . ." He moved up between the two knuckles, tracing the vein on the top of her hand, following the line to the joint of her wrist, and then he captured the wrist in his hand. "All the way to your neck."

Her chin had lifted, no words needed. She'd followed the vision he was painting her right to where he'd end up, with his hand wrapped around her throat. She swallowed as if she could feel its constriction and his hand tightened on her wrist.

"Did you ever buy Roy a collar?"

She shook her head. "That wasn't . . . something he wanted."

"But it's something you want, isn't it?"

She nodded, a quick jerk as if he had his hand there, limiting her mobility.

"We'll see about that. Open your eyes."

When she did, his attention was on her face. She'd noted his concentration when he'd been handling Willow, but it was far more powerful to have it up this close, and focused on her. She also saw a hint of what he'd been talking about, what exercising his skill as a Dominant gave him personally. She'd found pleasure in being Roy's Mistress, but she hadn't found this, an internal zone that was perhaps a related form of what a sub found when they completely let go. Within these bare few minutes, he'd stepped inside that zone for a Dom, and he'd very nearly taken her with him, by doing nothing more than touching her hand.

It overwhelmed her, not so much the newness of it, but how easily he'd made it happen. How easily she'd let it happen. She pushed away from the table, pulling from his hold. She rose and took a few steps away, drawing a deep breath. She was facing the house, her gaze fastened on the turrets that rose to the blue sky, pointing toward fluffy clouds. Tomorrow she was hosting a tea for the Daughters of the Confederacy. Afterwards they'd visit Metairie cemetery to do their monthly tending of the graves of the men that no longer had families to watch after them.

"I can't let this affect my personal life. It has to stay separate."

"I wasn't planning to spank you in front of your staff. Or tie you down on your boardroom table."

She gave a half chuckle at that image, though she was a little appalled by how it flooded her mind. Him stripping her naked and binding her on the table where she'd overseen so many decisions. He'd take a switch to her as he'd done Willow, such that her nails would gouge the wood, her perspiration seeping into it. Then he'd make her beg to come by putting his mouth between her legs.

She told herself not to be carried away. Reminded herself she knew nothing of him. A momentary impression at the club had become this lunch, this significant turning moment of her life. If a submissive at the club had told her she was contemplating such a course of action, she would have chided her for being too impulsive, even unsafe. But she could trust Dale with her physical well-being, couldn't she? He'd already proven that.

"Hey."

She turned. His penetrating look seemed to recognize every one of the churning emotions she was experiencing. And though his tone was gentle, he maintained the unrelenting expression, telling her he still held the reins. Like how a confident rider held the reins on his horse, communicating to the complex and responsive creature that she was safe under that restraint. Able to gallop and fly without fear—as long as it was at his command.

That was another key difference, she realized. A Dom had no desire to let go of those reins. He reveled in holding that control, seeing what the horse would do under his skilled touch, how far they could fly together.

"We all have lives that stay separate from this, Athena. But if what you're trying to say is that whatever feelings develop between us have to stay separate, that's something I can't help you with. Feelings go where they want to go. Neither Dom nor sub has any control over those. If that's your main worry, we have lunch and walk away from this."

Sensible, intelligent, logical. A touch of inexplicable sadness gripped her. "Okay. Fair enough."

He lifted a brow as she came back to the table. "So?"

She sat down, unfolded her napkin, smoothed it over her lap, even though there wasn't yet any food to make it necessary. She needed the action. He waited her out until she raised her gaze. "I don't want to walk away."

He nodded. "All right. You promised me lunch. I'm hungry."

It made her smile, and she saw the humor flit through his gaze in response. It calmed her nerves a little more. They'd have lunch. One step at a time.

Lynn had prepared a salad with ham-and-cheese bread as appetizers, followed by her incomparable stuffed crab. There was a homemade sherbet promised for dessert. When Dale complimented her cook's skills warmly, Athena was amused to see Lynn flush with pleasure beneath his regard almost as quickly as she did.

Roy would laugh at both of them. She remembered a particular day he'd complimented her on a dress. He'd gazed at her longer than the usual habit for a man married almost two decades to the same woman. It had made her blush. He'd lifted her hands to his lips, kissing both of them. *"I am the luckiest man in the world. And now you look like a lovely young girl."*

"You made me feel that way."

"I should do that every day." Then he'd kissed her mouth.

Dale had a similar way of paying attention to a woman that made it impossible not to feel . . . well, womanly, in all the right ways.

During lunch, he eased away from the more intense subjects. He asked her about the history of the house. The 1700s plantation home with antebellum Greek revival architecture overlooked the Mississippi River. Its extensive grounds had once been a sugar plantation. She told him anecdotes about the various families that had lived in the house, the exaggerated rumors that claimed Queen Victoria had given them a bathtub as a gift. She told him the story had been spun by one of the past owners who was drinking heavily with gambling companions. They'd all ended up in the bathtub, singing bawdy sailor songs and "God Save the Queen."

He chuckled over that, the velvet timbre of his voice twining around her. She'd slipped her feet out of her shoes as they were eating, and when he shifted his position, she realized her bare foot was within an inch of his boot. Not giving herself too much time to think about it, she slid her toes over the top of it. She did it lightly, not wanting to be caught indulging such a whimsical, intimate gesture, but then she realized what was under the leather didn't feel exactly like the foot she expected. Curious, she moved up a little farther, above the ankle, her toes sliding under his jeans' cuff. The boot gave easily beneath the pressure, as if what was beneath was mostly empty. What she felt was more like a rod than a leg. There *was* no leg there.

"I notice a woman playing footsy with me a lot quicker on the right side."

He'd noticed pretty fast, given that all of it had all happened within the past few seconds, with barely a pause in the conversation. Now she lifted her eyes to his. "Your eyes are like sea glass," he said. "That soft green color." Reaching out, he made her left eye close when he brushed her lashes, lightly. "These are almost blond." Then he pulled off another piece of the ham-and-cheese bread, offering it to her.

When she shook her head, he took it instead, his healthy male appetite warming her. Lynn would say he was a man who was a pleasure to feed. Athena could cook quite well herself, and if there were evenings they'd be spending here alone during the dinner hour, she might like that opportunity.

"May I ask about it?"

He picked up his sweet tea to take a swallow, then wiped his mouth with the cloth napkin before answering. "Right now you can ask me whatever you'd like, Athena."

Right now. The qualification reminded her that the clock was moving toward the five o'clock hour. If he'd intended to tighten that little screw on the wire of sexual tension that strummed between them, he'd succeeded admirably. He didn't seem visibly concerned that she'd figured out his handicap, but then he didn't really act like it was one, did he?

"How did it happen?"

"The details of the mission are still classified, but basically it was the result of an underwater explosion. A dislodged boat prop sliced into it and the docs couldn't save it, not by the time they got me to them."

"How long ago?"

"A few years before I was eligible for retirement. I was able to do other work, serve as an instructor, help with tactical planning for missions, but I was no longer in active combat situations."

No, discussing the leg didn't seem to bother him at all, but being cut out of active missions was a different matter. He'd made his peace with it, but in the tone of his voice, the way shadows darkened his eyes, she saw how hard-won it had been. "I'm sorry."

"Being a SEAL is a calling." He shrugged. "You know you'll retire one day, and I was able to do it after I served over my full twenty years. But even so, getting your legs cut out from under you before you're ready for it—a bit literally, in my case—it's tough. You miss it like a drug. It's hard to find anything to match it. I met an astronaut once who described going into space the same way."

She thought of those first days without Roy, figuring out who and what she was when what seemed like ninety percent of how she defined herself, motivated herself, structured herself, was gone. She still cried for him most nights before she went to sleep, hugging his pillow hard to her chest. "So how did you figure it out?" she asked softly.

He reached out, sliding a fingertip down her cheek with exceptional tenderness. "I dealt with it day by day, same as you. Some days I was a total bastard."

Matter-of-fact as his tone seemed, she expected the information was something he rarely shared. Perhaps the fact he was helping her embrace something she'd never shared with another gave him the comfort to speak plainly with her. She liked the idea of that connection, though thinking of him coming so close to a fatal injury made her heart hitch in her chest, no matter that it had happened some time ago.

"Ever been married?" she asked.

"Once. She left me about ten years into it, before this happened to my leg, thank God. I'm glad she didn't have to deal with that. Being married to a SEAL was hard enough for her. No children," he added. "You?"

She shook her head. "Our lives were full enough without them. We both have brothers and sisters with children, and we handle the operating costs for a children's home in Louisiana, so we can enjoy their company whenever we wish. We've hosted picnics and carnival days for them here. Why didn't you and your wife choose to have them?"

"Never had enough motivation to make it happen. Guess we should have seen that as a sign, too, like we both knew we weren't going to make it for the long haul. As a result, I'm glad we didn't take that step. I came from divorced parents and remember how much it hurt when they split. Kids are tough, they get over things or figure it out, but Pam and I were the types who would have stayed with one another to prevent doing that to a kid, even when the marriage fell apart. And kids pick up on that shit, no matter how much we tell ourselves they don't."

She nodded. "So was there anyone for you . . . when it happened? To your leg."

His eyes warmed on her. "Trust you to think of that. SEALs are a family. The guys in my unit, other guys I'd worked with along the way, they helped me pull through. We don't let one of our own wallow in self-pity. If I even thought about it, one of them was there to kick me in the ass, remind me of the ones who come back without both legs, paralyzed from the neck down or in a box. And if I was too pathetic, they'd pull out the big guns. They'd make me go hang out in the children's cancer ward."

She winced, and he nodded. "Yeah. Anybody who can pity themselves after seeing how those kids deal with things just deserves a headshot to put everyone else out of the misery of dealing with him."

At her smile, he gave her one of his own. "So I made it work. Turning a loss into a win is one of the codes we live by."

We. He didn't speak like he was retired, but he'd called it a calling, and one never left behind a calling. She thought of him, though, his leg being cut away on an operating table, waking up to face how that changed his life. She was glad he'd had others to stand by him.

"You had a little bit of a limp that day, after you helped me at the gas station. But you're not limping now."

"Yeah. The prosthesis and the gait training I've had let me walk pretty normally. Only time you'll notice anything is if I've overdone."

"Like the gas station." At his look, she shifted topics, recognizing the typical male desire not to linger too long on any perceived weakness. With private amusement, she expected that trait would be exacerbated considerably in a SEAL, retired or otherwise. "So, the Dom thing. When did you figure that out?"

"I don't remember the exact day, but I remember some key pivotal moments." He tilted his head, considering. "I was at a buddy's barbecue. One of his neighbors was there with his spouse, and something about the way the two of them interacted caught my attention. Whenever the husband needed something—another beer, another plate of food, whatever—she would go get it for him. When she came back to him, she'd settle at his feet on a folded towel, like she was more comfortable sitting on the lawn. At different times, when he was talking to people, he'd have his hand on her shoulder, his thumb inside her shirt collar, playing with this pewter choker she was wearing. It nagged at me, as if I was seeing some kind of secret code happening, and of course that was exactly what was going on."

She agreed, since she was attuned to those nuances herself.

"Other Doms told me figuring it out was like opening up this whole part of themselves that had always been there," he continued. "Driving them in their real lives. When I looked back at the way I drove myself to excel in the SEALs, how I took charge of so many missions, how I was with my wife . . . SEALS are pretty much alpha personalities, and though that's not a given for a Dom, we're also trained to evaluate, to notice details, to follow as well as lead. It's a balance, a give-and-take of power to accomplish the mission, and that give-and-take was something that was second nature to me. More than I realized."

He shifted his legs into a more relaxed sprawl under the table, one that aligned his booted feet on either side of her chair. It put her in the center of his attention, and felt that way. They were getting close to five o'clock, and his movement suggested how closely he was tracking the time. The fact he kept his tone mild, conversational, only enhanced the underlying tension between their two bodies.

"I approached the guy later, eased into the subject matter, and he confirmed he and his wife were part of the D/s lifestyle. He directed me to a few reputable clubs, gave me some direction, and I went from there."

His gaze moved from her face to her throat, sliding with casual pleasure over her upper body, down to her legs. "When we're down range—on a mission—we're in a hyperalert mode, a sustained intensity. Sometimes, when we get back, we have to hang out at a buddy's house, defuse, until we're fit for civilized society again. It's not a good thing to evaluate everyone in Walmart as a target."

"As tempting as that can sometimes be," she said wryly.

"Especially during the busy times," he agreed. That shadowed look returned to his expression. "When I retired, I threw myself into work, a million volunteer jobs, working like a reformed drug addict to fill the hours, but it didn't ease the ache. You miss the adrenaline rush in a way that's indescribable. I didn't want to just rock climb or run a triathlon. I wanted something that felt meaningful to more than myself. The camaraderie, the bond between you and your team when you're active, the way you depend on one another, it's hard to replace that. You help take care of SEAL families while your buddies are deployed, hang out with them when they're home, but it's not the same.

"When I was evaluating a sub in a club environment, working with her, taking her to subspace, I found that quiet space inside, where I could be focused on every single detail, like when on a mission. Her well-being is completely in my hands. She's depending on me to get her through it. And that bond brought it all together. Not the same, but enough to give me peace."

Now he straightened, his hand dropping back over hers, fingers on her wrist. She went still, and he cocked his head. "For instance"—he stroked her wrist bones—"if you were tied, I'd notice your circulation, how the knots are tied. Your facial expressions, the acceleration of your heartbeat. Every single thing I do creates a reaction. If I lean forward, just a few more inches into your personal space"—he did so, bringing his face closer to hers—"your breathing changes, and the tension in your body increases. Staying aware of those details determines what my next step will be, how I'll approach the next task, how to keep you safe, and deliver you to the end goal. Mission accomplished."

When he eased back, she took a breath. He noticed that, too. He'd mesmerized her, as effectively as a snake charmer. She cleared her throat.

"Have you been involved with anyone since your wife?"

"Nothing serious."

"Are you gun-shy?"

"On the contrary. I'm very comfortable with guns."

She narrowed her gaze at him and his lips curved. "You're the one who spooked about setting limits," he pointed out. "Spouting off about paying me."

"Spouting off?" She lifted a brow and the smile turned into a grin. It made him even more handsome. Then he sobered.

"I've already said I won't agree to you turning this into a

compartmentalized club session. You accepted that. Now you're asking questions that are cycling back to that again. Will this be a relationship or simply about the Dom/sub stuff? The purpose of your question is to control the situation, define it. That's not your job. You understand?"

The nebulous set of feelings she was letting out of a box that had always stayed closed seemed to understand. Yet he was correct; another part of her was uneasy and struggling with it, wanting to find some way to respond that put things on even ground between them, manageable, at her pace. Under her control.

Being at the mercy of the vacillation of her own mind was wearing on her nerves. She glanced at the carafe Lynn had left plugged in to keep the contents hot. "May I get you some coffee?"

She didn't ask as a hostess. Perhaps she was testing his acuity, but if she was, he aced the test. "It's ten minutes to five, Athena," he said mildly. "Are you trying to move up the clock?"

She paused, then nodded. How would he react? Would he make her wait? "Please," she said. Her voice had a tremor in it.

"No. Ten more minutes."

FOUR

s Athena pressed her lips together, looked toward the pond, Dale could see her mind working in ten different directions. Though every submissive was different, she was an exceptionally unique package. According to Jimmy, she was an accomplished Mistress. The irony was that skill came from being a down-to-the-bone submissive. Even so, actively performing as a submissive was going to be new to her.

While he might have barked at another sub for trying to rush the clock, galvanizing her into the right mind-set with an immediate show of discipline, he understood the level of conflict she was experiencing at this juncture. It wasn't yet time for heavy-handedness. The pacing needed to be as precise as the way he knew she'd pour him a cup of coffee. That was part of the pleasure of this, yet he felt an anticipation to it that was new to him. Sharper, sweeter—a sense that the stakes were higher. He wasn't gun-shy about relationships with women. Just very, very selective.

He shifted his chair so he could look out at the pond, study the view and the gardens. Ostensibly, he was ignoring her, treating her as part of the furniture, here for his use. Though he'd said they'd wait until five, it gave her enough of a taste of it to quiet if not calm her. Her fingers were in a knot in her lap. Without changing the direction of his gaze, he reached out, covered and untangled them, closing his hand around hers. He simply held it, rubbing his thumb over her cool fingers as the birds twittered and the clouds drifted across the sky.

His watch ticked to the appropriate hour. He waited a solid thirty seconds, then spoke.

"Bring me a cup of coffee."

She jerked at the sound of his voice, probably pulling herself out of frenetic, internal-narrative ping-pong, but then she composed herself, rising in that serene way she had. He noticed that she waited until he withdrew his hand to do it. Her undiluted natural instinct for submission was absorbing to watch. It was also a serious test of his self-restraint.

Circling the table, she lifted the carafe. The faint tinge to her cheeks showed all that was going on beneath the surface. She poured the coffee, not spilling a drop, then brought it back to him, placing the cup and saucer before him. She'd remembered he took it black. Damn, she was going to kill him.

She waited as he lifted it, tasted. Then he nodded at her. "Very good. You can sit down now. At my feet."

Just a brief hesitation, then she sank to her knees. His groin tightened, cock hardening so rapidly he'd have gotten dizzy if standing. *Jesus.* Yeah, a submissive like this could get him revved up, but even for that, his reaction to her was unexpectedly strong. If she could see how hot his blood was boiling, the things he wanted to do to her, she might run screaming. Or not. The thought of her embracing anything he threw at her only made things worse.

He put his hand on her hair, stroked a lock, twined it in his hand. She didn't put a lot of goop on it that made it stiff. It was fine and silky, with a natural wave from her face. He liked the brown-bird color, the way it had gleamed in the sun when she'd walked out of the garden toward him. She had a sexy walk as well, wearing that pencil skirt and heels in a way that turned a man's thoughts to fucking, no help for it. All the more so because it was unintentional. She was one hundred percent class.

"Seventeen hundred hours," he said, reminding her. Then he waited.

To his intense approval, she pulled the blouse from her waist-band, revealing a creamy band of skin as she reached up beneath the shirt. Her back arched, breasts thrusting outward in involuntary display as she unhooked her bra, worked the straps down through her sleeves and pulled the whole thing free. She folded and handed it to him. His thumb slid over the inside of one of the cups, feeling the warmth her breast had left there, and then he lifted the garment, inhaling the fragrance left by her skin.

She had to stand to accomplish part two of what he'd demanded, but as he gave her a nod to permit it and she rose, he caught her hand, stilling her. Her attention followed his, to where Lynn was walking out the side entrance, over to the garage. She was talking to another woman, perhaps the assistant Athena had mentioned, and they were carpooling. As they got into the car and pulled away, Dale returned his attention to Athena. It looked as if it had surprised her, his paying more attention to protecting her privacy than she herself had.

He tightened his grip. "Your job is to obey my will, follow my direction exactly and immediately. Mine is to make sure you don't have to focus on anything other than that. Understand?"

She nodded. She wasn't pulling away, and he decided to use that, shifting his grip to her wrist. "Take off the panties one-handed," he ordered.

Watching a submissive struggle with a logistical difficulty was another way of putting them off balance, taking up more of their attention, getting them in the right headspace. Plus it was a pure pleasure to have her putting her weight against his hold, relying on him for balance as she worked the skirt up to hook the thong pant-ies with one set of fingers. She couldn't screen herself from his view as much this way, so he watched the skirt bunch up over her thighs and then higher until he saw the point of her sex, covered by a smooth silky fabric, a tiny swatch of lace across the crotch panel. She was quite ladylike, his Athena.

She worked the thong down, and he won another brief glimpse of her clean-shaven pussy before the skirt draped back over it, barely. Now that the requested garment was at her knees, she straightened as if to pull the skirt back in place, but he shook his head. "I asked for the panties. That's your first priority."

Her hand shook in his, just a tiny tremor. The stress in her expression was a combination of arousal and uncertainty. She was all right; merely getting used to the new feelings.

Stepping out of the thong, she bent to retrieve it. Her arm remained in his grasp as she handed it over, but then he shifted that hold. He placed both hands on her thighs, fingers sliding beneath the folds of skirt to grip firm, silken skin. His thumbs pressed on the seam of her thighs and she adjusted so they were open to him.

"Good girl."

He sat back then, the underwear in his lap, and picked up his coffee. "You can adjust your skirt and sit at my feet now."

She complied, her cheeks a fetching pink as she wiggled the amount needed to accomplish the task. When she knelt at his feet, he saw her notice his arousal beneath the jeans. When he casually adjusted himself, straightening his cock beneath the denim, she moistened her lips.

It would be so fucking tempting to have her suck him off right here. He had a feeling she would do so the moment he commanded it, but it would be too much. She was handling herself well, but if what she implied was true, he was the first man she'd ever trusted with this side of herself, and she'd been married—and monogamous—with the same guy for over twenty years. It showed her strength, that she was reaching out this way. The gift she was giving him was priceless, and it came with a lot of responsibility. He had to protect her every step of the way.

The power of taking time was that it could wrap around a submissive, cocoon her, intensify every feeling for the both of them, and create a lasting experience that both would want to repeat, no guilt or regrets. It wasn't a race, but a journey, and one that worked best if they stayed together during it, progressing to the point that they wouldn't know where one of them stopped and the other started, the power exchange intertwined.

He took one more sip of the coffee, then set it aside. "Give me a tour of the property. I want to know the resources I'll have at my disposal."

"We don't have a playroom or dungeon. I know it seems odd, for as much space as we have, but . . ."

"That's fine. I actually prefer to work with the environment the woman in question provides."

"Oh." Though she nodded, there was an expression on her face that had him reaching down to touch her cheek, draw up her bemused gaze.

"That's a rare pleasure for me. Most of my time with subs is spent in a club."

Her shoulders eased. It mattered to her, that this was a relatively unique experience for him. Even more intriguingly, it had mattered to him to set her straight on that. He was correct—this relationship was going to be more. Whenever she sensed that possibility, like now, he noticed she became more nervous, but it was the good kind of nervous, the kind that was an aphrodisiac to a Master.

He slid his fingertip down her jaw, to her throat. "Every time you touch a particular chair, or walk across a rug, or handle a spatula in your kitchen . . . I want you to be thinking of me."

She phased out on him at little bit at that, her busy mind obviously caught up in the possibilities, but she recalled herself. She drew back. "I expect we should talk about rules and boundaries. Limits."

An entirely different matter from her earlier erroneous attempt to define the relationship itself. What she meant now was the structure that would guide her submission to him. Of course the word "limits" sounded forced from her lips, but he understood that. Most new subs wanted to get completely lost in the fantasy of total surrender, which was another reason a Dom needed to keep a firm hand on the reins, to keep the sub safe. Athena might have that temptation, but she had the wits and maturity to take it back to that track herself. They were on the same wavelength. He'd been about to suggest the rule discussion as part of the tour.

"Want to do that while you show me around? You seem like a good multitasker to me."

"Most women are." Her eyes smiled, even though the rest of her looked a little wound up.

"Athena." He set the coffee aside, leaned forward and clasped his hands between his knees. "You know there's nothing to be afraid of here, right?"

"I think I want to be afraid, a little bit."

"Yeah. I'll take care of that, I promise." The dangerous surge he felt at her admission must have shown in his face, because her color went high again, the pulse jumping in her throat. A strong Dom had a predator's instincts, such that he had to tamp down the desire to push that adrenaline reaction. Today wasn't going to be about that, he reminded himself. Again. "Let's get started on that tour."

She'd planned to take the paved walkways, not wanting to make uneven terrain an issue for him, but he was the one to step off the path, drawn by the various sculptures and how her landscaping was designed around them. She'd helped with those plans, so she was pleased to see his interest. He came to a stop at the section where a gravel path of white stone spiraled around the focus piece, a large bronze statue of a griffin. Its wings were spread, head lifted to the sky in a defiant cry. Standing a few paces away was a life-sized man with a drawn sword. His posture said he'd intended to engage the griffin, but his expression suggested hesitation, as if the beauty and sav-age power of the creature had overwhelmed him, or some other conflict held him back. The man wore a suit, like a contemporary businessman.

Dale looked from one to the other. "When the sun goes down, do they come to life and fight each other until dawn?"

"If they do, they're quiet about it. My bedroom window's right there." She nodded to the second level of the house. "The artist called it *The Choice*. He provided no other explanation than that, leaving it to the viewer's interpretation."

"As the best artists do. It's also a good way for the lousy ones who create junk to cover their asses."

After that dry comment, Dale reached up to touch the griffin's wings, the curve of the head, the texture of the feathers sculpted on his convex chest. He pivoted to look at the view beyond the griffin. Past the swordsman, the garden path passed between two large crepe myrtles and continued along a winding view of more flowers and trees, inviting the viewer to come that way, get lost for the afternoon. She knew such a wanderer would find benches tucked into leafy arbors, more statuary to study. Her gardens were always on the New Orleans spring garden tour. She loved following the tour groups, seeing how people reacted to what she, Hector and a landscape architect had created here, the designs evolving from year to year.

She trailed behind Dale for the same reason now, and for some additional ones. She was letting him form his own impressions, but she was also sorting out all the feelings he'd raised in the gazebo. On one level, she needed him to leave so she could take time to digest the momentous changes that had happened to her in the course of one meal, the things he'd awoken in her. Another, far stronger part of her, didn't want him to leave at all. She was very aware of the loose movement of her breasts beneath the blouse, the friction of her thighs against her bare sex.

He'd shifted direction, moving toward a rotunda with a copper roof. She thought about distracting him, leading him to another section, but she'd let him get too far ahead of her.

Inside the rotunda was a beautifully detailed, marble three-foot-tall sculpture of the goddess Athena. She had her shield and spear, a lion at her hip. Her owl rested on her wrist, wings spread. The statue was mounted on a platform, water glossing the disc and falling into a fountain pool below. Dale's head dipped as he studied the plaque beneath it. She swallowed, knowing the words he read.

For my Athena,
who brought the strength and wisdom
of a goddess to my life.
Thank you for giving a mortal man your heart.
Love you forever. Roy

"He had the rotunda built while he was sick. Told me he'd commissioned a very special statue and fountain for it. It was delivered a month after he died, with the plaque."

She turned away and moved toward the house, leaving Dale to explore the rest of this portion of the gardens on his own. When she reached the patio built in front of the sunroom that connected two wings of the house, she sat down on a bench there. Closing her eyes, she took a steadying breath. Then another. She was in the middle of the third when the bench shifted, telling her Dale had joined her. She tensed, but he didn't touch her. Just sat there quietly until she collected herself.

"I'm sorry. I didn't anticipate my reaction to you intersecting with . . ."

"You owe no one an apology for being in love with your husband, Athena. You gave a hundred and twenty percent to every part of the vow. I'm honored that I'm the first you're trusting with all of this. Ready to look at the inside?"

"I'm not sure." She gave a half laugh, then shook herself. "Of course. We can go in through the sunroom."

"All right."

He rose, held out his hand. When she offered hers, he laced their fingers, gave her a smile and tugged her to her feet. As he opened the sunroom door, he released her, but only so that he could shift the touch to the small of her back, grazing her hip as she moved inside.

The sunroom was more of a nook, her favorite reading spot. It held one roomy easy chair, a side table and a walnut portable heating unit, a rug laid on the floor before it. There was a small bookshelf that held both her electronic reader in its charger and some print selections, the latest in her reading list. There was enough wall space for a couple of paintings, watercolor studies of anemones.

Roy had called it her nest. On rainy days in particular she loved sitting here reading, watching the drops slide down the glass and the garden view change with the movement of the wind. In the past couple of years, she'd spent a lot of her time at home here, wrapped in a blanket, dozing over her books, wishing she never had to leave the room, never face the emptiness of the rest of the house.

"That statue . . . it's quite wonderful, but I'm not perfect, Dale." She felt a little foolish, stating the obvious. It made her sound egotistical.

As Dale turned toward her, he hooked a thumb in his jeans pocket. "But you strive to be, in all aspects of your life. Where do you relinquish control, Athena?"

Because of the size of the room, he stood close to her, the walls behind each of them reinforcing that proximity. When he shifted toward her, the smallness of the room increased considerably. The forest green color of his shirt filled her vision. "I'm thinking you carve out pockets of time," he continued. "Like when you're in this room, reading a book for your own pleasure or looking at your garden. It's your space, your time. That's your moment to breathe. But that's not the same as putting yourself in someone's hands, letting them take the reins, is it?"

She shook her head, though she wasn't sure how to answer his initial question. He didn't press her for a response, however. Instead, he clasped her hand again. "I certainly hope you aren't perfect. Else I'll have to make shit up to punish you."

The comment startled a laugh out of her, and his eyes twinkled. "Doesn't that break some kind of Dom code?" she asked.

"Not mine. Now show me the house, woman. It looks like it'll take days to get through it."

"Hardly." But she took the lead at his gesture, and began to familiarize him with the different rooms. Library, parlor, living areas, kitchen, bathrooms.

She mentioned polite details about the uses of the rooms, things she might have told any guest. After a few comments, he shifted his grip to her wrist, gave it a squeeze. "No more talking, Athena, unless it's something I need to know. Be quiet and let me form my own impressions."

He'd done the same in the gardens, only here he clearly had a different agenda. As they proceeded, she thought she might be watching how he approached missions. Evaluating terrain, resources, contingencies. Only this mission was one that involved her intimately.

He examined the tools Lynn had in the kitchen, drawing out a broad pancake spatula and slapping it against the flat of his hand, making her jump. He paid her no mind, however, putting the spatula back and moving to the refrigerator. On its stainless steel surface, Lynn kept a magnet clip to hold reminders of the week's menu. He removed the clip, checked its grip on his fingers. Opened the freezer to study the shape and size of the ice in the icemaker.

With everything he noticed, her mind filled with provocative images. Him putting her on her stomach on the butcher block table, tying her arms and legs to it so he could apply that spatula for her "less than perfect" moments. Letting the ice glide along her back, melt and trickle down the valley of her spine as she wiggled and squirmed. He'd give her several more sharp slaps for moving. When her clit was engorged, he'd clamp the magnet clip on it, making her beg for mercy from the discomfort and overwhelming sensation at once.

They moved on to the bathrooms. He tested the strength of the shower rod and filled up the Jacuzzi tub the few inches necessary to run the jets. Reaching down, he ran his fingers over them, checking the water pressure and how easy it was to adjust the direction of the stream. In turn, she saw herself on her back in the tub, her knees pulled up over the side, her arms tied to the safety bar on the wall as he held her spread legs centered in front of a jet until she came, screaming from the inexorable water pressure.

"How many of these tubs do you have? Are they the same model?"

"Three." Her throat was dry. "Yes."

When they reached the second level, she showed him the guest bedrooms as well as the upstairs library she used as her home office for days when she worked here, on either Summers Industries' matters or fund-raising efforts. He studied the neat arrangement of her desk, her closed laptop. In the guest bedroom, he ran his fingers over the sturdy wood posts of the canopy bed. Another guest bed had a wrought iron head- and footboard. He spent extra time with that one, lifting the mattress and box spring to see horizontal supports beneath. Without the bedding, the thing looked like a medieval instrument of torture. Her heart thumped a little faster, thinking of the more extreme things she'd seen done at the club with racks.

There was only one more room on this hallway, but when he moved toward it, she spoke for the first time. He'd told her to speak when there was something he needed to know, after all.

"Not that room," she said. "It's our bedroom. I mean, my bedroom."

He paused. "I'd like to see what your private space looks like. It tells me important things about you."

"I . . . Not this visit. All right?"

He gave her a close look, but he nodded, moving past her and back toward the stairs. When they reached them, he moved down the steps first. She thought about putting her hand on his shoulder, using that broad expanse to steady her descent.

She'd offered to pay him to avoid this, this confusing mix of the emotional with . . . what she was seeking. Okay, what she sought was emotional, but it was supposed to have limited boundaries. It had to, right? This felt . . . out of control. Things were getting mixed-up again.

She sank down on the top step, staring at him. Though he was several steps below her, he stopped immediately, proving how aware he was of her. He turned, one foot braced above the other, his hand on the rail. "You move like you have two real feet," she said. "I wouldn't have even known."

"Yeah." Coming back up the steps, he sat next to her, the stair wide enough to accommodate them both, though their hips were brushing. He bent his leg to put his hands on the toe and heel of his boot. The prosthesis was a tight fit down in the boot, because it took him a moment to work it off. When he did, her eyes widened.

"Oh. I guess I expected it to look . . ."

"Like a foot? Yeah, some do. I think at some point they realized it was far more important to make it work like a foot than to look like one. You saw that guy that ran in the Olympics with the blades? The guy who designed those based them on a cheetah's back legs."

She studied the prosthesis, momentarily distracted from her agitation. A pair of rectangular metal plates formed the "foot," the upper one curving up to form an "ankle" with a coil between the plates for shock absorption and to provide different adjustments that would allow it to articulate like a foot and ankle.

"There's computer programming in it, to help with different terrain and propulsion. You can adjust the ankle height for different shoes, so I can wear my boots. I was really lucky. Even with my benefits, I couldn't have afforded something like this, but I got into a special prototype study. Having the ability to flex the ankle piece gives me more options on everything, even something as simple as wearing boots. When you're wearing a prosthesis that can't flex, you can't really wear a shoe or boot that goes above the ankle."

"It's remarkable." She reached out toward it, then hesitated. "I'm sorry. I don't want to be rude."

"You have my permission to touch, Athena. At least my Lee Majors leg."

That attractive crinkle at the corners of his eyes almost made her smile. Sitting here on the steps like a pair of kids, things were easier. She touched the metal, followed it up above the ankle, where it attached to a rod.

"That goes up to the socket, where my knee rests."

"Does it hurt?"

"Only if the socket is fitted wrong or I do the wrong things. You also have to change out the stump socks at different times, use different thicknesses, because your leg changes shape throughout the day." He shrugged. "Like anything else, once you figure out how to maintain the equipment, it becomes routine. I shower only at night, because if I do it in the morning, my socket doesn't fit right."

"So no morning showers together."

"Unless we're planning to go back to bed for the day." His gaze heated on her, and the uncertain feeling returned. She clasped her hands together as he replaced the boot, pulled down the cuff of his jeans. When he straightened, he put his hand on the banister, his other resting loosely on his knee. "Are you reconsidering, Athena?"

She shook her head, then nodded. Then shook it again. Laughed at herself.

"If it was just about sex, it would be easy," he said quietly. "Where you've been, your marriage, you can't do dating or casual anymore. Right?"

She nodded, swamped by a sudden sick feeling. She'd been too craven; he was about to call it off. But then he curled his hand over hers on her knees. "Everything you've told me today, everything I've seen, tells me you're what I call a power sub. You crave submission, but it takes a hell of a firm and steady hand to bring you to that level of trust, because in order to please everyone, you've had to stay in control of every freaking detail. That's why I asked you about relinquishing control. To make it work, Athena, you're going to have to learn how to do that. And as you do, no matter what limits you and I set, a lot of emotional stuff is going to unfold."

A hell of a firm and steady hand. Those mesmerizing blue-green eyes projected a thrilling danger quality when he said that. She couldn't decide if she wanted to run toward or away from it. She looked at her hands, twisted back into a knot beneath his, and sighed. "I'm sorry, Dale. I've been a Domme for so long, but here I am, one moment acting like a newbie sub, so high on the idea of a Master that I don't care about contracts or limits. The next moment, you see my closed bedroom door and I want to make you leave, pretend I never did this."

He shrugged, unoffended. "As far as experience, you *are* a newbie sub, which is why you were smart, choosing to work with an experienced Dom."

"I didn't really choose at all. I just saw you and knew . . . felt, that was what I wanted. In that moment."

"An intuitive choice is still a choice. Sometimes better than a conscious one, especially for this." He leaned against her shoulder, nudging her. "I'll keep you safe, Athena. I can help you manage those initial feelings. You just have to trust me, girl."

She turned her gaze up toward his attentive face then. Reaching out, she caressed his jaw, her fingertips touching his hair, the shape of his ear, the pulse in his throat. Those few sensations alone overwhelmed her. He watched her, not stopping her, but not encouraging, either. She withdrew her hand.

"I'm sorry. I . . . wanted to touch you."

"Then you should ask me properly, Athena."

Despite giving her the structure, the boundary, he had heat in those blue-green eyes, reminding her of his arousal in the gazebo. He would remain in absolute control, but he wanted her. He wasn't detached at all. It was a heady awareness. Those "rash feelings" would help her move forward where she wanted to go, no matter how that path frightened her. But he'd told her he'd keep her safe.

A proper request came with a proper address, but he hadn't given her specific direction on that. Perhaps he was waiting to see what would come most naturally to her.

"Please . . . may I touch you . . . sir?"

"No. But I'm going to touch you."

Closing his hands on her upper arms, he pressed her back against the stairs, shifting so his knee pressed into the stretch fabric of the skirt, pinning her there. He loomed over her in the dim light of the stairwell, broad shoulders filling her gaze, his scent around her. When he leaned down, her helpless fingers curled against his sides, digging into his shirt.

"No touching me, Athena. Let go."

She opened her fingers, so aware of how close he was to her. At first she thought he was going to kiss her, and she froze, but he moved lower, and that feeling eased. His chest slid against her breasts, then his mouth was on the pulse pounding heavily in her neck. The first contact of his lips made her shudder like a climax, intensified by his requirement that she simply lie there, held down by his strength, hands open and empty at his command. He traced that pulse with his tongue, making her whole body strain toward his without movement. When his hip bone pressed against her mound, she moaned.

He raised his head, his eyes holding hers. "You're not sure about kissing yet. You tensed."

"I—"

"I wasn't asking a question, Athena."

He bent again, moved to her jaw. Her skin was on fire, flame racing across her breasts, her thighs. "How do you masturbate, Athena? With a vibrator? Your hand?"

"V-vibrator."

"Efficient, just like you. Until I come back for our first proper session, you won't be using it. If you wish to have an orgasm that I haven't ordered, you'll use your hand. Your nondominant one." He lifted her left hand, telling her he'd noticed she was right-handed. "If you can't bring yourself to a climax with it within five minutes, you have to stop, and you can't try again for twenty-four hours. You understand?"

"Yes sir."

"All right." He rose, bringing her back to a sitting position, then he lifted her to her feet, holding on to her wrists until she steadied. He was two steps lower than she was, so they were at eye level. "You have stationery? The pretty, girly kind?"

She nodded.

"Between now and our next session, you'll write out what you think your hard and soft limits are. No erasing, no crumpling, no marking out. If you change your mind, write it all out. If you say "No paddling" but then you think you might want to try that, add "well, maybe some." Pure stream of consciousness, no editing. No rereading. I'll go over it before I start."

"How will you know to plan that session . . . without that?"

"That's my area to figure out. Relinquish control, Athena. That's your area."

As he reached the bottom of the stairs, he turned to look up at her. She was standing on the same step, clutching the banister. "I'll let myself out," he said. "Lunch was good. Is sex part of our agreement?"

The man really needed to learn about segues. She blinked. "I don't know. I thought . . . maybe it's not the right thing for our initial sessions, because . . ." Well, he'd said it. She had no desire to date, no ability to . . . be casual. Sex was for intimacy, to express emotion. Not just to have a climax. "I didn't know if our first sessions are supposed to get that personal."

"Hmm." Those eyes seemed capable of tunneling under her heart, uncovering all the aching uncertainty putting pressure on her chest. "Slide your skirt up to your waist and sit down."

If he'd only told her to sit down, she could surmise it was because he'd noticed her knees were suddenly not so steady. She managed the skirt part, and because of the skirt's snug fit, pulling it up to her waist left her naked from the waist down, the fabric gathered in her hand. At least the stairwell was shadowed.

"Lean back, put your elbows on the stair and plant your feet third step below where you're sitting. Spread your knees as wide as they'll go. Drop your head back and arch your back."

By complying with his commands, she could no longer see him, but she felt the vibration when he moved back up the stairs. She heard the sound of his measured breathing, sensed him standing in touching distance of her spread knees. He would be staring at her bare pussy, at everything she'd exposed. With her back arched and without the bra, the thin silk of her blouse would delineate her nipples like the cherries on top of ice cream scoops for a sundae. Hard, firm cherries.

She imagined having a collar on her throat, a taut tether holding her head in this drawn-back position. A human pet, helpless to whatever her Master wished to do to her. The shocking idea intensified the coil of need in her belly, the arousal between her thighs.

"Beautiful. Your pussy's wet. I can see how slick it is from here."

She closed her eyes, swallowed, aching for one touch, the pad of his finger sliding over her labia, collecting that honey for a taste. He didn't touch her, however.

"Yeah, you're feeling it good, aren't you?"

She nodded, a quick jerk, not able to articulate it. But he wasn't requiring that. Just that she feel and listen.

"Stay that way for the next five minutes. Then put your fingers inside yourself, bring them to your mouth and taste yourself. You think about how I'll taste you, the next time we see one another." He paused. "I want to fuck you, Athena. If I took you right now, I'm worked up enough I'd leave you sore as hell for the next couple days. So you think long and hard about that sex question. I'll be in touch."

He left her then. Descended the stairs and left her throbbing. She clung to the sound of him moving through the lower level, crossing into the kitchen, the door opening and closing. Never in her life had she not walked a guest to the door, but he'd put her on the stairs like this, her legs spread and shaking, her pussy wet and nipples hard. She wasn't sure she could get up.

It was way more than five minutes before she could.

FIVE

Friday, first session. She'd stayed away from the club this week. Not unusual for her, given that she'd only been going about once a month, and had gone hardly at all in the first year after Roy's passing. But she wondered if Dale was there. Was he having sessions with Willow or other subs? How did she feel about that?

Did she have any right to feel anything about it? No matter what Dale had said, or her own conflicted feelings, she had initiated this like a session appointment, not a date. If she were being brutal with herself, their interludes might end up being little different from a therapy session. She wouldn't wonder who else's brain her psychiatrist was examining when he wasn't with her, right?

She absolutely refused to revert to a high school girl's naïveté, thinking a boy liked her when she was just his lab partner. Dale was a great fantasy. He was sexy, charismatic, fascinating. He was also insightful, kind, had a good sense of humor, and a missing leg that seemed no more impediment to him than a birthmark.

He was coming to her house for a session that he would be orchestrating, based on the notes she'd made. He'd given her no other instructions than that. Or so she thought, until the delivery van pulled up to her house on Friday morning.

She saw it from her office window. It was a private courier service. That wasn't unusual, though she typically knew when to expect a package. Lynn came out to accept it, and then brought it up to Athena, her face wreathed in a smile.

"It's from Mr. Rousseau."

It was obvious Lynn already liked him, but what woman in her right mind wouldn't? Picking up her letter opener, Athena slit the tape, noting the box was marked "fragile" and "keep cool." Inside, it was lined with a disposable cooler. As she opened it, Lynn sidled up to her elbow. Belatedly, Athena realized she should have opened it in private, since Dale could have sent her something she might not want to share with her household staff. Fortunately, her lack of foresight didn't result in embarrassment.

She lifted out the basket. It was an arrangement of yellow carnations on a bed of mint leaves. The carnations had been shaped in two mounded clusters, and black pipe cleaner and buttons for stripes and antennae turned them into bumblebees. White daisies with cheerful yellow centers were planted around them.

She remembered him in the potting shed, the variety of planting tools, the private courier. This wasn't an order from a florist. He'd done this.

"Isn't that a delightful, clever thing?" Her housekeeper's crisp British accent mirrored her own feelings on the matter. "Oh, don't forget your card." Lynn pulled it out, laid it next to the basket. "Do you want me to take the box out of the way? You'll want to keep the basket here so you can enjoy looking at it."

Athena nodded. She laid her fingers on the card, stroking the mint leaves with her other hand. As the woman moved to the door, Athena cleared her throat. "Lynn? What did you think of him?"

It was a ridiculous question of course, given that Lynn had met him for only a few minutes. It also made Athena appear too vulnerable to her staff, but as she'd told Dale, Lynn was quite more than that.

The woman turned, gave her a look. "I think he's the type of man that makes a woman's heart beat faster and her cheeks flush when he looks at her. You deserve that, even if you only want it for a little while." Lynn hesitated, her blue eyes kind in her lined face. "Sometimes that kind of man can get a woman's heart started again, if you understand my meaning. All right, then?"

"Yes." Athena squared her shoulders. "Thank you, Lynn."

She opened the envelope. It contained a blue note card, with a header stamp showing a pair of dogs and EJDS, Inc. She puzzled over it, then her expression cleared. Eddie's Junkyard and Dog Shelter. Was it a true nonprofit? Was there an Eddie? She'd heard more dogs barking elsewhere on the property, suggesting there was a main kennel area, so the "few" Dale had taken out for play and training weren't the whole population. She didn't know many people who could handle that many dogs at one time, but they'd been riveted on Dale like he was the pack leader. Who did the fund-raising?

Picking up her reading glasses, she smiled a little, seeing that his handwriting was a sprawling scrawl. Her gaze strayed to the carnation bees again, then went back to the note.

> *I'll arrive at eight. Meet me at the door wearing a robe, something thin and silky. Nothing under it. I'll be coming from the rec center so I'll be hungry. Make me a good sandwich and have beer. See you then.*

Well, a poet he wasn't. But poetry wasn't what she wanted. She could hear the command behind every word. There was nothing casual in this note. All the times in their life together she'd done things for Roy, poured him a drink, made him a sandwich, he'd always asked, never told her to do it.

Did he know you're a submissive, Athena? As she reread the simple order, her pulse fluttered in her throat, the same jumpiness happening in her stomach.

I want to fuck you.

Her body had been wound up like a spring when Dale left that night, but her mind had been so muddled, her balance so off center, she hadn't tried to do what he'd told her she could do, within the limits of his instructions. Her body had been on a low hum ever since, a state that became far worse at bedtime. Yet still she'd done nothing about it, hesitant to confront an arousal caused directly by Dale's effect upon her.

As she held his instructions in her hand, her mind running away with imaginings of how the night was going to go, the hum of her body became an urgent purr.

She locked the office door before she went into the private bathroom. Laying the note on the counter, she glanced at herself in the mirror, seeing that telltale flush Lynn had mentioned. Sliding her hand beneath the waistband of her skirt, down into her panties, she found herself wet, where moments before she hadn't been. One note from him, several almost-coarse commands—wear a robe, make a sandwich, have beer—had done that.

That was the power of a good Dominant. He could take a simple thing and create an explosion of response. It made her think of a couple who'd come to the club one night when she was there with Roy. It had been the woman's first time, but her boyfriend, the Dom, had been highly experienced. When she was looking around nervously, he'd put a hand on her shoulder. Placement of his palm had been precise, the juncture of shoulder and throat, his forefinger against her carotid, the others wrapped firmly over her collarbone. He'd leaned in, murmured two words, delivered with a direct glance. "Sit down."

Athena had been close enough to discern the words, but more importantly, she'd seen the look on the woman's face. It was as if all those worries and doubts vanished, all the scattered threads suddenly twisted together into an arrow that pointed directly at him for everything she needed for things to be okay. Her face had eased, her gaze lowered, and she sat down on the couch, her ankles crossed like a proper lady, her hands folded in her lap, back straight, obviously a posture he required from her. He'd touched her hair, warm approval in his face. When she dared a glance up, Athena had seen adoration and joy in her expression. Surrender.

She sat down in the wicker chair in the corner of the large bathroom, bracing her feet on the garden tub. Caressing her labia, she moved her fingers up to her clit, tugged on it. That first touch made her suck in a breath, arch at the dense wave of sensations. But stoking her arousal and achieving a climax were different matters. It really was so much easier with her vibrator, and . . . oh crap, she was using her wrong hand. She switched, and that of course made it more awkward. She had to go slow, be more precise with her movements, but her body was eager, needy.

She thought of Dale's expression when he'd told her she could give herself relief like this. She thought of him being here, watching her. He would sit on the edge of the tub, thighs spread in that casual male way, maybe a hand braced against one of them. He'd put himself between her spread legs so she had to spread them wider, so he could watch every movement of her fingers, the way her labia got slicker, how her cunt sucked on her fingers when she pushed them inside herself.

His gaze on her would be sharp as a laser. With Willow that night, he'd been thick and hard, the denim molded over that tempting bar of steel. Some of the Doms wore untucked shirts so as not to reveal their state to the sub. He had been deliciously unconcerned about it.

She thought about his arrival tonight, what he might wear, what they might do that would get him aroused like that. What he would do to her to make himself that way.

It was a titillating shift of perspective, and she responded to it, her hips lifting, the wicker emitting its quiet strawlike noise, which sounded loud as a squeaky door. There were two doors to the bathroom, one leading to the hallway. She'd locked it, but what if one of the staff came by, heard her doing this? But . . . oh God, it felt good. She played her fingers over her damp flesh, body quivering.

She imagined herself in the shoes of the nervous girlfriend, and Dale was the Master who'd told her to sit down. She kept rising up to her touch, getting closer, closer . . . Her gaze strayed to the clock.

Six minutes already? *Noooo*. She was so close . . . she couldn't help herself. She worried about going over his imposed time limit, and that worry grew as her fingers refused to stop. Would seven minutes really be so much worse than six? *Oh* . . .

The climax rocked her, a tiny, intense thing, not nearly satisfying enough, but enough to have her curling around her hand, pressed between her legs. She breathed hard through the aftershocks. "Oh . . . oh . . ." That syllable became a reassuring mantra while she rocked her body.

It took a little while for her to settle, but when she did, she rose unsteadily, returned to the note on the counter. The air-conditioning vent had tipped it into the thankfully dry sink. There was something written on the back. She squinted at it.

> *PS—if you bring yourself to climax today, don't wash that hand unless absolutely necessary.*

She brought her fingers to her face, inhaled the musky scent of her orgasm. Dominance and submission. She'd been a Domme and now she was trying out submission. It was merely an exercise to see how she liked it. An adventure, like a vacation, where there'd be a beginning and an end, and then she'd come home. Only she wouldn't have pictures, except in her mind.

Why was she lying to herself? She heard Dale ask the question again. *Did he know you're a submissive?* There'd been a tightness to his voice, as if he might have judged Roy in the wrong if her husband had known that about her. But there was no right or wrong to it. There'd only been love, a love she missed intensely, which conflicted with the strong, pulsing anxiety and need she felt toward tonight. She didn't know how to reconcile it. A part of her knew she should call this off, that it would go badly in the end because she couldn't manage her feelings, couldn't get a proper hold on all of it. But she wouldn't call it off. She wanted it too much.

Leaving the bathroom and returning to her desk, she fitted her hands-free to her ear and dialed her assistant at the office. "Ellen? I need you to do me a favor, when you have time. See what you can find out about Eddie's Junkyard and Dog Shelter, Incorporated. It's local. Not a first priority, but maybe look into it between tasks or next week. Just email me what you find out. Thanks."

There. She could do something with that. A little more settled, she took a breath, sat back down at her desk. Thinking, she opened a drawer, looked at a pair of thin gloves she kept there. Roy had given them to her to wear in the wintertime indoors, when her hands became cold and achy. She wore them to type at her computer. She slipped one on her left hand, a reminder not to wash it. Now she could touch other things, but she'd also retain the scent for Dale. For her Master.

She backed away from the startling thought like an electric shock. What was she doing?

Time didn't help settle nerves the way some people thought. In certain situations, the wait made it worse. Throughout the week she'd alternated between a pleasurable kind of excitement and uncertain anxiety. By seven, the latter had taken over. She prepared as he'd ordered, taking off all her clothes, sliding on a robe, brushing out her hair. Athena threaded her fingers through the thick strands, tightened the belt of the robe. It was green with a soft satiny feel, and it clung to her curves. It was also short, just past midthigh. It was something she'd bought herself some time ago for whatever reason. When she'd pulled it out of the closet, it still had tags.

Seven fifty-five. When she removed the glove, she found she'd been correct. She could still smell the lingering scent of her climax on her fingers, the unmistakable scent of her sex. The dampness of her palm intensified it.

The security chime in the lobby told her a vehicle had turned into the drive. She opened and closed those moist palms, and went downstairs. Opening the front door, she left the storm door unlatched. Now she sat down on the padded bench in the foyer. Her folded stationery, displaying the list of things he'd told her to write down, was next to her. In hindsight, the few pages she'd written didn't feel like enough to start. Not enough structures and rules to keep things moving as slow as they should, but it was too late to change it now. She hadn't brought a pen down with her, so she couldn't scribble a caveat: "All the above are null and void if I completely freak out, like I'm about to do now."

She shook her head at herself and focused what she could see through the open front door. There'd been an old beater truck by the office at the shelter, so this must be his personal use vehicle. He drove a dark blue Ford that looked shiny and less than a couple of years old. She didn't know how much it paid, working as caretaker at a combination junkyard and dog rescue shelter. She assumed he received a pension of some kind from being a SEAL. Whatever the sources of his income, it was apparently enough, but then she'd also seen his place. He kept it clean and neat, but he didn't spend a lot of money on obvious things, and that kind of person usually made a dollar go further than most. Maybe he did floral arrangement as well.

In truth, she knew almost nothing about him. Except that he'd been a SEAL, and that he'd mesmerized her with the way he'd taken over Willow, enough to invite him to her home and ask him to do the same to her.

Maybe this was a midlife crisis, exacerbated by Roy's death. Everyone knew how well midlife crises went. At best, a person looked back on them with chronic embarrassment. At worst, they could destroy lives.

She remembered waking up in Dale's house. She could trust this man. If it went terribly wrong, embarrassment would be her worst punishment. Which simply meant she'd never return to the club, and she'd close this chapter of her life. She could do that.

Her throbbing pulse, her shortness of breath as his door opened, told her that might not be the case. Which escalated her to near panic. She could bolt up from her seat, lock the door and run back up to her room. There was still time.

Her, Athena Francesca Summers, running away from anything? Really? What would Dale do if she did such a thing? She had a vision of him kicking the door down, pursuing her up to her room, pushing her down on the bed, ready to punish, to claim . . .

Okay, she'd just shifted straight to the fantasy of the pirate captain ravishing the beautiful heiress. It didn't help that she could easily imagine him in tight black trousers, shiny boots and a billowing white shirt unlaced at the neck. Technically, he already had the peg leg.

There was a structure for all of this. Controls and safe words. So why did she feel like a bug in a jar?

He'd stepped out of the truck and pulled a tote bag out of the back. After shutting the door, he circled around the grille, coming toward the front stoop. Like the night with Willow, he wore belted dark jeans, snug black T-shirt and his boots. The T-shirt was tucked into the jeans. Unpretentious yet severe, suggesting functional intent.

He saw her through the storm door. What did he see in her face? She wasn't sure herself. He came up onto the porch, stood in front of the glass door. He nodded to the latch.

"Open the door, Athena."

It was unlocked, but she expected he knew that. He was making a point, one that her subconscious understood well. She rose, smoothing the robe over her thighs. She thought of the first board meetings she'd chaired when Roy became sick enough he had to step down. She'd gone from vice chairperson to overseeing the board solo. She'd been nervous then, too. A part of her had wanted to run, to avoid the significance of what standing at the head of that table meant.

If she'd decided it was all too much, turned it over to someone else, board members like Mel would have been happy to step into that gap, take over the company Roy and she had built. But she hadn't run. Even at her lowest moments, she'd known she would take responsibility, be strong. That was who she was.

Crossing to the door, she pushed it open. She took it further, stepping outside, gesturing to him to precede her into her home. An instinctive decision. His gaze swept her and then he stepped in. But he turned to hold the door open for her and draw her into the recesses of the house, a different kind of gesture. One that almost made her smile except the working of her face muscles felt painful.

He closed the main door, flipped the deadbolt. "Athena."

"Sir." Thinking about the others she'd seen at the club, and considering it an attempt to calm her nerves through emulation, she sank to her knees on the marble floor. Looking up the length of his body, she thought he appeared so strong and confident, so sure of himself. Those blue-green eyes were watching everything she was doing, and probably reading her like a manual. Only men didn't read manuals, did they? They proceeded based on mechanical aptitude, an instinctive understanding of how things worked, of what things to tighten, which to loosen.

"I told you I'd be hungry," he said.

She nodded. "I have a plate ready for you. Where would you like to eat?"

"Kitchen." Noticing the pages she'd left on the bench, he picked them up, glancing over her handwriting. "Take me there."

She rose, leading him to the kitchen. As she passed the pictures hung in the foyer, she saw her and Roy's wedding picture, Roy's parents. Why was she doing this?

Because kneeling at his feet hadn't had anything to do with copying the actions of other subs. It had been as natural to her as breathing. She was padding across the floor barefoot. She never went barefoot in the house. Even at night, she wore slippers.

As they entered the kitchen, she gestured to the stools arranged at the island, and then pulled the plate out of the oven. She'd kept the heat on low so the turkey sub she'd made him would stay warm. A side of sliced and fried potatoes went with it. She added a sprig of mint from the arrangement he'd given her, which had a prominent display position on the counter.

"Thank you for the carnations." She turned toward the refrigerator, retrieved a beer. At his house, he'd had Bud Light, so that was what she'd bought, adding a couple more varieties from the wet bar in case he wanted something else. "You didn't have to send me flowers."

After opening the beer, she found a napkin to wrap around the base. He'd placed the bag on the floor next to the island. When he nodded to the counter next to his plate, she put the beer there. He laid his hand on her wrist, holding her. "Did you follow my instructions about writing these? And the other commands I left you?"

She flashed to the memory of being in the bathroom. "Yes. No. I . . . we need to talk about this more." She drew her hand away. "I'm not sure this is going to work. I need things more defined."

He grunted. "Like a car race on a closed track, where the circles are predictable, and when you hit the finish line, the race is over?"

"Don't judge me," she snapped.

Where had that come from? She nearly clapped her hand over her mouth like a cartoon character. She needed to steady her nerves. She needed to . . .

At the shift in his expression, she almost took a step back. "I wouldn't suggest using that tone with me," he said pleasantly. "I'm likely to react exactly as you're hoping I will."

A giant bunny leap of adrenaline from her stomach into her chest made it hard to determine if she was reacting to that with dread or anticipation. With effort—though she was pretty sure she was losing her mind—she found her dignity and laced her fingers together before her. "I apologize for the outburst, Dale. I'm just . . . This is all very new to me."

"I know that. I'll address your concerns, Athena. Right now, I'm eating. Sit here." He pointed to the floor next to him. "And be quiet. I'm going to read your notes."

She hesitated, then closed the distance between them. He hadn't chosen a stool, but was instead standing at a clear spot in front of the island. Sinking to her knees felt like what she was supposed to do. Structure. Order. She was beside his left leg, the one where half of it was missing. She found it hard to wrap her mind around that. He'd shown her the prosthesis, yes, but the man seemed so solid, it was inconceivable that any part of him was absent.

Her gaze slid up to his knee, noticed the difference between the stretch of the denim around that area and the other one. The left was somewhat thicker, she expected because of whatever socket held the knee. She'd looked up some things about it on the Internet, and knew a removal below the knee was called a transtibial amputation. Those sites said that was better than above the knee, because below the knee had far better prosthesis options, ones that caused less strain on joints and muscles.

She was scrolling down the recalled computer page like an automaton. It was a nervous, bug-in-the-jar reaction again, so she shifted her focus back to Dale. His scent, his nearness, what he was doing.

He was looking down at her notes, but he made an appreciative noise when he took his first bite of the sandwich. The incoherent compliment cracked open a tiny ball of warmth in her stomach. He ate while standing, wiping his fingers on the napkin she provided before he turned each page, reading the back, switching to the next page. His obvious intention to dive straight into the reason he was here tonight tangled more anxious things around that ball of warmth.

Like a session, not a date. What she wanted, yes?

He'd been so matter-of-fact about it, ordering her to kneel next to him. She hadn't really said anything in her notes about the degree of subjugation she wanted. She expected she was okay with what she'd seen him do with Willow, so she hadn't felt the need to spell it out, but maybe he'd tailored his intensity to that specific sub. While Willow was pretty hardcore, maybe Dale's preferences were even more so. She hadn't witnessed his aftercare process. Had he attached a leash to her collar, led her to a booth and had her sit by his knee, idly stroking her hair while he talked to other Doms? She liked that vision, imagined herself there, exhausted, thrilled, sated. Athena wished she could jump to that relaxed, somnolent state. But another part of her didn't want to miss the journey to it. Bug in a jar, bug in a jar . . .

She really wanted to lean against his leg, stroke it with her fingertips. Could she do that on this side? She laid her fingers above his knee, finding the firm, heated flesh that was Dale, then slid down over what she realized was the sleeve for the socket and then the socket. All of it was part of him.

He turned over another page. "Did I give you permission to touch me, Athena?"

"No sir." She withdrew her hand.

"Untie the robe and take it off your shoulders so I can see your breasts. Spread your knees."

Her stomach knocked against her rib cage this time, her breasts prickling with heat, nipples tightening. Was she going to do this? She put her fingers to the tie, but she couldn't make them move. "Dale . . . I . . . I don't think I can. Maybe it's too soon."

She was going to ruin it before anything started. But before she could scramble to her feet, withdraw, he set aside the pages and slid onto a stool at last. Stretching his leg out to one side of her, he bent the right one to brace himself. "Come here."

As she rose on her knees, he pinched the lapel of her robe between two fingers, a little tug to bring her to her feet. When she was standing between his thighs, he had his hands on her waist, holding and steadying her.

"Close your eyes, but keep your head up." His voice was low, firm, but not unkind.

Once she complied, he drew her closer. He captured her jaw with one hand, holding her face still. "Moisten your lips for me."

She did so, and began to shake. "Dale . . ."

"Shh. We're just going on a boat ride, Athena. It's a lazy, sunny day, and you're lying in the bottom of the boat. The sun is so warm and bright, your eyes are closed, and you feel the heat on your skin, the breeze." His breath touched her. Her heart was battering her ribs, her stomach tight and uncertain.

"I'm controlling the direction, the speed. The oars are dipping in the water in that easy rhythm. You have a pillow resting on my feet so you can put your head there and I can give you shade by leaning over you when the sun is too bright for your eyes. I'm taking care of you. Do you feel safe in the boat with me?"

"Yes." She whispered it.

"Good." He made a humming noise in his throat, as if he were singing to her. She imagined the boat rocking on the current, the unobtrusive noise of the oars. She could turn her head, brush against his leg, reach up and curve her hand around his calf . . .

The world steadied. She wanted to do this. The main reason she was so unsettled about it was exactly because of *how much* she wanted to do this.

His touch dropped, and he was untying the robe. He pushed it off her shoulders, but since his grip dropped to her elbows, keeping those held against her sides, it stopped there, the fabric pooling on her hips and lower back. "All right. Kneel on the floor the way I ordered. Knees spread shoulder-width apart. But Athena?"

She lifted her lashes to find his intent gaze so close she couldn't help imagining him closing the distance for a kiss. She wasn't sure she was ready for that, but that wasn't his purpose.

"When your eyes are closed, it's me touching you. Doing this to you. Not Roy. You understand? I can be a mean son of a bitch when it comes to things like that. When we're together, you're mine. I'm not a surrogate. Got it?"

She shook her head, but not to deny him. "Roy never would have done this to me," she said. She couldn't even imagine it.

It was a simple, honest answer, but one that seemed to satisfy him. Enough that his change in expression sent that thrill through her vitals again. She knew this was just a session, that she couldn't extrapolate from that, but she remembered her latent desire to see that sense of ownership in a man's eyes. She saw it clearly in Dale's.

"All right. Kneel the way I told you."

As she sank back down, his grip made sure it was a controlled descent. When she reached the floor, she adjusted her thighs as he described. Looking down, she could see the heavy weight of her breasts. Through their cleft, she saw the robe had parted so her inner thighs and shaved sex were revealed.

He touched her hair. "Lift your head, stare straight ahead. You're interfering with my view."

She obeyed, swallowing on a dry throat. The moisture in her body seemed to be collecting in one key part of her. She was still shaking a little. The first couple of times, Roy had shook. Maybe that was part of a sub's journey.

He'd gone back to reading the notes. He'd commanded her not to reread them, but since he'd told her she couldn't change anything, she hadn't known why that would matter. However, she'd only managed to get through one front and back page and part of the next before she was cringing. She'd stopped reading, but a pounding urge to toss all of it had followed her around most of the week. The only thing that prevented that was imagining Dale asking her if she'd followed his directions exactly. She couldn't lie to him. Lies disrespected the Dom and, more than that, undermined what was being built between Dom and sub in every session. Absolute trust.

Then there was the pride issue. Explaining why she'd destroyed previous versions would have been too difficult to articulate, too mortifying for an exercise she was already unable to review without acute embarrassment.

He'd told her to be quiet, but she needed to say it. "I disobeyed your instructions. Twice."

"How?"

When she didn't immediately respond, he lifted his head from his reading. Though she was staring straight ahead, which gave her a view of his hip and length of thigh where he sat on the stool, she could feel that inexorable gaze pinned on her.

"I started to reread the notes. I only read . . . I read three pages and then stopped. And . . . I used my hand for seven minutes, not five."

"When?"

"Today. A few hours ago. I didn't wash it . . . like you said."

He lowered his hand, snapped his fingers and then opened his palm, a clear directive. She laid the offending hand in it, which quivered as his thumb swept over her palm, her wrist pulse, his other fingers closing around her arm. He tugged her back up to her knees and she bit her lip as he brought the hand up to his face. He pressed his nose briefly into her palm, then rubbed his jaw over it, turning his head so her fingers passed over his lips. He kissed her fingertips, squeezed her hand, then used the same hold on her wrist to compel her back into a kneeling position.

"Hmm." He returned to reading the notes. Since he said nothing further, she remained silent as ordered. He pushed them away, finishing up the sandwich. He didn't speak again until he was done with his plate and had wiped his mouth. "Did you make this or Lynn?"

"I did."

"Good girl." Rising, he moved to the sink, washed his hands, dried them. Then he reached over and plucked the pancake spatula out of the pottery vase where it resided with all of Lynn's other kitchen implements. He twirled it, smacked it against his hand. Now as before, it made Athena jump, though her backside tingled in uneasy anticipation this time.

"I punish for a couple of reasons, Athena. One is for mutual pleasure. One is for discipline. You've earned the discipline side, which means this waits for another day." Putting the spatula back in its spot, he came back to the island, sliding a hip onto the stool.

"From reading your notes, I can tell you're not quite sure what you want, but you have the fever to the point you don't want to rule anything out. That's pretty normal. So we're going to let this evolve organically. Your safe word is *griffin*. Use it only if you want me to stop. I'm not going to give you an interim safe word yet, something to slow things down, because when you're all over the map like that, you need a tighter circle to decide if something is a hard or soft limit. Knowing what I already do about your personality, your determination and courage, I know that having a stop-go safe word will accomplish that."

She was looking at her hands, clasped and twisting around each other. He touched her shoulder, a firm tap reminding her to bring her chin up again. "Back straight, hands at your sides. Keep your thighs open. What do you think *The Choice* means? The bronze in your garden."

Athena was glad he added the clarification, though she had to struggle to catch up with the change in direction. Fortunately, she'd mulled on the piece's meaning enough in the past to have a formed opinion. "I think it represents every person's struggle to choose between fantasy and reality, what they wish for life to be and what it is. The man in the suit, holding the sword, is deciding whether he'll slay the fantasy, his dreams and wishes . . . or choose otherwise."

"What other choice does he have? Getting lost in the dreams?" Dale had shifted so his legs were stretched out on either side of her. He seemed to like doing that, hemming her in. She liked it, too. She wanted to put her hands on his knees, look up into his face. He'd been close enough to kiss her earlier, but he hadn't. Maybe he'd felt her uncertainty about that or, like the spatula, he was just really good at putting an image in her head, then taking it away, keeping her guessing—and anticipating.

"I like to think we live in a world where both can exist. When you hold on to your fantasies and dreams, your perception of the real world is transformed by them. Whether you achieve them or not, holding on to that magic gives you a different way of viewing everything. A better way, I think."

Dale twined a lock of her hair around his hand, knuckles brushing her face. He was good at that, mixing tender gestures with sensual threats. One moment talking about punishment and ordering her to silence, the next helping her visualize a lazy boat ride to calm her down. What had he thought of her admission about breaking his rules? What kind of discipline was he considering? The fantasy versus reality of *that* was elevating her heart rate. Or maybe that was simply his touch. He cradled her jaw, stroking his thumb over her bottom lip.

"We tend to limit our vision of ourselves, don't we?" he mused. "We decide what we are, all the things we can be. We think we have to be one thing or another, never realizing how many things we simply *are*. Like you. I've seen all the articles about your business, your fund-raisers. Even the personal stuff in the society columns. I saw the one about you and Roy taking his father out to the theater. He lived here, and the two of you cared for him until he died."

"Yes." Athena tried to wrap her mind around another subject change, though she had an inkling they were all related in some way. She was just too scattered to figure out how. "He was a good man. Roy's mother was a good person as well, though she was a little more difficult at times."

She and Elaine had had a cordial relationship, though Elaine saw Athena as competition for her only son's affections. On the other hand, Robert was so much like Roy, the obvious evidence of it when they'd both lived under this roof had amused her.

"During the tour of this place, two places spoke to me," Dale said. "One was your reading room. That's your breathing space, the place where you go just to be. Right?"

"Yes."

"Whenever I'm doing something that unsettles you, Athena, I want you to go to that place in your head and think it through, before you put up a shield. Understand?"

The words tweaked her subconscious, telling her that at some subliminal level she did. So she nodded. He stroked her hair behind her ear, teasing the tender area beneath. Sliding along the side of her throat, he caressed her nape.

"Let's practice it. When you watched me at the club, how does it connect to what you want here? Go to that space in your head, think it through, then answer me."

Closing her eyes, she remembered the last book she'd been reading in her easy chair. It was a book she'd read as a child. She'd found it when she was helping set up a thrift store for the women's shelter. A story about a horse . . . *Blaze*. That was it. When she was a child, she'd read it on a rainy afternoon, falling asleep curled in her father's recliner. Her mother's hand, stroking her hair, had woken her for dinner. A different kind of stroking from Dale's, but with that same protective, reassuring element.

"When I was watching you," she said slowly, "I had a feeling, a need. I don't know, I've never been on that end of things, you understand? I just felt a desire for what you were doing to Willow, how you made her step out of her head. You were whipping her, and you drove everything out."

"Do you think you want that level of pain?"

"I don't know. I just knew what you were doing felt like what I wanted, but I can't explain how." She stopped, feeling foolish. "I'm so used to being decisive, Dale. I think the reason I'm trying to keep you at arm's length, make this a more businesslike arrangement, is the fear that if you become too personal to me . . ."

"I'll become one of the expectations. Something you have to be a certain way around. I'll want more from you and you'll have to take on another role. Good girl. *Really* good girl. See, it's there, just waiting under all the storm clouds."

She felt absurdly pleased by the praise. She couldn't have this conversation with someone who'd known her as a Domme. But he had no history with her, no perspective from which to judge her. No expectations. So she kept talking. "Anyone else would assume I'm still a Domme, that it's a temporary switch, a change of pace. It's not unheard of."

"But that's not how you see it, do you?"

She shook her head. But as ill fitting as the Domme coat was, she'd made it fit. Taking on a role had a certainty to it, a safety. With the duality that seemed to be attending every step of this, she was torn between the security it provided and wanting to shed it forever.

He touched her chin, bringing her eyes up to him. "All right. I have a couple boundaries of my own, different from these." He glanced toward her list, then shifted his attention back to her face. "First, within the boundaries I set, you have the freedom to be whatever you need to be. You're not going to be ashamed of anything you say and feel around me. I'm in control, so you don't have to be. All right?"

She nodded. He tugged her hair lightly. "I expect a *yes* or *no* to a question."

"Yes."

His gaze intensified. "I do want something from you, Athena. And what I want will likely expand and grow. But I have only one expectation. For you to be exactly who you are. If who you are, who you become, doesn't have a need for me in your life, then you tell me and our arrangement ends. For my part of things, I'm here because you fascinate me, I like you and I'm attracted to you. The thing you can expect from me, at all times, is honesty."

He wanted things from her. For a single, insane moment, it made her want to give him everything.

"When in session, you address me as sir or Master," he added. "Those are your two choices."

She pressed her lips together under his touch. "What if I want to call you that outside of session?"

"Let's start with in session," he said. "Remember what I said about a sub getting overwhelmed by her feelings at first? Containing them to a certain extent helps settle you down, helps you decide if you really want to expand the D/s behavior beyond play and into lifestyle. That balance between fantasy and reality."

He tapped her cheek, drawing her attention to the color flooding there. "You're already breaking my first rule, Athena. Nothing you say to me should cause you embarrassment. I'm in control, you're not. It's clear you're going to need some discipline to recognize that."

When she'd snapped at him and he'd cut his eyes at her, he'd given her every reason to believe there'd be consequences for bad behavior. It had thrilled as much as terrified her.

"I'm not used to that."

"What? Giving up control?"

"No," she said. "Having someone to whom I can give it." Had she ever? *When do you relinquish control, Athena?* Perhaps the better question was, was she capable of relinquishing control?

She kept her eyes down, unable to meet his gaze after such a personal admission. His fingers grazed her hair.

"All right, then." He stood up. "You read three pages you weren't supposed to read and went two minutes over the limit I set for you to masturbate to climax. Did you climax?"

She nodded.

"You're just adding to the punishment, Athena."

Her spine snapped up straight. "Yes sir."

"The climax makes the infraction more severe. While I was reading, you also spoke when I told you to be quiet. You could have told me about your disobedience when I gave you permission to speak. Then there's breaking my first boundary rule and the rule about addressing me. So, eight for the individual infractions, and four for the climax."

Had she really been that bad? Summed up like that, it made it seem so. She was never bad. He put his hand under her elbow, brought her to her feet. With a perfunctory motion, he pulled the robe all the way off her body and tossed it on the stool, leaving her completely naked. Just like that, all her physical imperfections exposed. She was in good shape, but there was a difference between showing that off in the right kind of clothes and having nothing to sculpt or mold things into more appealing lines.

Shouldering his bag, he took her elbow again. "Come with me."

He was all business now, which actually helped her self-consciousness. He remembered the layout of her home, moving with purpose down the wide hallway to the indoor rec room, where there was an array of comfortable furniture, a large flatscreen, music system and pool table. Roy had often played pool while he listened to the news and grumbled about how many idiots there were in the world.

Dropping his bag on the floor, Dale took her to the padded footrest in front of a large cushioned chair. "Put your stomach on the footrest, breasts just over the end, palms flat on the floor. Your knees aren't going to reach the floor on the back end, so rest your thighs against the cushion and press your toes into the floor. Are you familiar with yoga?"

"Yes sir."

"Like a down dog, only your stomach will be on the cushion, so your knees will be bent."

It was still a precarious position, vulnerable, made more so when his tone sharpened. "Legs spread. Anytime I punish you, unless I say otherwise, you spread your legs. Shoulder width. I'll tell you if I want them wider."

Now that she was facing the reality, emotions were starting to roil in her stomach. "Dale . . ."

"Shh." He helped steady her stance, then stroked a hand over her hair. "Have you ever been disciplined, Athena? Punished for being bad?"

"No." Her voice was nearly a whisper, entirely unlike herself.

He let his knuckles glide down her back. "Then you're giving me a gift. Sweet as a virgin offering up her innocence. All this gorgeous, baby-soft skin. Count it off for me, and breathe."

She put her palms onto the Berber carpet, her toes digging into it on the other side of the footrest. In this position, her ass was lifted and, with her legs spread, she was as exposed to him as she could be. No clothes, no robe, nothing. He ran a hand down her back again. Cool air followed his touch on her buttocks, the flesh between her legs.

"Slick and swollen. This excites you, Athena. Your pretty cunt looks ready for whatever your Master wants."

She'd seen this done, but having it done to her was very different. Her breath started to rasp in her throat when, in her peripheral vision, she saw him put his hand to his belt, unbuckle it and slide it free. He doubled it over. "Count them," he reminded her.

The first strike was a lick of fire across her hindquarters. The last time she'd had her backside blistered, she'd been a child. Since being well behaved was the result of such prudently administered corporal punishment, it had rarely been required. The burn made her jump, her nerves scream in shock. Her brain demanded that she move away, turn, stop him. Instead, she dug her fingers into the carpet. "One."

Then came the next, and the next. The pain intensified. When she began to squirm on strike five, he put his hand on her back, pressing her to the cushion, showing how easily he could hold her down. She was panting, tears swimming in her eyes. "It hurts . . . hurts."

"Yeah, I'll bet it does. It's making your ass a beautiful shade of red. Keep counting. Six to go. Was that extra two minutes worth it? The climax?"

Oh God, no. It had been a tiny, pitiful thing next to this. To deliver the last strokes, he banded an arm around her waist to keep her backside in the air and her body in place. She was struggling involuntarily now, but his powerful grip held her fast.

"Nine." *God . . .* "Ten!"

The tears had spilled forth, and she was hooked to the carpet like a cat with claws. When the last blow landed, it had all become one fiery burn across her buttocks. He kept that strong arm around her as she sniffled. He steadied her, a warning that he was about to let go and he expected her to hold the position he'd mandated. When he released her, he moved behind her. Putting his hands on her buttocks, he settled his thumbs in the crease between labia and the pocket of her thigh. With no preamble, he dropped to a knee behind her and closed his mouth over her sex.

Her pussy was juicy as a peach slice, and when his tongue thrust inside of her, she came apart. He gripped her hips, holding her in place even though she was wheelbarrowing on the other side of the footrest, bleating and screaming as his relentless sucking and flicking of her clit catapulted her to a hard, fast climax. One far more intense than her infraction and far more desirable, because it was him making it happen.

She scrabbled for purchase on the carpet. He kept suckling her past the aftershocks, when she was jerking from the sensitivity, but he didn't stop until he was good and ready, even when she was making pleading noises in her throat. It wasn't until she quieted, accepting the crazy mix of discomfort and pleasure as part of her punishment, that he stopped.

He eased her down so she was draped limply on the footrest. The unease and emotional turmoil she'd felt since he'd arrived had mostly vanished. Was it possible her agitated state had been as much about violent arousal as uncertain feelings? His punishment and the cleverness of his mouth seemed to have cut her concern about the latter tenfold.

He drew her to an upright position on her knees, brought her to her feet. She was unsteady, but it didn't matter. Shouldering the bag he'd brought from the kitchen, he scooped her up in his arms. "That takes care of your punishment. Now let's get to your session."

SIX

What? He was going to kill her, and she'd let him. Out of pure gratitude, she wouldn't leave a single clue to betray him to the authorities. She really should have reminded Lynn where she kept the original copy of her will. Thank goodness she hadn't adopted that dog she'd seen at the local ASPCA. The terrier mix had been a mop of hair, with soft brown eyes that promised she'd be the perfect companion, a warm body sharing the bed. Athena had instead found her a wonderful home with a family. Since she was going to expire from the things Dale was doing to her tonight, she was glad she hadn't put that poor dog through the stress of such a temporary home.

Temporary. She'd assumed this arrangement with Dale was a temporary matter, something he kept gently—and sometimes not so gently—reminding her couldn't be defined. She couldn't help it, though. From bittersweet experience, she knew all things had a beginning and end, and when those experiences were wonderful, one always wished for a wider span between the two points. There was no way to brace for the loss, but it was human nature to try anyway.

Dale's skills, however, could draw the excruciating and the pleasurable out on the same rubber band, so the mind was torn between *please stop* and *never stop*. She was caught between in a way that ensured she'd never use her safe word, no matter how strenuously she was stretched between the two points.

He carried her through the house to her reading nook. He'd

turned at the appropriate points so her head or feet were protected as they moved through doorways. Now he reached under her and turned the latch of the sunporch, stepping right out into the gardens with her unclothed. There were no neighbors within viewing distance of course. It was just . . . she'd never been naked outside.

He didn't let her down until they reached *The Choice*. "Turn and face the griffin. Reach above you, see if you can grab the crest of his wings."

To do that, she had to lean full against the creature, put her forehead against its throat. Even then, she had to strain for the crest, going onto her toes. Dale came and pressed against her back to adjust her grip lower, on the slope of the wing edges. Now she was flat on her feet, but she was still stretched out. She wanted him to keep the heated strength of his body against her like that, but of course he stepped back.

"You're going to be here awhile. I don't want to put too much stress on your ankles or shoulders."

Dale gripped her hair then, using that hold to lift her upper body away from the griffin and reach around her, put his fingers on the metal. When she glanced down, she saw he was testing those metal feathers, verifying they were smooth and not sharp. His questing hand was close enough that his wrist and the heel of his hand brushed her nipple, the curve of her breast. While the contact might be incidental, that, combined with the knee-weakening clasp on her hair, sent a frisson of arousal through a body that should still be depleted by her last climax. Maybe the newness of the situation, the excitement of it, was refueling her faster. Or Dale alone had that effect on her, him exercising his Mastery over her.

He returned her to a full lean against the griffin, readjusting her hands on the wings once more so her arms were stretched as far as they could go without taking her off her heels. The griffin's chest rounded out her back, and the ridges of the feathers were a cool friction against tender skin.

Leaving her in that position, he went to his bag, unzipping it. Since he was in her field of vision, she saw him withdraw a coil of rope. Unwrapping the end from the figure eight coil, he shook it out in a deft move. Then he returned to her side and began tying her to the statue.

He moved with harrowing efficiency, binding her wrists with a knot that didn't slip, winding the rope around the griffin and her, eventually cinching her firmly to the mythical beast in a series of cross ties and knots he lined up on either side of her spine.

It took a while and, as he did it, her body reacted as if he was stimulating her in a much more intimate way. The restraint was turning her on, every incremental restriction making her breath shorter, her heart pound, her flesh heat. She wanted him to keep tying her endlessly, more tightly. The more immobile and helpless he rendered her, the more aroused she became. *Oh God.* No wonder Roy had loved it when she tied him up. It held a euphoria all its own.

Dale left her backside free of encumbrance, but pulled the ropes through her legs, positioning a rough, titillating knot right against her clit before he split the rope around her labia, putting further pressure there. It increased when he began wrapping her thighs. Whatever he did pulled her legs open another inch or two, which made her grip on the wings more of a stretch, providing a feeling of suspension, even though she stayed on the ground. He brought her ankles up close to the statue, gripping her ass in one hand to guide her into a more severe C-curve over the griffin's chest.

He knew his rope suspension techniques well, because the way he'd tied her, her shoulders weren't bearing her weight. The rope harness over her back, hips and thighs had formed a cradle, as if she was a baby bird in a closefitting sling against the griffin's puffed chest, her knees pressed against its lower abdomen. If he cut her loose right now, she'd fall, because she was no longer in a sturdy right angle with the ground. The sense of once again being simultaneously off balance and at his mercy was overwhelming.

He hadn't spoken throughout, and neither had she. She'd never felt such a complete lack of need to speak. The way his hands moved over her body held all her attention. As well as his even breath, the way he stopped at different times to study her face, gauge her reaction. When he tested tightness, the angle of the ropes, the stress on her joints, the functional task felt remarkably erotic. Arousal trickled down her thigh, and it wasn't from her last climax.

He put away the excess line. When he returned to her, he cupped her bottom once more, making her moan as he squeezed her hard enough the belt marks throbbed, then he stroked them.

"I like knowing your ass will be tender tomorrow because of this. You'll have a lot of muscles hurting you haven't used this way before. I'll enjoy thinking about that, too. I'm going to leave you instructions to deal with it. A hot bath tonight, a couple aspirin. You'll rub a liniment I give you into your arms and hips. Do you have someone who can help you do that?"

She shook her head. "I can manage."

"I'll come by in the morning and do it."

"You . . . could stay."

Her earlier impulsive state had obviously been exacerbated by the climax, her aroused state. She'd babble anything right now, but the idea of him in a bed with her was irresistible. But not her bed. Not yet.

"Not yet." He echoed her thought, which gave her a pang of uncertainty and disappointment both, but her body's intense reaction to her bondage didn't let it gain much traction. He gripped her hair anew, tilting her head back so she was gazing up into his unsmiling face, those piercing eyes. "Too soon. I'm not him, Athena."

A pang of mortification speared her. Seeing it, he shook his head, taking her chin in firm fingers. "What did I tell you? Are you acting within my control?"

She nodded, then remembered. *Damn it.* "Yes. Yes sir."

She was relieved he didn't put his hand on his belt, but he might be the type of Master who'd store such infractions away, pull them out at a later time. "Then why are you embarrassed? When I first arrived, what were you thinking, sitting on that fussy little sofa in front of the door? You looked like you were about to bolt."

"I was. I thought I might lock the door, run upstairs. Then I wondered what you'd do."

"What did you imagine me doing?"

She couldn't help flushing a deeper rose at that. His fingers tightened in her hair. "You'll answer me immediately when I ask a question, Athena. No hesitation, no thinking the answer through."

"I imagined you kicking in the door, following me upstairs and . . . pushing me down on the bed to . . . punish me."

His eyes glowed in a way that made her ache. God, she wanted that mouth on her. Her body tensed, feeling every line of the ropes holding her to the griffin. The sculpture had been cool when he first placed her against it. Now her inflamed flesh had warmed the metal.

"If I'd done that, I'd owe you a door tomorrow. And that looks like a pretty damn expensive door."

"What . . . would you have done?"

He stroked her hair, traced her lips. She parted them, eager to feel him on the moist inside of her mouth. He obliged her, sliding his forefinger partly inside, and she sucked on it. His gaze darkened as her tongue flicked against it.

"You'd like to be on your knees, servicing your Master's cock, wouldn't you?"

She nodded, hoping she'd be excused from saying "Yes sir" since his finger was in her mouth. She expected the look on her face gave him the answer, regardless.

"We'll see whether you deserve that. I wouldn't have kicked the door down, Athena. I would have sat on the porch, waited until you came back down. You would have gone upstairs, turned in circles, been scared, but then you would have come back down to me, because you'd know I was the one who could make it better, make that tornado happening in your head die down, get still again. Though before I did that, I probably would have tipped you over my knee and given you a sound spanking for making me wait."

He gave her that half smile again, the one that didn't dilute the truth of his words at all. He enjoyed giving out pain as part of pleasure. When he'd helped her up from the footrest, his cock had been a thick bar straining against denim. The way he had her tied right now, her face pressed close to the griffin's neck, she couldn't dip her head enough to see, but from his total attention, the way he touched her, it was obvious he was still stirred up that way.

"Time to explore these limits of yours."

He left her, going back to the bag. She heard him rummaging, heard the unsettling clang of metal, then a rustling. When he returned, he stayed behind her, but then he deprived her of any sight at all, sliding a blindfold over her eyes. "You're mine to look at," he said shortly. "But you have to earn the right to look at me."

"Yes sir." She liked how he said "mine." She wanted to wrap herself around it like a dragon guarding treasure. She knew what was happening to her, because she'd seen it happen to other subs. They might come in nervous, jittery, overly chatty. Then their Master or Mistress would start to bind them, and with every cuff wrapped or rope cinched, that negative tension would start to leave their bodies, their expressions getting both more vacant and focused . . . vacant of anything but their total focus on their Dom. When the physical chains were put upon them, the mental chains they wore outside the club dropped away.

Maybe she hadn't expected it to happen to her so much the same, or so easily, but she'd always been a submissive. Now that her subconscious had released that news flash to the rest of her mind, every cell was embracing this. They'd just been waiting for her to make the step into that room. No, not a room. An endless amusement park, or a quiet meadow on the planes of Paradise where she could simply . . . be.

She thought of how she'd struggled with this throughout the week, her conscious mind clinging to the paradigm she'd always had. Would it return in full force when she was untied? She was starting to understand how someone could have a split personality.

His hand dropped, sliding between her thighs, tugging on the knot over her clit. She whimpered, hands opening and closing in the bonds. When his fingers furrowed between her labia, she tensed; she couldn't help it. Every woman felt trepidation when a man first started probing her more tender crevices. Would he know how to do it right? Would he thrust his fingers in too fast or at the wrong angle? She had no way of stopping him except by calling out the safe word, and doing it before he even tried wasn't very sensible.

She needn't have worried. He eased in slowly, feeling his way, and she was so slick with arousal he burrowed into her cunt like he'd been there before. He withdrew, then slid back in again, setting a slow rhythm, emulating coitus. Her hips shifted, jerked, tried to move with his movements despite her restriction.

"Good. Hot and eager. You're ready for this."

When his fingers came out this time, the blunt head of an inanimate object replaced them. She had no time to worry about it, because he eased it in as smoothly as he had his digits, despite the fact it was a much thicker dildo that stretched her out as it pushed in deep. She'd used her vibrator inside herself periodically, and now she was glad she'd done so, else her channel would have been much tighter from lack of use.

As the dildo reached a certain depth, another piece, a smaller shaft, pressed against her anal rim. His fingers parted her buttocks, allowing it access. It didn't go inside, merely putting delicious pressure on that sensitive ring. He slid his hand to her front, then down her abdomen to adjust another curved piece over her clit. He tucked it beneath the rope knot, the soft gel of the device pressing into that nerve bundle. A series of straps were used to keep all of it in place, and when he tightened them, she moaned, rocking forward. He popped her buttock, a hard smack on one of the belt marks. The pain startled her.

"No moving until I give you permission." He wasn't messing around. It was his way or else. "Just feel it, Athena."

She nodded quickly. She'd be still. Still as a mouse. But it was so hard. She was quivering all over, and a fine sweat had broken out on her limbs. Another hard smack made her yelp. "*Yes sir.*"

"God, you have no idea how fucking gorgeous you look. Maybe I'll sit on that bench over there and jack off, make you my personal pinup fantasy."

A noise of protest was on her lips before she could stop it, and he seized her hair again, his heated breath against her lips. "You don't like that, Athena. Why not?"

"I want . . . to see you. And you said, if I was good, I could do that . . . for you."

"So I did. We'll see. That's a vibrator in your cunt and against your ass. I'm going to turn it on now. If you want to earn the right to suck my cock, you can't come. No matter what. Got it?"

"Yes sir."

She could do it. She would do it. But when he turned on the vibrator, she realized there was no way in hell she could stop herself from coming. It started with a low hum, but a building wave pattered against her clit with increasing strength, to the point she felt she was right on the cusp of an immediate, hard climax. Then it ebbed, starting over again. It was a diabolical rhythm, but she reevaluated, thinking that strategic ebb might keep her from climaxing, even as it destroyed her sanity.

The rope, the hard metal, the vibrator, it was all-powerful, physically overwhelming, but the higher she got, the more she noticed something missing. Visualizing Dale watching her helped, but it wasn't enough. When he'd spoken to her, everything had become more intense. Better. She needed him. She needed his touch to be part of this, so that the emotional reaction building in her chest, her stomach, her mind, bringing an ache to her throat, a sobbing gasp, wouldn't shatter her when her body shattered.

She didn't know if he knew it, or if it was just miraculous timing, but when her emotional response was close to overtaking the physical, giving it a sharp, painful edge, he stepped up against her, so she was no longer alone in the darkness. He put his hands on her hips, then moved up to her breasts, teasing the nipples.

The downside was that her body shot up toward that cliff edge as if his touch were rocket fuel. The rhythm of the vibrator no longer mattered. She couldn't resist her need for him.

"I can't . . . I'll . . . sir . . ."

"Call me Master, Athena." His voice was rough against her ear as he put himself full against her, pressing the rope into her flesh. "I want to hear you say it. Convince me you're all mine."

His. His slave. There were those at the club that called themselves that. For some, it meant a functional thing, a different form of service from a submissive. For others, in the way they said it, it was a desire to prove their devotion to their Master or Mistress with the strongest word possible. His harsh tone said he might be experiencing a need just as primal.

"Master," she gasped. "I'm so close . . . I can't . . ."

"You can. You won't. I want you on your knees, sucking my cock, Athena. Are you going to deny me that by disobeying, by giving in to your climax?"

She shook her head, hard, even as her body was jerking, screaming at her to come. She clung to his command like the word of God. She could do it, she could make it through, even if the damnable man seemed to be trying to force her failure. He captured her taut nipples in his long fingers, beginning to roll and tweak, tug.

"Master."

He molded himself against her curved body, forcing his erection against the crease of her ass. The weight of it pushed that piece deeper against her rim. She wanted him inside her. Wanted him in her mouth, her cunt, her ass . . . she wanted him to fill her everywhere.

She tried, she fought, she screamed in frustration, but then that scream became something else as the climax rolled over her. With the vibrator pulsing against her clit and her body immobilized, there was no reining it back, no easing the pulse or pressure. As the intensity built, she was crying out, begging for a mercy she knew she wouldn't be given. She was flying, crashing, fragmenting. Tipping her face the small amount her bindings allowed, he captured her lips in a hot, demanding kiss. His tongue plunged into her mouth, absorbing the vibration of her screams. She sobbed harder, tears streaking her cheeks as her body bucked in tiny movements, telling him what it craved, even if they weren't joined together.

He was kissing her. She recognized it after the fact, that she hadn't tensed but had instead opened her mouth to him, welcoming the invasion, needing the strong stroke of his tongue, his teeth clashing with hers, as she moaned against his flesh.

It went on for quite a while. With the vibrator still going, she was writhing in her bonds, gasping, eventually begging for mercy again because it was too much, her clit pulsing and overly sensitive, her inner tissues clenching to try and shield her against the strong vibration.

He slid the blindfold off her head but backed away, his fingertips grazing her flanks. When he moved into her field of vision, it wasn't to rummage through his bag. He sat down on the bench, his expression that of a man who was hungry for a woman's cunt. But it also reflected his terrifyingly fierce control over himself, his complete command of her.

"Please . . ." She pressed her forehead against the griffin's throat, her eyes clinging to Dale. She thought about how the creature's head was tipped back, roaring to the sky. Perhaps that roar was his claim that, regardless of whether or not the man killed him, the fantasy would endure. That the man's reality would always be a mere shadow, chasing the fantasy . . .

She'd closed her eyes, her wet lashes a reminder of her sobs. When Dale put his hand on her face, telling her he'd returned to her, she turned her lips to his palm in fervent plea, her emotionally raw state taking away any reserve. Had it always been possible for her to achieve this, or was it something he brought forth in her? All those months she'd sat in Club Release, and it wasn't until she'd seen Dale that she'd had the will to reach for this.

Some tiny corner of her mind was sensible enough to realize she was overwrought. But he'd said within his boundaries she could be anything she wished. So she kept kissing his hand, his wrist, as the tips of his fingers caressed her brow.

"Time to untie you." He removed his hand, stepped behind her and began to loosen her bonds. She didn't want him to let her go. Was that usual for a sub as well? She realized she hadn't really plumbed Roy's mind on these things. She'd notice if he needed to take it slow, sitting up after a climax, sipping water, leaning against her as he came back to earth. Disorientation was part of subspace, but she didn't really know what thoughts and feelings he had experienced.

The bonds loosened, the ropes tumbling off her, forming coils at her feet. Dale turned her, and she was a limp doll as he lifted her off her feet. She felt him pause, shift, and realized he'd had to make an adjustment in stance. This wasn't the first time he'd carried her tonight, but should he be doing that at all with his leg? He had fabulous upper body strength, but even so . . .

"Should you . . . Can I . . ."

"No." His forbidding countenance silenced her. "Don't do that. If I require anything of you, I'll tell you."

She was to rely on his strength, his control. That was part of the deal. Perhaps that was part of what he desired and needed, as much as she desired and needed to feel it, a perfect meshing. But the edge in his voice told her she'd struck a nerve. Even in her muzzy state, it was a reminder that Dale was more than the role he was playing for her. She frowned. She didn't like that term, *role-playing*. Being a Dom was an integral part of him. Obviously. She might as well say he played at being a SEAL, or she played at being Roy's wife. Maybe they were all roles, but they were vital parts of their personalities as well, like being happy or sad.

While she was rolling over those thoughts, he'd carried her to her reading nook, to the easy chair there. Because it was a large chair, it was a comfortable size for Dale and her together, especially with her in his lap. He worked the afghan she kept draped on the chair around her. Then he wrapped one arm around her back. Her head was on his shoulder, his other hand beneath the covering, stroking her bare hip, the line of her thigh. "Part your legs," he said. "You always keep your thighs open around your Master."

Of course. She should have known that, but her experience was with a male sub, where leg parting wasn't so much an issue. Her thighs loosened. She sucked in a breath as he pushed two fingers inside her slick cunt without hesitation, resting them there, while his other fingers stroked the outside like he might stroke a favored pet.

She listened to his heartbeat, inhaled the clean, male scent of him, pressed her face into his neck. She realized she was making little humming noises when she breathed, some form of self-comfort, a way of balancing. He shifted his arm so he could support the back of her head, tilt it back.

He met her gaze. "This time I kiss you and you accept it honestly, Athena."

She knew what he meant. The previous ones had been heat of the moment. He kept his eyes open, watching her face, watching her for any sign of tension. She wanted him to kiss her, needed him to kiss her, and that made her throat thick with emotion. It was hard to accept this sign she'd let another man into her life, that he was in the intimate territory that had been Roy's alone for so long.

But it was okay. The kiss was a long, slow fall, swirling in a soft wind. Everything steadied, the humming dying away. It went on for some time, him exploring her lips, her tongue; fingers caressing her face, her neck, catching tendrils of her hair around her face. When she lifted her hands, he made a negative sound in his throat, an obvious command for her to stay in place, not to touch him. Though she was trembling under his touch, she was otherwise required to stay still, not expected to do anything other than obey him, allow him to take his pleasure. As a result, the warm ball in her stomach expanded. The anxiety was still there, but it changed composition, became a different kind of urgency.

He pushed his fingers into her a little more firmly and her lower body responded. Aroused wasn't the right word, not exactly, because that suggested a progression from a nonaroused state. She'd gone straight from an orgasm into a state of . . . readiness. Her body was on a low hum, like what had escaped her lips.

"So you climaxed when I told you not to do it."

He'd intended her to do so. The satisfaction about it was in his voice. He wanted to be able to punish her. She remembered the belt, the spatula, and wondered if this punishment would be discipline or pleasure. For her, that is, since either kind brought him pleasure. Of course, she'd come so violently from all of it, maybe it was the same for her. Even so, her sore bottom was hoping for a gentler discipline. Regardless, Athena knew she'd accept either from his hand, which was kind of disconcerting.

"You tried like hell not to do so, though. I like that. You don't brat on purpose for punishment. You wanted to suck me off. I could punish you by denying you that, but I think you'd like to earn that reward, wouldn't you?"

The body she'd thought was too exhausted to do more than lie in his arms, slack and open to his desires, prickled with heat at the thought of it. Kneeling before this chair, going down on him, feeling his seed jet against the back of her throat. When she sat here later in the week, reading, daydreaming, she would remember his big body here, his cock thrusting into her mouth.

"Yes sir." She met his gaze. "I want that."

"Good." He withdrew his fingers, though he caressed her thighs with the slickness he'd drawn from her. As he did, he studied her with his unusual eyes. "I want to take you out on a date."

She blinked. "Now? Naked? Is that going to be my punishment?"

He chuckled. "No. I just thought of it. Separate issue."

"Segues," she suggested, her heart rate settling down from a panicked flutter. "You need to work on those."

"Sorry. It feels like you're in my head."

That, too, was unsettling, in a pleasant and scary way. "I'm not into public humiliation," he continued. "I'm also not real enthused about other men seeing you like this." His hand slipped to her buttock, gave it a firm squeeze.

He hadn't seemed averse to playing publicly with Willow, but then Willow embraced exhibitionism.

"Is that . . . I'm sorry, may I ask a question, sir?"

"You may. You learn fast, girl."

"Not letting other men see me. Is that your preference, or are you doing it because it's what you think I want and need?"

"To a good Master, they're one and the same, Athena."

"I know, but . . ." She was simply too fumble-tongued to figure out how to say it respectfully, but she needn't have worried.

His hand had been resting on her thighs. She gasped as it shifted, those fingers pushing back into her, a deep and demanding thrust, making her shudder, bite her lip. His eyes heated on her response. "Yes, Athena. I want to keep you to myself. That's my preference."

She liked the idea of him stating it that way. So blatant. Maybe it was only because of that uncontained flood of emotions she was experiencing right now, but that was okay. She reminded herself once again he'd said she could be any way she wished. Tomorrow, when he was gone and she had to handle her day as usual, that would be the time for rational thought. This was her moment, her fantasy, anything she wanted it to be.

"I meant I intend to take you on a real date," he said. "After the date, you can tell me whether or not it was a punishment."

She smiled at that. "As long as it's not a fancy, expensive dinner where the menu's in French and there's valet parking."

He frowned. "Athena, I can afford to take you out to a nice dinner."

"No. It's not that." She lifted a shoulder, trying to marshal her thoughts. It wasn't easy with his possessive hold on her, inside and out. "I like diners," she managed. "Roy and I . . . we used to get up in the middle of the night, and drive until we found one we hadn't tried. One night, we went all the way to Baton Rouge, didn't get back until past dawn. We'd get a meal if we were hungry, but most of the time, it was pie and coffee. It's best late at night."

"Of course." He slid his fingers from her, stroked her bare flank with his knuckles as she gave him a half smile.

"After he was gone . . . I didn't sleep well, not for a long time, so I kept doing it. At first it was hard, feeling like he should be there, but I'd take a book or something like that . . . and it was just me there, amid all these other late-night people . . ." She trailed off at his steady expression. "I'm sorry. I don't know why I brought that up."

"It's the type of thing that's hard to talk about. It's like . . ." He paused. "There was this day we were monitoring a river, and a group of targets started crossing. They were coming to join the insurgents, the guys trying to kill us. Well, the boat was an old rickety wooden thing. There they were, paddling across. We had kill orders to take them out, and the sniper team I was with could do that without breaking a sweat, but instead they did target practice on the boat, blowing holes in it until it was foundering. Then they picked off the guys when they jumped in the water. One guy made it to our side, tough bastard, but they put him down once he reached dry ground."

He met her gaze. "I tell most people that story, they'd think we were bad guys, making a game of something as serious as taking another person's life, but it's different when you're in it. When every day you're dealing with people who want to kill you, who hate you without even knowing anything real about you. And sometimes even the people you're trying to help turn on you, too. So you figure out ways within the boundaries to blow off steam. The rest you have to deal with later, when you wake up in your bed back home and think, 'God, that was fucked up.'"

The stories were entirely different, but in essence, the same. An experience carried that couldn't be shared, because of the difficulty of conveying what it meant, or why it was so important. She touched his face, sliding her knuckles down his jaw. She did it without thinking to ask this time, but he didn't tell her not to touch him, so she kept doing it, fingers moving up to the soft hair at his temple. He'd been hard beneath her when they sat down. During their conversation, that had died back a bit, but now, when she slipped her hand down his neck, she let her nails dig into his flesh, just a bit, and shifted her buttocks against him in deliberate provocation.

"I'd like my punishment now," she murmured. "So I can have my reward."

"You might have some brat in you after all." His eyes sparked with humor. "And I might just be glad about that. Go get me that spatula, and the clip magnet on the fridge. Keep it to a walk, but hurry. I want to see your tits bouncing when you come back."

The crudity didn't dismay her as she'd expect. Not the way he said it, with that voracious growl in his voice. She scrambled off his lap, with him helping her to her feet. She hurried out of the room, through the house, past the dining area where she saw the reflection of her pale body in the marbleized mirrors above the beadboard. In the kitchen, she plucked the spatula from the counter and the clip from the fridge, dumping the recipes it had been holding into the fruit bowl. As she returned, she had to remind herself to walk, since part of her wanted to fly. When she glimpsed herself in the mirrors again, she could tell her hair was loose and swirling around her face, her body flushed, nipples taut, clit still swollen from her climax. She looked wanton, sexual . . . appetizing. She glowed. She couldn't wait for Dale to punish her. She wanted to take his cock in her mouth, to serve him . . .

"Athena."

The bark of command catapulted her into motion again, and she was smiling, she couldn't help it. When she hurried down the breezeway from the dining area, she was in his direct line of sight. She'd left the door to the reading nook open and her blood ran hot at the way his gaze coursed over the movement of her naked body, his eyes full of lust. He'd be hard again now, she was sure of it, and she moistened her lips, thinking of his salty taste against her tongue.

There were two steps at the doorway of her reading room, since it was on the same grade as the sunporch. She jumped down, rather than using the stairs. The decision gave her breasts a healthy bob of movement. As she straightened her knees she saw laughter in his eyes, as well as deliciously dangerous things.

"Careful. You keep doing things like that, I'll make you jog in place. Come here, woman."

He bade her stand at the arm of the chair and took the spatula and clip from her. "Spread your legs."

When she did, he clasped the lips of her sex in firm, sure fingers, compressing them before he opened the three-inch-wide clip and slowly let the jaws come back together, holding on to her clit and labia. The compression was uncomfortable, but it also jammed all those aroused nerves together, making dense sensation arrow up through her core.

"Bend down, toward my lap."

She did so, and he took hold of her hair, wrapping it around his fist and guiding her all the way down so her mouth was pressed, blissfully, on the straining denim over his erection. She could smell the heavy, musky scent of it, knew he'd likely spilled some milky precum against the fabric of his shorts. She wanted to taste him more than she'd ever wanted to taste anything. His hand tightened in her hair. "Fold your arms beneath your breasts. Press your knees against the side of the chair."

It put more of her weight forward, so her forehead was pressed to his opposite thigh. Her fingers dug into the chair cushioning as she adjusted her knees so her thighs stayed open.

"Good girl. You learn fast. This will help you remember what happens if you come before your Master orders it."

The spatula strike made her jerk. He'd said there was a difference between discipline and a punishment for pleasure, but he didn't seem to hold back on either. Her capacity to absorb the pain seemed greater now, though, her ass lifting toward it, wanting more, even as every strike made her cringe and think, *Ow ow ow . . .*

He didn't tell her how many he was going to do this time, and by the time she was trying hard not to writhe, her ass singing with pain, she was about to beg. Her clit was pulsing beneath the hold of that clamp, her pussy tingling. When he dropped the spatula and pulled the clip off, she cried out at the painful rush of blood back to the area. It was mitigated by his touch, the clamp of his fingers over her clit, worrying it, making her hips lift up to him again. *Please . . . oh God . . . It feels so good.*

He pushed her up, shifted her so she was down on her knees between his feet. She watched with eager desire as he opened his jeans, adjusted them and the boxers beneath enough that he freed his cock, levering it out to stand tall and thick before her gaze. Roy had been a good size, more than capable of filling a woman, and Dale was the same. Her gaze coursed over the thick vein along the base of the shaft, the hint of the heavy ball sac still nested in his shorts.

"Hands behind your back, Athena. You'll suck me off with your mouth alone."

She desperately wanted to touch him, learn him with her fingers, but she was starting to understand his diabolical strategy. The tighter he held the reins, the more powerful the wanting became. The more she wanted, the more it turned him on, a closely intertwined strand that drove them both.

Clasping the base of his cock in one hand, he brought her down on him.

Steel and velvet, musk, salt. Lust and heat. She savored that first contact between the cushion of her lip and the broad head, the dampness of his slit. He kept total control of her movements, pushing her down deep on him. He did it slow, so she had time to adjust, but he still went all the way up against her gag reflex, making her fight not to choke.

"Relax your throat. Take all of me. There you go. That's my sweet girl."

She sucked that salty-musky taste, reveling in it, and when he let her slide up, she worried his slit with the tip of her tongue, sucked on the ridges of the corona, and then she was pushed down again. She worked within what his grip would allow her, flicking her tongue along his length, sucking on him so hard she hollowed her cheeks as she did it.

"Fuck, you're good at this. I might keep you on your knees all the time."

How crazy was it that she loved hearing that? She redoubled her efforts. She wanted him to come in her mouth, wanted to swallow his seed. She was wet and throbbing yet again, ready for another climax. It was exhilarating, terrifying, the way her body responded to this, to him. But would he allow her that? Or would he leave her hot and wanting, because he was immersing her in what it was to be a submissive? His kind of submissive, commanded by the inexorable will of her Master.

His thigh muscles were starting to flex and twitch in that way that told her the climax was close. His grip showed that as well, as if men lost an awareness of their own strength as they reached that crest. Or perhaps they realized getting rougher was something a woman craved, feeling his loss of control in that aggressive power. She sucked and licked even more ardently. She wished her hand was where his was, wrapped around the base of his cock, so she could feel that vein pump when the seed started to come through.

With a groan, he thrust up hard into her mouth. His ejaculation flooded her throat, several long, strong spurts that kept her swallowing frantically, trying to make sure none of it escaped her lips. Her chest heaved with the effort, her throat fighting against that gag reflex.

His animal noises of release kept her working to please him. When his touch finally eased, her scalp was stinging from his grip and her eyes were watering from the effort, but all she wanted to do was keep at it. Instead, she did the next best thing. She started to clean him, licking more gently, absorbing with pleasure the post-climactic shudders of his body, the way his fingers stroked her hair, yet also paused to do short, quick pulls, a pleasurable discomfort to her scalp. Then he had her under the arms, dragging her into his lap to grip her neck and hold her to him for a hard, deep kiss. The zipper of his open jeans bit into her sore ass, his damp cock mashed against her pussy, and she loved it, the visceral, sticky perfection of it all.

Pulling back, he stared into her face, caressing her lips with a knuckle. He caught the edge of his T-shirt, dabbed at her eyes and wiped her nose with it. During the tender gesture, her hand naturally fell on his abdomen, the ridges of muscle. When she stroked him, taking advantage to slide her palm up to his chest and curl her fingers in his chest hair, doing her own tugging, he gave her a mildly reproving look, but the indulgent light in his gaze said he wasn't going to tell her to stop.

He'd said they'd be more than a club session. What he was doing now, giving her free rein with a natural intimacy, confirmed it. This was a different emotion from what they'd shared a few moments ago. Softer, a lot of need behind it. Overwhelmed by it, she lowered her gaze.

He put his hand on the side of her head, guided her to settle back down in his lap, her temple pressed to his shoulder as she continued to stroke his chest.

"How about lunch on Wednesday?" he said at long last. "And it won't be a fancy French restaurant or a diner. We'll picnic in one of the parks. Wear sneakers. I plan to push you on the swings and make you hang from monkey bars."

The man really wasn't going to work on those segues, but then she remembered how often she and Roy hadn't needed them, following the track of one another's thoughts like they were on the same meandering garden path together.

"I'd like that. Just don't put me on the merry-go-round. I get nauseous."

"Roger that. No hurling from the merry-go-round."

She closed her eyes, content to be held. Even so, an uncertain thought managed to creep in, the idyllic moment ironically summoning it. This wasn't in a club, but she was still pursuing the fantasy in the dark of night, in isolated scenarios. Was that because she knew it wouldn't survive the light of day, the daily demands of her life, the expectations of others?

She'd held on to control too long to believe that she could leave it all in Dale's hands from beginning to end. At some point, she'd have to make some decisions and choices. But not tonight.

Tonight, this was enough.

SEVEN

Dale had stayed with her until near dawn. He'd carried her to a couch in the living room, kept her coiled and dozing in his arms as he surfed cable, pressed light kisses to her head. Eventually, he stretched her out on her stomach and kneaded her shoulders, her back, hips and legs, giving her the massage and liniment he'd promised earlier. It served the purpose of putting her in a deep, blissful sleep, probably the best she'd had since Roy had passed.

Her cell phone alarm woke her. She found herself in a guest bedroom, the one with a yellow coverlet and pale butter-colored sheers at the windows, tied back with blue ribbon. He'd respected her desires and hadn't entered her bedroom. As she fumbled for her cell and shut off the alarm, she saw it was seven a.m. While they were on the couch and he was massaging her thighs, his fingers sliding intimately against her damp core, he'd asked her when her housekeeping staff arrived. "Eight," she mumbled sleepily.

He'd lived up to everything he'd promised. He'd cared for her, shielded her privacy, respected the few boundaries she'd set, even when he could have overridden them with her full consent. At certain times last night, she would have unwisely cracked herself open to her very soul, and he'd protected her from making that rash jump.

She ran her hands through her tousled hair. He'd held control in every way, and she'd pretty much given up all of it. Probably the first time in her life, so as wonderful as last night had been, she felt like she was waking up to a massive sugar crash. Why did there have to be a morning after, with all its doubts and worries? And what exactly *was* she worried about?

She sat up in the bed, and dropped her hands into her lap. A little puff of air came out from under the pillowy comforter he'd pulled over her. She remembered what he'd told her about the insurgents and the boat. That led her mind to another part of the evening; when she'd been concerned that she should walk, rather than be carried, to spare his leg. It was the only time she'd seen a crack in that armor, a sense of the man behind the Dom.

With all of it so new and amazing to her, she'd been happy to be within those boundaries. But had she been like a kid playing in the maze at McDonald's, lost in oblivious fantasy while the parent sipped coffee, thinking about the less than three hours of sleep last night and whether the mortgage would get paid this month?

She was being silly. Dale had obviously been fully engaged and enjoyed their interlude last night. She'd wondered what his own unique preferences were, and he'd given her some of them. His desire to keep her to himself, for one thing.

She wanted to know more about him, though. While she never again expected to find the level of intimacy with a man she'd enjoyed as a married woman, it didn't mean she didn't hope for it, grasp at it like a naïve child snatching candy when a semblance of it was offered. He was right. She was ruined for casual dating, probably even for the idea of having limited "sessions" with a Dom. She wanted more.

So maybe that was the source of her vague unease. She was afraid of rejection, of risking her heart on a man who, despite saying they could give this free rein, see where this led, might himself only see it going a certain way down the road, when she might want it to go further. She could easily distort the relationship in her mind, amped up on the new experience or hormones or what have you.

She rubbed her brow. Often, when something was worrying her, she'd put the shoe on the other foot to clarify things, balance her concerns. Dale Rousseau was a divorced, middle-aged man, a retired SEAL who'd taken lives, who'd had to accept losing his leg. He loved dogs. He was very comfortable holding control over any situation. Did he have no reservations about meeting outside a club setting because he could impose an equally structured setting in any venue? Yet he'd implied he rarely conducted sessions outside the club.

He was an incredibly skilled Master and he'd given her an incomparable fantasy. What would it be like, if it were balanced and intertwined with the reality? Every time she came back to that thought, the yearning she felt intensified, as if her heart were seeking something she'd glimpsed last night, but hadn't quite grasped. Something she'd have to cross a mine field to obtain, and things were good enough on this side of the field she couldn't really justify risking her life, could she?

Time to be an adult again, Athena. Sighing, she picked up the silky robe he'd left her, slipped it on and headed for her bedroom. She had a full schedule for the next couple of days, so if a dose of reality was what she needed, she was going to get more than her share.

Unfortunately, her anticipation of their lunch together on Wednesday was dashed Monday, by a text Dale sent to her while she was at her office.

> Have an adoption on Wednesday. Let's reschedule for later next week. Will call you. Be good until then. Or not. I'll deal with either contingency.

"Problem?"

She looked up to see Ellen, her administrative assistant, giving her a questioning look. Athena shook her head. "No, just a cancelled lunch for Wednesday."

"Oh." Ellen lifted a brow. "The one you told me to block out but didn't tell me who it was with. The one that's had you glowing all morning."

"And how do you know that's the reason I've been glowing?"

"Because when you read that text, the light went out." Ellen picked up the papers Athena had just signed. "Hope he doesn't screw it up, doing the things that men typically do."

She should give Ellen a pleasant but nonencouraging look, keeping their relationship on its usual friendly but professional footing, but Ellen was a hard worker and a good woman. She was also a widow, which had given her and Athena a bond. She'd hired Ellen the year before Roy got sick, yet she remembered Ellen during that time as a quiet, efficient source of help on so many levels, the one person who never said the things that were well-meaning in their intent but such a painful effort to answer.

Athena also remembered a visit by Nancy Allen, a woman who'd always flirted outrageously with Roy. Nancy had come by to see Athena on a business matter, and had asked about Roy's illness. At that point it was advanced, Athena only in the office the bare minimum needed to keep things handled. When Athena necessarily explained that Roy's illness was terminal, Nancy Allen had put a familiar hand on her wrist.

"Oh, Athena, don't give up on him like that. You need to be positive for Roy. Who knows what will happen?"

Athena had nodded, detached herself, and returned to her office. But she'd come back to the door a moment later to find Ellen had stepped in front of Nancy. Neither woman noticed Athena.

"With all due respect, Ms. Allen, you don't know a damn thing about their relationship or what she's handling. She loves that man more than the sun and the moon—if he's dying, she'd be the first to know it, and she's doing her best to help him through it and not fall apart while he needs her. That's *not* giving up on him. That's loving him in every way she should, even while her heart is breaking every day. Your job, if you consider yourself her friend, is not to tell her what she should or shouldn't be doing, but figuring out how to support her. You shooting your mouth off about things you've never experienced makes you no kind of friend at all."

Athena had the unique experience of seeing Nancy Allen pale like a vampire under her airbrushed makeup and flee. Her assistant's fists unclenched and she swore softly, an obvious self-admonishment for losing her cool. When she turned back toward her desk, she started, seeing Athena.

"Mrs. Summers . . . I'm so sorry, I . . ."

"No apologies necessary. If that woman never darkens my door again, it will be too soon." She paused, studying Ellen's flushed face. "Thank you, Ellen." Then she'd returned to her desk. It was the last they'd ever spoken of it.

Now, remembering so many other times Ellen had done exactly the right thing from that place of shared understanding, she cocked her own brow at her assistant. "Of those oh-so-many-things men screw up, what are we referencing today? You could create a male-bashing day calendar, Ellen."

Her assistant laughed. "True enough. This one would be the cold feet syndrome. They have an amazing time with you, then get spooked and decide not to call you for a few months, long after you've given up on them. I think it's because they've been burned before, but it's still aggravating."

"Hmm." If Dale was having cold feet, there'd only be one foot involved, wouldn't there? The wry thought made her consider her earlier thoughts. She might have a desire to be treated as a submissive, but that was not all she wanted from a man in her life. And he'd said he was interested in more.

"Go ahead and keep that two-hour lunch block for me on Wednesday," she decided. "Since I'll be working here until nine tonight on the details for the gallery benefit this weekend, I think I've earned it."

Ellen snorted and moved toward the door. "With the hours you work, you could take two-hour lunches forever and never catch up. Good for you."

With a woman's practiced eye, Athena knew she and Ellen could be sisters, since they both had brown hair and green eyes, but the structure of their faces were different, and Ellen downplayed her looks significantly. The woman was too thin and pale, and today as always she wore demure, monochrome colors and little jewelry. She didn't dye her short brown hair, so it had strands of gray that made it look mousy. She was as supremely competent—and utterly unremarkable—as the computer on her desk.

Athena thought about the effort it had taken her to even get dressed the first year after Roy's death. Ellen's husband had been gone far longer.

"Ellen, are you seeing anyone?"

Ellen turned, gave her a surprised look. "No, ma'am."

Athena pursed her lips. "I don't in any way want to commit the faux pas Nancy did, speaking of things she doesn't understand, so let me simply ask this as a friend. How long will you mourn?"

Ellen shrugged uncomfortably. "I just can't bring myself to date. All those games, and no man wants to feel like he's being sized up for a life fit on the first meet."

Ruined for casual dating. There it was again, a discomfiting reminder of herself in Dale's words and Ellen's mirror image.

The admin met Athena's gaze. "I had a man who loved me, who knew me, who cared about me as much as I cared about him. You and I know what a miracle that is, but it's a miracle that happened because of time and tears, years of being together. I'm not asking for all that in a first look. I'm looking for a sign, I guess, as silly as that sounds. If there's a man out there for me, he'll do or say something and I'll recognize it. It will feel like . . . the chance is there. But if that never happens, it's okay."

Though her eyes had a suspicious brightness to them, Ellen pressed her lips together in an attempted smile. "We're blessed if we get it even once. So don't worry about me, Mrs. Summers. I hope you've been fortunate enough to find that second round of blessings. You're a good person, and you deserve that kind of love again."

"So do you," Athena said sincerely.

Ellen gave her a nod of thanks and exited Athena's office, returning to her desk just outside of Athena's view. Athena turned her chair to consider the city, the document blinking on her computer temporarily forgotten. It did take time. Dale had been a surprise. The question was whether he was simply a jump-start to get her heart moving toward love again, or if he was in fact the type of man that would take a permanent hold on it. She had to be brave enough to find out, didn't she?

She'd decided to take lunch to him on Wednesday. If she arrived before the dog's new family did, she wouldn't mind watching him handle an adoption, hanging around until he was free to share food with her. She made sandwiches, boiled eggs and a good pound cake. She also added in some raw veggies, dip and other appetizers he'd probably like. Lynn had given her an odd look when she insisted on baking the cake herself, but she remembered his approval when he'd asked her if she made the sandwich herself. Of course, if she'd proven herself a lousy cook, he might have changed that stipulation. Men were funny that way.

On the flip side, with all this largesse, he might accuse her of trying to make him fat, but from the muscled body she'd had too little opportunity to touch, she was sure he was in no immediate danger of that.

They hadn't had sex that night. Dom/sub sessions often didn't involve that, especially if the couple weren't romantically involved otherwise, but he'd made it clear with the condom comment on the first night that he hadn't ruled it out. She imagined what it would have been like, straddling him before his climax, sinking down on him . . .

Easy girl. Her heart was tapping like a metronome on allegro, and she'd only driven up to the front gate. From here, she could see a big Caddy with no wheels under the shade of a sprawling oak inside the junkyard. During the massage that night, his voice had rumbled with soothing pillow talk of this and that. He'd mentioned on pretty nights he sometimes put a sleeping bag on the hood of that Caddy and slept there. Thinking of what they might do there, beneath the stars, she found her cheeks heating.

The gate was unlocked, but still closed, so she parked on the shoulder and decided to take the arbor gate that served as an entrance for foot traffic. Locking the car and slipping the picnic basket over her arm, she wandered under the arbor, pausing to reach up and touch the clematis vine he had winding through the wooden slats. The arbor looked hand built and recently repainted. The man certainly had a wealth of talents. Passing through the gate, she closed it securely after her and proceeded down the driveway toward the main office. He might be somewhere else in the junkyard, but she could certainly wait on the steps. Though the last group of dogs had met her, she hoped if there were any new ones loose, they wouldn't decide she was an intruder. She had enough turkey sandwiches to ransom her life if necessary.

The drive was about a quarter mile, a nice walk on a breezy New Orleans day. When the curve in the road resolved itself to reveal the office area, she discovered she didn't have to worry about Dale's whereabouts. He was leaning against the railing of the stairs, playing with the dog she expected was waiting for his new family. A young tan-colored shepherd mix with one pointed ear and one that flopped over. He and Dale were engaged in a tug-of-war with a stuffed sock that had been knotted on both ends and once in the middle.

She was approaching downwind, so the dog didn't scent her right off. Dale did, however. His gaze flicked up, and he straightened.

He wasn't wearing the prosthesis. He was leaning on crutches, and the leg of his jeans had been pinned in the back so it wouldn't drag along the ground. His expression gave her a mental pause, and suddenly she wasn't so sure of herself.

No, she hadn't called ahead, perhaps because she was testing the whole "structure" of their arrangement, but she hadn't completely abandoned her manners. She'd already decided if she arrived and had the sense she was intruding, she'd simply say she was dropping him off lunch on the way to something else. Easy enough. She didn't like lying to him, but she wasn't going to put him in the uncomfortable position of bearing her company when it wasn't welcome.

Oh hell. She could rationalize it all she wanted, but she'd followed pure impulse, wanting to surprise him, and hoping that was a good thing. She felt like a fool, but pushed down the dismay and ignored the cold knot in her stomach. As she came within speaking distance, the dog trotted over to her to say hello and check out the basket. She petted him, straightened. Dale still hadn't spoken, but then neither had she.

When she met his gaze, she knew she wasn't going to lie to him. She wasn't sure she could.

"I thought I would surprise you with lunch, but I apologize," she said with calm dignity. "I should have called and found out if you were all right with that. There are turkey sandwiches in here, potato salad and dessert. I wasn't sure what condiments you liked, so I put those in small containers to add the amount you prefer. There's a really good spiced mayonnaise. I'll just leave all of it upstairs and you can eat it when you're ready."

The sound of a car trundling down the driveway had her turning. Dale bent to take hold of the dog's collar so he wouldn't run toward it. The occupants of the vehicle looked like a father and son, and from the anticipation on the boy's face, the animated way he was pointing and talking to his dad in the car, Athena had no doubt the dog's new family had arrived.

"You're busy, so I'll go ahead and get out of your way," she said briskly. "The little boy looks very excited."

She added that with a practiced smile. Then she moved toward the stairs to his apartment, cutting a wide swathe around him. He watched her mount the stairs, she could feel his gaze, but he still hadn't said anything. Her heart felt like a stone, weighing her down.

The car doors opened, the boy jumping out. She turned at the top of the stairs, holding on to the rail tightly, just in time to see Dale let the dog go. The shepherd mix and his new master greeted one another with equal enthusiasm. The father was smiling at them both, talking to Dale, reaching out to shake his hand. Her gaze lingered on the set of his broad shoulders, his back to her in this position, and she swallowed, hard.

Letting herself into the apartment, she put the basket on the table. He might not be upstairs for a while, so she went ahead and unpacked the perishables, put them in the fridge. The man really did keep a neat place. The shelves were clean, not a crumb or stain on them from a ketchup bottle or orange juice carton. He kept beer, juice and milk, the usual sandwich staples, and what appeared to be the remains of a vegetable beef stew he'd cooked for himself.

She left the cellophane-wrapped pound cake on his kitchen table, in a basket that held a stack of napkins. She decided to keep the bottle of white wine, because it was obvious he was more of a beer drinker and she'd really brought the wine as her beverage.

The dryer was turning in his laundry room, and the apartment was small enough it heated the kitchen, bringing her the pleasant scent of drying clothes. From here, she could see his open bedroom door. He hadn't yet made his bed today, and there were a couple of breakfast dishes in the sink, suggesting he'd risen late. Well, neat didn't mean he wasn't a man.

The thought would have made her smile, if she wasn't nursing hurt feelings, a condition she fully accepted she'd brought upon herself. "Time to get going, you silly woman," she murmured. But she did take the circuitous route, stopping by his bedroom door. She could hear him talking to the boy below, snippets of conversation about care for his new family member. She slipped into the bedroom, knowing she was being entirely inappropriate, but she had to do one thing, even if she never had the opportunity to do it again.

She sat down on the bed where the sheets had been pulled back, so she was sitting where Dale would have lain as he slept. She smoothed her palm over that expanse, laid it on the pillow that still bore the indentation from his head. With his hair so short, it wouldn't really be tousled when he woke, but it might stick up here and there. He'd have that appealing dark stubble that would make him look more than a little dangerous.

Her gaze drifted across the floor, and she saw the prosthesis. It was the first time she'd seen the leg part completely unclothed, a metal shaft and a plastic mold socket. As her gaze drifted over the night table, she noticed there was a tube of a topical antibiotic.

The prosthesis clearly made walking and dealing with the dogs easier, so perhaps the medicine was an indication of why he wasn't wearing it today. She wanted to ask him about it, but things were strange and this wasn't the right moment to explore more about him. Maybe at a time when they were both more prepared for it. If they ever reached that point.

With a sigh, she rose and left the apartment, carrying the basket. Dale was going over some paperwork with the father at a picnic table while the boy and dog were chasing one another around the open area. The boy had a toy he'd obviously bought for his new friend, and he was alternating between throwing it and playing tug-of-war like Dale had been doing before they arrived.

Athena wasn't going to disrupt them. She was skirting the area, intending to head back up the drive to her car, when Dale's voice reached her. "Athena."

She turned, that same bright smile on her face. She felt like a lightbulb, the kind that hurt the eyes, such that a person turned it off at the earliest opportunity. "I put the sandwiches in the fridge," she said. "You don't need to worry about—"

"Can you hang around a few minutes? I'd like to talk to you."

Despite her hurt, something in his tone, in the whole situation, pricked her intuition. If she put aside her own insecurities, she knew the way he was acting wasn't quite Dale. Yes, she only had a couple of meetings to go on for that conclusion, but now, at the simple statement, the way his gaze met hers, she was sure she was right. It gave her the confidence to answer him in a way that was calm . . . and pointed. Challenging him to respond to it.

"Yes." She took a breath. "I'll do anything you tell me to do."

Emotion kindled in those blue-green eyes, telling her she'd struck a spark. "Wait for me upstairs," he said.

She nodded. She managed not to say "Yes sir," given that her remark had probably already raised the curiosity of the father. Regardless, she hoped Dale saw her desire to address him properly. From the tightening of his jaw, she expected he did.

While she waited on him, she made his bed, washed those couple of dishes, straightened up. The clothes were still going in the dryer, so she sat down in the chair, listened to the rotation in one ear, and his voice rumbling below in the other. From where she was sitting, she could see him finishing up the adoption. When they loaded the dog in the car, the boy sitting in the back with the happy canine, Dale lifted his hand in farewell. She saw the dog pause, look back at Dale, suddenly realizing what he'd known was changing yet again. The boy tousled his ears, reassuring him. The father also twisted around in the seat, giving the dog a pat.

As the car disappeared around the curve, Dale turned, using the crutches to get to the stairs. Once there, she heard the vibration through the apartment's thin walls as he maneuvered up each step. When he approached the top, she rose to open the door for him, pushing open the screen so he didn't have to manage that with the crutches.

"You don't have to open the door for me," he said shortly. "I do it all the time. Sit down."

"I don't mind." She retreated as he moved into the kitchen, taking it over with his size and presence. "They seem like they'll be very good to him."

"Yeah." He paused, looking at her. She'd sat down when he'd told her to do so, and now her fingers curled in her lap. It was an effort not to fill the silence, but she made herself wait on him. "It's a good adoption," he said at last. "I don't adopt to kids. The adult has to want the dog for himself. That's so when the kid starts getting into cars, girls, soccer, whatever, I know the dog doesn't become a piece of the furniture. Bert—the dad—picked Rusty out. Reminds him of the dog he had when he was a kid."

He shifted. As the silence drew out, Athena rose. "Well, I guess I should be going."

"Why did you come today, Athena?"

She drew her brows together at the almost accusatory tone. "I thought it would be fun to surprise you with lunch. We seemed to be developing the kind of rapport that would welcome that. I was mistaken. I'm sorry."

"You already apologized. You don't need to do it twice." He noticed the dishes in the drainer, and his lips pressed in a thin line. "And you don't need to do my goddamned dishes."

She blinked. "I was occupying myself while waiting, being helpful. Serving."

His gaze snapped to her. She wasn't sure what was happening here, but she was obviously missing something. "I'm going," she said. "I shouldn't have come. Perhaps all of this has been a mistake. I obviously . . . I'm making more of this than it is, which suggests I've let my emotions run away with me like a schoolgirl. I wanted to see you. That's all. I wanted to make you lunch, to do something for you. Watch you during your normal day, be a part of that day before I have to return to work and be who I am for everyone else.

I've intruded where I'm not invited, and I've made you uncomfortable. So I'm going."

She was being repetitious, but an ache was growing in her throat. There was too much pressure behind her eyes. She picked up her basket, but Dale was in front of the door. She'd just slip past him, was all. There was enough room to get past.

She'd almost made it when his arm snaked out, caught her waist, bringing her to a halt. She went rigid. "Please let go of me."

He shook his head. Stared straight ahead and just held her there. His fingers flexed against her lower back, his arm pressed under her breast. She closed her eyes, amazed at how strongly her body reacted to his merest touch, how she wanted to melt against him, put her fingers against his strong throat and reach up on her toes to kiss him with all the heated passion she'd been imagining when she drove up to the gate.

To hell with it. She dropped the basket and lifted a hand to his face, drawing his gaze to hers before she used the strength of his arms, the way he'd planted himself in the floor like a tree, his one leg and the crutches braced against both their weights, to lift herself up against him. She buried her fingers in his short hair, nails scraping his nape.

She kissed him with longing and need, with desire and pure pleasure in the heat of his mouth, which increased as he began kissing her back, muttering an oath against her lips. He smelled like grass and soil, old rusty cars and a little bit of dog and Old Spice.

His hand dropped to her ass, pulling her to his front so she was fully against him instead of locked to his side. Her lower abdomen contracted at the pleasure of his hard response pushed against her there.

He let the crutches fall, gripped the sink edge and pulled them both the necessary step to it so he was leaning against that, the better to keep an arm around her waist and put the other hand to her head, taking over the kiss. His fingers slid along her jaw, down to her throat. She made a needy sound there, vibrating beneath his fingertips. He was just as hungry for her, in a raw, undisciplined way that she embraced, all her earlier uncertainty driven away before it.

Before they could get too out of control, he broke the kiss, his chest expanding from the effort of drawing a deep breath, even as his hands remained clamped on her. "I'm sorry, Athena. You shouldn't be apologizing because I was being a bastard."

She didn't care. She just wanted him to keep kissing her. But he tightened his grip, keeping her still. "I've never Mastered a woman without two legs to stand on. I wasn't prepared to be that exposed."

Her spinning world came to an abrupt stop. She stared up at him. "You thought it would matter to me?"

Apparently seeing her utter lack of comprehension did him a world of good. The set of his strong jaw eased significantly. "Yeah, I did. That's what I assumed when you started acting so funny, talking about leaving the lunch instead of sharing it with me."

Oh, God. She was such an idiot. It made so much sense she almost started laughing at herself, at both of them, even realizing that would be entirely inappropriate.

"I was acting that way because you were being so remote. You looked like a storm cloud." She put her hands on his face. "Dale, you're not dealing with a child. I was married for over twenty years, which is plenty long enough to realize a man's character lies in his heart, his soul, not his body. Though your body packs more than enough fantasy for me. If you had a second leg and smelled like brownies, you'd be too perfect. I couldn't wait to be with you again. With . . . my Master. And now I am being a little schoolgirlish, but if you're going to be insecure, I get to take a turn, too."

That and the brownie comment made him chuckle, dissipating her worries. He put his forehead down against hers. "Fuck, I made a mess of that. I thought I was long past this kind of thing. Turns out all I had to do is get stupid about a woman again and all that old bullshit tried to pile back on."

Get stupid about a woman again . . . It was amazing how few words a man actually had to say to capture a woman's heart and earn her total forgiveness. "Seems like only a brief relapse," she said. Lifting his palm to her lips, she met his gaze as she shifted against his body, rubbing her stomach against his still-turgid response. His fingers tightened over hers.

"Are you trying to misbehave?"

"No sir." But she smiled.

"So what you said outside. That you'll do anything I tell you to do."

"Yes."

"I didn't tell you to do my dishes or make my bed."

"No," she admitted. When he waited, obviously expecting more of an explanation, she lifted a shoulder. "It's like the submissives who do the bootblacking," she said, referencing the particular segment of the D/s community who took great pride in the art of shining their Master's boots. They could spend an astonishing amount of time discussing how to keep them in top form. "Or the one who always brings her Master his drink from the bar. The sub who folds his Mistress's clothes precisely according to her specifications before she has him kneel before her, service her with his mouth."

"You're not here to be my maid or my nurse, Athena."

She shook her head. "I didn't mean it like that. I don't think they do it for that reason, either."

"I know you didn't. I'm telling you to keep the distinction in mind." He nodded to the dryer. "Hang up my clothes, then come down to the yard. We'll have lunch after you help me with the dogs. They're raring to get out a little bit, since they've had to be in the kennels this morning for Rusty's adoption."

Using admirable muscle control and balance, he picked up the crutches and fitted them under his arms. "I liked hearing you call me Master."

Leaning down, he pressed his lips against hers for another lingering kiss. She barely breathed, hands closed into balls against his chest in the small space between them. He hadn't given her permission to touch him, and the order he'd just issued had switched her mind to the submissive mode, waiting for his cues and direction. Whereas so much of the past few minutes had felt wrong, precarious, now things felt right. She badly wanted to straighten her fingers, touch him, but waiting for his permission to let her do so just made the wait all the sweeter.

"There's a lotion in my bathroom. It's not sweet smelling like yours, but use it, since you washed my dishes. I expect my sub to keep her hands soft, and that dish soap will strip tar off paper."

He moved past her, back out the door. She tried not to worry or hover, though after he started down the steps, she did watch him through the blinds. He managed the stairs by putting the crutches in the opposite hand, taking hold of the railing and hopping down each stair so capably she could tell he'd done it plenty of times. Just as he'd said.

When he returned with six of the dogs, she noticed how they maintained a couple-foot buffer around him, more than they did when he was walking on the prosthesis. Part of it was what he was, of course. With their enhanced faculties, animals could detect a lead alpha with little difficulty. It resonated off Dale such that even the comparatively handicapped senses of humans couldn't miss it. Even so, the dogs' extra attention when he was hampered by the lack of the prosthesis made her love them even more. She was going to help him find every one of them a wonderful home.

After she hung his clothes in the closet, she couldn't help moving back to the bed and lifting his pillow to her face. She inhaled a deep scent of Dale before she adjusted sheets and cover again. Even with his bed unmade, his blanket had been folded at the end of the mattress, suggesting he slept only under a sheet. He also had the windows open. The junkyard was filled with metals and gravel surfaces that absorbed the heat of the Louisiana sun, so she expected he received more than his share of warmth from that, but he didn't seem dependent on a controlled climate, regardless. She found an air-conditioning unit in a closet.

When she came back outside and descended the stairs, only one dog remained with him. The others probably had dispersed with the "free" command, so he could give this one his undivided attention. It was a mixed golden retriever with three legs.

"This is Perry," he told her. "Lost his leg because somebody shot him with a BB gun. It was too infected to save when he was rescued. My hope is that karma kicks in threefold and all the shooter's appendages rot off."

She considered that. "Wouldn't threefold mean he loses three limbs, not all four?"

"The rest would be a bonus," he said. "And if he lost all of them, it would be five."

She chuckled at that. Dale smiled in return, and she thought he looked very fine and masculine, standing there with his eyes squinted against the sun. When he reached out, touched her face, she could feel her eyes softening on him. His expression relaxed further. They were all right. She supposed they'd weathered their first fight, of sorts.

"You said you wanted my help working with the dogs?" she asked, before she embarrassed herself.

He nodded. "With Perry specifically. Ball throwing helps him keep his muscles in shape. He gets the basics of it, but he starts to gets a little distracted after two or three tosses."

"No ADHD medications for dogs?" she asked.

He snorted. "No, with dogs we do it the old-fashioned way. Instead of using drugs, we teach them to pay attention. In SEAL training, facing a few hundred push-ups or additional boat drills in fifty-degree water if you fuck up tends to focus you. I go with a bit nicer approach with dogs, but repetition works for them as well. Anyhow, speaking of attention"—he gave her a narrow look and she tucked her tongue in her cheek—"if he doesn't go for it, you run and grab it. Make it seem like bringing it back to me is the coolest thing ever, so he'll start competing with you to go get it. When he brings it all the way back to me, we both make over him like crazy. Goldens thrive on approval, but his confidence has been shaken. You okay with that?" He gave her a critical look. "You look like running's part of your workout regimen."

His eye for detail continued to impress her, and the veiled compliment was bolstering. "Yes. And swimming. I haven't done my workout today, so this will catch two birds in one net. Right, Perry?" She bent down and tousled his ears, and Perry laughed up at her, mouth open and eyes bright. Even so, she saw a wariness in his expression that most well-loved goldens didn't have, evidence of the confidence problem Dale mentioned.

"Just don't throw it over the fence, Mr. Overachiever," she teased Dale. "I don't scale barbed wire."

"Don't worry. My throwing is a bit hampered" He wiggled the crutches under his arms. "Though I can throw it far enough to enjoy the way you run after it. If you get rid of that shirt, I'll enjoy it even more."

She laughed, but then his expression changed, making the sound catch in her throat. He nodded. "I mean it. Take it off, Athena."

Her blouse was a rose-colored flowing fabric that hid the fact her bra was a pale pink satin thin enough to show the shape of her nipples, especially if they were aroused. The sheer upper panels of the cups were wide enough to give him a hint of areola. When she shed the blouse, his gaze lasered in on that area. She didn't know a straight man alive who had an attention disorder when it came to breasts.

He directed her to hang the delicate garment on a hook inside his truck, parked beneath the apartment. As she moved back toward him, he was fondling Perry's head, but he tilted his own toward her.

"That's right, Perry. She's all ours. It's a good day, isn't it?" He put out a hand and entwined his fingers with hers. "God, I'd love to see you run without the bra, but I'm not a total sadist. Most days. You dressed up for me. The panties match?"

"Yes sir."

He nodded. "All right, then. Let's see if we can give Perry a good workout."

Now familiar with the dusty gravel of the junkyard, she'd switched from heels to canvas sneakers in the car. She was glad she had, since she wouldn't have been suitably prepared to help him otherwise.

Perry went after the first few balls enthusiastically enough. When his attention started to flag, she began to race him. Just as Dale had predicted, he embraced the competition. She had to be quick footed, because he'd even try to trip her to get to the ball first. She accused the dog of foul play, even as she laughed and dodged around him, trying to outwit his three legs with her two. Sometimes she encouraged Perry to jump at the ball, try to wrestle her for it. She was going to have to use her sticky roll in the car to de-fur her skirt, but she didn't care.

Despite the frivolity, she never forgot the deceptively lazy regard of the man watching them. Each time she and Perry ran back to him, and she saw his attention sliding over her body like sun rays, it spiked her adrenaline.

Dale finally called for a water break. He offered her a bottle from a cooler he had next to the steps and directed Perry to a bowl under them. As Perry lapped enthusiastically, she twisted her hair up on her neck, held it there while she fanned herself with the other hand. The position necessarily tilted her upper body and when Dale turned toward her, his blue-green gaze sharpened. She realized she wasn't the least exerted by her competition with Perry. Her body was fueled and vibrating, needy for Dale.

The object of her lust crooked a finger at her. As she came to stand before her Master, he slid his knuckle down her sternum, into the damp cleft of her breasts. "I think that will do for the day," he said. He snapped his fingers, bringing Perry to his knee, then lobbed the ball out over the cars. "Perry, *free*. Go play."

Perry took off, barking joyously. He was answered by dogs from various parts of the yard, so he headed off toward whatever adventures they'd found. Dale slid his touch to the small of her back, hooking his thumb in the waistband of her skirt so his fingers traced the elastic of her panties beneath.

"Turn your head away from me, Athena. Hold your hair off your neck."

Some tendrils had escaped, so now she scraped those together, held them up against the heavier mass twisted on the back of her head. His lips pressed against her throat, making her sigh with pleasure. When his thumb slid over the satin cup of her bra, over the nipple, she rocked against him.

"What do you want, Athena?"

"Whatever my Master desires."

"He wants to hear what you're imagining."

"You . . . inside of me."

She saw that enigmatic look cross his face again. This time, she wouldn't mistake it for the wrong thing. She met his gaze directly.

"When you look at me," she said softly, "you could have no limbs at all. It's not your physical strength that commands me, Master. It's you. Please."

His jaw flexed with emotion and arousal both, making her want to strain against his hands, show him her need. He tightened his grip at her waist, an implied command to keep her still. "Go upstairs," he said, low. "Take off everything but the bra and panties. Kneel by the bed."

EIGHT

She wanted to help him up the stairs, but she knew he wasn't going to let her take care of him, at least not that way. The way he *would* let her take care of him had her mounting the stairs quickly. As she slid into the apartment, she was already unhooking her skirt. She shimmied out of it, the socks and canvas sneakers, and put them all neatly in one of the kitchen chairs. Then she moved into his bedroom and sank to her knees. She parted them and laced her fingers behind her head, keeping her eyes down. Since he'd liked the way her body had arched when she'd held her hair on her neck, she chose this position over other possible permutations of the submissive posture, like palms flat on the floor or at her sides.

She heard him coming up the stairs, one at a time. Her gaze moved to the nightstand. Going on instinct, she scrambled across the room to put the antibiotic ointment and extra stump socks into a drawer. She also moved the prosthesis into the closet and closed the door, coming back to her kneeling position just as the door opened.

When he entered the bedroom, she kept her eyes lowered, wanting to give him the chance to catch his breath and be everything he wanted to be for her. The crutches and his one leg braced themselves in front of her.

"Look what someone left me while I was away," he murmured. "A gorgeous sex slave."

She trembled as he slid a finger along her bare shoulder, hooking the bra strap and caressing her collarbone. "Are you wet for me, Athena?"

"Yes, Master."

"Prove it to me."

She slipped her fingers into her panties and rubbed them against her slick lips. Lifting her hand, she rose onto her knees, still keeping her eyes down. He clasped her wrist, making her quiver harder when he drew her fingers into his mouth, sucking on them.

"Nice, but I want you even wetter. Masturbate while I get undressed. I want to see you touch your breasts, play with your nipples. Keep your eyes on your body, not on me."

She wanted to offer to undress him so she could feel the shape of him beneath her hands, but his tone of voice said she was expected to be silent, obedient. She vibrated with the desire to serve. She put her hand back into the panties, knowing the thin fabric and the spread of her thighs would show him the movement of her fingers over her cunt. With the other hand, she reached into her bra cup, cradled her breast, moving her fingers over the nipple as she squeezed and kneaded. Her body rocked up at the stimulation, her ass rotating against her calves as she sank back down on them again. A gasp slipped from between her lips.

"Don't get too enthusiastic, slave. Your orgasm belongs to me."

"Yes, Master." From the squeak of protest and the scrape of metal, she knew he'd taken a seat in the kitchen chair. She heard the thump of his jeans as he skinned them off, tossed them to the floor. His shirt landed on top of them. He must have taken off the boxers with the jeans, because when he settled onto the bed, she had the brief impression of a bare, muscular haunch. He propped the crutches by the nightstand. Then he dropped a scrap of cloth on the ground next to her knee.

"Put that on."

Everything inside her protested. It was a blindfold. She wanted to see him, wanted to learn every curve and plane of him by sight as well as touch. She wondered if he wanted her to wear it because of his amputation. She hesitated, putting her fingers on it.

"Please let me see you, Master." She didn't want to break the mood, or push him into a place he wasn't ready to go, but she also wanted past this hurdle. She never wanted it to interfere with their time together again. She wanted to prove to him it truly didn't matter. He was a warrior who'd lost a limb in battle, that was all.

Long moments passed. Since she assumed he was thinking it over, she let her hair down so it spilled over her shoulders, down her back. She put one arm behind her, bracing herself so she could arch up and undulate with greater flexibility against the manipulation of her fingers on her sex. Slipping her slick fingers into her mouth, she then brushed those wet fingers over a prominent nipple, pushing the bra cup back with her knuckles so he could see her do it. "Please, Master," she breathed, hips lifting up as she dropped her hand between her legs again. "I need you inside me. Please."

She wouldn't look until he said it was okay, but she wanted to be immolated by the heat she was sure would be in his eyes. He was the type of Master who would be intensely turned on by begging, that whole alpha-male-testosterone thing. She was the type of sub who loved to beg, so it worked out perfectly, didn't it?

"Come here." The animal growl of his voice confirmed it, and she had to restrain herself to keep from scampering to the bed like a puppy, as eager to please as Perry.

He'd stretched out on the mattress, so her gaze fell on the arch of his right foot. Aware of his weighted silence, of the time he was giving her to look, she slid her attention slowly up that toned calf and then moved over to the other leg where it began, just below the knee. She knew the worst thing she could do was try to school her reaction, make it anything less than honest feeling. His left leg down to his knee looked like any other leg. Well, the leg of a man with Dale's level of fitness. Muscled, a light sprinkling of hair.

It was paler than the other leg, but the stump probably wasn't supposed to be overexposed to the sun, such that he took more care to protect it. She saw the scar, the seam where the skin had been lapped over the end. She also saw abrasions, several sores on the pale skin. Perhaps that was the reason he'd had the topical sitting out, and why he wasn't wearing the prosthesis.

"May I touch you, Master?" she asked. Though his apartment was small, her voice echoed in the utter stillness that cocooned them both.

"Yes." His voice was thick. Still her Master, still certain of himself, yet there was another note to it. This was new to him as well, which made it all the more precious to her.

She molded her fingers over his knee, slid them down to the stump. She didn't touch the sore spots, mindful not to cause them any further irritation. Shifting onto the bed, she sank to her knees between his, which he spread further to accommodate her. She braced her hip against his right leg, rested her hand on his left knee again.

"I'm so glad that you're alive." She didn't try to disguise the keen emotion in her voice, and when she lifted her gaze, she most wanted to see his face. As gorgeous as his body was, all virile male, his cock in a promising semierect state despite the emotional distraction, she needed to see what he was thinking and feeling.

He was staring at her face, so when she raised her lashes, their eyes locked. His expression held something deep, painful, powerful, but he wasn't displeased. He was . . . maybe he didn't even really know what he was right now. She just knew it was right, whatever emotions were weaving them together. Staying in the clasp of that brilliant, unfathomable gaze, she let her fingers drift down her sternum, to her abdomen. His gaze held hers an extra moment, then he followed her fingers to where she slid them over the outside of her panties, drawing his attention to how the panel had become soaked with her response. She caressed herself, catching her lip in her teeth at the sensation of pleasuring herself before him, at his command.

"Take off the bra."

She obeyed, reaching behind her to unhook it. She dropped it off the side of the bed.

"Bring those gorgeous tits to my mouth. I want you to hold them while I suck on them."

Her breath shortened at the demand. She straddled him, sitting down on his abdomen, sliding back so his stiffening cock pressed against the seam of her buttocks. She wanted to get rid of the panties, too, slide her wet folds over him, but he hadn't ordered that yet.

He'd recognized this part of her almost instantly, and that had given her the confidence to admit she'd known it as well, though it had been unacknowledged for so long. Even so, every time he summoned it from her, she was amazed at how quickly she could be immersed in this, a need to be totally under his command, anticipating every word, every look, her body trembling and eager.

"Beautiful," he said, and she knew he was talking about that as much as how she looked. He was absorbed in it. Every level he took a sub under his command was another level he could reach in his own desires. She marveled at the revelation, even as his gaze flicked up, giving her that rough impatience that thrilled her.

"I'm waiting, Athena."

She grasped her breasts and leaned forward, moistening her lips as his gaze riveted on them. He gripped her hips, held her steady. Parting his lips over one nipple, he bathed her with the heat of his breath alone, no other contact, such that a measured flick of his tongue at last made her jerk violently. Her reaction became even more implosive as he kept doing it, so restrained. Her pussy wept and her nipples got harder, tighter.

"Please . . ."

He drew back, studying the strain in her face, the wildness she was sure was in her eyes. "Stay right where you are."

He lifted onto an elbow, reached into the crack between the top of the mattress and the headboard. He came back with a knife, a six-inch blade he must have scabbarded there. "Do you trust me, Athena?"

"With anything."

"Then don't move."

He slid the flat of the blade down her sternum, over her navel, then the tip of it was caressing the flesh above the waistband of her panties. When he reached her hip, he hooked the elastic. The panties parted, the steel cutting through the mesh effortlessly. He ran the blade over the top of her thigh, then moved to her opposite hip, doing it to the other side.

"Arch your back. I want those breasts on display."

She obeyed, taking a firmer grip on the curves, lifting them so the nipples tilted up at a more provocative angle.

"That's my girl." He pulled the panties free and set them aside, along with the knife. She glanced at them on the nightstand, the military-grade knife with its heavy black handle and guard, the thin swatch of her ruined panties draped over it, then her gaze was back on her Master.

He turned his hand over, sliding it beneath her so he cupped her pussy fully. She lifted up into that cradle, pressing her lips together as his fingers spread over the base of her buttocks and his thumb stroked her clit, sliding down to part her labia, tease inside those sensitive walls. Then he used the pressure of his palm to make her stand on her knees. The wet tip of his cock slid down the seam of her buttocks, then between her legs, to lie straight and stiff along his belly beneath her.

He withdrew his hand. "Bring your breasts back to my mouth. I want you to rub yourself against my cock like you're trying to make yourself come. Tell me when you're close, but you won't come."

"No, Master. Not without your permission."

"Damn straight."

She closed her eyes, loving that possessive growl.

"No more talking. Your only focus is my commands."

She leaned down, anticipating his mouth once more. As she did, her clit came against the hard shaft for the first time. It made her internal muscles convulse, milking out more slick fluid to ensure the slide along his length was more pleasurably excruciating. He tortured her the same sensual way as before, teasing her nipple with his breath, then the flick of the tongue, here then gone, followed by a slow lick around the areola. His hands landed back on her hips, their strength aiding her as she slid herself down his length, keeping her back elongated and arched so he had full access to her breasts.

Her pussy pressed against the heavy weight of his testicles, then she was sliding back up again, all the way to the friction of his ridged head. She wanted to keep going, wanted to close over him and sink down, let him penetrate her to the root, but that wasn't what he had commanded.

She cried out as he closed his mouth over her right nipple. It increased the pressure of her grip on her breasts, such that the peaks became even more sensitive, especially the one in the hot cavern of his mouth. When he began to suckle, her hips moved more frenetically against him. He gripped her buttock with the other hand, working her over his cock, not letting her hold back in the least. Her response built hotter, faster. He switched to the other breast, tormenting them equally.

The man definitely knew how to walk and chew gum at the same time. And probably juggle and figure out the theory of relativity. He worked her hard and fast against his cock, then directed her to make slow, sweeping circles over him, her ass rubbing against his upper thighs. Throughout all that, he never stopped suckling, licking, biting at her nipples and breasts. She was rocking on him, moaning, pleading in incoherent little noises. Her body vibrated, coiled . . .

"Master . . . I'm too close . . ."

He clamped both hands on her waist and lifted her, shifting

them so quickly and with such impressive strength her breath caught for a whole different reason. He'd lifted himself to a seated position on the side of the bed, and she was face down over his lap, the hinge between her thighs and hips hooked over the thigh of his half leg, her upper body draped over the other leg. One of her hands caught his calf, the fingertips of the other sweeping the floor. Those fingers convulsed as he spanked her hard, the sting and the power of her near climax making her writhe and gasp. His cock was a tempting steel bar against her stomach.

He rubbed firm circles over her abused flesh as he squeezed a breast with the other hand, fondling the nipple where it pressed against the side of his leg. "Who do you belong to, Athena?"

"You."

"And when you climax, who orders that?"

"You do, Master."

"Only when I command it."

"Yes sir." Oh, but she was hurting for it, and him holding it out of reach only made the need worse.

"Spread your legs wider," he said brusquely. "You hold still. No wiggling."

When she complied, he started spanking her again, only now he alternated between her ass and short swats of her wet pussy. Trying not to move was utter torture. She felt like an explosive device, the pressure to detonate unbearable.

"On the floor. On your knees, forehead to the ground, ass in the air. Face away from the bed, but stay close enough your feet are beneath the bedrail."

He helped ease her to the floor, which was a good thing, since she was so aroused she was unsteady. How long could he push her like this? She expected as long as he wished.

She'd seen what he did to Willow, had experienced a taste of it at her home, but she was starting to grasp the full depths of the kind of Master he was. Ruthless, taking her beyond her limits, teaching her to stretch herself to meet his every demand. He could make her his slave in truth, because at the moment she'd do anything for him, anything to relieve this burning need that he had stoked to a full blaze. But it wasn't a matter of mere physical release. She didn't want to put her hands or a vibrator between her legs to ease the pressure. She needed her Master's touch, his cock, his mouth . . . his command. She wanted to please him, wanted her release to belong fully and utterly to him.

She was in the prescribed position, forehead to the floor, haunches in the air, her feet tucked under the bed. He was straddling her, still sitting on the bed, one foot planted by her right calf, the other leg spread so his knee extended over the mattress on her other side.

"Stay like that, Athena. I want to look at what's mine. Pull your hair up over your head so I can see every inch of your beautiful skin."

She did it with clumsy, uncoordinated fingers. She was rewarded by him bending down to slide his hand from her nape to the valley of her spine, then up to her buttocks. He parted them with his thumbs, exploring her there in a way that made it clear no orifice was off-limits to him.

"Have you ever been fucked here?"

She shook her head.

Slap!

"No sir," she yelped. "No, Master."

"Good." His finger traced the rim, setting off a spiral of sensation. "I'll be the first. But not today. That pleasure will be for another time."

She hoped that didn't mean he wasn't planning to take her at all. She needed him filling her so badly it was like a lifelong, fervent wish.

"I want to do wicked things to you, Athena. Your submission brings out the beast in me."

Good. She felt like a wild animal herself.

"I'm going to take you back to Release one day. You'll go there as my slave. I also want to fuck you in your bedroom. You understand? Not today. Not tomorrow. But one day. If you fully surrender yourself to me, there'll be no half measures. Nothing held back. I want to own all of you."

She knew things could get exaggerated in scenes, but this didn't feel like that. The dangerous promise in his voice roused a nervous, uneasy response in her. No. She wasn't ready for those things. But he'd told her not today. Not tomorrow . . . one day. She could work with a forecast. All she needed, truly, was for this moment to go on forever.

"Move on your hands and knees to my closet. Open the door as far as it will go."

It was only a few feet away, but it made her feel so subjugated, in a crazy, thrilling way, walking away from him on all fours. He was seeing her flushed and wet pussy, the weight of her breasts swaying with her movements. When she opened the door, there was a full-length mirror on it. In its reflection, she saw he'd pulled a condom from the night table and was tearing it open. As she watched hungrily, he unrolled it over his thick, hard length, shifting his thighs out wider.

"Come back to me. Still on your hands and knees, moving backwards. When you get here, I want you to stand between my legs and face the mirror."

She'd stopped thinking. It was all feeling now. Heated, needy feeling, an ache in her chest, her lower belly. When she reached him again, she rose, keeping her back to him as he'd required. He gripped her thighs, let his palms glide up her body, caressing her hip with one then sliding across it to between her thighs, making her moan, her body sway, as she watched him do it in the mirror. He steadied her with the other hand on her hip as he worked her clit between his knuckles, stroked her labia with clever fingers, dipped them into her pussy. Her nipples were a dark color, so tight and aroused, her breasts like ripe, full fruit. When he slid both hands up to cradle them, pressing his mouth to her lower back, she whispered his name.

"Master."

His touch dropped back to her hips, and then he was lowering her to his lap. "Keep your thighs together."

He speared the tight opening with the skill of a man who knew a woman's most intimate places . . . pussy, ass, heart. She was being maudlin, but that didn't mean she was wrong. He stretched her, brought her all the way down onto him, pushing her upper body forward so her nipples brushed her knees. He shifted her as he went, achieving a full and deep penetration. She was folded over an ache growing in her lower belly and chest, at odds with the pleasure she was experiencing. He wound his hands in her hair, gathering it to him, his knuckles grazing her cheek, and then he bent, brushing his lips over the tender protruding bones of her spine. Her heart cracked.

"Shh. You're a treasure, girl. Be with me. All the way with me."

"I am, Master." Her voice broke. "Please, may I touch you? Please." She thought she might die without that contact.

"Yes."

She put her shaking hands on his knees, fingers curving into them, noting that there were some different protrusions in the left one, as if the knee had suffered some damage as well. But she tilted her head toward it, brushed it with her lips, her inner muscles clenching on the length of his cock as she did it. She was simply lost, but in a way hard to define as good or bad. It was all inside his sphere of influence, so she wasn't really lost at all. Just completely out of control, possibly for the first time in her life, relying fully on another to bring her back home.

His fingers tightened in her hair, then he let it go to slide his hands back down to her hips. "Hold on to my legs, Athena. You're going to need the anchor."

He began to thrust. Holding her close this way made his strokes short, intense. With her legs pressed together, it catapulted her reaction to an explosive level in a matter of seconds. But at this angle, the climax so perilously close was not close enough. Just close enough to have her screaming at every stroke.

He kept going, showing admirable control, while she was clawing his legs with no restraint at all. With each full penetration, she pressed the soles of her feet into the floor, her inner muscles squeezing him like a vise. His breathing was harsh, and several times she heard a muttered, reverent curse, which just took her higher.

When he brought them to a halt, she almost wailed, even knowing she wasn't going to get a climax until he was damn good and ready. Using those impressive biceps and stomach muscles, he lay back on the bed, unfolding and taking her with him, shifting her body to adjust to the new angle. He was stretched out with her face up on top of him, back to his front, his foot braced on the floor to anchor them. She kept her thighs tightly closed at his brusque command, the balls of her feet barely reaching the floor between his. The position pushed him up high and tight inside of her. One hand went to her throat, the other to her clit, and his hips pumped up against her, slow, torturous, careful movements for them both. Too wide a range would break the connection. But the moment he started rubbing her clit, things started to unravel.

"Master . . . please . . . may I . . ."

"Yes. Come for me, Athena. Let me hear it."

Because she couldn't move much in this position, the waves kept coming, higher and more intense, so she was crying out in prolonged agony, one of the most extreme climaxes of her life. He released when she was at the height of it, and drove her even higher, his powerful body shuddering beneath her, every muscle going hard to match the rigidity of his cock, so deep inside her.

She was a shaking mess in his arms. When he eased her off him, he shifted them both so they were together on the mattress, his head on his pillow and her turned toward him, cradled in his arms. Her muscles had no strength to help him at all. He was stroking her hair, murmuring to her.

"Shh, girl. It's okay. Easy, love."

She kept jerking a little bit now and then, a combination of aftershocks and nerves. He slid his hands over her, slow, easy strokes, cupping her bottom, teasing the side of her breast with his knuckles, massaging the nape of her neck, pressing kisses to the top of her head. Her nose was running and he had a box of tissues by the bed, but her limbs were too numb to reach for one. Since she hadn't lost enough of her sense of decorum to use his flesh as a handkerchief, she kept sniffling.

He rolled against her so she was squashed with wonderful pressure between him and the mattress. It was a brief moment, allowing him to reach over the side of the bed to the floor. When he caressed her cheek with a soft cloth, an unexpected sob choked her. It was his T-shirt. She pressed her face against it and him, letting the shirt absorb her physical reaction and his chest hide the emotional one.

At length he spoke, with tender amusement. "So, was it good for you?"

She must be on the edge of hysteria, because she started laughing. It was a painful transition, like trying to run after drinking a full glass of water, but he held her tighter, so that whatever was trying to tear her apart, laughter or tears, wouldn't gain the upper hand.

"It's all right, girl. It's all right. Shh."

"Yes," she managed at last. "Quite satisfactory." Her words were slurred, like she was drunk, but she fought to get them out. "We should do it again in a month or so, when I've had a chance to recover."

His chuckle was a soothing balm. "I'm going to want you again, far sooner than that. You're going to have to build up some stamina."

"You're going to kill me."

"No. I promise I won't do that." Another kiss on her forehead, this one lingering. When he lifted his head, she tilted her chin to find him studying her with an unfathomable look, one that went on for some moments as he slid his fingers along her lips, her cheeks, her wet lashes.

"What?" she whispered.

"I was thinking of a song. It's one the kids play at the community center. I don't pay much attention to it usually, but I've caught the chorus a few times. 'You must be the reason I'm alive.' The way you looked at my leg, what you said . . ." He shook his head, tightened his arms around her, pushed her head back to his chest. "It was good for me, too. Athena. Better than anything I've felt in a long time. Thank you."

They dozed for a while. At some point Athena realized her two-hour lunch was going to run way over. She didn't have any appointments this afternoon, but she still needed to let Ellen know she hadn't disappeared off the planet. Well, in a way she had, but she didn't want Ellen thinking she'd been kidnapped, since she was obsessively punctual.

She was sprawled over Dale's chest, and when she began to move, his arms tightened around her, his grunt telling her what he thought of her leaving. She whispered she'd be right back, that she needed the bathroom, and those blue-green eyes appeared, lingering on her in a way that warmed her to her toes.

"Don't be long."

She fished her phone out of her purse, then slipped into the bathroom. When she sent Ellen the quick text, letting her know she'd decided to take the rest of the day, the response was instant and brought a smile to her face.

Understood, Mrs. Summers. (you go, girl!)

Shaking her head at her assistant, she set the phone aside and took care of some necessities, including using Dale's brush to comb her hair and his washcloth to clean up her face. His medicine cabinet was typically male. Shaving gear, toothpaste. A couple of prescription meds, including an antibiotic and a painkiller. She assumed the first was for his leg and guessed the latter dealt with days where joint pain might be an issue, though the man gave the impression he was all but invincible. They'd last been refilled about six months ago, so he wasn't regularly taking either one.

Thinking about that, she left the bathroom. When she crawled back on the bed next to him, she folded her legs under her and looked at the truncated limb, those sores at the surgical site.

"Was that why you cancelled our lunch date?" she asked. Though his eyes were closed, she knew he was awake and aware of what she was doing. A man didn't keep a knife like that behind his mattress and sleep deeply. Her gaze touched it briefly, still tangled with her ruined panties.

"Yeah. It was stupid. I'm sorry." His eyes opened then, his hand reaching across the mattress to clasp hers, a loose hold.

She shook her head. "We're still getting to know one another, Dale. Crazy as that sounds. So did we overdo the other day, when we were at my place? Is that what caused them?"

"Yeah. That and taking care of the dogs that same day. I just didn't do some of the things for it I'm supposed to do. It happens every once in a while." Then he got that warning look. "Remember what I said. You're not my nurse, Athena. Don't go there."

"No, I'm not. But I am your submissive. At least as long as you want our sessions to continue."

"These aren't sessions, Athena." He reached up, caught her chin in thumb and forefinger. "Did you call them that because you didn't want to make me feel boxed in, or because you believe that's what they are?"

"You really don't leave a girl anywhere to hide, do you?"

"Not my job." His gaze held hers. "Athena."

"No. I don't feel like they're sessions." She put her hand over his, and he shifted it to take a grip on her fingers as they came to a tangled rest together on her knees. "But I'm afraid to assume too much, too soon. I don't know you well enough and . . . these feelings are pretty new to me. I'm not sure of myself, either."

He nodded. "It's one of the reasons I'm keeping a tight rein on things. You realize that, right? For now, my job is taking care of you. Period."

The words made her feel so strange. She had to breathe in and out a few times before the vise around her chest loosened. "I think I understand that. But I want to serve you as well. It's different from taking care of you, isn't it, even if they look a lot the same?"

"Yeah, it is different, but my understanding of that isn't the concern. No matter what you say, I don't think you're far enough away from the nurse side of it that *you* recognize the difference."

She could have been insulted by the comment, but he didn't sound patronizing. He was stating flatly what he'd observed, and could she really argue with it? As she'd just said, she was dealing with so many new feelings when it came to this. Yet she couldn't help but wonder if his judgment on her was affected by his own situation. He'd obviously dealt with the painful memories and emotions associated with his injury, accepted his situation and refused to call it a handicap, but he was a proud man who would have no patience with any kind of limitations.

She didn't want to get into another argument today, so she tried to explain it a different way. "When I saw you with Willow, I wasn't sure what kind of Master you were. Since Jimmy said you worked with a variety of submissives, at different levels, I figured you like the challenge of determining what each woman wants, what type of submission she needs. Like you told me, the intense attention to detail, the in-depth understanding that requires . . . each one was a mission, even if that mission extended over a few sessions or only one."

She took a deep breath. Did he know how intimidating his silence could be, especially combined with the piercing regard of those eyes? "But what I wondered was what kind of Master you truly are, at the core. What you want for yourself. If you had a permanent submissive, what would she provide for you? Just now, I thought I felt it. You wanted everything. You were reaching down into my soul and I could actually feel your hand closing around it. It was frightening, and overwhelming."

She met his gaze. "Submission, service, was so important to me, the gift I needed to give to the man I loved, to the extent that I became a Mistress to him. No half measures, like you said. In every way he needed, I became that for him. It seems . . . we may be a yin and yang to one another, but whether it's a good mix, or a self-destructive one, I don't know. But I do know it makes me want to say everything and anything to you. Be everything to you. No, I'm not your nurse or maid. But I can be far more than that, all that and anything more. And I think that's what you want. Eventually."

If you learn to trust me, and I learn to trust myself.

She didn't add that, thinking it might be too argumentative. She'd said her peace, probably more than she should have at this juncture. She looked down at their clasped hands, waiting on him. At length, he shifted onto his elbows, reached up and touched her face with the other hand. "Maybe." He sighed. "You're the first woman I've let cross this line with me, Athena."

The revelation amazed, thrilled and slightly terrified her, but he shook his head, telling her he wanted her to keep silent until he finished. "You said it. You have such a deep well when it comes to this that you became a Mistress to your husband, because that was what he needed. It makes you a superlative sub, but you crossed the line into a place you didn't really belong, that didn't meet your heart's desire. And if he's as good a man as I suspect he was to deserve someone like you, he probably saw it at some point, even if he didn't completely get what you were."

Demand as much for yourself.

Her hand tightened on Dale's. They were Roy's words, from a fairly significant moment in the life they'd shared. As if summoned by Dale's comments, the memory attached to them returned as well.

Roy had been pretty sick at that point, and it was one of his bedridden days. She'd brought him a mostly liquid lunch he'd barely touched. She'd thought he was dozing, but then his hand twitched under the light grasp of hers and his gaze turned to her, holding the sorrowful knowledge that their time was getting shorter.

I was able to be everything I am with you, Athena. Man, boy, happy, sad, hero, bastard. Roy had smiled a bit at that. *You took me over when I needed to give up the reins, and handed them back at the right moments. You knew me, down to my soul, and you gave me everything. I hope . . . You deserve better than that. It should be a pane of glass, not a mirror. Love is about seeing one another clearly through everything and accepting each other. What you gave me, you should have the chance to have that, too. It's not a closed circle unless you can give as much as you're given. I wish I'd been able to do that for you. But you make me a promise. If the opportunity presents itself, do what I know is so damn hard for you to do. Demand as much for yourself. Demand to be given as much as you're willing to give.*

He'd been on some strong painkillers, so she could tell he'd struggled with what he was trying to say. She hadn't really understood what he was saying then, any more than she completely understood Dale's point now, but both sets of words resonated with her.

"A Master is about more than demanding every corner of a sub's soul," Dale said gently. "He needs to be about protecting that soul as well."

"So I can't help with this." She touched his leg, feeling strangely desolate.

"Maybe one day. But not now. I take care of that part of things myself. That's part of who I am, who I need to be. But anytime you want to bring me food, you can knock yourself out."

She smiled uncertainly as he lifted her fingers to his lips, kissed them. Then he squeezed her hand and winked, dispelling the somber mood. "Let's eat that lunch. Fucking you has given me a hell of an appetite."

She'd never thought of herself as the type of woman who'd respond to crude talk like that, but the way he said it, so sexy and male, his hot gaze sweeping over her, put her already broken antenna into another spin. He didn't let her put on any clothes. Instead, he had her bring the lunch back to the bed and ate naked with her, feeding her bits of sandwich, reaching out to touch her breasts or telling her to keep her legs open so he could see her pussy as he consumed the food she'd made him. He kept that Master-sub dynamic so out front and center between them, such that the unsettling topics he'd raised were beyond her concentration. As a result, she was able to quell the uneasy sense of paradigm shift and just enjoy being with him. She'd deal with the rest on her own time.

He'd told her he expected her to build up her stamina, that he'd want her again. It didn't take long for him to prove it. After lunch, he pushed her to her back without preamble and stretched out between her legs. With his strong hands curled around her thighs and one foot braced on the floor, he put his mouth on her cunt and brought her to the brink of another pleading, writhing climax in no time. When she was so close to release the heat of his breath on her quivering tissues might have pushed her over, he rolled over onto his back and made her turn so she straddled his face, her knees pressed into the bedding above his shoulders. He ordered her to take his cock in her mouth while he resumed feasting on her pussy. The command to come came with her lips stretched over him, vibrating against his cock as she screamed. She shuddered through the aftershocks while still frenetically sucking him. He kept licking and teasing her well past her climax, not stopping until she brought him to release as well.

The man was diabolical. By the time he decided he was finished between her legs, she was quivering with renewed arousal, as if he hadn't wrung two extreme climaxes out of her. And that was apparently the state in which he intended her to remain.

For some Masters, that was a vital part of the turn-on. While a lot of men were done once both partners found satisfaction, Dale obviously liked to take a sub through the whole roller coaster multiple times. But instead of letting her get off the ride at the logical ending point, he took her past that and hit the brake at the peak of that first huge hill, right before the thrilling fall. It was enough to make a woman hit him with a blunt object, except for the fact she'd wait until the end of time for him to do it all again.

It was late afternoon when she dressed, collected her picnic basket and prepared to depart. He insisted on walking her to her car. She tried to dissuade him from it, not wanting him to go that far using the crutches. The look he gave her was one he'd probably used on SEAL recruits. At some point, she was going to prove to him she wouldn't be so easily cowed, but she wasn't going to rock that boat today.

Especially when he rewarded her by rocking her world a wholly different way. At the BMW, he pressed her back against the car door and kissed her so thoroughly, she felt the tingle all the way to the soles of her feet. He took his time with it, drawing it out such that the sun had dropped another notch in the sky when he finally released her. His last words, breathed against her ear, merely confirmed his agenda to drive her to distraction.

"I'm going to be so fucking hard this week, remembering how hot and wet you are right now. No more touching yourself when it's not my command. You save it all for your Master."

"When will I see you again?" she asked. Their fingers were laced together and her heart beat a little faster as he lifted her knuckles to his lips, brushed his mouth over them.

"I'm glad you came to see me, but for our next visit, you wait for my call." He stroked a hand over her hair, his mouth softening as he gazed down at her. "I have to handle some prior commitments, but you'll hear from me in a few days. I promise."

She was a busy woman with many demands upon her time. Work, meetings at home, offsite and in the office. Yet there were certain things for which there was no distraction large enough. Dale Rousseau was one of those things. Several days later, her focus still wasn't on her responsibilities but on Dale's hands, his eyes, voice, the powerful body and, most importantly, the way he made her feel. Her skin felt exposed and tingling, the friction of her clothes just exacerbating it.

She was as besotted as she'd been as an eighteen-year-old, when she'd met Roy and developed the crush that would ultimately result in falling head over heels in love with him and into a life together.

Troubled by the thought, she rose from her desk. She'd been staring into space—again. When she moved to gaze out the window at the New Orleans business district, her fingers were twitching where they lay against the base of her throat, her other arm wrapped around herself. The first couple of days, she'd told herself her agitated state had to do with how new this all was to her, like a first love, but each day her feelings were more out of control. The waiting was agony. Dale Rousseau was turning her into a basket case.

She was more disciplined than this. She was a middle-aged woman, for pity's sake, not a teenager. Truly irritated with herself, she went back to her desk. She glanced at her accounting software on the screen and noted Ellen had flagged the charitable giving ratio to profits in the first quarter. They had a surplus, which meant she could give a little more to one of their existing charities or do a onetime donation.

No big surprise, Dale's shelter was the first thing that crossed her mind. After their lunch and before she'd left, he'd taken her to the section of the junkyard where the kennels were. The runs could be opened to allow the dogs to play in a communal area when he wasn't letting them explore the junkyard. He'd landscaped around the area with a wealth of fragrant bushes that helped minimize the kennel odors. He and other volunteers for the shelter, some of them fellow SEALs, had poured the concrete pads and installed the necessary plumbing so he could keep the runs clean.

They'd also built a small supply building for food and other necessities, and he'd mentioned their plans to build a bigger building, perhaps one with an indoor exercise and training area, an examination room where a vet could visit and examine the animals on site. But her questions had revealed they didn't have a capital fund at this point. Most of the donations given went to operations, like vaccinations, getting the dogs spayed or neutered before adoption and some efforts to publicize the animals up for adoption.

Ed Senior, the former owner of the place, was the father of a SEAL with whom Dale had served. Eddie had died in action. Though Dale didn't say so, Athena had a feeling it was the same mission where Dale lost his leg. During his last years as a SEAL, and then through his retirement, Dale had checked in on Ed Senior, helping him with the maintenance and management of the dog shelter. The old man had stopped operating the junkyard as a business about five years ago, except for the occasional hobbyist or mechanic looking for an old car part. When he'd died a few months ago, he'd left the place to Dale.

Dale had moved onto the property and taken over the dog portion of it. There were a total of fifty dogs there now. Adoptions and donations were coordinated by word of mouth, and most of those came from the military community and their contacts.

Athena was very good at nonprofit management, and had helped improve the operations and fund-raising of a variety of New Orleans charities, first as a volunteer, and then later as a sitting member of several of their active boards. Sitting back in her chair, she considered the potential of the place, especially with a man like Dale running it. Their relationship was so new, she wasn't sure how Dale would react to her advice, but increasing the publicity would improve funds as well as adoptions.

If the board voted on it, that tidy surplus from this quarter's earnings, plus a hundred thousand from the discretionary funds she controlled through a foundation she and Roy had established for such efforts, would give Dale more options.

She buzzed Ellen, asking her to get her banker on the phone. Once her admin patched him through, she initiated the paperwork with him. She asked him to deliver the first check to Dale, provide him notice of the account and how it was set up. She wanted to give Dale a call, let him know about it herself, but he'd been pretty clear, telling her in that unmistakable Master voice he would contact her. Oh well. If he called her before the banker reached out to him, she could tell him. Otherwise, it would be a nice surprise for him. She couldn't wait to see what he thought.

Nodding, pleased with the decision, she returned to work in a better frame of mind. She could do this. She could handle the type of relationship she was cultivating with Dale and keep her life in perspective.

Balanced.

NINE

When she arrived at the office the next morning, she came down the hall on brisk heels, her mind already on the things she needed to do. Since she'd be meeting with the board at lunch, she was wearing her pearls and dark suit, anticipating her usual power struggles with Mel and the other handful of members who wished she would retire from the board and tend to her gardening. Maybe Mel would be better due to their last interaction, and the others would fall in line behind him. She didn't put a lot of stock in it improving Larry's behavior, however.

Ellen was at her desk as usual, but she had an odd expression on her face. When Athena entered her reception area, she rose, looking flustered. "Ah, Mrs. Summers. You have a visitor this morning . . ."

As she glanced past Ellen, she was startled to see Dale. He'd risen when Ellen had and now stood squarely facing her. He was wearing his boots and a dark T-shirt tucked into belted jeans. It seemed to be his preferred fashion statement, one she personally felt worked on him anywhere. The mere sight of him made everything flip-flop, like she was sitting naked on his bed again, doing his bidding, doing any unspeakable, incredible thing he demanded.

The fact those blue-green eyes were cool, direct—a Master's eyes—didn't mitigate that feeling in the slightest. His body language broadcast it as well. Surely he wouldn't act inappropriately at her place of business. Or would he? As her pulse ramped up, she told herself not to be ridiculous. She was in control of this situation.

They weren't Master-sub at the moment, no matter that his very presence made her feel like they were.

"Dale," she said, summoning the appropriate smile, which of course felt inordinately fake. "What an unexpected pleasure. Did you—"

"We need to talk about this." He lifted a thick envelope that displayed her bank's logo.

Though his tone was blandly courteous, he didn't smile. Before she could think of another polite response, or invite him into her office, he'd taken a step forward, closed his fingers on her elbow and was directing her there. Just like that, he'd taken control of the situation. Catching the bemused expression on Ellen's face, she managed to speak with a calmness she didn't feel. "Hold my calls, Ellen."

"Yes ma'am."

Once inside her office, he released her elbow, but only to close her door. She moved to her desk, pivoted to stand behind her chair and face him. In hindsight, she wasn't sure why she'd chosen to put such a barricade between them, but he recognized it as a shield, his gaze narrowing upon her. "Come out here, in front of me."

His tone had sharpened like a knife, the eyes even cooler now. She lifted her chin. "What if I say no? You didn't strike me as the type of man intimidated by a businesswoman."

"Does anything about me suggest I'm intimidated, Athena?"

Not a damn thing.

He bared his teeth in a smile, her expression apparently giving him the answer to the question. "If you refuse to come out from behind the desk, I have two possible responses. One, I leave and we're done, because if you say no and mean it, that says you're not ready for what you claim to want from me."

Her reaction to his walking out the door was strong enough to make her put tented fingers on the back of the chair to brace herself. Images of everything going back to exactly what they were like before their first meeting at her house flipped through her mind like one of those cartoon books, the ones where the characters moved at the pace of the riffled pages. Every page a slight movement, so the frames helped the character move forward . . . or backward.

She'd always thought the painstaking work of the artists, their passion, had to be akin to monks illuminating manuscripts, one perfect letter at a time. Did they ever recognize that connection themselves, or was it just tedious? Maybe the monks had felt the same way. Maybe they hadn't seen it the way those who admired it did. As a complex process, step by step, to create something amazing.

"And behind door number two?" she said, noting her voice had a strained note to it. His gaze caressed her face, even as his expression remained uncompromising.

"I come behind that desk and get you. Whatever you imagine, I promise you will *not* like that option. You're not going to yank my chain and not get bitten."

She didn't know what he meant, but for some reason she didn't want to ask him to clarify. "I'm not afraid of you."

"Yeah, you are. Not in the way you mean, though. You know I'd never do anything to truly harm you, and I'd break the fucking arm of anyone who did." The different tone sent a ripple through her. "You're afraid of what I'm doing to you, who you become when you're with me. Come out from behind the desk. Now."

She obeyed. She wasn't sure what to do, if she should lean her hips casually on the front of her desk like a cat pretending she'd meant to fall off a railing, when she'd really lost her footing and ended up where she hadn't expected. He took the decision from her, surprising her by closing his hands over hers in a gentle way. Her slim fingers looked small inside his grip. She'd missed that. Roy had been a big man, and she'd always liked the difference in their sizes, the way it could make her feel so feminine.

Dale rubbed his thumbs over her palms. "How were things this week? And I'm not looking for a rundown of your itinerary. Was it a good kind of crazy? Like a teenage girl waiting for roses?"

She flushed, but he squeezed her hands. "Answer me, Athena."

"Yes."

"But it wasn't all good, was it? There was something bugging you, eating at your gut."

When she didn't say anything, he sighed. "The first day, maybe you felt like you were at a carnival, thrilled with how unpredictable things are. But after that, it started to feel like it does when it's getting late and the carnival is packing up. The fantasy is over, so where does that leave you? You did this thing with the trust, the check, and then you felt way better. Glowing."

He was right. Startled, she ran it over in her head, feeling him watching her, waiting on her, waiting for it to make sense. She pressed her lips together. "I don't understand."

"Yeah, you do." He tapped the top of her hand with a thumb. "When you acted as a Mistress for Roy, I bet you were like a sponge, absorbing every impression. You learned from other Dommes, from their subs, from Roy's own responses. You have great intuition, and the fact you're a successful businesswoman tells me you're good at reading people. It's really not so hard to understand both sides of the coin once you're born into at least one side of it. So what were you doing, Athena? Put yourself in a Mistress's shoes and evaluate what you did."

The shift brought a click, like a key turning a lock. The moment it did, she wished she could close the door, but she couldn't, because he'd made her open it, face it.

She'd been holding on to control. Taking it back from him, afraid to let him hold the reins. Damn it. It was pitifully obvious. How could she be so stupid?

"Hey. Look at me."

It was too difficult, but he put a hand on her face, guided it to obey his direction. "If you give yourself shit for it, you'll have an even bigger punishment coming than you already do."

Her stomach fluttered at that, but she couldn't suppress the self-castigation. "I'm sorry, Dale."

His lips twisted. "You have to do everything exactly right, or you've fallen short, haven't you, Ms. Perfectionist? Failed yourself, failed me."

She pulled away, moved to the window. She resisted the desire to cross her arms, assume a defensive posture. "You're right. I'm new to this. It's not an excuse, but—"

"Stop talking."

She closed her mouth, startled by the mild command, when his expression wasn't mild at all. Those blue-green eyes had gone laser sharp. As he stepped up beside her, she quelled an absurd urge to hide behind her desk again, but the implied threat in his proximity wasn't entirely unwelcome, given that her fingers were curling against her sides, wanting to touch him.

"You put yourself together so well, Athena." His gaze coursed over her, from the light flush in her cheeks to the tips of her polished heels. "Nice outfit, appropriate for an office setting. The skirt a little snug, enough to show you have a good ass, but not flaunting it. The blouse exposing those delicate collarbones, reminding a man you're a woman. And more, reminding him he's a man, and all those differences between you. Proper and enticing, all at once. Don't even need that hint of lace you can see at this angle."

She started to glance down, but he intercepted her, fingers catching her chin. "Your body belongs to me, girl," he said. "And you don't have permission to look at it right now."

When he released her chin, she kept her eyes fixed on his, her head up. He nodded in approval, slid his knuckle down her sternum, then over, inside the collar, teasing the lace under the silk. Her nerves tingled at the heat of the direct touch. "You didn't fail me, Athena. Or yourself. By the time I leave this office, you'll understand that. And you'll feel much better about everything. In a real way this time. Even though the carnival packed up, you'll know there's something even better in that empty field. Do you want to trust that I'm right?"

"Yes. I want to trust you." She wanted to trust him with everything she was. She wanted to say yes, she *did* trust him, but of course he'd just proven that she didn't.

"All right. Does your office door lock?"

She nodded. His lips firmed into a line. "Yes sir," she corrected herself. Just like that, the environment shifted from any uncertainty about their roles to a clear line between Master and sub. There was a relief to it, even though it scared her, too, given she was right in the heart of a place that was all about her being in control. Dale had obviously intended to confront her here for that very reason.

"How much can your assistant hear through the walls?"

"They're not soundproof, but the walls are well insulated. Conversation sounds like a distant murmur when the door is closed." Her heart was moving up in her chest, closing in on the pulse in her throat. She needed to tell him they couldn't . . . not here. But she couldn't seem to say anything. A war was going on in her stomach. That uneasy, uncertain feeling she'd experienced before she decided to send the check was back now, but it was competing with her response to what he was implying. She didn't know how to resolve it, or feel right about it, so she did nothing. He'd put her in a position of waiting to see what he would do. How *he* would resolve it.

She was giving him control.

She was amazed at how that cold ball became a little less painful at the realization. It wasn't gone, but something was on the right track. That feeling intensified when he settled his hand at the base of her throat, collaring her.

"Do you know where I'm going with this, girl?"

"I—I think so. Maybe . . . no."

His lips twitched, his thumb sliding along her jaw. "Send your assistant out to get an order of fresh beignets. Does she lock the outer office when she's not at her desk, even if you're here?"

"Yes. There are files that—"

The pressure of his fingers increased, his gaze steady on hers.

"Yes sir."

"Good." He leaned in, and her lips parted. His gaze flickered, as if he'd felt the soft exhalation of her breath on his skin, and a shiver went through her. Her hands were still tense balls at her sides. "How long do you think that will take her?"

"About twenty-five minutes." She glanced at the clock. "More, if there's still a morning crowd."

"So a half hour. That will be sufficient." Releasing her, he reached back, pulled his wallet from his jeans pocket and removed a twenty from it.

"Oh, I can—"

"No. You won't. Not ever with me." When he so chose, he had a gaze like a tiger's glittering in the dark. His fingers closed over hers, transferring the bill to her palm. "Go do what I told you to do."

She was surprised her quivering legs obeyed her, but they did. She moved toward the door, having the presence of mind to take a few steadying breaths, something that would hopefully make her cheeks a shade less than scarlet, before she opened it and stepped out into the admin's area. "Ellen, I need you to . . ."

As she relayed Dale's instructions as if they were her own, she put the money on the edge of Ellen's desk, not trusting herself to hand it over. Ellen would certainly feel the tremor in her fingers. Athena had a lot of practice at staying cool under fire, though, and it stood her well now. Except for the speculation she could tell Ellen was entertaining, having wisely deduced this was Athena's Wednesday lunch date, her assistant didn't show any surprise at the request or her boss's expression.

"It may take a few minutes. You know this is their busy time of morning."

"No problem. Mr. Rousseau and I will be working out the details of the trust for his shelter, so he should be here for the next half hour at least."

Ellen nodded, already rising to gather up her purse and the

money. She did offer Athena a playful look of female conspiracy, mouthing *wow*. It didn't take any brain cells to know Ellen was reacting to Dale's appearance, and of course *wow* fit. He wasn't a pretty man, but he had the rugged looks and confident, powerful bearing that would turn any woman's head. Plus, there was that dominant, purely sexual quality to him that drew female attention, whether the woman in question recognized it for what it was or not.

"You want me to lock my door like I usually do?"

"Yes, go ahead and do that. I'd like to get this done without interruption, and you know Larry might decide to ambush me before the meeting to dry run some of his usual power plays."

Ellen rolled her eyes. "Yes ma'am." And then she was gone, making sure the button lock was in place before she drew the heavy wooden door closed behind her.

Athena pivoted, came back into her office. She emulated Ellen's actions, pushing in the button lock and closing the door. Now it was just the two of them. Dale was standing at the window, looking down on the New Orleans business district. But he turned as the door closed, with that look that made her knees even weaker and her mind scatter.

"Take off everything but the pearls, heels and stockings."

The trembling she'd mostly contained in front of Ellen took her over then, every limb quivering. She removed her jacket and shell, unzipping her skirt. As she took off each piece of the uniform she'd donned to deal with her board, she felt like his attention was removing any layers or shielding beneath it, stripping it all away. She reached back, unhooked her bra, let it slide off her arms. Then her panties. Her windows were tinted, so facing buildings couldn't see what she was doing, but it was still perturbing to look at the bank across the street and see people so clearly through their non-tinted windows. Employees working at their desks, secretaries running copies, meetings in progress in posh boardrooms.

Dale began to close her blinds. They allowed filtered light, but to such a lesser extent it created the sense of a hushed cave, underscoring their privacy. He left one blind up, a three-foot-wide section of the facing building and sky backdrop still visible, and shifted in front of it, drawing her attention to him. "This is about you and me," he said.

"Yes sir."

"Stand there, just like that." He moved across the room to her desk, gazed at the files on it, the computer screen. She knew he was seeing her screensaver, a montage of different flowers slowly opening their blooms. He looked in her middle drawer, found what he was seeking. Withdrawing the wooden ruler, he slapped it against his hand. The crack made her jump.

A million things were going on inside her. Uncertainty, anxiety, arousal. She didn't realize she'd closed her eyes until his fingers brushed her lips, making her lift her lashes. "I'm scared," she said.

"Why?" His voice was tender now, and tears stung her eyes.

"Because I'm afraid of how all this makes me feel. I can't control anything."

"You control everything, Athena. You tested me, to see what I'd do. These are the consequences you wanted. Proof that I'm your Master."

At her distressed look, he shook his head, sliding his arm around her waist, settling his fingers over the curve of her buttock. She leaned into him and he allowed it, brushing a kiss over her forehead. Her bare thigh was pressed against his denim-covered one, her breasts against the T-shirt stretched over his broad chest. "I'm not saying you manipulated things deliberately. This is part of the way it works, with a sub like you."

"So I'm predictable?" She tried to rally some spirit about it and was rewarded when he smiled, those eyes sparkling at her like Caribbean waters.

"Not a chance. I didn't anticipate you taking that exact tactic, though I knew you were having trouble with our conversation. That's why I wanted to give you a few days, see what you'd do with it, where it would take us next."

"So you're not really going to hit me with that?" She cast a dubious look at the ruler.

"Oh, hell yeah." He chuckled, a wicked sound. "I want you sitting on a sore ass during your important meeting, thinking about me." He lifted a strand of hair off her forehead. "But if you want me to corner Larry in a dark alley and make him scream like a little girl, I'll be happy to do that. I don't like to hear that anyone is giving my girl a hard time." At her ironic look, he grinned. "Except me."

Stepping back, he nodded toward the one window that wasn't covered by a blind. "Go over there. Put your palms flat on the glass, and then step back as far as you can from it without taking your hands from the window. Raise your ass and spread your legs shoulder-width apart. Your Master plans to play with what's his during your punishment."

The particular part of her anatomy he was referencing liquefied. Her breasts felt tender, her nipples getting tight under his close regard.

"Don't keep me waiting. Unless you want Ellen to hear you getting your bottom whipped for trying to control things with your Master."

She moved to the window. She felt disembodied. Yes, she'd had punishment scenarios with Roy, but this . . . had it felt like this for him? She didn't think so. While Dale had been almost kind when she realized she'd actually solicited this, his intentions were inexorable. What's more, the war in her lower abdomen between need, arousal and anxiety told her she craved the definitive reinforcement that she was the submissive in the relationship.

She put her palms on the glass, and walked her feet back as he'd instructed. She was leaning toward the window, her body stretched out. When she spread her legs, it was both uncomfortable and exposed, which she was certain was his intention. Her vacillating reactions intensified.

Dale moved into her field of vision. He'd removed the stress ball from her desk. It was the size of a small apple and yellow, with the Summers' logo printed on it, a sun against some decorative elements. Dale nodded to her mouth. "Open wide. You're going to be scream- ing by the time I'm done, and this will keep the rest of the building from calling security."

It was bigger than her mouth, but he squeezed it down enough to get it past her teeth, and then it expanded, pressing against her tongue and the roof of her mouth, filling that cavern completely, as if its intended purpose was being a ball gag. Too big to cause a choking risk, but muffling any sound she made, it increased her sense of vulnerability. A safe word wasn't possible, and he didn't seem inclined to suggest a safe gesture.

"You need the punishment," he said, as if reading her mind. "You don't get an out for that. Trust me to know what you can handle. I can read your body language, Athena. That's your safe word."

He ran his hand over her buttocks, gripping the left one, his thumb sliding along her labia. "Higher, girl. Show me how pink and wet you are, thinking about your Master punishing you, mak- ing things right again."

She lifted her hips to a more extreme angle, whimpered against the ball as he slid two fingers inside her, proving how slick she already was. "There she is. My gorgeous girl."

She liked it when he called her *girl*. He used the same tone as other Masters or Mistresses did when they called their subs *pet*, *slut*, even *slave*. It wasn't a debasement, but a mutually craved sign of ownership. *My* girl, my pet, my slave. He'd called her that earlier, hadn't he?

"I'm going to give you fifteen smacks with this. I think that'll cover it. Then I'm going to fuck you, right here in your office. You're not going to get to come. This is about you understanding that I'm your Master. You serve me. That's how you find what you're seeking, Athena. By giving it all to your Master, trusting him to take you where you need to go, give you what you need."

Her fingers curled against the glass, those tears threatening again. Remembering the last punishment he'd given her, she had a feeling they were about to be doing more than threatening.

He put his palm against her abdomen to hold her in place. On the first strike, she curved over that touch, her ass tucking down at the outrageously painful sting.

"Ass up," he snapped. "Don't you hide from your punishment."

On trembling legs, she obeyed, crying out against the gag as the second blow fell on the opposite buttock. He alternated, though a few landed solidly over both, a couple on her upper thighs, sending a stinging echo through her pussy. His hand slipped down, his fingers now pressing on her clit, not manipulating or caressing it, simply capturing it between his knuckles, squeezing with firm pressure. "Don't you move," he warned her. "Every time you move enough to shift my hold, you'll get one more strike."

Oh God. Did he realize how impossible it was to keep the body from reacting to pain with movement? Of course he did. While rationally she knew she wasn't being permanently maimed, that the marks he left might be gone in a day, the pain activated a flight instinct hard to defeat. She couldn't stop herself on stroke fourteen, cursing against the ball as her jerk of reaction made his knuckles slide off her clit briefly. Her swollen clit.

He clamped back down on it, gave her the next two in quick succession. Fortunately, he didn't count the penalty shot against her, because she twitched again. Her ass was on fire. If he kept going, he'd have to go on forever, because she knew she couldn't bear it in stillness any longer.

He'd said he wanted to think about her sitting on her sore ass. Sitting was going to be out of the question. She'd be doing a lot of standing at that meeting. Unless he ordered her to sit, since his mind tended to work that way. She cursed and craved it at once.

Her hands were pressed so hard against the glass she knew she'd need to pull down the blind until she could wash off her prints. It was a fleeting thought, because Dale's grip left her clit as he shifted behind her. She heard him unbuckling his belt, unzipping his jeans. A condom being ripped open. He was really going to do everything he'd promised. He—

No dramatic pause, no slow easing this time. He slammed into her, pressing his pelvis tight against her throbbing bottom. He caught her breasts in both hands, tweaking the nipples, squeezing them with rough male pleasure as she moaned in an entirely different way. Now she would have welcomed that touch on her clit, but he'd promised she wouldn't get a release out of this. This was about serving her Master's pleasure. That thought made her hotter, her clit throb even more than her abused buttocks. Her sounds of pain had become ones of needy pleasure.

"That's my shameless girl," he muttered. "Fuck, your cunt feels like heaven. I missed you like hell this week. Even if you hadn't done a single . . . thing . . . wrong"—he punctuated every one of the three words with an extra hard thrust—"I probably would have whipped your ass for having to be away from you."

She cried out against the gag. He'd missed her. Being away from her hadn't been easy for him. He was so laconic yet brutally honest, such a brief statement unleashed a whole flood of new emotions inside her. He was ruthless, tough, totally in control. Her Master.

He climaxed then, and she wished he hadn't donned a condom. She wanted to feel him jet inside her. She reveled in his harsh groan, the way he grunted with satisfaction as he received the full measure from her. Her inner muscles milked him, one of many ways her body was communicating how much she wanted to keep him there, even if she missed the board meeting or if Ellen came back. Now she understood why teenagers were so irresponsible when they were falling in love. It wasn't that adults didn't feel exactly the same way—adults just exercised better control. Mostly.

The thought snagged her. Was she falling in love with Dale? She couldn't address that. She'd lost control of everything, particularly her thoughts and feelings.

When he pulled out, her shaking legs buckled. Her fingers reflexively tried to grip glass, but she needn't have worried. He caught her around the waist, holding her steady. "Easy, girl. It's all right. Let's put you down here a moment while I take care of things."

He eased her down to the carpet, her shoulder against the window. She lifted her gaze to see him strip off the condom, tuck himself back into his clothes. Tugging up the zipper so the jeans were held loosely on his hips, he grabbed a couple of tissues from the box on her desk to wrap up the condom. He put it in his jeans pocket, finished buttoning and buckling, tucking in his shirt. She was still vibrating, her clit swollen and pussy wet. She wanted him back inside her. She was also fixated on that small lump in his pocket. She'd worried he would act inappropriately at her place of business. Instead, he'd even avoided leaving behind any evidence of impropriety on her part, no matter that it was evidence someone would have to dig through her trash to find.

He'd told her, though, hadn't he? *A Master is about more than demanding every corner of a sub's soul. He needs to be about protecting that soul as well.*

She had tears on her face again. It seemed every time she was with him, he gave her a cathartic cry as well as a shattering climax. She was helpless to quell either reaction, her mind spinning in too many directions.

Leaning down, he slipped a finger into the corner of her mouth, worked the ball out, helped by the pressure of her tongue pushing against it. He put the gag aside, then he slid his arms beneath her legs and back and lifted her. She felt the shift as he accommodated the action on his two disparate limbs, but other than that, as always, her weight felt like no issue for him. Moving them over to the couch, he lowered himself to it, holding her in his lap.

"It's all right," he said, keeping his arms tight around her. "Just let it out, girl."

She kept hiccupping over the sobs, the tears pouring out for a good five minutes before things slowed down. Her ass hurt, but her heart felt easier, things more . . . in balance. Just as he'd promised. She was still wound up as a teenager, though. Days of thinking about him, and now this, and still, no permission to . . .

He slid one hand between her thighs. The arm around her shoulders shifted so he could close his hand around her throat, nudge her chin up with his knuckles. He held her there, with her looking at him, as he found the heated flesh between her legs, began to stroke. And circle. And press . . . and pinch . . .

When she wanted to avert her face, self-conscious about how she must look, her makeup ruined, her eyes red from crying, mouth slack with desire, he shook his head. He pressed more insistently on her chin, increasing the strain on her neck, the sense of restraint.

"You'll keep looking at me, Athena. All the way to the end. If you look away, I'll stop."

Her body twitched, her sore ass pressing down against his legs, then lifting, then dropping, starting to work in rhythm with him.

"Dale . . ." She needed to say his name. Her fingers had latched into the front of his shirt, her nails digging in.

"I'm right here with you, girl. Everything is safe with me. Everything you are."

It happened so fast and hard, she barely had time to warn him, to beg, but he rode over top of the gasped words.

"Come for me. Come hard." Then he had his mouth on hers, swallowing the scream, his hand shifting to cup the back of her head to hold her fast to him. His fingers never stopped their skillful manipulation of her clit, the stroke of her labia, the press of his knuckles between them. She was rolled over and over in the waves of her climax, the buildup of the week making it intense, long, and so incredibly satisfying that when it finally ebbed away, she felt like a sunbaked creature on a flat rock, so replete she never needed to move again.

He was still kissing her, his fingers making slow, soothing strokes over her pussy. By now she knew what her Master liked when it came to this. Despite the sensitivity of her tissues, she made herself stay still and kept her legs open to him. He shifted to hold her nape, pull her back. From the fierce male satisfaction in his face, she was sure she had a glazed, overwhelmed expression. His reaction gave her a different kind of heat, one no less welcome.

He helped her dress. She had a bathroom attached to her office so she could touch up her makeup, her hair, and while she did that, he sat on the commode lid, watching her silently. When she was done, she thought she'd pass inspection, though to herself she looked like a woman who'd been thoroughly pleasured and thrown off her axis, a little wild-eyed and sated at once.

He rose, tucked a piece of hair behind her ear, leaned in and brushed his lips over hers. "I'll be going. I'll pick up my beignet on the way out."

"Ellen hasn't . . ."

"She returned right when you climaxed. I heard the door unlock. You were a little preoccupied."

"But she didn't knock. She . . ." Athena turned scarlet. "Oh my God, if she . . ."

"She didn't. I muffled the sound with my mouth, remember?" He smiled. "She was making enough noise out there to let you know she was back. Closed the file cabinets twice, made a phone call. She was smart enough to realize we'd open the door when we wanted the beignets."

"You heard all that?"

He shrugged. "It's my job to pay attention. She's a good assistant."

"I don't know if I should be mortified or impressed. With both of you." She'd tensed up, thinking of Ellen's reaction, but he put both hands on her shoulders, drawing her attention back to him.

"I expect she was respecting your privacy. She obviously cares for and admires you. I don't think you've done a thing to tarnish your tiara."

She caught the slight edge to his tone. "Dale, I wasn't implying that I was embarrassed to be here with you. Just . . . doing something like that in my office. The board members are all male. They're good men, most of them, but even so, I have to maintain certain expectations with them."

"I get it. I do." He touched her face. "But I'm going to go now."

He slid past her, leaving her unsure if she'd offended him or not. "Master?" He turned at that, the look in his gaze intensifying at the address. "Can we . . . I'd like to see you again, sooner rather than later. May I?"

His jaw eased, making her feel better about speaking her feelings. The man encouraged an appalling level of honesty from her. "Yeah. You can. You like movies?"

She nodded.

"What's your favorite movie of all time?"

"*Ben-Hur.* With Charlton Heston."

His brow lifted. "A little before your time."

"My mother took me to see it when I was little. I watch it every year at Easter."

"Hmm." He cocked his head. "Favorite scene?"

"I have a lot of them. But my most favorite is when he and Esther meet in the upstairs room, both before and after everything that happens." She recalled the quote with a poignant smile. "'If you were not a bride, I would kiss you good-bye.' And she replies . . . 'If I were not a bride, there would be no good-byes to be said.'"

"And he takes her slave ring, and promises to wear it until he meets the woman he'll marry."

She raised a brow. "You've seen it."

"The gorgeous Israeli woman playing a slave caught my attention."

She chuckled, she couldn't help it. He closed the step between them, brushed her jaw with a fingertip. "We'll plan on a movie or something like that, something a little less intense. Let me get some crap off my schedule and we'll figure it out. Until then, I'll call you every day. All right?"

She gave a half smile. "You don't have to do that. I'm not that needy." But she certainly didn't object to the idea.

"I am. I want to hear your voice." He gave her jaw a little squeeze. "Thanks for the money for the shelter, Mrs. Summers. The dogs appreciate it."

"You're going to take it?"

He blinked at her. "Of course I am. I never intended not to take the money—that's for them, and I know you want to help. It was how you did it that caused the problem."

She pursed her lips. "So I just *paid* for my punishment?"

Those attractive lines around his eyes creased. "A win-win, don't you think?"

She swatted at his broad chest, and was caught to him for another thorough kiss for her trouble. She melted into it, reveling in the way his fingertips slid into her hair, the male noise he made against her mouth, how his scent surrounded her, the strength of his body.

When he released her, she knew she was ridiculously starry-eyed, but he looked pretty caught up as well. Confirming it, he gave her a reproving smack on her ass that made her wince. "Wanton. You should probably use a pillow for that board meeting."

She'd do no such thing and he knew it. Thank goodness the chairs were cushioned. Regardless, she thought she'd be getting up and doing a lot of moving around during agenda points. He was headed for her office door, allowing her to thoroughly enjoy the view. Coming or going, he was a feast for female eyes.

"Leave me a beignet," she said.

"Not a chance. You're hard work, woman. I built up an appetite."

Even so, when she headed out to her meeting later, she found he'd not only left her one of the pastries, he'd given Ellen one as well.

The man really was quite something.

TEN

A couple days later, the phone rang midmorning. Surprised to recognize Club Release's number, she picked up, even more surprised by the identity of the caller.

"Jimmy? Good morning."

"Hey, Lady Mistress. I'm sorry to call you at home—"

"Not at all. It's a nice surprise. How are you?"

"I'm good. Management's just having me do some call arounds, the quarterly thing to make sure the membership's happy with how things are going. I've never done it with you because, well, you were dealing with Roy's passing, and before that, you guys visited pretty regular, but . . . Oh hell, why am I bullshitting like this? Hank, the guy doing security the night you were here, told me about the trouble at the gas station. He said MC took care of it and waved him off when he came out to see if you needed any help."

She didn't remember that but, in those first few moments after the attack, a marching band could have gone by and she wouldn't have noticed.

"Anyhow, he said you seemed okay, but it's been a couple weeks and since you hadn't been back to the club since . . . I know you've only been coming about once a month, but . . . I'm sorry. If you think this is inappropriate, I apologize, but I consider you a friend and I was worried. That's all."

Genuine warmth, tinged with regret, touched her. Jimmy's awkwardness was likely due to her silence, the fact she was simply listening instead of taking control of the conversation. Remarkably, she'd stopped thinking of herself as a Mistress, almost from her first interaction with Dale.

"Oh, Jimmy, that's very kind of you. Yes, I'm fine. It was my own fault for not thinking about how dangerous it was to stop for gas so late at night."

"Don't ever apologize for other people being assholes, Mistress," Jimmy said staunchly. "I told MC that if he'd caved in their skulls and dumped their bodies behind the club we would have taken them out with the rest of the trash and not said a word about it."

"He's been there since?"

"A couple times. If you've been checking your club email account, we had a Japanese rope-tying demonstration last night and he was one of the presenters. It was pretty awesome. They're doing another one tonight. You should come." He paused. "Do you think you'll be back anytime soon?"

"I'm sure I will," she said automatically. "I'm sorry, Jimmy—I'm getting ready for a luncheon at my house, so I have to go, but I'll look forward to seeing you again soon. It really is so nice of you to check in on me. It means a great deal to me."

"Hey, you're welcome. See you then. I'll have your virgin Diet Coke waiting," he added, teasing her. Then he hung up.

Athena held on to the phone, pressing it to her chin. She was sitting in her reading room, an opened book on her lap. On the days she worked at home, it was a relaxing morning ritual, reading and watching the garden unfold its daily routine with bees, birds and butterflies, as well as the incursions of other wildlife like squirrels and deer. Having her cell phone with her was a new addition to the ritual. She'd kept it with her in case Dale called. Though if he'd gone to the club last night, he'd probably had a late night, hadn't he? *A couple times* . . .

Whom had he tied up for the demonstration? What did he do with her afterward? What had he done during the time he was there?

Stop it. No matter what was implied during the heat of their moments together, it had never been clearly stated their arrangement was going to be exclusive. The man himself had told her the challenge of working with submissives with unique needs was what helped him deal with the vacuum retiring from the SEALs had left in his life.

She understood that. Yet she felt stabbed in the heart, was even now kneading her palm over it in reflex. She could go to the club, pick out a sub, prove that if he was going to treat their arrangement as nonexclusive, she could do the same. Mature, reasonable adults.

No, she couldn't do that. Being with Dale had removed any doubts about it. She had no interest in being a Domme again. Further, she couldn't present herself there as a submissive. She cringed from the visual, anticipating judgment, reactions. But it was deeper than that, wasn't it? It felt like a betrayal of Roy, though she couldn't understand why she felt like that about the club environment, when she didn't feel like that when Dale had mastered her in the very home she'd shared with her husband.

She hadn't allowed him into her bedroom, though, had she? So she was holding him at arm's length as well. *Oh, Athena, for heaven's sake.* They'd only had three . . . whatevers together. Date, meeting, session. She didn't even know what to call them. Even so, she thought of him at the club with another woman and she didn't like it. Intensely. Didn't they make movies about women like that, women who boiled rabbits?

All right, fine. Maybe she was being unreasonable about this right now, but what if they were together three months from now? What if she at last invited him into her bedroom and every corner of herself—he was already further into that territory than she would have expected—and he still didn't see any problem with going to the club?

She rubbed her forehead, feeling a stress headache starting. To hell with it. She threw off the blanket. She'd go tonight. If nothing else, she could enjoy talking to Jimmy. She'd watch and appreciate Dale's skill and technique, the way she'd done the first night she'd seen him. Then she'd imagine picking up Jimmy's ice pick and stabbing "Master Craftsman" right between those broad shoulders, to inflict the same sharp pain on him that Jimmy's few words had given her.

Before she headed upstairs, however, she made a detour to the kitchen. Lynn lifted her head from the list she was making. "Good morning, Mrs. Summers. I'll be hitting the market this afternoon. Anything in particular you want me to pick up?"

Athena shook her head. "When the landscaping crew arrives today, would you mind talking to Hector about what he'd charge to have his crew switch out the bed in the master bedroom with the one in the yellow guest bedroom?"

Lynn lifted a brow, but she proved she was worth the money Athena paid her by not asking any questions about a topic she had no desire to discuss. "As often as you've given them bonuses—and my cooking—they'll be happy to do such a quick job for nothing. Do you want me to change out the linens, put the master set on the other?"

"No. Just leave it as is. The colors of the guest spread will work fine with the master bedroom. You can go ahead and wash the master set and store them, though. If we don't have anything suitable to replace it, draw on the household account and get something that will work."

"You don't want to do it yourself?" Lynn's surprised expression reminded Athena it was unusual for her to have staff pick out specifics like that.

"No." She didn't want to be involved with it in any way. She didn't want to see it happen. Bidding Lynn a good morning, she headed for her bedroom and a shower. As she moved up the steps, she laid out a list of to-dos to fill up the day, a track the train of her mind could follow without focusing on the destination. A train arrived regardless, because there was no jumping the track, was there? A train couldn't move without its track.

Tonight, she would wear a demure outfit as she'd done in the past, to ensure she wasn't sending out signals she was interested in playing. According to the club's strict rules on harassment, stating it was enough, but she knew how men could be. That thought dragged her mind unwillingly to Willow. Fifteen years younger than Athena, the woman had a lithe, perky body and fresh, unmapped face.

Moving to the back of her bedroom closet, she pulled out a sleeveless black sheath with a skirt that stopped at midthigh. It had a zipper from the low scoop back to the hem, following the seam of the ass. As Dale had so kindly pointed out, she had a very hot body, thanks to her daily running and swimming regimen. She'd never worn this dress. She'd bought it for New Year's Eve, intending to wear it for Roy. No matter how sick he was at that point, she wanted to dress up, show him that being attractive for him was still important to her. He'd died before then and she'd stayed in New Year's Eve, the dress forgotten in the back of her closet.

She closed her fingers on it, thinking how stupid she was being. Maybe she wouldn't go after all.

No, she had to go. Dale had said she could trust him to take care of her. That might be true during their intense . . . get-togethers, but Jimmy's phone call reminded her she couldn't abdicate her responsibility to take care of herself at other times, particularly if Dale's version of being her Master couldn't cover everything she might hope for it to be. She knew the difference between dreams and reality, and though she wasn't a cynic, and she did have dreams, she also understood only an idiot let them obscure reality to the point she'd let herself be blindsided by a moving car.

Whatever their relationship was, she needed to see it not just as a besotted submissive exploring her cravings, but as a woman who had to protect her own heart.

Apparently, his demonstrations were quite popular, because there were about thirty cars in the parking lot. Club Release only had around a hundred members, so a normal weeknight might host twenty guests, maybe thirty or forty on weekend nights. Having up to sixty in the club at once, as there appeared to be when she came in, was a very good turnout.

As she came to the top of the short set of steps that led from the hostess area to the club floor, she saw him over the heads of the crowd gathered in the main playroom. He was by the large suspension frame. Built by member volunteers out of heavy oak, the wood beams were polished to a gleam. It always reminded her of the inner workings of a tall ship.

If the participants gave permission, instructional workshops like this were filmed and put on the members-only section of the website for viewing. Accordingly, both Dale and the sub serving as his model wore concealing eyemasks, in the event the demos were ever hacked. Even so, she was familiar enough with Sally, a twentysomething blonde, that she recognized her right away. As for Dale . . . he was unmistakable, wasn't he?

He'd already started, was explaining the different ties and loops as he did them. Sally's hands were above her head, tied to an eyebolt in one of the vertical beams, a nonsuspension position where her feet remained on the floor, though her body was stretched upward in a nice display. All she wore was a black thong.

Sally's visible facial features reflected that rapt internal focus Athena now understood from a much more personal viewpoint. That expression merely intensified with each knot. He was making a diamond pattern down her front, similar to what he'd knotted across Athena's back when he had her bound to the griffin.

As he cinched a braided length of rope against Sally's pale pink clit, splitting her labia with the pressure, she swayed. Despite her secure position, he steadied her with a firm hand on her hip. He murmured to her. Making certain she was okay, Athena was sure.

"Hey, there you are." Jimmy's low greeting dragged her attention to the bar. He had her drink already prepared, and she wished she'd brought a shot of something stronger for it. Putting a small straw into the glass, he slid it into her usual spot and gestured to her to join them. There were several other people at the bar, watching the demo on the flatscreen on the wall. Dale had a mic clipped to the neck of his T-shirt, so the audio came through clearly, the deep voice rumbling out of the flatscreen speakers, vibrating through every cell of Athena's body.

As she forced herself into movement, descending the steps, Jimmy's gaze swept over her. He gave a quiet whistle. "Wow. You're dressed to the nines, Mistress."

"I have to attend another party," she lied. "But I thought I'd stop in to see the demonstration first."

"Oh." Jimmy didn't cover his disappointment quickly enough. She expected he, like some of the other subs who glanced her way, had hoped she might be here to play when the demo was over. It had been a mistake to come. She couldn't handle their expectations, their disappointment. Not combined with her own. She'd spend a few moments here, sip her drink, then head back home.

The rope-tying part of the demonstration was now done, but usually, to increase the pleasure of the crowd, the teacher would engage in a session to show how the sub reacted to additional stimulation. Dale had picked up a switch, was testing it. He would apply it to Sally's toned thighs. Perhaps have her spread her legs and give her a few taps there. She would writhe and cry out from the pain, as Athena had done from the ruler. The braided rope he'd positioned snug between her labia would get even more soaked with her fluids when she came. Her nipples were already hard, her eyes behind the mask following Dale's every movement. He had that effect on a sub, didn't he? He was like a sorcerer, bespelling any woman he chose.

She couldn't watch this. She couldn't. She took a swallow of her soda, the carbonation burning, and put it down with a five. "Thanks, Jimmy. I have to go."

"You just got here."

"Sorry, my schedule was already tight. I didn't realize . . . I just have to go." She turned away from his puzzled expression and fled the play area. As soon as she was out of Jimmy's sight, she increased her pace, practically trotting down the hallway toward the hostess station. She couldn't bear to hear that first strike fall, Sally's ecstatic cry of pain.

It was never going to be like it was with Roy. Falling in love so young, growing up together, becoming everything to one another. Ellen was right. So many people never had that dream even once; what right did she have to expect it twice? This was karma slapping her in the face for her greed. She was a submissive, yes. Dale had been right about that. But she wasn't like a Sally or Willow, enjoying play with different Masters as part of their club membership, then returning home to their lives the rest of the week. She wanted one man, one Master, and wanted to be his sub. Committed and faithful to one another, a closed partnership. Intimate in a way that was pure fantasy, because it couldn't happen overnight.

She should have made that clear, and maybe she wouldn't be hurting like this now, but then she hadn't really known what she wanted until Dale opened it up inside her, had she?

She was nearly running, and of course that was never a wise idea in high heels. The thin point wobbled and then her ankle turned, making her stumble. She caught the wall, cursing softly at the pain that shot up her leg. *Damn it, damn it, damn it.* Though it didn't feel like a bad sprain, one more step told her she wasn't going to be able to walk a step further in the sexy shoes. She yanked them off, resigned to the fact her stockings would be torn up by the parking asphalt, and proceeded at a slower pace.

Fortunately, some other members were coming in when she

reached the hostess station, so she nodded a quick good-bye to Susan. A new person she didn't know was working the door, so that, too, was a perfunctory farewell. She moved toward her car, fumbling for her keys. When she looked up, she started back two paces. Dale was leaning against her car door.

He had to have come out the side exit, circled around. And he would have stopped practically midsession, leaving Sally hanging there. *What in the world . . .*

His attention coursed over her, touched briefly on her shoes, but then he made a more thorough perusal of the dress and something else entered his gaze. Heat and storm clouds.

He straightened, coming toward her. "You shouldn't come out in the parking lot alone," he said shortly. "Why are you limping?" When he reached for her elbow, she jerked away.

"I can take care of myself. You didn't have to leave what you were doing to provide me an escort. Who's watching over Sally?"

"Gerald. He was assisting with the demonstration. Since he taught me the technique, he's more than capable of taking it over. He's been talking to me about sharing the load, because he's getting requests for so many demos lately. Not just here, but at different clubs and a couple cons. There's good money in it."

"I'm sure there is. I'm late for an engagement."

"Athena, hold up. What the hell is this?" He caught her by both elbows, refused to let her go when she struggled against him. "Settle down. Why are you dressed like this? Were you planning to . . ."

She stopped, raising a gaze to him. "What?"

"Were you here to be a Mistress? Or a sub?"

"Why would that matter to you?"

"Because the outfit says you intended to let a man touch you in some way. In a lot of ways." His blue-green eyes flashed dangerously. "That matters a hell of a lot to me."

"Really? You're in there, tying up a naked twentysomething, and *you're* being possessive?" She yanked out of his grip, glared at him.

"What about aftercare? Were you going to cuddle her, stroke her hair? Hold her in your lap when she cried, like you held me?"

The hurt welled up so strong, she felt sick with it. "Get away from me. This was all a mistake. Please just leave me alone."

He planted himself between her and her car, taking her purse in a smooth grab that suggested a lucrative career in petty theft if he were so inclined. "I'll give it back to you after you listen to me."

"No. I don't want to listen. And don't you dare give me that look. I can be as irrational as I want to be. It's no concern of yours."

"Gerald wasn't just taking over because I went after you," he said. "He took over because that's how we set it up. I explain and demonstrate the rope tying, pick out the punishment, and then he takes over from there. Including aftercare. I'm interested in doing this as a way to improve my skills, to teach others the right way to do it, and to earn some extra cash." His gaze slid over her again. "I'm doing another one next Saturday. Why don't you come as my sub, and I'll do the whole thing on you, beginning to end? He's been pushing me to do solos."

"Jimmy said you'd been here more than once over the past couple weeks, not just yesterday."

"So you were checking up on me?"

"No." She set her jaw. "He called me. He brought up the fact he'd talked to you and that he'd seen you here a couple of times. I didn't ask."

"Why not, Athena? Did you think you didn't have the right?"

"We didn't agree to be exclusive." Drawing her dignity around her, burying her hurt with effort, she told herself she *would* be an adult. "I know I'm reacting irrationally. That's my problem, not yours. I apologize. If you want to continue to have sessions with other submissives, I just can't do that. I didn't realize it about myself until tonight. I should be able to keep it separate in my head, see you the way Sally or Willow do, but obviously I'm still too emotionally vulnerable. Please move."

He nodded, slid to the left. But when she stepped closer to the car, he caught her wrist, shifting their positions so she was up against the side of the vehicle, and he was standing in front of her, his broad shoulders shielding her from any eyes but his.

"Why did you wear this dress tonight?"

She shook her head, and he put his hand on the side of her face, tilting her chin up with his thumb. "Answer your Master, Athena."

Her gaze snapped up to him, met that steady, no-nonsense stare. Why was he doing this to her? Didn't he understand? Her body trembled at the words, yearning toward them, a shameful betrayal of her heart.

He wasn't waiting for her answer. Or rather, he was occupying himself while he was. His other hand was on her bare back, sliding down over her right buttock to take a firm hold. That storm-cloud look increased. "Christ, you're not even wearing panties under this thing."

"No, I'm not. I wore it . . ."

Oh, for the love of all things, she was not going there. She was not going to humiliate herself. She shoved against him. "Let me go. Please . . . just let me go."

"Athena." The tone of his voice changed in that instant, from that of hard Master to puzzled lover, a far more devastating tactic. When his hands gentled, closing over her upper arms, she went still, staring miserably at his chest. "Athena, look at me."

She shook her head, and he sighed, putting his mouth briefly on the crown of her head, then resting his chin there, so her face was in the curve of his throat. She closed her eyes, feeling the timbre of his voice through her cheek. "I agreed to do the sessions with Gerald a month ago. The original plan was for me to do them beginning to end, on my own. But earlier this week, I told him I was seeing someone, and it was getting serious. I asked him to do the handoff after the punishment choice because I wanted to talk to that special someone about this, see if I could get her to agree to be my submissive for future demos. But I wasn't going to leave him in a lurch this week, since I'd agreed to help him. If you want, you can go in and ask him, verify I'm telling the truth."

She said nothing, though her cheeks were warming now. He slid his hands back down to her waist, thumbs sliding over her hip bones. "You wore this dress to piss me off, didn't you? Make me think that if I wasn't going to limit myself to you, that was a two-way street."

"I'm refusing to say anything."

"Fifth amendment and all that?" There was amusement in his voice, but it wasn't patronizing. When she lifted her head, dared a quick look at his face, there was a rueful expression there, even as his features remained tense, a little angry. "I'm sorry, Athena. I should have told you about this ahead of time. I was trying not to be presumptuous. I wasn't sure you were ready for exclusivity. But then I saw you in this dress, and I realized, whether you were ready or not, I sure as hell was. When I saw you, I couldn't finish up with Sally quick enough. If you'd made a move toward another guy . . ."

Things were feeling a little better now, but she'd gone so far down the other road, it was hard to call herself back from that tangle of turbulent emotions. She did put a hand on his chest, tentative though it was.

"Hey." He slid his fingers into her hair, tugged it so she was looking up at him. "Can we avoid the risk of homicide toward each other and innocent bystanders and confirm we want this to be an exclusive thing, for however long it lasts?"

"I told Lynn to have the bed in my room changed out with one in the guest rooms."

She wasn't sure that was an answer, but it was what came out of her mouth. He nodded. "Which bed?"

"The one in the yellow bedroom."

"The four-poster. Good choice." Possibilities kindled in his gaze. That heat found its way into her lower belly, tendrils teasing other sensitive parts of her. "You still haven't said it, Athena. I want to hear the words. You're mine and only mine."

She stared up at him. "I'm yours and only yours," she said softly.

Even so, she pushed out of his grip, establishing a little space between them. She rubbed her arms where he'd touched her, realizing she wanted him to keep touching her, but that she also needed him not to do so. Her feelings were too large, things too much.

"You need to retreat?" he asked shrewdly.

She didn't want to nod, but her head was already moving that way. "It feels different, being in there, watching you . . . knowing that I'm different now. Not what they all think I am. I need to go home and think it through, get a little space away from this."

He glanced back at the club, then at her. "You're building this place up too much in your own head."

"Probably," she admitted. "It just stands for a lot of things, I guess. Who I was, who I'm becoming."

"Their expectations of you."

Sometimes his ability to nail the point could be as irritating as it was helpful. When she didn't say anything, he reached out, squeezed her hand. "I'll let you off the hook tonight. But that's not going to last forever."

"I meant what I said," she said quietly. *About being yours.* "But I have to think about this some. I don't act as impulsively as I did tonight. I need to slow things down. All right?"

Since she had no idea what she really meant, she couldn't expect him to do so, but he fished her keys out of her purse and unlocked the car door. Opening it, he leaned in and put the purse on the passenger side, then straightened, gesturing to her to take the driver's seat. "All right," he agreed.

After a brief pause, a weighted silence between them, she stepped inside the shelter of the door. He took advantage of his height to reach over it. He slid his fingers into her hair, drew her up to him for a kiss. She resisted, but not enough. The mouth he put on hers was full of barely restrained tension and need. Those emotions linked with similar feelings in her own chest. When he lifted his head, she had her fingers curled over his wrist, and she didn't want to go, as much as she knew she needed to do so.

"I'll be as close as a phone call, girl," he said. "You reach out when you're ready. But wait too long, and I'll come looking for you. Say it again."

She knew what he was demanding, because the mere command made those emotions leap in her chest like a deer bounding across a cloud-covered meadow at night. Rushing and fast, mysterious and dark. "I'm yours," she whispered.

He nodded, his fingers slipping down to caress her throat. "That tether's there, all the time. You'll feel me tugging on it."

She gripped his wrist harder, then let go, feeling the loss of his touch as he let her get into the car. He closed the door and stepped back, remaining in place while she turned the engine over. When she was driving out of the parking lot, he was still watching her, the shadows cast by the parking lot lights etching out those relentless planes of his rugged face. His words were burned into her brain; his touch felt branded on her skin.

She thought how crazy she was for leaving him standing there. Then she decided not to think at all.

That stasis only lasted until three a.m., when she woke, her body aching and her mind in a whirl. She thought about everything they'd done since she first saw him at Club Release. The lunch at her house, their first session there, the time at the junkyard, in her office . . . the club last night.

Even though she smarted a little from that, remembering his kiss and expressions, the way he'd touched her, helped soothe some of those raw wounds. When she drifted back into a fitful sleep, she held his words to her, let them steady her.

His. More than that, he'd made it clear he considered himself hers exclusively.

Stepping out of the shower in the morning, she studied her backside. The bruises from the ruler beating were fading. She wanted to cup her breasts, stroke between her legs, aroused simply from looking at them, but he'd said that was forbidden. Why had she gone home last night? Why had she gone home alone?

Because she fell to pieces so easily with him, that was why. She'd never been a woman who fell to pieces at all.

It reminded her of a conversation she'd overheard at the reception after Roy's service. Amy, Roy's niece, had been comforting Evelyn, Roy's sister. Evie had kindly mentioned that they should check on Athena.

She's fine, Mom, Amy had assured her. *You know how she is. Aunt Athena can handle anything. I think if the whole world stopped tomorrow, the first thing she'd do is make a list on how to get it running again.*

Yes. That was probably true. But Dale kept turning her toward her own needs and desires, and that was a volatile, far deeper well than she'd realized. It was good to take a breather, not let the bucket descend further until she was ready to explore more of that darkness. She wondered what Dale would say to that.

You won't be exploring it alone, girl. Will you?

God, she missed him. But she'd drawn her line in the sand and she was going to make herself observe the boundary, even if only for today. She decided she'd work in her garden.

She kept her phone with her, though. She received a couple of emails on her private account from Release, reminding her of the monthly munch and another rope-tying demonstration. His name wasn't featured on that one, making her think he'd told Gerald he needed to pull back entirely until . . .

Until what? Until she said it was okay? Until she agreed to do it with him? Once again, she recoiled from the idea of appearing within those walls as a submissive. She deleted the emails, though she felt a twist of guilt, thinking of Jimmy and some of the others there who'd supported her so staunchly during Roy's illness. She'd address that another week.

As she worked in her garden, she closed her eyes and lifted her face to the sun, thinking of Dale kissing her . . . of Roy touching her hair, tugging on it. She recalled a day she'd been tending her roses and Roy brought her a wildflower he'd seen on the side of the road. He'd pulled it from the dirt, roots and all, putting it in a plastic beer cup he had left over from the day's golf outing. Kneeling next to her, he planted it in the ground among her roses.

"Those fancy, well-tended plants need to remember what it is to grow wild, to see something beautiful spring up somewhere unexpected." He'd touched her face at that, making her smile.

She'd tended his offering as carefully as her roses, so now, two years later, that little yellow wildflower was a bushy edging around their perimeter.

Her eyes were wet, she realized, pulling off her gloves to swipe at them. Dale was a new and special part of her life, but there were days she missed the man who'd been in her life for over twenty years so very much. What would he think of Dale? She thought he'd like him, tremendously. They'd probably share a beer, play pool together.

But that was the crux of all of it, wasn't it? Not just what she'd been or what she was becoming, but what she'd been all along, and how she would deal with that part of her coming to life, competing with her past, challenging her future.

Her phone buzzed and she glanced down at it, hoping it wasn't Ellen. The week after the board meeting was usually a quiet one, allowing her to handle most things from home. When she saw it was Dale, the leap in her chest was a good feeling, simple and pure. "Hi. I'm glad you called."

"Hi." He paused. "Are you okay?"

"Yeah." She sniffled. "Just working in the garden. Allergies."

He stayed silent and she glanced down at her spade, resting in the dirt next to a clump of the yellow flowers. "I was just thinking about Roy. It makes me tear up a little. I didn't want you to think I cry all the time."

"Do you?"

"A lot less these days than I used to." She hoped he could hear the smile in her voice, the truth of it.

"I'm flattered."

"Oh, you thought I was talking about you? It's actually because of my new pool boy, Stuart, and my German masseuse, Gunther. We have three-ways every afternoon."

He snorted. "Didn't we go over this?"

They were teasing one another about it, which was a good sign. "I guess I just wanted to verify. The way you military types do when you're on a mission and you're checking coordinates. I've seen it in the movies."

"I'll bet." His voice became husky. "I'm not sharing you, girl. If you think I will, you're going to get well acquainted with my belt. I'm pretty damn good at corporal punishment, and I enjoy the hell out of it. That enough verification for you?"

She had to clear her throat. "Stuart and Gunther who?"

He chuckled. "Much as I like flirting with you, I did call for a different reason. I wanted to ask your advice on something, since you seem connected to a lot of the area charities."

"Anything," she said, pleased. "What do you need?"

"A couple buddies of mine had a field trip to the local Y planned for some inner-city kids, an ice cream/pool party thing. The Y had an issue come up with their pool and it's shut down for the next week. Do you know somewhere else we could take them this coming weekend? The Y was going to give us a three-hour block of private time. It's about thirty-five kids with behavior problems, mostly just rough edges from hard lives. Neil and Lawrence are trying to give them some good experiences, ease them into environments different from what they're used to."

She thought it over. "I do have somewhere, but I don't know how you'll feel about it. My place."

"What?"

"We didn't visit our extended recreation wing the night you were here. We have an Olympic-sized pool, with a playroom annex. Roy put arcade games in there. Foosball, Ping-Pong, a pool table . . . you name it. He was a big kid about things like that, and our adult guests loved the parties we hosted there. We've held a couple events for the Louisiana children's home we support, so it's not the first time it's been used for something like what you're proposing. I should do even more things like that with it, because I mainly use the pool for my daily laps now."

"Which explains that hot body of yours, Mrs. Summers."

Her nerves prickled pleasantly at that, but she could sense his hesitation. "I'm not doing . . . what I was doing, right? Trying to control things?"

"No, not at all. I just don't want anything to happen to your property. Some of these kids are a bit rough."

"They're just things. They can be replaced. How can they learn to appreciate nice things if they're never given access to them?"

"Sounds like something I said to my prom date."

She chuckled. "Did it work?"

"Not as much as I thought it should have. Look, are you serious about this?"

"Yes. This Saturday?"

"Yeah. Is three hours too long?"

"Well, if you're going to bring them all the way out here, why don't we make a day of it? I can have a lunch prepared for them, and they can watch a movie in the theater room after they get tired of swimming."

"You have your own theater."

"Of course," she informed him loftily. "That's where I watch *Ben-Hur.*"

"You're scary rich, aren't you?"

"One of the evil one-percenters, if you believe anticapitalist propagandists. One that employs thousands of people in eleven non-unionized plants across the country. Plants that provide excellent health care, day care benefits, scholarships . . . Oh, and jobs. Dumb stuff like that."

"Careful, Mrs. Reagan. Your teeth are showing."

She grinned at that, confirming it. "You don't seem scared."

"I like your teeth. And everything else. Okay, I'll tell Lawrence and Neil it's a go."

"Will you be coming with them?"

"Two single SEALs in their sexual prime coming to your house? You bet your sweet ass I'll be there."

"Sexual prime, hmm?" She laughed. "Don't trust me?"

"Just taking precautions. A smart man protects what's his."

A heated weight took up space in her chest, resting low in her stomach, spreading to the sensitive place between her legs. She swallowed. "Would you . . ."

"Would I what?"

"I wanted . . . I just want to be around you." So much for her resolve, but he was enough of a gentleman not to point out her "breathing room" had only taken the space of a night. He merely sounded pleased she'd changed her mind.

"Come over today, have Chinese takeout with me and spend the night. No expectations, one way or another. Maybe we'll watch a movie, like we were talking about. We can see how it goes."

"So you don't do that kind of thing often."

"No, Athena. I don't."

She gripped the phone, holding it as if she were holding on to him. "Yes, I'd love to do that. Can I pick up the takeout?"

"Nope. They deliver. Just bring yourself and your toothbrush. No PJs. I'll keep you warm."

He'd already managed that, raising her core temperature by about ten degrees. "I'll see you in an hour or so."

ELEVEN

H e had the gate open. Figuring it might be that way for the takeout guy, she left it open, drove up to the office and apartment building. He was sitting on the bottom step, a pair of dogs at his feet. The canines, who looked like a blend of shepherd, chow and lab, were watching him cut up an apple. He was offering pieces to them between bites for himself. He also had an open bottle of wine behind him, with an extra glass. He'd filled one with a rich red and had apparently been sipping on it, a change from his normal beer.

He looked so good. His blue-and-white-striped button-down was worn to that softness which had the fabric molding his upper torso, the tails loose over jeans. His booted feet were braced out wide to accommodate the dogs. Men really didn't have to futz much with the details and accessories. A handsome man could wear the same outfit every day, observe decent hygiene and still turn heads wherever he went. It was his attitude, his charisma, that made the man. It could make a woman hate the entire gender, if she hadn't had the experience of being in love with one. She saw many similar qualities in Dale. As well as some very vital—and appreciated— different ones.

Getting out of the car, she was struck by a wave of longing for him so strong it almost made her dizzy. She'd left so abruptly at the club, and the last time she'd seen him before that had been in her office. He'd said no expectations, no planned session, just Chinese takeout and being together, but when she came toward him, her body felt tight all over, her throat thick with things she couldn't say.

He set the wineglass aside and reached for her, nudging the dogs to the side with his boot. That was all it took. He'd pulled her into his arms and she was straddling him on the stairs, the dogs nosing her ankles in greeting as she put her mouth on his; hot, open and delving deep. His arm went around her waist, his other hand taking a firm, proprietary grip on her ass. She made a needy noise, pressing herself against him.

When she came up for air, she didn't speak, just stared down at him, wanting him to see it all, understand it all.

"I need to put the dogs up."

"Okay."

"The takeout guy should be here in the next ten minutes. Go upstairs and get in my bed. I expect you to be naked under my sheets." His eyes held hers. "Play with yourself. I want you even more hot and bothered than you are now. Get yourself as close to coming as you can without doing it."

Holding on to her waist, he rose and put her on her feet with the strength of one arm. Then he sent her on her way with a healthy, stinging slap to her ass that reminded her of the marks he'd put there earlier in the week. She felt like she floated up the stairs, which was kind of a miracle given that her body was weighed down with lust.

Pivoting at the top, she saw he was halfway across the open area, the dogs at his heels. She let herself into the apartment and went right to his bedroom. She took off everything, folded it to the side, and then savored his sheets against her bare flesh. She lay on her back, but turned her head, pressing her nose into his pillow. She moved it on top of her body, hugging it to her, sliding it across her breasts and then down, the weight of it against her wet pussy. She wanted him to have her scent there.

Turning on her stomach, she pushed the pillow beneath her so she could use the pressure of it against her body to do as he demanded. Slipping her fingers in between the pillow and herself, she began to slowly rub her clit, work herself against the pillow, the movements of her body creating friction between the mattress and her nipples. He'd said not to let herself come, and yet she might come from merely thinking about him. She hoped the takeout wasn't late.

It was a nice day, so the windows were cracked. In no time she was gasping, such that there was a chance the delivery guy would overhear her. He might think it was the wind, but she imagined his male instincts would hone in on the erotic quality of it. If Dale was as territorial as he seemed, he'd cover it with casual conversation and send the guy packing.

The pleasures of male possessiveness weren't new to her. It was a myth that a male sub wasn't as testosterone driven as any other man when he thought someone was sniffing around what he thought of as his female. Roy had wanted her to be *his* Mistress, and definitely considered her *his* wife. She liked that feeling of belonging, liked the shape of it with Dale, the sharper sense of it as his sub. But she had to agree with Roy's viewpoint as well. She felt just as possessive toward Dale as her Master, which her reaction at the club had proven. Now that she'd confirmed Dale's feelings agreed with hers, she didn't feel as foolish about it.

She heard the vehicle arrive, the male voices. She worked herself harder against the pillow, reveling in the sound of Dale's voice. He'd follow the guy back to the entrance and lock the gate, because he was careful that way. She stroked her breast, tweaked the nipple, which made her hips jerk. She'd be leaving more than her scent on his pillow at this rate. She might end up having to wash it for him. She wouldn't mind that, either.

She heard his feet on the steps, the slightly uneven tread. Her heart went from pounding to racing. When he came in, she couldn't see him, because her head was turned toward the window, cheek pressed to the bed. Cool air touched her as he drew back the sheet, watched the undulation of her slightly perspiring body, the rise and fall of her hips against the manipulation of her hand.

He slid his fingers down the line of her spine, over the curve of her buttocks. "Keep doing that, girl. Christ, you're a picture." He pressed a kiss between her shoulder blades as he slipped his hands between her body and above the pillow to cup both her breasts. She cried out at the intimate contact, lifting her bottom higher, such that she brushed his hip in the rough denim. She wanted to make circles against the front of his jeans, dampen them with her arousal, but he was at the wrong angle. He was staying out of range. She was performing for him, all of it for his pleasure. Keying into that, she spread her knees even wider, teasing him with the sight of her fingers working her pussy. Never in her whole life had she been so blatant and shameless with a man.

When he withdrew, she turned her head to the opposite cheek, in time to see him reaching inside the night table drawer for a condom. "Can you . . . not use that? There hasn't been anyone for me, since Roy. And I had my tubes tied a while ago."

He paused. She knew how careful he was. Even if he'd had other partners recently—something she didn't really want to know—she expected the risk would be nonexistent. She trusted him.

When he nodded, closed the drawer, she let out a sweet, soft sigh. He came back to the bed and grasped her arm to turn her over. He removed the pillow, putting her on her back in the center of his bed.

"If it's the first time we're doing it that way, then we do it different," he said. "Stay like that for me."

She watched him remove his shirt, that glorious ripple of muscle across his abdomen. Opening his jeans, he sat down on the edge of the mattress. He removed one boot, setting it aside, then he pushed the pants to his knees, reaching in to lift his left leg out of the socket of the prosthesis. He peeled off the stump sock, letting it disappear down the leg of the jeans, and then pushed the denim all the way off both legs, leaving the clothes crumpled around the prosthesis and other boot. Now he turned to her, as bare as she was. He slid his fingers down her stomach, making her quiver. So many things were going through her mind now, images of Dale and Roy twisted together, a lot of emotion with them. He shifted onto the bed, put himself on his knees between hers, and lay down upon her.

His upper body strength had him managing it all smoothly, and though a worry passed through her mind about his knee, she was going to trust what he'd said. He considered that issue his to handle, a part of who he was.

When he settled between her legs, his cock nudging at her entrance, she wrapped her arms around his broad shoulders and lifted her hips, making a guttural noise of pleasure as the head pushed inside her. He stopped there, a blissful, anticipatory pause until she looked up into his face, met his eyes.

He slid in deep, stretching her with his size, a snug fit she loved. "Yeesss . . ." she whispered, and earned an answering glint of pleasure from the blue-green irises, a tightening of that firm mouth.

"All mine," he said, pushing in a little deeper to emphasize it. "My girl."

She nodded, giving him a tremulous smile as he bent, covered her lips with his, a swirling, long kiss as he moved inside her. Slowly, easily, like floating on waves. She'd been so worked up, so hot. Now, though her body was still intensely aroused, the emotional weight countered it such that everything became slow and languid. It was a surreal, perfect, isolated moment. They were the only ones in this world, their bodies moving together toward that crest when the wave would surge and crash, rush them over the edge.

Her fingernails bit into his back. "Don't be afraid to mark me, girl," he growled. "I'd love to carry your scratches."

She was glad of that, because he left her no choice. That slow, blissful spin started to change to sharp, demanding spikes. He captured a breast in one hand, his back curving so he could seal his mouth over a nipple, suckle. She worked herself even harder along his length, clasping him tight, wanting to feel every delicious inch of him.

It wasn't kinky, acrobatic, or exceptionally original. It was a perfect coming together, totally driven by instinct and the need for intimacy, and she loved it. In some way it cauterized and closed the wounds opened at the club. This underscored once and for all that what they were experiencing together wasn't just a series of defined sessions between Master and sub. What they were sharing, building together, wasn't defined or limited at all. It might crash and burn. On the first day, that possibility had scared her, but now she liked that the flight was open-ended. It made her want to soar.

She loved the way it felt, her legs spread for him, heels locked over his back and flexing buttocks, his arms caging her on either side, the rough scratch of his jaw on her tender flesh. The sound of his breath, getting harsher, tighter, as his arousal built with her own. Even as her body's responses accelerated, her mind braked further, taking in all of it. Did anyone ever appreciate such intimacy until it was gone? The pleasure of having a man lying upon you, holding you, breathing with you through the long, dark night? Not just any man, but one with a strong thread of connection to your heart and soul?

Time had not yet tested or strengthened that thread for her and Dale, yet she could feel the stitch had been made. The connection was there, enough to make this a hopeful, poignant moment, as well as an erotic and pleasurable one.

He put his mouth on her throat. She'd already seen his control was substantial, but she'd done a little research on that missing limb and knew it wouldn't be good for him to stay in this position indefinitely. He was taking care of her; she was going to return the favor.

She began to tilt her hips to meet his thrusts, tightening down on him, lifting her breasts up further, displaying herself for him.

Men were visual, after all, and when she turned her head, giving him even more access to her throat, the obvious gesture of full surrender locked in tandem flight with his craving to dominate. His thighs hardened against the insides of hers, and she heard the fluctuation of breath.

"Together, girl." He nudged her cheek so her eyes lifted to his burning ones. Once their gazes locked, he slid an arm under her, arching her further into his mouth as he suckled her nipple harder, his hand gripping her buttock. One of his fingers pushed into that intimate seam to tease her rim as he worked himself deeper into the tilted angle of her hips.

It swept over her so fast, she barely had time to gasp it out, but he was already there.

"Fuck, yes. Come for me."

She did rake his back, caught in a pounding surf, the climax strong and uncontrolled. He matched her screams with his hard groans as he released inside her, giving her that desired jet of hot seed bathing her channel, her cervix, transforming her aftershocks into minor orgasms. When she finished, he was still thrusting, ensuring she had the full measure of her release, and she was bearing down on his cock inside her, trying to do the same for him. Her limbs were trembling. His back was slick with perspiration, but it was also sticky. Lifting her fingers, she blanched. "Dale."

She *had* marked him, because she had blood smeared on her hands. "Oh, God. I'm sorry. I didn't mean . . ."

"To do exactly as you were told?" He gave her a look that eased her heart, especially when he took that hand and kissed each fingertip. She sank back into the mattress, watching him. When he shifted off her at last, she caught his arm before he rolled to his back.

"Do you want me to get a towel from the bathroom, to protect the sheets?"

He touched her cheek with a fingertip. "Sure."

When she returned, spread it out beneath him and he lay back, he took her with him. The insistent move made her smile as he settled her firmly against his side. She put her hand on his chest, moved down to his abdomen and let it rest above his softening cock. She couldn't resist gliding a fingertip over it, feeling how her juices had made him sticky in a different way there. Some of his semen had trickled down her thigh, escaping her slick and swollen core.

They didn't say anything for a while. She was giving him time for that postcoital somnolence men required, and truth, she was drifting with him. She'd been wound up since being with him in her office, wanting this, wanting him.

Yet as lust's driving demand eased, something else penetrated their newfound intimacy. She slid her palm back up his body, over the sectioned stomach muscles, the well-developed chest with the light mat of hair. When she pressed her nose to his flesh to smell him, her stomach shifted like an uncertain cat on a new lap. Her fingers curled, drew in to themselves. During her arousal, it hadn't even crossed her mind. In their earlier couplings, the newness of the Dom/sub dynamic had apparently kept her from noticing it. The focus had been on assuaging that need for one another. But in the slower pace now, she felt a perverse, unwelcome need to draw away. Not out of the bed, but enough to establish some space, consider him from a distance.

When she shifted to do that, his arm tightened around her and he tilted his head to look down at her. With a Master like him, not much escaped his attention. In this instance, that could be as much curse as blessing. He touched her chin, her cheek, but she continued to stare at his chest, her fingers curled in a ball in the space between her curved body and his. "What is it, Athena?"

"It's . . . I'm not sure I can say it right."

"You don't have to worry about that with me. Just say it. Are you okay? Did I do something you didn't like?"

She shook her head, thinking how kind it was for him to ask

such a thing, not in the tone of a man seeking ego stroking, but a lover concerned about her well-being. "It's . . . Roy was . . . softer than you. He stayed fit, but the way a normal man does. You know, working out on the weights and treadmill, staying active enough to stay trim. Whereas you . . . well, you obviously work out a lot." An understatement. The man was pure muscle. "Is that a SEAL thing?"

"Maybe. You get in the habit of it, to stay prepared, and it's hard to let it go. Though I don't think any of us stay as fit as we do when we're active. And young and gung ho." He gave her a faint smile, but his serious eyes were still tracking her expression, waiting to see where she was going with this.

"Touching you, sometimes I feel . . . decadent. Like I'm fifteen again, the girl with freckles and glasses who's looking at the quarterback, wondering what it's like to be the cheerleader who gets to touch him. It's fun, exciting."

She lifted her gaze to him, answered his faint smile with one of her own, but then she sobered. "Then there's another part of me that—and please don't be offended—feels wrong. I'm expecting to feel my husband's body under my hands. Women always talk about wanting an Adonis, but when you love someone, their body becomes the body you desire, no matter how much you enjoy looking at the others. So in a way, I almost want your muscles to feel softer, to make me feel more comfortable, like I'm with him. But you're not him, and I really don't want you to be the same as him. It's just . . . different. Odd. It took me by surprise. It's only in moments like this I notice it. I'm sorry . . . I'm really not saying this right."

"You're doing just fine."

Pushing himself up on his elbows, he caught her wrist. Keeping that steady gaze upon her, he drew her hand back to his body, laying her palm on his chest. He left his hand over hers, slid them both down his chest, over his stomach, so she followed every ridge. He took his time about it, murmuring a quiet reassurance as her fingers curved into the hard terrain.

Then they were at his cock, his testicles, and he molded her hand over them as she caught her lip in her teeth. She stared at the way it looked, her hand touching him there. She could feel his eyes still on her face. He didn't appear to be watching their hands at all, only her reaction to what he was doing. He moved her hand to his thigh, back up over his hip bone, his rib cage. He kept it to a leisurely pace, a not-so-casual tour, giving her ample time to expand the exploration. She traced a strip of pale skin, stroked the fine hairs of his body, seeing the more vulnerable places among the less-so ones as she went along.

The contact brought back the sensual intimacy of a few moments ago, with a different flavor. By the time their layered hands returned to his chest, she felt a little less uncertain. He laced his fingers with hers, squeezing them together as she lifted her lashes to meet his gaze again.

"I'm not your husband, Athena. I'm your Master. This is my body, and you can explore every part of it." He turned to his hip, putting his arm around her waist, drawing her close enough to put his mouth to her ear. The position let her press her face into his neck as her hands slipped over his hip and buttock, his scored back. "It's time to figure out how to love a new body. A new man." He paused. "I can't imagine how much you must miss him."

She closed her eyes, her lips against his collarbone. "It's gotten better this year. Maybe the third year is the charm. But the first two years, I didn't want to get out of bed, get dressed, do anything. I didn't expect to lose him when I was still . . ."

"Young enough to want to love again, to want someone again."

She nodded. "It felt like a betrayal, to start to think that way again. But when I saw you, it was as if he was standing in the back of my mind, saying, 'Yes, Athena. That's the one. He's the right one.'"

Realizing how that sounded, she drew back, met his eyes. "I'm sorry. I don't mean I'm seeing you as a jumpstart. Or trying to trap you into something more than you intended us to be."

"You're saying what's in your heart. I'm a man, Athena. I won't overanalyze, I promise." He smiled again, making her smile back.

"Okay," she said. Putting her head back down on his chest, she tried to believe the strength of his arms would slow the world down. Keep her feelings for him manageable, in perspective. "Okay."

TWELVE

Dale had told her what Neil and Lawrence had budgeted for food for the ice cream/pool party. She'd bought groceries within that range, carefully keeping the receipts for them, and then she'd bought a whole lot more. The thirty-five kids were all boys, and she knew enough about adolescent appetites to prepare for an army. The tables in the game room were loaded with snacks, as well as the ones the staff had set up beside the open French doors that led back to the pool area. As the boys traveled between locations, they could grab a handful to keep them fortified.

The tennis courts were equipped with extra rackets and several wire baskets of balls. Basketballs sat at the ready beneath the two hoops. Roy had poured the pad for them between the pool house and tennis courts. Beyond them was a driving range and putting area.

Her husband had been a big kid when it came to his sports, and she loved watching him play there with friends. As well as playing there with him herself. As her gaze passed over the driving range, ensuring the staff had put out enough balls and clubs, she remembered the day Roy had tried to teach her to swing. Holding her from behind like that had led to a different type of athletic activity.

"Ma'am?" Lynn buzzed her phone. "The invasion force is coming up the drive now."

Athena chuckled. "Don't worry, Lynn. We have three SEALs to contain the attack."

She cut around the side of the house to get to the driveway, arriving in time to see a battered activity bus park with a rattle of the diesel engine. One of the men, presumably Neil or Lawrence, stood up inside to give direction to the boys so they spilled out in a reasonable order. Dale pulled up behind them in his truck, giving her a wink as he got out. She thought she gave him a proper smile and nod back, but the amusement in his gaze told her she might not have quelled a blush. Or perhaps she'd overdone the propriety, such that he was already devising ways to get her into a far less proper position. That thought *did* make her blush.

Neil and Lawrence made the boys line up and introduce themselves to her. They ranged from ages eleven to fourteen. She understood the SEALs' intent today was as much about developing good social behavior as having a play day away from the stresses of their difficult home environments. Therefore, she responded appropriately, asking each boy a couple of things about himself, shaking his hand and making eye contact. Most were wary of the respectful adult greeting. Some were shy, but intrigued by her attention. They were all fidgety, their eyes wandering everywhere, wanting to explore. In short, they were active boys.

Stepping back, she told Neil how to get to the recreation area around the side of the house. She raised her voice to explain the pool house had bathrooms and a locker area for changing. She noticed many of the boys had brought suits, but she'd provided a few extra, as well as a wealth of towels. When she mentioned that, more than one expression brightened in the faces of the boys who were empty-handed. Dale gave her his look that told her he knew she'd gone beyond what they'd asked her to do, but she hoped he understood her motives. She wanted to do her part to make this a wonderful day for all of them.

Lawrence wasn't tall, only about five seven, but he had the ripped body that all SEALs seemed to possess. He had a good way with the boys, too, and they were attentive and respectful to him, despite the shifting bodies and wandering eyes. They were like a pack of young dogs, wanting to run. She couldn't blame them.

"For those of you interested in taking a look inside the house, Mrs. Summers said she'll be happy to give tours throughout the day. However, unless you're with her or with one of us, you stay in the areas we've just talked about."

"Yo, we ain't going to steal nothing," one of the boys called out.

"It's not about that, Elliott," Lawrence said patiently. "Part of moving ahead in the world is showing you can respect boundaries. This is Mrs. Summers's home. We respect that. You're not going to see me, Neil or Dale going in her house without her permission, either. Now, we have a good day planned here. We're going to swim, play games, use the courts and driving range, have lunch. Later this afternoon, you'll get to settle down in Mrs. Summers's home theater to watch a movie, and we'll cap off the day with an awesome pizza dinner."

His gaze swept them all. "But that's contingent on you guys using the manners we've talked about. You say please and thank you, and if you want to do something you're not sure is okay, you ask *first*. You break the rules, you sit on the bus for fifteen minutes, which means whichever one of us is babysitting you is going to make you do push-ups in the aisle, because we'd rather be out here having fun, too. Got it?"

He received a fairly amenable response, a few eye rolls, but more for form than to be disrespectful. Even so, he pinned a couple of the eye rollers with a stare that had them straightening up. Athena pressed her lips against a smile. When Lawrence gave her a significant glance, she thought she might be getting that chastising stare, as if he sensed the mirth she was suppressing, but he was merely doing a lead-in for his next point.

"I'm sure all you rocket scientists have noticed Mrs. Summers is a woman."

The expected comments and some attempts at whistling were handled by Neil. He was taller than Lawrence, with a lanky quality that didn't detract from his powerful build, reminding her of a young Gary Cooper. He administered a few head slaps that quieted them back down. "You show extra respect to her," Lawrence said, his stern look suddenly very much like what she'd often seen on Dale's face. The boys responded to it almost as she did, with cautious attention. "You watch your language. That's what comes out of your mouth, what gestures you make . . . you can put together the rest. You learn to be respectful around women, you'll get a lot further with them."

"Don't see either one of you with a woman," one of the boys teased.

"Cause he don't trust them around us," another called back. "He knows we can steal her away because we got moves Neil and Lawr only dream about."

Neil rolled his eyes, dishing out another set of head slaps, but the way the boys ducked and laughed told Athena the teasing was part of the bond they had with the men. Everything within the proper boundaries.

The thought made her gaze slip back to Dale. He was leaning against the side of the bus, listening and watching, riding herd on the boys closer to that end. Feeling her regard, he met her eyes again, gave her a slow smile. Her toes curled inside her sneakers.

"All right, we ready to do this? Give me the answer I want to hear."

"Yes sir!" They shouted it at once and with great force, like a basic training platoon. Not expecting it, Athena jumped, and Lawrence slanted her a grin, some of the other boys laughing at her reaction. She chuckled at herself, shook her head.

"Anything else you want to say, Mrs. Summers?" Lawrence asked.

She stepped up beside him. "I'm delighted to have you boys here in my home. At the tennis courts, you'll meet Maryann and Chuck. John and Carl are at the driving range. They teach tennis and golf lessons and said they'd be happy to teach anyone who doesn't already know how to play. Don't be shy. They love getting new students.

"Also, throughout the day, please help yourself to the food that's sitting out. Don't worry about us running out. We'll restock anything that gets empty, and you'll each go home with a bag of left-overs at the end of the day. Have fun."

More of those wary looks, but she knew they'd loosen up as soon as they felt safe in the environment, which was the whole intent. Nodding to Lawrence, she stepped back again.

"Okay, whoever wants to swim first, follow me to the changing rooms," he said. "Those who want to go to the arcades and courts, follow Neil. *No* stampedes. Believe me, you'll be tired as hell by the end of the day. Spread it out."

As the boys split up as he indicated, their obvious charge checked by his warning, Dale moved toward her. His attention slid over her T-shirt, neat jeans and sneakers. She'd put her hair in a ponytail and applied light makeup, intending to look more motherly than womanly today.

"Did you intentionally go for the MILF look?" he teased.

She arched a brow. "You better behave. Lawrence told me to report anyone acting inappropriately to him right away. No telling what kind of punishment he has planned."

"Usually push-ups or sit-ups. It worked great in BUD/S. You got so you hated the word push-up."

She gave him a considering look. "I wouldn't mind seeing you do some push-ups. Shirtless, of course."

"Now who's misbehaving?" He winked at her. "Of course, if that munchkin had the balls to give me a punishment, it'd be knee bends. All SEALs have a sadistic side."

At her startled laugh, he took her hand, leaned in and brushed a kiss over her lips. "You did too much. Maryann, Chuck, Carl and John?"

"Maryann and Chuck teach the youth tennis division at my country club. Carl is one of our golf pros and John is one of the caddies, but he's an excellent golfer as well. They owed me some favors, but more than that, they were enthusiastic about helping. They've done it before, with the Louisiana children home visits. As for the rest . . ." She shrugged. "What good is having lots of money if you can't do fun things like this with it?"

"It's more than money. You could have thrown that at a bunch of people and then spent the day getting your nails done somewhere off-site. You look ready to get hands-on."

The observation obviously carried more than one meaning. When he brushed a thumb over her cheekbone, drawing her attention to the fact he'd made her cheeks warm, she shook her head at him. "I think Lawrence is going to be making you do those knee bends."

He snorted. "He can try." Linking hands with her, he nodded toward the recreation area. "Let's go join the fray."

I t was utterly exhausting, and tons of fun. She went where she was needed, and by late morning, that was the tennis courts. A few braver souls came to learn about the game, and then, when others saw them having fun, they flocked over as well, such that having a third instructor was useful. She wasn't on Maryann and Chuck's level, but she was a good player and knew enough to provide basic instruction.

Most had basketball hoops in their neighborhoods, so throughout the day there was a regular rhythm of sound coming from that area, the echoing metallic sound of baskets being made, the shouted directions and exclamations as the boys passed and feinted. The arcade area was likewise well attended, with a profusion of beeps, explosions, gunfire and theme music from the various machines drifting out the open doors of the building.

There were a few who didn't swim, but teaching that wasn't difficult for a pair of SEALs. Neil and Lawrence took turns giving lessons. Watching them, she thought about being in the pool with Dale, just the two of them. In the water, she expected he'd be far less concerned about his leg, the buoyancy compensating for its lack. She'd twine her legs around him, his arm cinching her close, nothing between them but water droplets . . .

She brought herself away from that with a firm shake. Definitely not the environment to be having such thoughts.

Dale was like her, floating from station to station, pitching in where needed. Since Lynn and Beth kept a good eye on the snacks and drinks, Athena wasn't surprised she had very little to do for that area. She was surprised by how well the boys cleaned up after themselves, but apparently that was one of the rules Neil and Lawrence had set. Her suspicion was confirmed the first time a boy missed his three-point throw of his wadded up napkin into a trash can and tried to walk away without dealing with it. The sharp-eyed Neil caught him by the collar and brought him back to pick it up. Then he made him do ten push-ups right there, to the good-natured teasing of the other boys.

It was then she noticed one boy who kept coming back to the snack tables. He'd caught her eye several times, because he'd merely been wandering from place to place without really getting involved in anything. He'd watch the other boys engaged in activity, and then move onward. It made him look like he was participating when he really wasn't. The men had noticed it as well, trying to draw him into things, but he'd preferred to stay on the periphery. Now, as he went by the snack table once more, glancing around to confirm he was by himself, she put together what he was doing.

When he was ambling away from it once more, she intersected his path. "Jason?"

He looked surprised that she remembered his name, but that had been the point of her questions about each of them, helping her mark their names in her mind. It was an effective tool for fundraising parties. She'd asked him his favorite thing to do, and he'd said basketball. Yet he wasn't at the courts. He was a tall boy for his age, taller than her, and had the beginnings of broad shoulders. From the way he studied the ones playing basketball, she expected he was a good player.

"Yeah? I mean, yes ma'am?" He said it dutifully, obviously

coached by Neil and Lawrence, but not really sure of the importance of the honorific.

"I notice you're not joining the other boys."

"I'm not really into all that." Yet his eyes tracked the boys in the pool, visible since she'd had the staff latch open all the entrance doors so the pool house was a pavilion today.

"Why are you hiding food in your clothes, Jason? It's all free, and you can have as much as you like. There's no reason for you to worry about that."

His gaze cut back to her. Before the hard, defensive look to his mouth could become a denial, she held up a hand. "You're not in trouble. Food isn't the same thing as electronics or a pair of high-tops. You're taking it for someone, aren't you?"

Behind him, she saw Neil and Dale had noticed their conversation, registered Jason's tense shoulders. She gave them a subtle head shake, telling them she had this under control and didn't want their involvement.

When Jason set his jaw, she nodded. "It's good of you to look out for them, whoever they are. Why don't we do this? Put back what you're carrying and just focus on having a good time today. I promise, before you leave this afternoon, I'll take you to the kitchen, and we'll make up a box of food for your family. That's what we planned to do for everyone, but if you need it, we'll put extra in yours. Neil and Lawrence are taking you all home, so they'll make sure you have additional hands to carry it."

At his suspicious look, she reached out, laid a light hand on his arm. He didn't skitter away, but he stared at it like he wasn't sure if it would bite him or not. "Jason, can you look at me? Meet my eyes?"

He did it, and she nodded in approval. "You look like you have a lot on your shoulders," she said gently. "You're not betraying those you love by taking a day for yourself, by rewarding yourself for your care of them. Go have fun with the others, and let us help you take care of them today. All right? Can you trust us enough to do that?"

The uncertainty that entered his gaze made his expression far bleaker than a thirteen-year-old's should look. It twisted her heart, but she kept her attitude matter-of-fact. When they'd been arranging the event, Lawrence had called and given her a lecture, his tone amusingly not too much different from what he'd used on the boys when they were lined up outside the bus.

These guys go through hell every day where they live, but they don't need your pity. To get out of their world, they're going to have to learn to pull themselves out of it, and the right way, with honor and integrity. Strength of character. You don't get that from being babied or pitied.

"So, that's decided," she said. "Put the food back on the table, and change into a suit. All right? The pool temperature today is too good to waste."

A small smile appeared on his face, nervous and wary, but there. "Yeah, okay."

"Yeah, what?" She gave him a little pinch on his arm and won a small smile.

"Yes, ma'am."

"All right."

She didn't watch him return the food, but when she was a suitable distance away, she glanced back. He was headed for the changing room. He fell in with a couple of boys coming from the arcade who'd decided it was time to do the pool. He seemed a little easier, exchanging banter with them. One good day might not change his view of the world, but as she well knew, one good day could make a lot of bad days more bearable.

The rest of the day was a blur. Dale teased her about it, but in truth, she was having as good a time as the kids. The boys also became far more comfortable around her, though she noticed the men were quick to correct any who became too familiar. She understood they were making sure the boys saw her as an adult to respect, not an easy mark. Though she adjusted her behavior accordingly, she couldn't resist an occasional hug of a younger boy or teasing the older ones right back as they made comments about her being a "rich white lady" who couldn't play basketball or beat them on the *Star Wars* arcade. She impressed them with her serve on the tennis court, however.

She conducted a handful of tours through the house and grounds. A couple of boys had more than a passing interest in her library and the gardens. One asked her specific questions about the art pieces scattered throughout the house. Finding out he was an accomplished graffiti artist, she showed him some of the books she had about art history and let him hang out in her reading room to look through those.

She'd been told plenty of times she'd be a good mother. She knew the best way to interact with children was to be attentive and not patronizing, and project a firmness that came with the expectation of respect on both sides. By teaching children like this about a world larger than their own, they were learning the behavior that would help them succeed, if they developed that critical strength of character Lawrence had mentioned.

It made her think of the submissive cravings she'd kept so well hidden, channeled into something else for so long. Dale had helped bring her into that world, and was showing her she could exist there and still keep who she was. Actually, she could be more of who she was, by integrating both. When the graffiti artist paged through one of the books, he unconsciously dropped his tough street talk and attitude to ask questions and respond to her own enthusiasm about it. Everyone assumed disguises to cope, to meet expectations. How rare a gift it was, to be truly oneself with another.

She'd been able to be herself with Roy, except that one part. Could she be all of herself with Dale, not just the submissive side she was exploring?

Take your own advice, Athena. Just enjoy the day, and the time you have with him. This was her first relationship after her husband's death. It was possible it was nothing more than a bridge to what she'd eventually settle on, but she didn't like the word *settle*. Did she still feel Dale was too larger-than-life to be a permanent part of her life, that the strong Master was merely her tour guide on a fantasy? When she had that thought, she was leaning against the chain-link fence at the tennis courts. Turning her head, she saw him on a bench by the basketball court, calling out encouragement or insults while Neil played a scrimmage with several of the kids. One of the younger boys was sitting next to Dale, unconsciously mimicking his pose as they razzed the players together.

Dale's concentration was on the game, his expression changing for quick smiles or sneers as Neil threw back insults. His body language was easy. He was having a good day. She had intimate knowledge of that body. She'd likely have intimate knowledge of it again sometime very soon. Maybe tonight. They hadn't slept in her master bedroom since the bed had been changed.

The first night after Hector and his men had done the switch, she'd gone to the guestroom. Lynn hadn't yet changed out the bedding, so she'd slipped under the covers of the bed that had been hers and Roy's for so long. But the bed was in a different room. The surroundings changed the feeling of it, telling her she'd made the right decision.

Though she'd shed a few tears as she returned to the other one, she'd since become used to the different feel of it. Even so, each night when she lay down to go to sleep, she ran her hand over the empty side, registering how it was no longer sculpted by the hollows Roy had left there. Would Dale be part of her life long enough for that side of the bed to bear his imprint? An imprint that would deepen from nights of passionate lovemaking, expand from her sleeping close to him, draped over his body. Or would it bear a couple of different imprints over time?

Her mind recoiled from that thought. She was amazed she wanted Dale there so soon, but perhaps it said something about her state of mind toward him that if she envisioned anyone there, it was him. She wasn't sure she had the strength to be involved with a man who didn't understand her the way Dale seemed to know her.

Deciding she was just worrying herself without purpose—because none of her thoughts changed a damn thing about her feelings or actions today—she threw herself back into play with the boys.

By the time they all settled down for pizza and movie time in the theater room, she was worn out, but in a good way. When she was sitting on the back wall, Neil and Lawrence came and sat down on either side of her. She offered them both a smile, noting they didn't look as tired as she was, but it was obvious the boys had given them a workout.

"You are utterly awesome," Lawrence stated frankly. "The kids have had a great day."

"That's your doing," she said. "I just provided the venue. I had a great time, too. I've been thinking about making it a monthly event."

"Not weekly?" Neil teased. Close up, he had tawny brown eyes and close-cropped sandy hair, as well as a sprinkling of freckles. If he wore a bill cap and she saw him lounging shirtless in a bass boat on the bayou, it would match her image of him as a Louisiana good old boy, reinforced by the drawl to his words. She chuckled.

"I'm not energetic enough for that, but I think we could work out doing something like this on a regular basis with the Y. There's a city grant to fund inner-city youth programs and . . ." As she fell into a conversation with them about that, another idea sparked in her mind, one she filed away to discuss with Dale at a later time.

Speak of the devil. He'd appeared at one of the entrances to the theater and was scanning the room, even as he engaged a few of the boys in conversation. When his gaze latched onto her, making it obvious whom he was seeking, her body and heart tightened in all the right places. Seeing him at a distance all day, not being able to touch or kiss him the way she wanted, but getting close enough to enjoy his scent, the sound of his voice, all that was enough to spike her libido.

Watching him work with Neil and Lawrence had just enhanced it. All three of them were powerful, charismatic characters. Their clean, direct communication, the dry humor they enjoyed, and an unmistakable sense of brotherhood that synced their movements and thoughts in a fascinating way, increased their magnetism. It gave a woman a good feeling just to be around them. Though Dale had said Neil and Lawrence were still single, she couldn't imagine how difficult it was for the wives and children of such men, having them half a world away, deployed on dangerous missions for months at a time. Maybe she'd plan another pool day for Dale and his fellow SEALs and their families.

While her motives were certainly pure, she couldn't help imagining her pool area full of muscular men like these three. Playing pool volleyball, muscles sleek and wet, swim trunks weighed down so when they went up for the ball, she'd see that strip of pale skin below the hip bone, the upper curve of tight buttocks . . .

She imagined the three of them surrounding her, Dale commanding her as her Master as Neil and Lawrence removed her clothes, all three of them touching her, kissing her . . .

She started out of the unexpected daydream. Being shared was something she'd never contemplated, and she didn't think she was really doing so now. It was just too nice a fantasy to resist, given that she was being flanked by two sweaty, muscular young men, and she had her Master eying her across the room the way the boys had eyed the juicy burgers and fries she'd provided for lunch.

When Dale moved in their direction, she noticed his gait was more pronounced. He'd been on his feet quite a while today, doing a variety of physically exerting tasks. However, his expression said he wasn't going to give her time to nurse that thought. As he drew closer, he offered his hand. She immediately put her hand in his grasp, let herself be tugged to her feet. That first touch was so welcome, it shivered across her skin. He registered it, his blue-green eyes flickering.

"If you two don't mind, I'm going to take Athena off for a little break. She looks beat."

"And if we do mind?" Neil teased him, latching onto the hem of Athena's T-shirt as if he was going to tug her back down on his knee. It was so close to her fantasy, her body responded to the flirting, her fingers tightening on Dale's. "She's too awesome, Master Chief. Lawrence and I have decided to keep her."

"I'd rethink that, son. This old frogman is more than capable of taking both your legs off at the knee." Dale gave him a half smile, but he moved Athena decidedly into his grasp and away from them, making the other two men grin.

"You ever get tired of his cranky and overbearing attitude, Athena, you know where to find us," Lawrence put in helpfully.

"Yeah. In an unmarked grave, you keep that up." As he guided her out of the theater, Dale threw a look over his shoulder, leaving them chuckling.

He guided her with purpose away from the recreation area, into the northwest gardens and well away from the area the boys occupied. Bemused, she saw he was headed to one of the potting sheds placed at strategic points through the extensive grounds. The moment they reached it, he pushed her against the outside wall, his mouth capturing hers with hot hunger. She made a matching sound in her throat and gripped his shoulders, hanging on. She *was* tired, but need was pulsing between her legs, in the aching cavern under her breasts, all of her craving to be filled by his touch, his desire.

"Christ, I've wanted to do that all day. C'mon." Now he opened the shed door, drew her into the small space with him and closed it securely. Enough light came through the window to allow the moonlight and solar lights to frame his silhouette. As her gaze shifted to the floor, she saw two spare lounge chair pads had been laid out, covered with a trio of towels. He'd even smuggled out a couple of throw cushions to use as pillows. He'd prepared for this. The knowledge only intensified the needy feeling inside her.

He wasn't ready to take her down yet, though. Instead, he lifted her onto the workbench. This was the shed where Hector kept his tools, and there was a vise on either end of the bench. Dale looped something around her wrists, zip ties for tomato stakes. He threaded two lengths of ropes through them before cinching the ties to a more snug fit. Tugging one of her arms toward the end of the workbench, he secured the rope ends in one vise, turning the handle so it clamped down, held them fast. Then he did the same to the other side so she was sitting on the bench, her arms spread out to her sides and held by both vises. He did it so efficiently, with no wasted effort, it took her breath away. She had no time to react. Well, her mind didn't. Her body reacted with eager pleasure.

"Dale . . ."

He pushed up the T-shirt, shoving her bra cups down to capture her breasts in his hands. She moaned, pressed into his grip. When he put his head down, nipping at her throat, he squeezed her curves. "I'm feeling a little mean, girl. I caught you hanging out with those two young studs, and I think it's time I remind you who your Master is."

The rough threat made her arch into his touch even more. She turned her head, trying to tease his brow with her lips, the tip of her tongue, and then made a soft cry as he bit her throat. When he lifted his head, locking those blue-green eyes upon her, she grasped the challenge with both bound hands. Tossing back her hair, she gave him a sultry look.

"How can you do that if I'm up here, rather than down on my knees where I can serve my Master best?"

He muttered an oath. Rather than responding with words, he pulled open her jeans and slid his hand into her panties. He'd made her wet merely by looking at her in the movie room, but he tsked at her slippery state, giving her a stern look. "Just as I thought. You were fantasizing about them, weren't you?"

"Just about the two of them . . . touching me . . . under your command."

His fingers stilled, his gaze sharpening on her face. She wasn't sure if she should say such a thing, but he'd made it clear that he expected honesty from her. "Is that something you think about, girl? Me sharing you?"

"No." She put the truth of it in her voice, her eyes. "I like the fantasy, but the reality is . . . just you."

She could imagine a wide range of things, but when it came to what she wanted when she woke in the middle of the night, whose hands she wanted on her, demanding her surrender, this was all that, with nothing lacking.

He studied her, as if verifying she wasn't stroking his ego. Whatever he saw made him put his mouth over hers. Her fingers tightened in her bonds, curling over the ropes as he kissed her endlessly, fingers plunging into her hair, slipping over her throat, her nape and shoulders. The man knew just how aroused a woman could get from being touched from the shoulders up. Done right, everything below the shoulders caught fire. She kissed him back with the fervor of an inferno. "Please tell me," she whispered. "Please."

He pressed his mouth to her temple. "Tell you what?"

"What did you think when I said that? The truth."

Tugging her head back with both hands snarled in her hair, he bit her throat again, sharper this time, making her suck in a breath. His body pushed urgently between her legs, and she flexed against him, her legs wrapped around his thighs. "I told you, I don't share," he said. "Not you. That may make me a selfish prick, but . . ."

When he began to kiss her again, he put the passion behind the thought into the kiss, a thorough branding with mouth and hands that left her trembling.

"Let me please you, Master. Please."

"You don't do anything but, girl." Cutting the zip ties with a box cutter on the workbench, he slid his hands under her arms and lowered her to her knees on one of the cushions. She rested her palms on his thighs and looked up. His face was in darkness, but she sensed he was thinking about her words. He was a confident man, one who didn't cut himself any slack about having half a leg. She'd spoken of her fantasy about his two friends without hesitation because she'd never thought of Dale as anything less than a whole man. But when it was silent like this, she knew it would be in his mind. She'd seen hints of it when he watched Neil play basketball, his whole, healthy body feinting and spinning with the kids.

He'd believed her, rationally, yes, but she wanted to prove it. With actions, not words.

Her fingers slid up his thighs, thumbs drifting along that intriguing crease of denim between testicles and hip. Then she unbuckled his belt, and slipped the button, drawing down the zipper. When she found him under the soft cotton of his boxers, he drew in a gratifying breath. He helped shove the jeans down a little further, making it easier for her to put her hungry mouth over him. The moment her lips touched the broad head and spread around it, drawing his thick cock into heated moistness, his hand dropped to her crown. He gripped her hair hard, growling as she sucked him in, hollowing her cheeks and flicking him with her tongue.

This time he was letting her put her hands on him, and she was going to make sure he liked it enough to let her do it again. A lot. Circling the thick base of his cock with her fingers, she used the other hand to grip the side of his thigh, fingers teasing his buttock as the muscles shifted under her grip, thrusting him deeper into her mouth.

He had a wonderful organ, so hard and pulsing, wide enough to stretch her lips, long enough to take him to the back of her throat and beyond. He put his other hand on her shoulder, thumb sliding beneath the collar of her T-shirt to catch her bra strap and tug as she serviced her Master. Her panties had soaked through to the crotch of her loosened jeans, such that she felt the dampness as both rubbed against her when she shifted. All the pent-up pleasure of watching him from a distance today was now channeled into this. She made little needy noises against his steel flesh as she worked him in her mouth, drew him toward climax.

"Fuck, as good as that is, I want your cunt. Right now." He caught her arm and brought her to her feet, despite her noise of protest. In a movement too swift to follow, he'd yanked her jeans to her knees, and brought them both down to the lounge cushions. He didn't give her time to take the pants all the way off. Instead, he rolled to his back and, with the strength of his upper body alone, slid her on top of him. He guided himself between her closed thighs, held that way by the jeans and panties still up at her knees. It made the channel even more narrow, so his angle of penetration was high, his cock rubbing against the wall of her cunt as he pushed into her. The feeling was indescribable. He put both hands on her ass and started shoving her down on him fully, controlling all her movements, rubbing her clit against his rougher skin. She shot up toward climax in record time.

"Master . . . I'm too close. I'm going to—"

"Let me hear you," he growled.

She did, crying out her release. She gripped his shirt, feeling the solid man beneath, her thighs strained cords against his hips as he rocked them both to completion. She wasn't the only one driven crazy by their chaste proximity throughout the day. He thrust up into her, letting go with a groan, fingers clamping down on her bare ass to hold her pinned, working himself in her. She gasped and continued to make helpless noises of pleasure until he slowed to a halt with one last shuddering, satisfied grunt.

"Jesus," he murmured. He pushed her head down into the opening between his shoulder and the side of his head, pressing his face into her hair.

She couldn't agree more with the reverent expletive. She held on to his shoulders, balanced on his body like the firm deck of a ship, the world around still rocking, making her dizzy. She turned her lips to his ear, but she wanted to do even more for him. Despite the constraints of her clothing, she pushed herself up and wriggled down his body until she was kneeling between his legs again. Cradling his semiturgid cock in her hands, she bent, put her mouth on him once more. She tasted herself and his seed, and began to clean him with caressing licks, suckling his flesh, making him twitch a little at the sensitivity, but he didn't stop her, merely reaching down to stroke her hair, fondle it.

"You keep doing that, girl, I'll put you on your back next."

"Why do you think I'm doing it?"

He chuckled, the sound vibrating under her touch. "I might have to call in Neil or Lawrence after all. Make them keep up with your demands. I think you'll wear them out first."

"I'd rather wait on you."

He gripped her forearm, telling her he wanted her to come up and lie next to him. She did, sliding her hand over his testicles and cock, offering one last caress before she put her hand beneath his T-shirt and rested it on his sectioned stomach. *A different man from Roy.* Recalling their conversation, she traced those muscles, the shiny smooth skin of a scar. Pressing her nose against his side, she inhaled his unique Dale scent. Then she rested her cheek over his heart.

"Master Chief?" she asked, remembering what Neil had called him.

His chest rumbled with a half chuckle. "My rating in the SEALs. I've told them not to call me that, now that I'm retired, but sometimes they forget."

She expected it was because he was still so obviously in command, and the world felt like a safer place to Neil and Lawrence—and her—when that was the case. *Master Chief. Master.* She liked it.

"Should we be getting back to the kids, help Neil and Lawrence?"

"Naw, they'll keep for a while. The kids are exhausted, too. Most of them'll probably doze off during the movie and we'll have to wake them up with a foghorn to get them back on the bus."

"They could stay here tonight—"

"Oh no." He gave her bare ass a firm squeeze. "You've been a very generous hostess, Mrs. Summers, but I promise you Lynn will quit if she has to confront the horror of three-dozen teenage boys using your bathrooms in the morning. Plus, we told their parents we'd have them back tonight. The ones that give a rat's ass, that is, which means about half."

She thought about Jason, the other boys she'd met today. How many of them would actually make it, given how few good influences they had in their corner? She'd be adding all of them to her prayer list.

"Are your parents still alive?" she asked at last.

"Yeah, my mom is. She lives up in Michigan, near my two sisters. She remarried after my dad died, and the new guy makes her happy, but he's always kind of rubbed me the wrong way, so we don't really see one another too much. Around the holidays, mostly. It's all right. My dad and I were much closer than my mom and me. My two sisters have also provided the all-important grandkids for her."

"How did he . . ."

"Lung cancer. Chain-smoker since he was a teenager, knocked him down in his forties." Dale turned his head, pressed an absent kiss to her temple. He stroked the line of her back beneath her T-shirt. "Lived long enough to see me graduate BUD/S, which meant the world to us both. He was an enlisted Army grunt, served in Vietnam. That was where he picked up the smoking habit, and he couldn't ever kick it. He was adamant about none of us getting hooked, though. First time he caught me with a cigarette, he ground up some with a couple raw eggs and made me drink the whole thing. Cured me forever of the urge. I thought I was going to die of puking."

"I'll bet." She smiled against his warm flesh. His heartbeat was slow and steady.

"So . . . I believed you when you said you weren't interesting in being shared. But I want to know why."

She considered it. "Why do you not want to share me?"

"That doesn't work as an answer." He took a proprietary grip of one buttock. "My reasons have to do with an overload of testosterone. You don't have any of that, thank God."

She smiled at that. "That's not all of it, though. You've shared subs with other Masters at the club. Like . . . with Gerald."

"Because they aren't mine. They belong to me for that session, and the session is about pushing boundaries, exploring the things the sub wants. Even though I'm completely involved, absorbed in it, there's a certain level of detachment. I'm facilitating what the sub wants, integrating it with my intentions and desires. I'm not trying to get into her heart and soul, just her body and mind."

She swallowed. "But you are trying to get into my heart and soul?"

He tipped her face up with his strong fingers, ran them along her jaw as his gaze caressed her face. "You invited me in, Athena, and I liked what I saw. That first time, the way you opened yourself to me, stripped yourself bare, inside and out; it called to something inside of me, something I haven't had before. That's why it's different."

He gave her a not-so-gentle pinch with the other hand. Her thighs were slippery against one another when she twitched in response. "You're not getting off the hook," he said. "Why don't you want to be shared?"

It took a few moments to marshal her thoughts, but he waited on her. "Women are supposed to be adventurous and want to do it all, these days," she said slowly. "Not think of sex as so significant. But to me . . . the marriage oath was sacred. Keeping yourself for that one person, and him for you. If you care enough about someone else to create that bond, that suggests that whatever you need, physically, you can find with one another, if you have the patience and desire to uncover it. I know we're not married . . . but I still view it the same way. If I want to be with a man, I want to belong to him, and only him. And him to see me the same way. As his and his alone. It sounds archaic, I know—"

"No, it doesn't. Or if it does, it's as archaic as an ancient temple. And just as sacred, like you said." He lifted her chin again. "I find you to be a remarkable woman, Athena. Honest and confident about what you want. That's rare, not old-fashioned."

The praise warmed her, and he bent his head, tasted her lips. "Will you stay tonight?" she asked when he broke the kiss.

He gave her a look of regret. "I have to help get the kids home. Do you have to work tomorrow?"

She quelled her disappointment that he wouldn't be sharing her bed. "Not until the afternoon. Why don't I bring you brunch?"

"Sounds like a date." He gave her a searching look. "I would love nothing better than to wake up with you, Athena. This is moving pretty fast between us, isn't it?"

"Too fast?" she asked. Had he read her mind, or did he share her concerns?

"Can't tell. It moves like it moves. The trick is to make the in-between time quick, but draw out every moment like this"—he leaned down, kissed her again, proving the point by keeping the kiss going long enough she was breathless when he was done—"so it feels like the kind of forever you want. Then you have no regrets."

THIRTEEN

She dreamed of him. She was on her knees at the club, gazing up at him. She was wearing a collar, a strip of velvet with a pendant, but a collar nonetheless, and she loved having it on, loved feeling his fingers brush against it. He snapped a tether to it, linking them together. Then she heard laughter.

Turning, she saw Jimmy pointing at her, a whole legion of Dommes staring at her with derision. Their glossed lips were stretched with cruel laughter as male Dominants eyed her with speculative avarice. As they closed in around her, Dale vanished, the tether loose on the ground for anyone to pick up. She scrambled for it, but a large booted foot stepped on it, and she looked up into the face of a bald-headed, beefy Dom she'd never seen before. He picked it up as one of the Dommes appeared next to him, cocking a latex-clad hip.

You gave up control. Now you're ours. Our little poodle bitch. Sit up and beg, bitch . . .

She woke up in darkness, her heart beating rapidly, fingers curled into her pillow. She didn't know any of the people in the dream except Jimmy. She knew Dommes in the club, but they were courteous and pleasant to her. Some of them she considered friends, at least inside the club. She had no idea how they'd react to her appearing as Dale's submissive, but of course they wouldn't react in such a criminally horrible way.

So the problem was in her head, wasn't it? If she publicly showed herself that way, she would be letting down a wall, letting them see her true self. When the Dom stepped on the tether, the way she'd felt in the dream was all too familiar to her. She'd struggled with it the first year after Roy died—a loss of security.

Having a significant other felt like a fence against harm, because someone had a permanent connection to her and was concerned about her whereabouts. Both her parents were dead, and other than Roy's father and his one sister, Evie, the rest of his family hadn't seen her as suitable for him. Roy hadn't cared about their opinion, of course. Once he passed, his brothers had made some noises about trying to take some of his self-made fortune. They claimed that since he'd capitalized on connections made through the family business, some of his estate belonged to them, but she'd had a lawyer viciously quash that attempt. That was the last she heard of them.

As for Evie and Amy, she'd set them up a trust fund to ensure they would never have to worry about money, including college tuition for Amy. Roy had asked her to watch out for them and she always would, both because it was his wish and because they'd loved him, with or without money.

After the unsettling dream, she left the bed, went down to her reading nook and wrapped herself in her blanket. She brought a cup of hot tea with her to settle her nerves. She told herself it was nothing; merely what the late hours of the night could do the mind, creating demons and nightmares where there were none. But she really wished Dale was here.

Too fast. You're getting too deep, too fast.

No. She was in control. It was all right. A dream held no power over her. She kept telling herself that, even as her subconscious beat an uneasy tattoo against her lower abdomen.

Too fast.

I n the morning, the dream lingered with her, but she did her best to outrun it. She rushed through getting dressed and showered, only to find there wasn't an overabundance of things to do at the house. The boys had done a remarkable job of cleaning up after themselves, chaperoned by the eagle-eyed SEALs. Her housekeeping staff had anything else needed well in hand, like putting away the extra equipment and furniture, tidying up the courts and vacuuming the theater and arcade area. Lynn even had time to help her make up the brunch she was taking to Dale.

They made omelets, bacon, sausages and biscuits. Lynn had suggested garlic pepper in the omelets, which Athena agreed gave them a little kick. The housekeeper sampled Athena's biscuits with an approving nod, then added a couple fresh tomatoes to the basket. "To cut up over the breakfast to give it color and flavor." She winked. "He's a nice man, Mr. Rousseau. He was so courteous yesterday, helping me carry things to the kitchen."

"He is a nice man," Athena agreed. Sometimes not so nice, in ways that made her shiver with pleasure. The thought didn't necessarily calm her nerves, though. They stayed on edge on the drive over to Dale's, but once she pulled into the junkyard, she shoved it all down, determined to enjoy her morning with him. It was only brunch, for heaven's sake.

He was already up, and on his second cup of coffee. Her timing was good. He'd just finished cleaning the dog runs and doing the feeding. As he came up to the apartment to join her and lowered himself into a chair at the kitchen table, the two of them making general conversation, she noticed he wasn't moving as fast as normal. She was right; he'd overdone it yesterday. Yet when her glance lingered on his leg, the way he was massaging the knee, she saw his jaw tighten in warning. Fine, she wouldn't take them down that road again. But why wouldn't the stubborn man let her help him? She could have come earlier, helped him with the dogs.

As she kept up a bright chatter of conversation, she reminded herself he'd been doing for himself for a long time. He'd told her quite clearly he didn't need her for that. He'd also implied there were other volunteers for the shelter who could pitch in. If he'd ask for their help. *Yeah, right.*

All right, fine. If he wouldn't let her pitch in on the manual labor, there were other ways she could help.

"When I was talking to Neil and Lawrence about grants for the kids yesterday, I had an idea for your place." She put his plate down in front of him, closing her hand briefly on his broad shoulder before turning back to the stove. "If you're interested."

"Why don't you stop flitting around the kitchen and come eat your breakfast?" he said, blue-green eyes tracking her. "You can tell me about it. Are you all right today?"

"Yes, certainly." She raised her brow as if surprised he'd asked. She hadn't gone back to sleep after her dream, but she was wired like she'd downed one of those energy drinks. She slid into the spot, picked at her eggs.

"You mentioned the storage building, and I know the trust will help cover that, but your main goal is to find good homes for the dogs, keep them rotating through here so you can help as many as possible. That's as important as maintaining the facility."

"True." But his look was wary. "What did you have in mind?"

"Think about the material you have to draw people here. It's perfect. The SEAL who died, his father running it in his honor because of the first dog he rescued. Now you, a veteran with one leg, continue to run it. It plays perfectly. It—"

His face turned to granite. "Whoa. Stop there. 'It plays perfectly'?"

"You know what I mean."

"Yeah, I do. No."

"Why not? If you just—"

"Athena."

"But it makes perfect sense. Why wouldn't you—"

"Because I said so."

She came up short at what was nothing short of a barked command, the tone he'd use to bring a raw recruit to heel. She saw herself again at the end of that loose tether in her dream. Was that what a submissive was to him? *You gave up control . . .*

"This isn't about your pride," she said icily. "I assumed you'd want what was best for the dogs. And—"

"That's not what this is. I will see myself in hell before I capitalize on what Ed and Eddie went through." He smacked his lower leg, the sound of metal making her flinch. "And if I wanted to be some sob story news program—"

"I didn't mean it that way. I'm trying to help."

"No, you're not. You're doing it again. You—"

"No, I'm not," she fired back. "Every time I disagree with you, it's not because I'm trying to run things. I am allowed to have my own opinions and ideas."

"Yeah, you are. Never said you weren't." He sat back, bracing his hands on his thighs. "This was why I knew it was a mistake for you to see me the other day, without the leg. And seeing me this morning, when you can tell it's hurting. It kicks off this mode in you."

"Don't you do that." The surge of anger that moved through her was so intense she felt lightheaded. "Don't you turn that day into something wrong and ugly. Don't twist it and use it against me right now because it makes you angry to be vulnerable."

His gaze narrowed, became dangerous. "Then don't use my perceived vulnerability as a way to grab the reins. You will lose that fight, Athena."

"It's not about winning and losing—"

"It's always about winning and losing," he shot back.

"If there's an enemy. You see me as your enemy." She saw it in his angry expression, his defensive body language.

"No. What the hell is—" He reclaimed his temper, perhaps registering the stricken look, but by then she'd done what she never did. She bolted.

S he could have run to her car, left him there, because as capable as he was, he couldn't run, not faster than her. But she couldn't leave. Instead she ran deeper into the junkyard, until her heart was pounding high in her throat and she was even dizzier. She'd gone up a hill, was standing at the boundary of the property. A high chain-link fence with barbed wire marked it.

She realized she was crying. It seemed she spent half her time with Dale crying or close to it. It couldn't be normal, could it? She also realized she wasn't alone.

The two Rottweilers had followed her. Had Dale sent them after her, making sure someone was watching over her amid all the piles of scrap metal that could pose a potential hazard to someone running blindly through them? She wouldn't be surprised if he had.

She lowered herself to a car's backseat, propped on a pile of tires like a weird retro couch. They'd probably pay a thousand dollars for it in New York City. She put her hands over her face and leaned forward against her knees, trying to get the aching to stop. Why hadn't she run toward her car? *An enemy.*

She'd learned to accept that sense of aloneness that came with being a widow, no matter how many people surrounded her. It was like there was an umbilical cord between married people, and the loss of one left it severed, dangling. In a matter of days, Dale had made her feel not alone, which made this all the more excruciating, a reopening of a carefully tended wound.

She knew he'd been about to ask her what the hell was wrong with her, and that was the question, wasn't it? That dream had unsettled her, but it was a symptom. So much was changing so fast, and one part of her embraced it, refused to slow down, while another felt like she was clinging to a cliff's edge, with no one to grab her if she let go.

She was being ridiculous. She shouldn't have come, should have made an excuse, backed out of the brunch. She'd known she was out of sorts, something not right with her. She shouldn't have inflicted that on him. He was probably wondering if being with the crazy girl was such a good idea after all. She should retrace her steps, make as dignified an apology as could be managed, get in her car and drive away.

When she heard his footsteps, it loosened some feelings and tightened others, more of the same thrilling and exhausting duality. She didn't know what to do, so she simply sat there, her head down, as the cushion next to her gave way under his weight.

"Come here." His arm was already around her shoulders, enfolding her. He didn't just bring her to his chest. He scooped her up, moved her into his lap and held her.

"I'm sorry. I know you think I've lost my mind. I'm not—"

"Shut up."

She shut up, pressing her face into his shirt, her shoulders quivering against the strength of his arms around her.

"Shh. Easy girl. Shh."

"I wasn't trying to be adversarial. I—"

"The last thing you are is my enemy, girl. I'd cut out my tongue if I could take back anything I said that made you think that." He muttered a curse, brought her closer. "Damn it. Fuck. Just . . . be quiet a moment. Let's both breathe."

"It's like a roller coaster. Everything's so perfect one day, and then the next I feel so afraid and unsettled. Things just keep going wrong. I don't think . . ."

"That's what happens when two stubborn, independent, middle-aged people are falling in love, Athena."

Her gaze snapped up to his. Though his expression was still tense, he gave her a wry glance. "You have a better explanation, Ms. Know-It-All?"

She closed her mouth, a weird tingle of sensation threading through her chest. She wanted to be with him every second, and thought of him when she wasn't. His kisses made her knees weak, and his gaze could make her breath stop in her throat. It wasn't the first time it had crossed her mind, but given that women tended to indulge romantic fantasies, and she and Dale hadn't known one another very long, it hadn't been totally credible. But by implication, Dale had said he was falling in love with her as well. Which made the possibility far more real.

She'd fallen for Roy during the first weekend of meeting him. He'd told her it had taken him only the first moment.

"Wow. Uh . . ."

"Here." He eased her into a sitting position next to him. Across from them, the dogs were lying down in the shade of a battered Ford Fairlane. Dale kept an arm around her waist. "Sorry. Didn't mean to knock your feet out from under you."

"Did you mean it?"

"It's how I perceive the issue. I think it's the truth." He met her gaze. "Only you can say what's happening in your own head. But the way you worry and fuss over me, and the few nights we've spent together, the way things take on a life of their own, it sure as hell suggests that's what's happening. I've been a Master awhile, Athena. I've seen the way it looks for people who are wrapped up in each other above and beyond the Dom/sub stuff."

"Yes." Session euphoria could easily be mistaken for enduring emotion, like teenage hormones, but during aftercare one saw the truth of it, in the way committed couples related when the session was over.

He rubbed a hand over his jaw. "Let me do a better job of saying what I was trying to say. We've talked about this. You were trained, so to speak, to run things, to handle things. An ultimate service sub, if you want to think of it that way, trained by your husband to be his Mistress. As such, you equate your worth with service. It's a fine, noble thing in ninety-nine percent of that incredible, amazing life of yours that gives so much to others. But that's not what I want from you. That's not what you came to me for. We both know it. I'm your Master, Athena. With me, you let go of all of it."

"But . . . what does that give you?"

"I've told you." He chuckled, but it was a grim sound. "It gives me everything, sweetheart. That's the way I'm made. When you surrender, when you look at me with that dazzling, mindless trust in your expression, when I feel how you hand over every part of yourself to me, and you accept pleasure and pain at my hand . . . That's like a drug to me. And I *do* like the service side of you. I like it when you make me a sandwich and sit at my feet in that thin, pretty robe of yours, or nothing at all, so I can enjoy looking at what's mine. I want to own you, Athena. That's my drug as well.

"You're a confident, independent woman, a remarkable person, and I respect all of that. But when you're sitting at my feet, I fucking love the feeling that you're my property. To protect and cherish, to fuck when I want. I know you get hot and bothered, thinking about it like that, too. There's nothing PC about it, but we both get off on it, right?"

She nodded. She was getting hot and bothered right now, hearing the words come from his distracting mouth.

"But because of what we both bring to the table—my leg, your husband—it's a fine line. I don't mind you caring about me, wanting to help me, any more than I expect you to mind me wanting to do the same for you. But . . . Roy sounds like a great guy, so don't take this the wrong way. I don't need to be handled like him, and when you get uptight about all this, you go into that mode. That's not the way it works for you and me. Understand?"

"I think so. I don't know. I still have trouble with that part." She let out an unhappy sigh, pushing her hair away from her face.

"That's the biggest step in letting go." He touched her cheek. "You have to decide you're ready to let go of one relationship and move into another. You keep straddling that fence. I don't mind it, much, because I understand how hard that is, but at some point you have to choose, Athena. Or I'll walk. That's not an ultimatum to push you. I just don't want to settle for less."

Hadn't she recoiled from that word herself? *Settle.* The success of her marriage, the failure of his, had brought them to the same point, the same resolve. "So what does that mean to you?" she asked. "How will it look and feel to you, if I've made that choice?"

"You'll know when I know," he said. "I won't be able to lead you to that, Athena. But when it happens, we'll both know you've given me everything, and not just when I have you tied up and you're lost in subspace. When and if it happens," he added gently, "it doesn't mean you don't love your husband. It means you understand you're still alive, and moving forward. Which I think Roy wanted, if he's the type of guy you described. I know if you were mine and I died, I'd want you to be in good hands, loving hands. I wouldn't want you to be alone in this world. In fact, no offense to Roy, but screw that. *I* don't want you alone in this world. You're becoming important to me, Athena, in a way that might get a little scary to you, because I don't do things halfway once I'm sure of myself, and I'm a pretty decisive guy."

"Really? I hadn't noticed." The corner of her mouth tipped up. "You seem to waffle over the littlest things. It's tedious and annoying."

He ruffled her hair. "Be careful, woman. You get too mouthy and I have ways of dealing with that."

She smiled. They sat silently for a few moments before she spoke again. "The aggravating thing is, I'm *really* good at this kind of stuff, the fund-raising and such. I just keep sabotaging it by offering it the wrong way, at the wrong times. Despite that, I hope you'll let me help. It doesn't have to be me trying to control things."

"You didn't ruin anything. The ideas are good ones. I trust you to help with that, when I ask for it. I just . . . I know that what you're saying would help, but I am *not* this missing leg." His jaw got that rock-hard look to it again, his eyes flashing. "Maybe it's selfish of me, but even for a good cause, I won't exploit it. Not when other guys came home in body bags, leaving widows and kids without dads, and I'm the lucky bastard who gets to still be here. You understand?"

She did, and it matched everything she already knew about him. It also gave her a twist of guilt and self-reflection. So much of what she'd done for Roy had been tailoring herself to his needs. At some point, had she'd stopped seeing Roy, the whole man, and instead defined him by the things he needed from her? Dale was very much his own man, and from his behavior yesterday with the kids, and even now, talking about it, she knew he was telling her the truth. He respected who and what she was. But he wouldn't allow it to adversely direct what they were becoming together. There was a relief in that, if she would accept it. She didn't have to run the show.

She saw that, but she also wasn't going to dump all that responsibility on him. She had to learn how to deal with uncertainty in their relationship better. Once she managed that, there were ways their roads could cross, intertwine, help one another. How a relationship was supposed to evolve.

She nodded, but she should have known he'd seen deeper than that. "Now that we've dealt with that," he said, "what was this about this morning? You were out of sorts. What was going on?"

"I can't really talk about it right now. Or rather . . . I wish we wouldn't. Can we talk about it at another time?"

He gave her a thorough look, one that made her cheeks flush a little, her eyes lower. She knew it was somewhat cowardly, but it was too much for one day. Her shoulders eased when he sighed. "All right. But we're going to have to talk about it more at some point. You don't get out of it forever."

She shook her head. "I'm sorry I interrupted our breakfast."

"Well, if you're really sorry, you'll run your pretty ass back up to the apartment and bring it back here. We can finish eating in these lovely surroundings." He nodded to the chain-link fence, the junk cars around them. "Best view in the city."

"I'll be back in a few moments." She smiled, but paused. "Can I do anything, for your leg?"

When he gave her his look, she met his squarely. "I want to help, Master. Please let me help."

"You're relentless." He gave her a look of wry exasperation though, making her feel better. "You are helping. It's hurting like a son of a bitch this morning. If you bring my breakfast back here, that will give it a break."

"If you want, you could take off the prosthesis and I could bring your crutches." She held her breath, anticipating a growl, but he lifted a shoulder.

"I may take it off when I get back to the apartment, but for now all I want is my breakfast. And your company. Those boys wore me out."

"You and me both. I felt stiff as an old woman when I got out of my chair this morning."

His brow lifted. "You slept in your reading room. Did you fall asleep reading?"

She shook her head. "No . . . . I had trouble sleeping. I went down there in the middle of the night, stayed there until morning."

"Athena . . ."

"You promised," she said, backpedaling toward the apartment.

His gaze narrowed. "I may not be able to run as fast as you, but the dogs are trained to bring SUVs to a halt. One small contrary woman is no problem at all."

She chuckled at the threat. Even so, she felt his eyes following her as she retreated. He wouldn't let it go, she knew. He was as relentless as he accused her of being. But one issue per morning was enough. He was right; there was a fine line of power between the two of them, and she wasn't entirely easy with how to reconcile them yet.

As she reached the apartment, her phone signaled an incoming text.

Look in the top drawer of my nightstand. I bought you a gift.
Put it on before you come back.

When she went to the drawer and saw what it was, her eyes widened. Given the emotional turmoil of the past few moments, she wasn't sure if she was up to anything sexual, but her body seemed to have different ideas after seeing his gift. He wasn't here to argue with, anyway, and she wasn't going to debate it over a text screen. With only another brief hesitation, she shimmied out of her panties to step into the straps and position the clit stimulator in its appropriate place. It was shaped like a butterfly, the body pressing against the insides of her labia, the antennae and shaped head snug against her clit. The controls were on the side. He hadn't said to turn it on, but just placing it against her body made it respond. When her phone buzzed again, her cheeks were pink and heated, much like the flesh between her legs.

Where's my food, woman? I'm getting hungry.

It would have made her laugh if she wasn't feeling like a rubber band, stretched between the earlier argument and now this. She put her panties on over the device, then packed the breakfast back in the basket. She transferred their juice into the covered cups that went with the picnic set. They locked into the cup holders on the sides. Nice normal tasks, while her body quivered and her mind fizzed like carbonated water.

Going down the stairs and walking back through the junkyard was an entirely different experience. The stimulator teased the petals of her sex and her clitoris as she walked. It altered her focus, and though she was still unsettled, the unbalanced feeling wasn't unwelcome at all. When she came into his view, the way his intent gaze logged everything only sharpened her response. Her nipples were tight against her bra, the flesh between her legs now slippery.

She put the basket down in front of him and he lifted a hand, keeping her on her feet. "Give me your panties."

Fingers still twitchy, she slid them off, handed them to him. He closed his hand over her wrist, ran a thumb over her wrist pulse. Then he nodded to a Lincoln Town Car about ten paces away. "Go and bend over the trunk. Tuck your skirt up into the waistband so I can see that butterfly and your gorgeous ass."

His look was direct, his tone uncompromising. He was settling all the debris of the morning in a way all her rationalizing seemed incapable of doing. She moved toward the Lincoln, gathering up her skirt.

"Actually, just get rid of it. I want you naked from the waist down. If I had my way, I'd keep you naked all the time."

She imagined Dale sitting at her dining room table, her kneeling naked next to him as he ate his meal, seemingly detached yet so aware of her being there, waiting on his desires while her own overflowed. Hour after hour of being accessible to his every demand. Her pussy became even wetter.

She stepped out of the skirt, set it aside, and then put her elbows on the trunk. Bracing her legs shoulder-width apart, she lifted her ass and was rewarded with a blast of heat from his gaze when she dared a look over her shoulder.

"Little tease. Hook your fingers in the edge below the rear window. I want you stretched out over the trunk, your hips pressed to the back bumper. Legs spread wider so you feel that clit stimulator tight against you."

As she did it, she heard him rise. He'd taken away her ability to look over her shoulder in the elongated position, which she was sure was his intent. He ran his hand down her back, over her backside, checking the straps holding the butterfly against her. He slid his fingers beneath her, verifying it was firmly in place, making her shiver again.

"You stay like this unless you get physically uncomfortable, and then you tell me what's going on. If I ask you a question, you answer it, no matter what else is going on. Got it?"

"Yes sir."

His firm swat left a tingling print on her buttock. "I don't think *sir* is going to cut it today."

"Yes, Master."

"Better." He put his hand between her legs again, and the stimulator began to hum against her clit and labia. She caught her lip between her teeth as he made some other adjustments. With her own vibrator, she usually focused on the clit, the hard and fast climax that direct contact could deliver. This stimulator proved how responsive the slick inner walls of her labia were, those nerve endings building toward the same end, only with a slower, fiercely sweet build that made her shudder in the restrained position he'd imposed.

"The longer it's on, the more the intensity will increase. Eventually it goes back to the original setting and starts over again. Since it divides its time between clit and labia, and I can adjust it so the antenna also tweaks you under your clit hood, I can spend the whole morning watching you go fucking mindless, Athena, your cunt gushing over and over. All while eating this great breakfast you made me."

He gave her another stinging slap, then moved back to the couch. She couldn't see him from where she was, and the angle of the window provided no reflection. But she could hear him taking a seat behind her to eat his breakfast and stare at her naked, exposed body. Her legs were already shaking, responding to the stimulation of the vibrator.

"So what did you do in the middle of the night? Read a book?"

She nodded, then remembered. "Yes, Master."

"Tell me about it." He was eating, because he sounded a little muffled. "Title, what it's about."

The man was a sadist. He'd likely endured interrogation torture as part of SEAL training, but he was no slouch at administering it. As she became more and more aroused, he demanded detailed answers about the book, her job, her childhood, the fucking weather. The intensity of the vibration grew, just as he'd predicted. She started pressing against the bumper in a coital rhythm, rotating her hips, unable to resist the stroke of that stimulator.

"That's nice," he said, his voice husky with heat. "Keep doing that. Lift your ass, show me that my girl wants to be fucked by her Master. Beg for it with your hot little body."

Her nipples were stiff points against the trunk lid, her fingers in a death grip on that edge. "Dale . . . Master . . ."

Roy had told her men liked food, beer and fucking. *Combine all those things? Heaven on earth.* She should have brought Dale a beer.

The orgasm was too close. "I'm going . . . to come."

"Yes, you are. Try to fight it, girl. I want to see you fight and lose."

She did her best, but the stimulator won without much of a contest, her body too revved and eager. She screamed out her pleasure, working her hips against the metal, feeling the sun's heat on her back, in the steel she gripped, but it wasn't yet so hot she couldn't bear it. When she came down, she was jerking, because of course the stimulator changed settings on its own schedule, and for a few excruciating moments it was on the same accelerated intensity. She let out a relieved sound when it at last settled down to the original hum. Even that was almost too much, but Dale didn't seem inclined to stop the device.

He didn't, not until she came twice more. By that third time, she'd lost her grasp on everything but the car. When he came to her, he had to unhook her hands, massage the stiff fingers. She was making little gasping noises like sobs, only she wasn't crying this time. When he opened his jeans, she adjusted her legs, lifting her hips automatically. He made another approving grunt as he slid into her from behind and pressed his big body down on hers, taking her right there against the car.

He was even thicker than usual, proving the effect her performance had on him. He came in less than a dozen thrusts. He had one hand tangled in her hair, the other sliding under her shirt to fondle her breasts in her silky bra. He lifted her off the car enough to spread one hand over both, grip the flesh to hold them together. One nipple was caught between his fingertips where they'd tunneled beneath the cup, the other pressed beneath the heel of his hand.

"There she is. That's my good girl. Sweet, gorgeous woman."

He slid out of her, adjusted his clothes, and then guided the clit stimulator off of her. When he lifted her upper body off the hood and turned her so her hips were propped against the bumper, she watched him slide her panties back onto her legs, then her skirt. He nudged her to her feet, guiding her hands to his shoulders to steady her as he restored her clothing to its proper place. He plucked open the buttons of her shirt, though, so he could continue to caress her breasts, tease her cleavage and trace the lace edges of the bra.

She swayed at the power of that simple sensation. In answer, he made another soothing murmur and drew her to him. As she leaned against his strength, he slid his arms around her, held her close, spoke in her ear.

"What woke you up in the middle of the night, Athena? What had you all wound up this morning?"

When he did this to her, it was easy. She gave him everything, no reservations. Which underscored what a leap of faith it would be when and if she could do it all the time, as he demanded.

"A dream." She mumbled it against his chest. "We were at Release, and you had a collar and leash on me. It felt good, but then . . . Jimmy was pointing, and the female Dommes, they were pointing at me, being unkind. Like I was a fraud. You disappeared, and there were all these male Doms, closing in on me, like they could all have me, because I'd lost control, given it away. I was scared, and . . ." She didn't know how to continue from there.

He sighed, held her closer. "Okay. We'll deal with it, all right?"

"But not today."

"No, not today." He touched her face, guided her gaze up to him. "At some point, we *will* go to Release, and you will go there as my sub. Even if we only go once, and never go again, that's going to happen. If you want me as part of your life, that means you let me into all of it. I don't need it all today, but I want to start meeting your friends, becoming part of your day-to-day life, the way you're integrating yourself into mine. Deal?"

She nodded. "I think I need to sit down."

He pressed a kiss to her forehead. "I'm a bastard, not giving you any breakfast before putting you through all that."

"Did you eat all of it?" Her words were slurred. Like being drunk, only much better. No hangover. Unless one counted how she kept crash-landing into her doubts and worries on the other side of such euphoria. She was going to work on that, though. That was one of her resolutions from this argument, wasn't it? He'd almost made her forget they'd had an argument, and that wasn't such a bad thing.

"I was tempted." He chuckled. "But I managed to have some manners and save some for my girl. I'm going to put you in my lap and make you eat it from my hand, though. Teach you to trust me for everything, one step at a time."

She had no problem with that at all. She'd be happy to stay in his lap forever. If only she never had to face anything beyond this blissful state of being he could give to her. However, if there was one thing she knew, it was that a love worth having required courage. She would find the courage to reach for what she wanted—as soon as she figured out once and for all what that was.

FOURTEEN

Over the next few weeks, she discovered what it was to have a man as a constant, regular part of her life again. Dale wasn't living with her physically, but he was in the forefront of her mind even when he wasn't with her. His words, his touch, his expressions, and all the things they were learning about one another.

They spent one afternoon gardening together. She'd had Hector transfer some azaleas from an area where larger shrubs were crowding them out, but she hadn't yet done anything around the relocated azaleas to blend them into their new location. Hector knew she liked to do that part of things herself, unless she indicated otherwise.

When she mentioned it at breakfast one morning, teasing Dale with the mock accusation that he was making her neglect her gardens, he said he'd help her with it. They came up with a plan together, walking the gardens and thinning out plants to fill in the azalea area.

As they were finishing up with that, Dale leaned on a shovel and glanced down at her, a half smile on his handsome lips. She patted soil around the last edging plant and braced her hands on her thighs, squinting up at him with a warm smile of her own. "This works really well. I think you have a future as a landscape architect."

"So do you, Mrs. Summers." He nodded toward the area she maintained for Roy's marker. "That freestanding wooden picket fence you have over there? I have some wildflower specimens that would make a great accent for it."

The decorative piece of fencing was set at an angle to a rustic-looking bench, the place she sat when she was visiting Roy. Shedding her garden gloves, she tucked her hair back behind her ear. "Oh? What color?"

"Several. Yellow, white and purple. They bloom their heads off every time it gets warm, which, down here, is pretty much year-round. Want to run by my place and grab a few? We can get some lunch while we're out."

She agreed. He didn't let her clean up beyond washing her hands. Instead, he lifted her into the seat of his old junk truck, both of them sweaty and dirty, and took them through a fast food drive-thru. He found them a spot at one of New Orleans's many parks so they could eat the greasy food while watching ducks and toss a few fries out the window to them. He wiped a touch of mustard off her mouth, then kissed it away before putting the truck in gear and trundling onward to his place.

She helped him dig up the wildflowers and check on the dogs. While she was there, she made another couple of suggestions for his own plantings out by the front gate, and then they were back at her house. After a quick stop at the Dairy Queen, that is, because he wanted dessert. She couldn't remember the last time she'd enjoyed a chocolate-dipped cone, and Dale gave her the cherries off his banana split.

Back at her house, Dale laid out a couple of towels and drew her down against his side on the grass next to the bench and freestanding picket fence. They enjoyed a short siesta, the newly turned earth nearby a pleasant perfume among the garden's many smells. He tangled his fingers with hers on his chest and she answered his questions about Roy's marker, the golfing statue. It was surprising how comfortable it felt to her, being in that area with Dale. It was almost as if Roy was giving them his blessing. The sense of peace and quiet companionship they shared working side by side seemed as natural as the flow of water from one of her fountains.

By the end of the afternoon, she had a new design for the fence and bench area to enjoy when she came there on pretty days to read and talk to Roy. Later that week, Dale brought her a family of concrete pigs. They placed them amid the waving stems of the wildflowers, a perfect addition.

During their times together—watching a movie at night, going to the French Market, playing with the dogs, Dale meeting her for lunch at the office—he also told her more about his experiences with the SEALs. He couldn't talk about mission specifics, but even still she received a harrowing picture of the cold, the danger, the hardships, though he treated those things with the matter-of-factness she applied to preparing a memo with Ellen. It was when he spoke of the men with whom he'd shared those experiences his strongest emotions came through. The sharing of such things had forged a bond he valued highly, a vital extension of the principles that had driven him to commit his life to the SEALs.

He also shared his impressions of the countries he'd visited. In return, she told him about her visits to temples in Vietnam and gardens in Japan, the churches in Barcelona. "When you look up at the ceilings, it's like looking inside a beautiful, scrolled teacup," she said, and he smiled at her.

He did that a lot. She would turn around, find him simply looking at her, and when she noticed, he would smile in that way that made things flip-flop in her stomach. They spent an afternoon in Audubon Park together and went to the zoo. She found out he liked the flamingos. When she suggested it was because of their propensity for standing on one leg, he laughed.

The Master-sub thing was also unfolding in an interesting way between them. She supposed every sub first explored it as a surface thing, a purely sexual expression, but as time went on, she recognized that as symptomatic of deeper cravings inside her, ones met by the fact his Master side ran just as deep. When they were working in the garden, things might be casual, but still, if he told her to bring him a spade, or to take a break, she'd detect that tone in his voice that she locked onto instantly and obeyed.

Of course, the sexual was still a delightful component of it. They might be cooking something in her kitchen, after the staff had left for the day, and he'd press up behind her, take over slicing the tomato. He'd order her to stand there inside the span of his arms as he wiped the knife, then ran the blade along her throat, down her side, up beneath her skirt. He'd give her thigh a tiny prick with the tip before he set the blade aside and replaced its cool touch with his far more heated one. She'd forever associate the smell of tomatoes with sex, since he'd taken her right there, thrusting into her as her fingers curled helplessly against the cutting board, getting the sticky juice of the tomato and its seeds on them. He'd licked all of it off.

Getting used to having him in her daily life, being under his command, put some of her demons to rest. It was the morning that he was reading the paper and he absently told her to get him his coffee that it finally clicked, what he'd told her about not being his maid or nurse.

It wasn't that he couldn't get his own coffee. He was underlining what lay between the two of them, as if between their more heated, sexual interactions, he was tugging on an invisible leash, reminding her that he was her Master, and she was his willing sub. It was provocative, distracting, and because he did it randomly, she was always eager for hints of it.

Testing it, she'd brought him the coffee. He put his hand on her arm, holding her in place until he took a sip and nodded his approval, telling her it was to his liking. Then he let her go. She let out a pleased sigh, quietly delighted that it was starting to make sense.

Even better, the more he recognized that she was grasping the concept, the more he allowed her to serve him. Her understanding expanded even further then. The act of her bringing the coffee to him reinforced both sides of the coin they each needed. Master and sub.

One roadblock remained. Well, two, if she counted the club, but she still shied away from that topic. They'd not yet slept in the master bedroom. They always ended up being somewhere else. Several nights it was in the living room, where he'd take her on the couch and they'd fall asleep there. Another night, he chose the west guest bedroom. He put her on her elbows and knees and tied her wrists to the iron railings of the headboard. Sitting behind her, he lifted her knees to his shoulders, holding her with strong, sure hands as he brought her to climax with his mouth, her balanced only on her elbows.

That night he introduced her to another first, something she'd never suspected could be as wildly pleasurable as it turned out to be . . .

As she came down from that oral-induced climax, still gasping, heart pounding, he eased her knees back to the bed. It was obvious he wasn't done with her yet. She knew enough about him now to know the man's stamina and control were terrifying. There'd been nights he brought her to climax three different ways before he thrust inside her and gave in to his own orgasm. Seeing her get aroused and go over was apparently as vital a pleasure to him as his own release, and it built his own, to push her to that edge again and again. A woman's fantasy for certain, though a little scary in reality. In the thrill-ride kind of way.

He dipped his fingers in her soaked cunt, collecting some of the slippery fluid before moving them between the seam of her buttocks. He painted that slick wetness over her rim. He'd played around that area several times, arousing her, but back when he'd asked her point-blank if she'd been fucked there, her flushed cheeks and uncertain look had answered the question. Roy hadn't been into that, and she'd never used a strap-on with him, either. He preferred to have her straddle him when he was tied up, ride his cock to climax, making him hold back until she commanded him to come. Now she tensed a little as Dale probed.

"Easy, girl. This all belongs to me, right?"

She nodded. "Yes sir."

"Any pain I give you is a good kind of pain. The kind that makes you hot and begging, right?"

She couldn't argue with that. So far tonight he'd used a flogger, a belt and a switch on her, and though the switch in particular had stung like crazy, he had a way of working her up before, during and after that had her remembering the pain with as much longing as the pleasure. He could be fierce and mean, but in a way that was controlled and exciting, a way that carried them both to an intense sexual experience.

"We're going to use the condom for this, because it's lubricated. I'll move slow, girl. You push out against me, releasing those muscles. I want to be all the way in, so my balls are against your pussy, and you'll feel them slap against your clit every time I thrust into that sweet ass of yours. Do you trust me?"

Her fingers curled in her bonds. Her pussy was still throbbing from the climax he'd given her, her body loose and willing. She was all his. Including every orifice.

He wouldn't hurt her. It might sound crazy to the fly on the wall who'd seen him strapping her until she was pleading for mercy. Or watched him do breast bondage on her, keeping the ropes tight until her curves were aching and swollen. When he released the bonds, the tingling pressure was a sweet agony, blood rushing back into them. But he'd kiss those sore places with such tenderness, rub balm into her skin to keep it soft. On the rare nights he wasn't staying with her or her with him, he'd call her and make sure she wasn't overdoing, that she'd taken aspirin and followed all of his aftercare direction.

Still drifting along the course of his question, wanting to be sure she was giving him an utterly truthful answer, she remembered cutting herself on the pruning shears. He'd held her finger under the tap, the cold water running the wound clean, and carefully wrapped a Band-Aid on the cut. He'd kissed it, then given her ass a slap and told her to be more careful with what belonged to him.

But the telling day was when she'd caught a bad head cold. They'd planned to have dinner together, so she'd called him, stuffed up and feeling miserable, and told him she'd reschedule when she was feeling better. When she got off the phone, she tried to shrug off the melancholy. She hated getting sick like anyone else, but she'd particularly dreaded it since Roy was gone. For some reason, it could make her feel a bit blue and alone, even though she knew that was self-pitying drivel. She had plenty of friends and a caring staff.

An hour later Dale arrived bearing chicken soup, several boxes of extra-soft, aloe-infused tissue, and herbal teas infused with echinacea and zinc. He relocated her to the couch in the TV room with ample pillows and quilts. He'd watched a trio of her favorite movies with her while she probably snored like a lumberjack, since she couldn't breathe. He plugged in a humidifier, added a eucalyptus oil to it that helped open her passages. Whenever she surfaced from her dozing, he was either under her, her upper body in his lap, or watching over her from an easy chair as he read or watched television.

"If you're angling to get at my wealth, it's really working," she'd told him, blowing her nose. "At this point, you have the kept-man position in the bag."

He grinned at her, and left the chair to come back to the sofa. He adjusted her pillows on his lap so she could put her head there, then leaned down to brush his lips over hers. "I'm the one keeping you," he corrected her.

t was all those moments added together that decided her. "Yes, I trust you, Master."

"Good girl." He added additional oil to her rim and then eased a finger into her, letting her feel the way of it. He teased her with the sensations, then withdrew, his hands gripping her buttocks to knead and massage, readying her for something much bigger than his fingers.

When he pulled open his jeans and put the head of his cock there, she let out a breath, trying to relax every muscle and obey his direction, pushing against him. He went slow, as promised, cupping her breasts, fondling and teasing the nipples as he eased forward. His cock's invasion stretched and burned a little, but it didn't feel all bad. Especially as his clever manipulation on her nipples and breasts, the way he held them with such familiar possession, aroused her anew.

As he moved deeper, the burning increased, but then he stopped again, dropping one hand beneath her to stroke her pussy, play with her clit. He leaned down over her, kissed her nape, her hair pooled on the mattress. The rough hair on his chest and thighs was a welcome stimulation against her back and legs, and she pressed up against the hard body they covered. He sank deeper into her, and she let out a shuddering moan.

"That's my girl. You want your Master deep inside you."

She did. No matter how deep Dale had gotten into her, at moments like this she thought it would never be deep enough.

He'd accomplished what he'd said he would. His testicle sac lay against her pussy, his cock lodged to the hilt in her ass. She was quivering, anxious with the unfamiliar feel of it, but he was over her, his body covering her, reassuring her.

"Perfect," he rumbled. Then he withdrew a small amount, pushed back in, eliciting a whimper and a wriggle. The sensation was different, crazy, and she wanted him to do it again. But when she tried to push back against him, he swatted her.

"You know better than that. I'll move at my own pace. I'm fucking your ass for my pleasure."

Ironically, when he said things like that, it made her spiral all the higher. Surrendering to him, letting him take them both on the journey he had planned, it was freedom within bondage like she'd never known outside it. She put her forehead down on her arm and moaned with frustration and need. He responded to both, continuing that slow move that made her come to pieces as she held completely still, until he was rocking inside her, and she couldn't help but move with him again. But at that point, he let her.

The way his testicle sac was hitting her labia and clit sent little shards of pleasure spearing through her lower belly, but it wasn't enough. She kept making those little pleading noises, not articulating it until he commanded that as well.

"I want to hear you beg for your climax, girl. Convince me you've been good enough."

"Please, Master. I've been very, very good. I want . . . oh God . . . please . . ."

"You are a very, very good girl." Yet still he held it out of reach, working her until she was simply crying out at each thrust in distressed need. At last, he put his hand beneath her, found her clit and started stroking. His middle finger sank into her pussy, adding to the pressure.

"Come for me, girl. Scream."

She did, no help for it, and as she was coming, his thrusts became hard and punishing, him taking his pleasure in the new orifice she'd surrendered to him. She felt the heat as he gushed into the condom, and hoped next time he wouldn't wear it, so he could mark her in every orifice with his seed. The thought made her aftershocks fiercer.

When he slowed at last, her rim was sore. She made an involuntary noise as he eased out, so gently. "Stay in that position," he said.

He went to the bathroom. She heard running water, and laid her head on her forearm again. Her haunches were still in the air, the coolness of the room making her shiver a little, but she wasn't alone long enough to lose the heat of his body entirely. A few minutes later, the mattress dipped as he moved onto the bed again. Sitting on his hip next to her, he parted her buttocks and put a hot wash-cloth against her rim.

Oh, God . . . it was heaven. She smelled the herbal rinse he used for inflamed tissues. Her fingers loosened in their hold on the blankets as the treatment eased her discomfort. Her limbs were still shaking, so once he finished that part of things, he eased her down to her side and untied the ropes. Setting them aside, he curled around her, holding her against the heat of his body as she drowsily gazed through the sheer panels of the floor-length window. The man-made pond and a section of garden were visible from this view. Beyond it, she could see the tennis courts, the pool house. A pair of rabbits hopped across a walkway, disappearing into her ornamental grass.

"I'd like to invite you to a dinner," she said. She dipped her head, brushing her lips against the forearm of one of the strong arms he had banded over her chest.

"Hmm." The grunt was sleepy, making her smile. She reached back, slid a hand down his thigh. He was still wearing his jeans. Despite that one day, he still tended to stay mostly clothed around her. When he spent the night, at some point—usually after he worked her into exhaustion and she'd fallen asleep—he'd take off the prosthesis and his clothes.

She wanted to feel bare skin while awake, though, so she turned in his arm span, reached down. He'd left the jeans unbuttoned, so she pushed the zipper down, letting her fingers settle on the boxers beneath, slide down his upper thigh, as far as she could go before the denim became too restrictive.

"Can I take these off of you, Master? Please?"

His eyes had opened at that. She'd added the *please* before he could say no, wanting him to understand it was important to her. He nodded. She understood now it wasn't a matter of trusting her; he was simply more comfortable as a Master with both legs, so to speak. However, the same way he was helping her understand and accept certain things about herself, she hoped in time she could give him the same gift. He would truly understand there was no difference to her. No, actually there was. She loved his Mastery even more when it was simply, only Dale, no trappings at all to embellish what needed no embellishing.

Shifting to her knees, she worked the jeans down. He helped her then, sitting up and removing his boots, giving the one with a prosthesis a firm, practiced tug to work it free. Now she could remove the jeans all the way off both legs. As she did that, she moved off the bed to kneel between his flesh-and-blood foot and the metal one. Cognizant of how closely he was watching her, she put her hand on the socket.

"How do I remove it?"

He showed her how to release the socket, take it and the liner off the stump, her fingers curling into his warm skin. The slight tension in his shoulders, the frown lines around his mouth, suggested how difficult it was for him, making her appreciate him all the more. He was trying to be fair, giving her as much as he was demanding.

When he was completely naked, that swept anything else away. As she gazed at the whole man, she made sure her deep pleasure showed, her attention sliding over both legs. Putting her hands on his thighs, she lifted herself up so she could place her mouth on his chest. His hand cradled the back of her head as she kissed him, nuzzled, worked her way over to tease a nipple, reveling in the feel of his hand tightening on her hair when she nipped him and he chuckled, a strained sound. She was pressed in between his legs, and his cock stirred against her.

"You never told me about that dinner. I think you have a short attention span, girl."

"Once you're like this, only one thing matters." But she settled against him, linking her hands around his waist and propping her chin on his chest, looking up at him. "It's an annual appreciation thing for our major clients and vendors. There's a charity auction and dancing, and the dinner is usually spectacular, done by the best chefs in New Orleans. Would you come as my escort?"

"Is it black tie?"

She nodded. "Is that a problem? If it is, you and Roy are a similar size. I still have some of his—"

"No, it's not a problem. I can rent a tux, Athena." He touched her face. "Do you still have a lot of his clothes?"

"Not so much, no. I donated most of it to the men's shelter after the first year. But there were a couple of things I kept. He always looked so handsome in a tuxedo, so I kept that in the back of the closet. Along with his favorite around-the-house shirt. It's an old, soft polo. During the first year, I'd wear it when gardening. Now I just keep it hung up in my closet." She studied his chest. "I've actually been wearing yours now and then. That T-shirt you let me wear home the night you ripped my blouse."

"Well, it seemed like the gentlemanly thing to do."

She smiled, lifting her lashes now. "Will you go with me? To the dinner?"

He'd said he wanted to meet her friends, spend time with her associates. So far that had been her household staff and Ellen. She hadn't been avoiding widening the circle because of any concerns about how he'd like them or vice versa. She'd merely been hoarding him, liking the way it felt when the two of them were alone. However, she'd attended the annual dinner the past two years alone, preferring it that way, but this year she couldn't imagine going without him.

"You're not concerned that I may look like a mutt among purebreds?"

"I have a friend who runs a dog shelter. He tells me that the mutt is the most loyal and well-balanced of the dog breeds, because he's a blend of their best qualities."

"Well, that may have been propaganda to get you to take home a couple Rottweiler mixes to protect you when he's not around."

She chuckled, but then she sobered, locking gazes with him. "I would be honored to be on your arm, Master."

"The honor would be mine," he said lightly, but then he clasped her upper arms, lifted her up to meet his mouth. It was a slow exploration, a reflection of the new territory they'd covered tonight, on a couple of levels. "You might have to tell me which fork to use," he said, when he at last broke the embrace.

"Whichever one you like. Roy said that kind of etiquette was designed to make people feel small, and the only thing that proves our size is the way we act toward one another."

Dale shook his head wryly. "It's hard for me not to like this guy."

"Are you trying not to like him?" Her brow creased.

"No, it's not that, girl." He followed the shell of her ear with his fingertips. "Come on back up here."

She obliged, clambering up on the bed and returning to their spooned position. She let out a small sigh of contentment when he snugged her into the cradle of his thighs and groin, his cock pressed to her buttocks. He could relax into her body more without the prosthesis, no worries about accommodating its more rigid structure or accidentally scraping her tender flesh with it. His arm was under her breasts, the other under her head, so she could rest her cheek on his firm biceps.

"It was hard for me to wrap my mind around the idea of a man pushing his wife to dominate him, when it was clear she was a submissive."

"No, he wasn't like that. He was—"

"I know he wasn't." Dale tightened his arm around her, shushing her. "The one thing I know about Dominants and submissives is they're unclassifiable. It's hard to fix one set of rules that fits any one of them, let alone all of them. You obviously loved him, and he loved you. I also think he was more of a bottom than a sub. He wasn't looking to submit as much as he was looking to let go during defined sessions between you. He needed the release of the pain and restraints, the psychological domination, but it doesn't seem like it was an integral part of his personality."

She shook her head. "Not like it is for you."

"Or you." He slid his hand down her abdomen and automatically her thighs loosened, giving him access to stroke her pussy. His fingers came to rest there, sending a quiver through the rest of her. "You can't imagine what it does to me, that shift in your expression, your body language, when I command you with nothing more than a word or a touch. You go into this dreamlike mode, where you let go of everything. It's like your soul is sitting right there, in my hand. It's intoxicating."

"To me, too." She tightened her thighs on his fingers as he rubbed her clit absently, sending those tiny spirals of sensation through her thighs and abdomen. "Master, why . . . I switched out the beds, but you haven't . . . it seems like you're avoiding the master bedroom."

"Not me. You. You're not ready for it yet. You switched out the beds, but you yourself haven't made the suggestion, or pushed it. Granted, you are not a pushy woman, at least not in that way," he gave her a teasing pinch, "but whenever we start in that direction, you get uptight. You start walking slower and doing the nervous-talking thing."

"I—" She stopped, thinking about it. He was right, she did. She tensed now, thinking about what he'd said. "I'm sorry. You said I have to choose. I'm trying. I just—"

"Hey." His fingers spread out to caress her thighs. "I expect you to make progress, Athena, not set speed records. I'm your first since him, and you were with him for over twenty years. I was in the SEALs for over twenty years. Every morning I wake up, I have to remind myself I'm not going to get a call to gear up and head out. And every morning I have to deal with how that feels."

Like her waking up and wondering if Roy had already gone down to start the coffee. Or thinking of things during the workday she intended to tell him. Over time, it had improved, but she still occasionally had to remind herself he was gone. "Was it difficult, when you first retired?" she asked. Her hand slipped to his thigh again. It was pressed up against hers, and she let her fingers trail down to his knee, feeling the scar tissue there.

"I had some time to get used to scaling down, when I'd lost the leg but was still on active duty. Since I couldn't be in the field any-more, I served out the last few years of my service behind the lines, doing the things I told you about—tactical and occasionally serving as a BUD/S instructor, things like that—but it's never the same. Those first few years after an amputation, the limb shrinks, changes, and so you deal with the constant doctor visits. Though my current prosthesis was a great improvement on the first couple I had, it still required a lot of initial coordination with the docs and the company that let me take advantage of their program. Then there's the phys-ical therapy, gait training, all of it. I don't feel the prosthesis touch-ing the ground, so I had to train my brain to deal with that."

At her quizzical look, he elaborated. "Think of swinging a tennis racket. You get used to how the ball's going to hit it because of muscle memory, so that the racket becomes an extension of your arm, but you don't actually have nerves in the racket. You don't have feeling in the foot, so there's no way to feel for traction. When I carry you up stairs, I always take it slow, relying on that muscle memory, so I don't take us both for a tumble."

"Hence the romantic pace with lots of pauses for kissing. I like it." She was hoping to make him smile, and he did, faintly, but then he sighed.

"It all made me irritable as hell, having this be such a big part of my life. I resented it like a son-of-a-bitch, my body slowing me down when it had been the thing that always kept me running ahead. But you figure it out. I was in my thirties and already start-ing to feel some of the creaks of getting older when it happened. The guys that face it in their early twenties, when they're still in that invincible stage . . . it can cripple them emotionally. But it does a number on you no matter what. I guess what I'm saying is, good or bad, when I did finally get to retirement, I was better prepared for it than most."

She linked her fingers with his hand up near her head. Did he realize he'd equated retirement with the loss of his leg, the two incidents apparently interchangeable? "Were you okay with me removing it tonight?"

"I wasn't, not really. I'm guessing you caught on to that. But it's time, Athena. I tell you that you have to trust me, but that goes both ways. I have to trust you at some point, trust that you won't see this as anything more than it is. It's functional, practical; it's not who I am."

Actually, it had sculpted some aspects of his personality in positive ways, but she held that thought for another day. For now, she just nodded, pressed her cheek into his biceps.

"I like you better this way," she whispered. "It's not your legs that make you my Master. Not at all."

His arms tightened around her. Though he didn't say anything else for a while and neither did she, she could feel him thinking about her words. She hoped he believed them, because they were simple, powerful truth.

FIFTEEN

The night of the dinner, Athena donned a sequin sheath and swept up her hair. She'd normally wear her diamonds, but she was worried that might be overkill. A couple of times this week, she'd wondered if she'd made a mistake. Perhaps this wasn't the best event to introduce him to her board of directors and society friends.

The dinner was being held at one of New Orleans's upscale hotel ballrooms. The guest list was over five hundred people, including most of Louisiana's top business people, government officials and some local celebrities. Which of course meant society reporters would be milling around outside to take pictures of the elite coming to play together and raise money for a good cause. Louisiana native Harry Connick, Jr. would be joining the full orchestra for a couple of songs.

She should have waited until she was having a private dinner with her board and their spouses to introduce them to Dale. But she'd followed her intuition in that quiet moment in her guest bedroom. What was done was done. However, she'd leave the diamonds in the box for the night. She settled for a simple gold chain and matching earrings.

Certain Dale wouldn't be comfortable walking the red carpet among the shouting reporters and their flashing cameras, she'd told him she'd meet him at the hotel. She'd added him to the list of those who would take the quieter entrance blocked off by hotel staff for more discreet arrivals.

Therefore, she was surprised when Lynn contacted her over the house intercom system and told her "Mr. Rousseau" was waiting for her in the foyer. "Thank you, Lynn," she managed. "Ah, see if he wants a drink. I'll be down in a few minutes."

"Already done, ma'am."

Of course it was. She didn't know why she told Lynn such obvious things, but perhaps it was simply to reinforce the courtesy.

She checked her hair and told the butterflies in her stomach to settle. As she hurried toward the landing, she told herself it was all going to be fine. Then every thought fled her mind.

She came to a full stop at the top of the stairs, even putting her hand on the banister to steady herself. When he turned toward her, she needed the support even more.

He hadn't rented a tuxedo at all. Instead, she beheld the breathtaking sight of a man wearing naval dinner dress blues, and Master Chief Dale Rousseau knew how to wear the hell out of them. Her gaze slid over a narrow lapeled, short black coat with gold buttons, worn over black bow tie and studded shirt, a gold cummerbund and perfectly creased black slacks. Gold striping and insignia adorned the left sleeve, and his gold Trident rested over his ribbons on the left panel of the coat.

She'd expected his military bearing and handsome, stern features to set off a tuxedo well, but seeing him in the uniform he'd earned, he was more than a formidable figure. She was swept off her feet.

He had his white hat with its black brim and gold anchor embellishment tucked under his arm, and now she realized he was carrying a trio of roses, tied with a ribbon. She made her feet move at last, though wisely she kept a firm grip on the banister. He cocked his head, considering her with those vivid eyes. The way they covered every inch of her in the form-fitting dress made every workout she'd done, every dessert she'd given up, worth it.

"It's a good thing you did invite me to this shindig," he said as she reached the bottom of the stairs. "If I'd seen photos of you in

earing that thing, and you without an escort, we would
problem."

d the possessive threat. "I told you that you could meet
me there."

"Yeah, you did. You were trying to handle me, make things
easier for me. We've had that discussion, a couple times now, haven't
we?" He softened the reproof by touching her face. "You invited me
so you wouldn't have to go alone, Athena. That means from beginning to end."

His tender caress, the knowing look, made her throat tight, her
heart expand painfully in her chest. "Actually," she said, "I invited
you to show you off. My gorgeous SEAL boy toy."

"Man toy," he corrected her, with a quirk of his lips.

Now that she was closer to him, she could see even more details
of his uniform, the ribbons and embellishments that reflected his
career with the SEALs, the honors he'd been given. They were a
map of who and what he was. "Dale, you look . . . amazing."

He ran a thumb along her cheek. "I brought a gift for you.
Something I'll give you later."

"Not now?" She'd never been good at waiting for gifts. Her visible disappointment was the right response, because the lines around
his eyes creased with good humor.

"Well, since you look even more gorgeous than usual, my resis-
tance is low."

He freed a small velvet bag from his clasp on the roses. Handing
the flowers to her, he loosened the drawstring and spilled the contents of the bag out into his hand.

It was a necklace, a beautiful choker of braided silver and gold.
The pendant was the SEAL Trident, one crafted by a jeweler who
knew his trade, every detail precisely sculpted. Now that she had
been with Dale awhile, she knew the significance of every part of
that symbol. The eagle with the bowed head, honoring the fallen,
the trident he grasped representing the SEALs' connection to the

sea. The cocked flintlock pistol showed the SEALs' state of readiness at all times. The pendant was gold, a scattering of diamond chips gilding the symbol to give it a more feminine look.

Dale let it drop into the waiting cup of her palm. As he did that, the pendant turned over, such that she saw the engraving on the back. Her breath caught in her throat. Though her other hand still clasped the roses, she found herself also clutching his sleeve for support.

At the club, a sub being collared by her Master was sometimes a ritualized public event, though for most it happened in private. To some, it was as sacred as a marriage proposal. She'd been going twelve different ways tonight, worrying about Dale, figuring out how to ease the experience for him, how to make sure he had a good time . . . handling him, just as he said. Underscoring firmly what he'd said from the beginning, he'd chosen this moment to give her a collar. He was in charge. He was escorting her, helping her not to feel alone at this event for the first time in three years. She was the one in his keeping, not vice versa.

She had male friends who could have taken her in years past, but it wasn't the same. She'd done what he'd wanted her to do from the first. Make a choice because it was what she wanted and needed, down to the depths of her soul. She'd acted as he expected her to do—as she wanted to do—relying on and trusting her Master, using his dominance as a form of confidence and shield both.

Property of Dale Rousseau.

She lifted her gaze from that remarkable engraving to meet his eyes. "I want you to wear my collar, Athena," he said. "I've never offered it to a woman before."

In answer, she put the roses on a side table, threading them into the vase of cut flowers already there. She unclipped the chain she'd been wearing, let it coil onto the table's surface. When she presented her back to him, her breath was shallow, her heart beating high in her throat. She closed her eyes. He put his hands on her bare upper arms, and she felt the coolness of the necklace between his palm and her flesh. As he stepped closer, the wool of his uniform was against her bare back.

She opened her eyes so she saw him bring the necklace down in front of her face. Tucking the dangling pendant beneath her chin, he clipped the choker at her nape. The pendant lay perfectly in the pocket of her throat, the choker snug enough to remind her of his ownership.

"I thought about wearing diamonds earlier," she said. "I like this so much better."

His fingers closed on her shoulders again as he put his lips on her throat, just above the choker. She quivered in his grasp, turning her chin to her shoulder to give him full access. "Did you think I wouldn't be comfortable with the diamonds?" he asked.

"Yes, Master. I'm sorry."

He slipped his hands around her waist, coming up to capture her breasts in the thin fabric. She arched into his touch, needing him, wanting him.

"I'll give you a pass, because right now you're just too beautiful and perfect for me to scold." He folded his arms around her then, holding her close. "I love you, Athena. Don't say it back. I know you're not ready to do that."

She wasn't, but hearing him say it made her grip him harder, digging her nails into those strong, callused hands folded across her abdomen. "Thank you for your collar, Master. Thank you so much."

"My pleasure." He turned her then, pulled a handkerchief out of his jacket and dabbed carefully at the corners of her eyes, saving her makeup. "None of that, now. I can't bring the hostess late to her own party. Are you ready?"

With him at her side, she felt ready for anything. She smiled, pushing back tears to please him, savoring the firm clasp of her hand on his. "Yes, Master."

"Then let's go to this party."

She'd read about SEALs, their missions, the situations where instant adaptation was the difference between success and failure, life or death. As such, she should have realized Dale was trained to make any situation work for him.

He'd never spoken of his rating before Lawrence and Neil called him Master Chief, but she'd looked it up after that day and learned it was one of the highest designations an enlisted SEAL could earn. She could only imagine the career of dangerous missions he'd had, proving his leadership ability time and again and demonstrating a success rate that proved he could get the job done, whatever was required. He'd known what it was to command men, to lose them. Even if she hadn't deduced that from her reading, she would have picked it up from everything she knew about him.

That aura of command he carried so well with the uniform resulted in a blend of intense curiosity and unconscious respect from the other guests throughout the evening. As well as a lot of female stares, which made her feel like Dale did about her wearing her sexy dress. With exasperated amusement, she quelled her possessiveness. Somewhat.

Dale fortunately made it easy to manage the feelings, since he rarely left her side. He was a good listener and engaging conversationalist with her guests, but she was keenly aware of his constant attentiveness to her as well. While they were talking to others, he'd often put a hand on her mostly bare back, sliding it provocatively along the low scoop edge of the dress, telling her he was very aware of the body beneath it. He held her chair to sit down for dinner, and when she was seated at the table, he dropped a kiss on her shoulder before taking a seat next to her, his knee pressed against hers. All not-so-subtle signs of possession that made her knees weak and the butterflies continue to roam pleasantly through her stomach.

During the appreciation speech she made, she noticed those sharp

286 JOEY W. HILL

blue-green eyes sweeping the crowd, as if he considered himself her personal security detail, same as the men who'd attended with the mayor and some of the celebrities. It was automatic to him, to be protective, but she loved feeling that safe. She should tell him that.

After dinner and the first set of award ceremonies, the dancing started. She was surprised when Dale rose from his chair and offered his hand to lead her onto the floor. It was a slow piece, allowing them to move in an easy four-step. She loved it, being held in the arms of a lover, dancing once again.

"I *can* dance," he said, noting her surprise. "Just don't ask me to jitterbug."

She chuckled. "I'm not sure I'd be up for that myself. So are you having a good time? I saw you met the mayor."

"Yeah. We both agreed the sausage and cheese things would make a great tailgate addition for the next Saints' game." He gave her a smile. "You were fantastic up there. You're a great public speaker."

"It always scares me to death. My stomach flip-flops like crazy, no matter how much I've done it."

"It doesn't show. But it does explain why you picked at your dinner."

"Well, that and this dress. There's really only room for me and one meal in it, and I already had breakfast."

He grinned. "Serves you right, trying to get all these men hot and bothered." He held her even closer and she slid her hand from his shoulder to his nape, caressing the short, soft hair there. Lifting onto her toes, she brushed her lips over his ear.

"I only care about getting one man hot and bothered," she whispered.

She'd taken steps toward claiming her identity as a submissive. She'd been timid with those first steps, mannerly, obedient. But over the past few weeks, a transition had happened, times like this when she embraced how broadly she could explore this sense of herself, teasing her Master at the same time. So now she pressed her lower body against his, managing a discreet rub against his groin as they made the turn.

His eyes glinted dangerously. "Just wait until we're where I can get you out of that dress. I'm going to remind you of your manners . . . and make love to you while you're wearing nothing but my collar."

She reached up, touched his mouth, connecting them like a kiss. "In my bedroom. Please."

She still had a mix of feelings about it, but overriding all of it was the desire to have him there, to wake up with Dale in her bed. She wanted to take that step with him. She wanted to make her bed their bed.

"We'll see." But in the past he'd simply told her no, so she knew he saw things were shifting for her.

"May I cut in?"

Seeing Larry standing beside them, she suppressed the surge of irritation. She'd been aware of his close scrutiny several times tonight, though he'd kept a fairly proper distance. However, with his impeccably poor timing, he'd chosen what anyone else could see was an intimate moment to interrupt their dance.

"I haven't had a chance to dance with the loveliest woman here tonight," he said, shifting his gaze between them. "I'd like to speak to Athena for a moment or two. If you don't mind?"

Dale glanced at her and she gave him a stiff nod. He tightened his fingers on her briefly, then stepped back. "I suggest the jitterbug."

She stifled a laugh, recognizing the comment was posed to her, not to Larry. As Dale relinquished her to him, she tried to hold on to the feeling. It wasn't the first time she'd danced with Larry, but she always felt a faint tension at his proximity, a woman's awareness of when a man wanted more, and she had no interest in that. And not just because he was married.

That didn't stop him from touching her during board meetings or sessions in her office. All of it casual brushes of her arm or back, the type of contact that couldn't be called inappropriate except for what she discerned was behind it.

She fixed a polite smile on her face. Larry was a good board member with excellent business acumen, an asset to Summers Industries. It didn't matter that personally he was a chore for her to handle. In the scheme of things, it was a minor aggravation, one she could manage.

Larry had never touched her while Roy was alive. Roy didn't give a rat's ass about maintaining the courteous Southern façade a woman often did in such a situation. He would have pulled Larry aside on the golf course, told him to stop touching his wife or he'd put a five iron up his ass. And break it off for good measure.

"As usual, the event has gone splendidly," Larry noted. "The guests look very happy, and the silent auction totals are already well beyond a hundred thousand. Your foundation is matching whatever's raised this year?"

"As always."

She was just sorry Roy wouldn't be there to present the check to the community center that Dale, Neil and Lawrence supported. He'd always enjoyed that part immensely. Not the actual check presenting, because of course the cameras had to be there, a necessary evil to help promote the charity in the community. Roy liked staying after the reporters left to take a personal tour, meet the volunteers involved, and learn even more about what they did. He'd enjoyed making money, but he'd equally enjoyed the results of what could be done with it, large or small. Surprising and delighting her with a rare bonsai, or giving the local Salvation Army a twenty percent budget boost, it didn't matter. He saw the value in either gesture.

"I visited the community center you chose to receive the funds this year. They seem in great need of the money."

"They are. I hosted an event for some of the boys at my home recently. And the board voted for that, not just me, Larry."

"Of course. But you are the tip of the spear, aren't you?" He gave her a friendly smile that she knew wasn't really friendly at all.

"Well, the tip doesn't get very far without the rest of the spear propelling it." She glanced past his shoulder. Dale was talking to Matt Kensington, head of Kensington & Associates, and his lovely wife, Savannah, CEO of Tennyson Industries. She wished she was over there. She'd only spent a brief amount of time with Matt and Savannah at events like these, but she'd intended to get to know them better, because their charity interests often overlapped hers. Interestingly, the way the two of them greeted Dale, it was as if they already knew him. She wondered how they'd met.

"I'm sorry, Larry, I was distracted. You were saying?"

"I said"—his brow creased, reflecting his irritation at her lack of attention, but he could be like that—"your escort was an excellent choice. Having a member of the armed services here makes Summers look very supportive of the military, always a good message to the community."

"Summers *is* very supportive of the military. It's why last year's auction proceeds were divided between the USO and Wounded Warriors, and we had fifty veterans and their spouses attend the event."

Larry had no sense of the true significance of that uniform. Or of the sacrifices that went along with it. Dale, a strong man in the prime of his life, had suffered a debilitating injury that forced him to find a new path when his life had been the SEALs. And he had. He'd refused to let his leg give him an excuse to be any less than what he'd always demanded of himself. She thought of what he'd said about trotting his injury and service out to serve a good cause. Hearing Larry talk about it just that way made her understand what he'd meant.

To add to her growing annoyance, Larry had made his predictable move, sliding his hand from its proper place on her waist. Not low enough to be improper, but low enough she felt the forced intimacy, the touch of his smallest finger on the upper rise of her buttock. It made her want to recoil from his touch. He'd done the same thing when she danced with him at the first of these events after Roy's passing. He'd invited her onto the floor, leaving her no polite way out of it, but that one dance had cured her of wanting to be in any other man's arms for the rest of the night. At that time, she'd wondered if she'd ever want another man to touch her, even in passing. She'd ached with longing for the unique intimacy of Roy's arms around her.

Over time, though, she'd realized it was just Larry that made her feel that way. Now she knew she didn't want Larry touching her anywhere that was her Master's alone to touch. She found herself fighting an overwhelming urge to end the dance with all the tact of a sledgehammer. Fortunately, someone else took care of that.

"Athena." Dale was back, and she barely suppressed her sigh of relief. She could certainly handle one middle-aged board member with wandering hands, but the night had been going so well, she resented having to do so. "I'm sorry to interrupt your dance, but Ellen says she needs you for a few minutes, to help sort out a problem with the vendor awards."

"Of course. Thank you for the dance, Larry."

Dale watched her nod to the man, her gaze meeting Larry's squarely. Good girl. She didn't avert her gaze from him at all, didn't give the bastard any sense he had the upper hand with her. Her dealing with him being an asshole was obviously a regular thing. He'd confirmed that with Ellen when he asked the assistant if she'd be willing to be part of his conspiracy to get Athena away from Larry without making the bloody scene Dale actually preferred.

The admin had followed his gaze, rolled his eyes. "Definitely," the woman murmured. "You'd think that married prick would take a hint."

As Athena moved away, he and Larry strolled with her to the edge of the dance floor. However, once they stepped off of it, he put out a hand to stop Larry from leaving his company. Athena disappeared in Ellen's direction.

"You seem like a very astute man, Larry."

The board member paused, his brow lifting. "Excuse me?"

Dale met his gaze. Larry had blue-gray eyes, and they tended to shift a lot, a common trait in a man who had specific weaknesses of character. "A woman who can care for her husband until his death, run his company successfully even while grieving"—*one who has the courage to reach out for love again*, though he held that thought to himself—"deserves your admiration and respect. I suggest you start giving them to her."

Larry curled his lip. "Is that a threat?"

"No." Dale shook his head, offering a smile he knew was more a baring of his teeth. "She doesn't need me to fight this battle for her. She can whip your ass any day of the week. She proves it with every board meeting, doesn't she?"

He shifted closer, laid a friendly hand on Larry's shoulder, and now his gaze became a lot less friendly, despite the casual pose. "I don't need to protect her from you in the boardroom or in your business, Larry, but I sure as hell will protect her from any man's unwelcome advances, because that part *is* my job. Starting now, the twisted passive-aggressive mating rituals end. She fully recognizes them for what they are, and she *and* your wife deserve better from you."

Larry's eyes were turning to gray frost, and somewhere inside his misguided brain he was probably thinking about a highly unwise remark. To thwart it, Dale increased his grip on his shoulder, a not-so-subtle warning. "If you don't listen, you and I will have this conversation again, only there will be a lot less talking. I don't really give a shit about your lawyers or your money. They only mean something to you, not to me. You take that however you want to take it, as long as it results in one thing—you never putting your hands on her again the way I and everyone else here just saw you do. Including your wife, despite the vodka tonic she just knocked back to try and blind herself to it."

"How dare . . ."

Dale held Larry's gaze, challenging him to finish the sentence. Whatever the man saw in his face, felt in the grip of the hand on his shoulder, made him shut his mouth. He pivoted on his shiny, expensive shoe and disappeared into the crowd.

Satisfied, Dale went to find Athena. She'd answered Ellen's question, some obvious thing the clever admin had made up, and though she was engaged in another conversation, more mingling, he could tell by her casual sweeps of the crowd she was looking for him. It felt good to have that connection with her.

She was a true Southern lady. A thickheaded idiot like Larry would mistake the unflagging politeness, the genteel manners, for vulnerability. He wouldn't understand that he continued to be defeated and rebuffed because of the steel core beneath. She understood what he was all about, but she was raised to deal with such things with a shield of politeness, not aggression.

Fortunately, Dale had a different code.

Stepping up behind her, he put his hand exactly where Larry had laid his. The easing of her shoulders, her slight shift that pressed her hip and buttock against his leg, made his reaction toward Larry all the more fierce, even as it made him all the more protective toward her. Since he figured he wouldn't win any points kicking the shit out of one of her board members behind the building, he focused on the latter, stroking her skin, letting her feel he was there, standing at her back.

Christ, he really was in love with her. Simple as that.

I t was a worthwhile but always exhausting event. The night air was a little cool when they left, so Dale shed his jacket, placing it over her shoulders. When Ellen came out to speak to the departing guests as well, Athena saw her note Dale's chivalrous gesture. She sent a woman's smile toward her boss, and it felt good to smile right back about it.

Athena held the heat and scent of him around her as they got into the limo. She fingered the stripes on the sleeve, felt the faint scratch of the wool against her skin. As he put his arm around her, she leaned against his shoulder, a wonderful thing to be able to do. He didn't make her talk, recognizing she was tired, and their silence was comfortable. He took her hair down, pocketing the pins, and then played with the strands. His fingers caressed her collarbones and shoulder where the dress left her skin bare.

She noticed Rex glancing back at them. He was her usual driver with the car service she occasionally used, and he was obviously making the same mental adjustment her staff had been making these past few weeks, seeing her with someone different. The good thing was they all seemed to like Dale. She did, too. Probably far too much for her own good. But he'd said he loved her, hadn't he?

She didn't want to go down the insecure and entirely female path of wondering if it meant the same thing to him that it meant to her. Or how long he would stay with her, what their relationship was about and what he was thinking—Lord, please not that. Pushing it all away, she brushed a kiss against his throat. She slid her arm around his waist, holding him closer as his arm tightened around her. He pressed his lips to her forehead.

"Tired, girl?"

She nodded. "Will you stay with me anyway?"

He touched her chin. "Nope, sorry. If I'm not getting some acrobatic sex from all this dressing up, I'm headed out."

His teasing gave her a tiny smile. But as he bent to let his lips touch hers, his blue-green eyes were a tropical night sky. His words, spoken low to share only with her, were serious and intent.

"I'm with you for more than that, Athena."

Her heart beat a little faster, her fingers curling into his side.

"That makes one of us," she managed. "I'm only using you for the acrobatic sex."

He chuckled. "Don't forget about my gardening skills. Those are pretty impressive."

"True."

She was still smiling as they pulled up to the house. Dale handed over a generous tip before she could reach for her purse. He really was stubborn about some things. It didn't rankle tonight, though. In truth, there was a part of her that respected his stance on such things, understanding the message he was sending.

She thanked the driver, then slid across the seat. Dale had exited the vehicle so he could take her hand, help her to the curb. As the car pulled away, he put his arm around her waist and they moved up the steps to the front door, hip to hip. He shifted away to give her room to program in the door code, but she stopped him with a hand on his wrist.

"It's thirty-two, thirty-three, pound."

He met her gaze, nodded. Keyed it in and opened the door for her.

Since it was after midnight, the house was quiet and dark, only low-level lighting illuminating the foyer and second-level staircase. She stepped out of her shoes, sighing at the feel of the cushioned carpet through her shimmery stockings. Then she sighed a different way when Dale drew her to him. He slid his hands down her sides, to her hips. He held her to him that way as he kissed her, a long, slow pleasurable drowning. She wanted him in a way that was quiet and intense, overwhelming, like the depths of the ocean. Her earlier words hadn't been the passion of the moment. She wanted that joining to happen in a specific place and, in this clear moment, she understood she didn't have to direct things. She could just tell him how she felt and trust he'd understand.

She reached up, framing his strong face with her hands. "Please make love to me, Master. In our bed."

He nodded, bending his head to kiss her again. This one was just as fathomless and swirling as the first, so that every part of her yearned when he finished. He drew back, but only to clasp her hand in his. They ascended the stairs in that fashion, him gripping the railing to balance himself, her holding his hand for her balance.

Her bedroom door was open. When she was going to be out late, Lynn or Beth always left on the dresser lamp. Athena had draped the shade in a blue scarf to give the room the sense of candlelight. The scarf was new, to go with the new décor Athena had been adjusting over the past few weeks. She'd changed out some of the pictures, moving those Roy had particularly liked to other viewing places in the house, replacing them with prints that might appeal to Dale as well as herself. One of those was the large watercolor over the bed. The painting was nothing but horizontal lines, but it combined all the colors of the sea, slightly wavering, so it was obvious that was what the artist intended it to represent. Dale glanced at it, his gaze sliding over the yellow bedspread, the blue and green pillows and the white area rug.

"The colors reminded me of your eyes," she said without embarrassment.

He curved his long fingers around the side of her neck to draw her to him again. As he kissed her this time, he slid down the side zipper of the dress and then pushed it off her shoulders. The fabric stretched, so that it could be taken to her ankles with little effort. But he wasn't yet ready to do that. He stepped back, retaining her hand even when they reached the full stretch of their arms. Her breasts were held up on display in adhesive cups that molded to her like a second skin, a necessary accessory to allow for the backless dress. The upper part of the dress was now folded low on her hips, a froth of glittering sequins. She held her breath under the slow, lazy perusal that made her feel like she was utterly his, and he was pleased with what he saw.

"Take it all off. Everything except my collar. But do it slow. I like watching the way you take off your clothes for me." Proving it, he sat down on a chair, waiting on her.

She might have been tired, but there were certain things he could do to her that would revive her body like electricity. Only tonight, instead of a jolt, the feeling lifted her like an ocean wave, a sense of sudden buoyancy.

She'd played with the necklace countless times tonight, touching the pendant, running her nails under the hold of the choker. She'd been like a girl looking at her shiny new engagement ring, only her obsession was tactile rather than visual. She'd been complimented countless times about the necklace. When one woman recognized the SEAL symbol and the obvious connection to her escort, Athena noticed her eyes and mouth had softened. It was an acknowledgment of the romantic implication, if not the deeper, more potent meaning behind the choker. Her collar.

Dale's eyes had flickered over it a few times as well. Once, when they were talking to a group of bankers, he'd had his hand on her shoulder, fingers brushing her nape. He'd slid two of them under the back clasp, tugging on it in a discreet, provocative way. She instantly lost her train of thought. He'd interjected a question, covering it, but then he'd given her a teasing look. The heat in his eyes said he liked knowing that his touch on her collar had been responsible for her distraction.

Now she slid out of the dress. The little shimmy she made to get it over her hips earned an intrigued look from his blue-green eyes. Emboldened by it, she slid the stockings off even more provocatively, holding on to the bed post as she freed one, then the other. Due to the fit of the dress, she'd worn a thong only, and a low-rise one at that, since the back of the dress was low enough to show the twin dimples just above the seam of her buttocks. Standing in thong and bra only, she peeled away the cups. The underwires had dug into her flesh, but she resisted the urge to massage the deep grooves she was sure they had left beneath her breasts.

Pivoting away from him, she hooked the sides of the thong and slid it down her legs, bending over as she did so. She walked over to her dresser as if she were floating through water, a sensual creature under his close regard. She laid her undergarments there and removed her earrings, bracelet . . . rings.

She looked down at the three bands on her right hand. She'd never taken them off, for exactly the reasons Dale had guessed. Until him, she hadn't been interested in encouraging any advances, and those who knew her widowed status had taken it for the message it was. Well, except Larry, but the man had no respect for marriage.

Dale was behind her now. His hand slid under her arm, closed over her hand. "You don't need to take those off, Athena. They can stay."

"No," she said quietly. "Not tonight." Slipping off the set, she laid them in the crystal dish where she'd placed the earrings.

He turned her to face him. When his hands bracketed her rib cage, his thumbs massaged the grooves the bra cups had left. She emitted a noise of quiet joy.

"You are just too good to be true," she said.

"Remember that next time I piss you off."

"You've only done that once. Twice. Okay, maybe three times. It really wasn't necessary to criticize *Stealth* like that. I enjoyed it."

"The military should be able to ban movies. Or require a disclaimer that the makers were clueless."

"The point was entertainment, not accuracy."

"And Jessica Biel in a bikini. That was the one redeeming quality."

"Don't forget Josh Lucas's blue eyes." She brushed a light finger along his cheekbone to make his own beautiful eyes glow.

"I'll have to take your word on the benefits of that."

Smiling, she rested her knuckles on his shoulder, the crisp white shirt. She'd hung his coat carefully in her closet and he'd removed his tie, left it on her dresser, so now he wore only the shirt, the T-shirt beneath and his slacks. "Did you really enjoy this evening?"

"Actually, I did. You attract good people, Athena. The few less-than-good ones are necessary evils, ones you manage admirably."

"I saw you talking to Matt and Savannah. I'd like to get to know them better." Her voice thickened as his thumbs slid out of that abraded area and over the curve of her breast, just below the areola. Her body quivered.

"Good choice. They're members over at Club Progeny."

She blinked, tried to sound casual. "Really? You go there?"

"Not recently." He gave her an amused look, making her flush. "Jealous girl. Over time, I've found I prefer Release's smaller membership, the quieter venue. Before that I saw Matt and Savannah there on a regular basis, though they play in the private rooms. Matt's pretty possessive. I know the feeling." He cupped her breasts fully, making her hum in her throat. His thumbs wandered in the cleft, his gaze zeroing in on the choker as she lifted her chin.

"I like seeing that on you."

"I like wearing it."

"Every time you touched it tonight, it made me want you. Hell, every time I looked at you, smelled you, heard your voice, I wanted you."

She trembled, moistened her lips. Stepping back from her, he nodded to the bed. "Go lie there. Wait for me."

She obeyed. Cognizant of her Master's gaze, she put her knee on the bed, moved to the center on her hands and knees. When she lowered herself to her stomach, turned onto her hip, his gaze could have burned her flesh.

"You're teasing your Master more often these days. I like it. It means you trust me more."

"I do," she whispered. Her need grew sharper at his expression. He freed his cuff links, opened the shirt. When he stripped it off, she enjoyed how the white tank beneath showed off the musculature of his upper body. He unhooked the trousers. Though he didn't do the striptease she'd done, he didn't hurry, either, building her desire with his casual but intent speed. His eyes rarely left her, even when he sat down on the chair to take off his shoes and socks. He stood to push the slacks and briefs down, sat to remove them fully. Then he was moving toward the bed.

Since he didn't have his crutches, he'd left on the prosthesis, the first time she'd seen him fully naked wearing it. Her Master was trusting her more as well. Responding to it, she slid her hand across the bed, a mute appeal for him to come to her. He closed those several strides, sat down on the edge of the bed. She caressed his hip, brushing his firm buttock with her knuckles as he bent to remove the prosthesis. When he rolled toward her at last, lying on his hip so they were facing each other, it was just Dale and Athena, except for her collar. They were in the master bedroom, lying on the bed she'd put here weeks ago, preparing for this moment. Yet tonight was the first time she was truly prepared for what it meant. He'd been right to wait on her, and his sensitivity, his intuition, intertwined with all the other things about him she'd been learning to love, overwhelmed her senses.

He ran a hand along her arm, his brow creasing. "You're shaking. Are you cold?"

She shook her head, and his mouth firmed. He slid his arm around her waist, drew her full against him. She made a soft noise at the heat and strength of his body. Sliding her leg over his thigh, she pressed her knee against the base of his taut buttock as his hand descended, fully palming hers to hold her against his erection. He gave her one of those deep kisses, soothing her trembling by banding his other arm around her, pushing her to her back, his chest a solid weight against hers.

Those emotions flooded her, increasing the pressure beneath her rib cage, the aching in her throat. She couldn't say it aloud, not trusting it.

I'm falling in love with you. I love you.

He shifted onto her, her legs parting to cradle him. So often during these past weeks, he'd built her response to an inferno with a wealth of foreplay, intense BDSM play. He'd consummate the moment only when she was like a wild animal, crazy with need and heat. Tonight, though, it was simple and perfect without any of that. He slid into her with the ease of a key, her body rising up against his, reacting to the pleasure of him stretching and filling her, locking them together. She put her arms around his broad shoulders, tilting her head back as he laid his lips on her throat, using his tongue to trace the skin above and below the collar he'd given her.

"Master . . ."

"Sweet girl. Mine."

He pushed deeper into her, and she lifted her hips, taking him further inside. He made slow, short movements, an excruciating, pleasurable build. Everything about this felt like it should. So good she was afraid of losing it, but fear had no place between them tonight. Still, he saw it, and he drove it away with the movements of his body, with the endless kisses that became more demanding, compelling her to trust him with all of it, body, mind and spirit.

She surrendered that and everything else, including her fear, and let him carry them both over that precipice. There was no fear then, because when all was quiet again, they were in the bed she could now truly think of as theirs. He was home to her, and she kept her arms tight around him, hoping she was telling him the same thing. She could be his home. That, more than anything else, told her the truth.

She truly was in love with him.

SIXTEEN

A thena paused outside of Release, shifting from foot to foot. Was this the right thing to do? Of course it was. Three months. She and Dale had been together for three months. Though it seemed like the relationship was progressing so well on all fronts, this remained a hitch. He commanded her in the bedroom and often out of it, when that gave both of them pleasure, but whenever the topic of the club was broached, she stalled, and he saw it.

He'd told her that she didn't need to worry about it. When she was ready, he would know, and then, objections or no, they'd go. She'd tensed up over that possibility, but as the weeks passed and he didn't act upon it, she relaxed. Until she started to feel like a coward. Crossing that last bridge with him was a signal she was ready to be his, unconditionally. He'd given her so much, she wanted to give him that gift. She didn't want to blight their relationship with one thorny trust issue. She needed to show she was ready to do this. So she'd decided on a test run of sorts, by herself.

It was a good time to do it. Dale was in Houston tonight, visiting and helping out a family where the husband and father was a deployed SEAL. She would have accompanied him, since she'd been invited, but she'd had a couple of unavoidable work issues.

Though being away from him was never easy, work had become more so these days. For one thing, ever since the night of the dinner, Larry had been noticeably better, less aggressive in the board meetings, demonstrating more of his pluses than his minuses. Whatever had changed, she hoped it was permanent, though she remained distantly cordial, not wanting to encourage him back to bad habits. When she'd mentioned that to Dale, she'd earned herself a frown and a rather thrilling punishment.

He'd told her that she didn't encourage the man at all—that his character was flawed, not her behavior. Then he'd stretched her arms above her head, hooking them on the weight machine in the rec room. He tied her up in one of those beautiful and erotic rope harnesses he did so well. When she was bound from throat to thighs, he had three knots placed strategically against her clit and labia, such that as he used a paddle on her with powerful, stinging strokes, she writhed and stimulated herself. He'd drawn it out, increasing the pain to balance the pleasure, until she was pleading with him to let her come.

He only gave her the command when she stated three times that she was not responsible for Larry's actions. She'd soaked the nylon of those knots with her climax. After that, he'd gagged her with that piece, tying it around her head. She tasted her release as he put her over the arm of an overstuffed chair and fucked her hard, making her come again.

She swallowed on a dry throat at the memory. Though they weren't in "active" session all the time, in some ways she thought of them as a 24/7, because the Dominant side of him and the submissive side of her was always there, right beneath the surface, in everything they did. It was as if being together so much allowed her to reveal how much of her personality went in that direction, and of course it was clear how much of his did.

They'd met Matt and Savannah for dinner one night, an invitation initiated by Dale. The lovely rose quartz and silver choker Savannah wore must hold the same significance as Athena's Trident pendant, since she saw Matt put his hand on her neck once or twice and do the same maneuver Dale did with her on frequent occasions, a light tug while sliding a finger between warm skin and the metal, a reminder of its significance.

A s she entered the club and drew in the familiar scents, she saw that they'd added a couple new pieces of equipment and changed out some of the wall art, keeping the erotic prints fresh and interesting. But Jimmy was behind the bar as usual. He was talking to a couple of the Dommes, that easy flirting he did so well with men and women alike. The man was a bit of a chameleon, all told, though she'd heard less magnanimous members hint that he was merely uncommitted, as if being a switch, keeping his options open, was a bad thing. As if a set-in-stone, black-or-white classification was necessary to gauge a person's value.

It was part of the reason she was here tonight, right? Actually, both reasons explained her presence here tonight. She'd decided to leave behind one classification and embrace another. The key had been in Dale's words. *Ultimately you have to make a choice. Or I'll walk.* No, he hadn't been talking about this, but she wouldn't let this one issue erode their growing relationship.

As she moved to the bar, Jimmy saw her. His eyes lit up, reassuring her. "Hey, Lady Mistress. What's up?"

It jarred her. She'd forgotten the name they called her. Wasn't it odd, that something she'd been called for nearly five years in this environment had slipped her mind, obliterated by what she'd become under Dale's command, something that felt so much more like what she was?

"Hi, Jimmy," she said with a casualness she didn't feel. Was this a good idea? Yes. She needed to do this, get the first obstacle out of the way, see how it went. No need to make Dale suffer through this awkward and potentially disastrous foray.

"Diet Coke as usual?" He reached for the bottle.

"That would be great." She nodded to the other two women. "Mistress Sheila, Mistress Amy."

"Lady Mistress. Good to see you tonight. Are you playing?"

She imagined Dale's reaction to that, the feelings he'd made clear about any other man touching her. She was his, utterly and exclusively. It gave her the courage to meet Sheila's gaze, shake her head. "Not tonight. Actually, there've been some changes in my life." She touched her necklace. She hadn't intended to use it to initiate the discussion, but in this environment, it was pretty clear what it was, so it might make some of the elaborate explanations she'd rehearsed on the way over here unnecessary.

It did that, and then some. The shift in their expressions from warm welcome to silent shock made it clear they'd understood the message. It also gave her a premonition that things weren't going to go as well as she'd hoped. Or maybe just as bad as she expected, given that a fearful tension broke loose inside her that was all too familiar. Over the past few weeks, she'd done such a good job of compartmentalizing it, she'd forgotten how deep her dread about this moment was. Those unlocked emotions surged up now, filling her mind to the walls during the silence.

Jimmy was the first to break it, giving the other two women an unfathomable look before he spoke. "You playing with the switch side of things?"

"Yes. No." She corrected herself, not allowing herself the out. She closed cold hands in her lap, covering their sudden trembling. *This was a mistake, this was a mistake.*

No, you can do this. You're being silly and melodramatic.

This was your and Roy's place. You have no place here anymore. You need to go.

She set her jaw. "Actually, I was a Mistress to my husband because that was what he wanted, and I wanted to be what he needed. I'm a submissive, Jimmy. I always have been."

He blinked, processing that. Sheila and Amy exchanged a glance. "Told you," Amy said to the other Mistress.

Athena's brow furrowed. "I'm sorry?"

Amy shrugged. "I told Sheila it felt like you were faking it sometimes. Don't get me wrong. It was a good fake, but it didn't come off right. When you were in session, you did everything right, but it was almost too perfect. Plus you didn't act the same way toward him after, when you were hanging out together here. Like you just turned it on and off. And you never had the same vibe toward any of the other submissives."

She couldn't argue with any of it, but the word *fake* felt wrong to her. It hadn't felt fake to Roy, and that was what was important, wasn't it? Even more vital, it hadn't felt fake to her. It hadn't been what she was, but she'd viewed it no differently than watching a football game with him or him attending a book reading with her, things neither of them would choose to do themselves, but they enjoyed because of how the other enjoyed it. They'd liked pleasing one another, and that was a different type of enjoyment, no less real, because it all was part of loving one another. How could she explain that? She couldn't of course. It was too personal, too intimate.

Sheila shook her head. "No offense, but do you know how often I have to deal with the 'you must have been abused by your daddy, that's why you're a Domme' or 'you just haven't had a real man'? Or worse, the guys who think I'm one step away from a whore, 'playing' Mistress to meet *their* needs? What you did just underscores that attitude."

"This is a private membership club," Athena said evenly. "I came here to serve my husband, not to make a public statement about being a Domme."

"Whatever." Sheila slid off the stool. "Go kiss your Master's ass. C'mon, Amy."

Amy gave her another look, an additional shrug as if to say, "it is what it is," then followed her. They were headed to the suspension room, probably to hook up with one of the watching submissives in there.

"Here's your drink." Jimmy placed the cup at her wrist. Another couple had sat down on the other end of the bar, and he gave her a nod before he turned to them. But his welcome had definitely cooled. Not him, too?

She could have moved away, but she wasn't going to leave it there. After he took care of them, she drew his attention by lifting the cup. As he returned to her, she met his gaze. "Jimmy, what's wrong? I expected some negative reaction from the other Dommes, but you?"

He made a face, spread his hands out in a conciliatory gesture. "Don't get me wrong. You have every right to be what you need to be here. Domme, sub, switch. But people have the right to also be disappointed by it. I didn't think you were faking, Lady Mistress. A lot of people didn't."

"I *wasn't*, Jimmy." Because Jimmy had been a good friend, she tried to take the edge from her voice, give him more. "It's hard to explain. I wanted to be anything Roy needed, because of the way he loved me. The way I love him. When I was acting as Mistress to him, it was all part of that."

"Yeah. When it was never stated up front, that's hard for a lot of people here to understand. Even me," he admitted. "But you know some Mistresses have strong feelings about a Domme suddenly claiming to be a submissive. Especially one who was good at it, who attracted attention. Who has a rep for it, as you do, no matter what Amy says. Yeah, Sheila's right about the attitudes they face, and you're right that this is supposed to be a private forum to be what you want, but . . ." He gave her a helpless look. "It throws us for a loop. You'll just have to let us deal, learn to see it differently, and you be what you need to be. I have another customer."

"Hey, girl."

Startled to hear Dale's endearment for her spoken in such a scornful female tone, Athena looked toward the doorway to the suspension room. Sheila was leaning against the wood, coiling a single tail in her long-nailed fingers. "Yeah, see? Guess Amy was right. You already respond to being summoned like a sub. Want to exercise those *real* feelings and let me top you? Maybe we'll find out what's real. Like maybe you shouldn't be coming here anymore, because you're just a vanilla chick who was your husband's doormat."

Conversation at the bar and in the sitting room came to a halt, the few members present staring between the two of them. Hearing the conflict, several more had come out of the various playrooms. She recognized at least half of the curious faces.

"Mistress Sheila." Jimmy spoke sharply. "We have strict rules about harassing any member. That's uncalled-for."

"What are they going to call you now, *Lady Mistress?*" Sheila asked, brown eyes trained on Athena's face.

Jimmy came out from behind the bar, interjecting his body in between the two of them, breaking Sheila's line of sight. "Keep it up," he said between his teeth. "She can have your privileges suspended by the membership committee. Is that what you want?"

"Jimmy, that's not necessary." Athena slid off the stool. She appreciated his stepping up to defend her, but from the wooden expression he turned toward her, she thought he was just doing his job. She put down money for the drink and a tip, and shifted to meet Sheila's gaze. Sheila had hugged her the first time Athena returned to the club after Roy's death, but their relationship was defined by the location, the setting. It wasn't like she and Sheila were the type of friends who visited one another's homes or had shared interests outside the club.

During Roy's illness, she'd discovered which of his friends were true and which were fond acquaintances or worse, hangers-on. When things changed so dramatically, all but one's true friends disappeared, didn't they? "Thank you, Jimmy. It's clear I'm not welcome here, so I won't be returning. Good night."

She thought she saw a look of regret on Jimmy's face, a protest rising on his lips, but she was already turning, walking up the corridor, nodding politely to the hostess as she took her leave.

She reminded herself Sheila had resented her decision in a way that was disproportionately personal. Everyone knew she had some issues with authority, which was one of many reasons she'd embraced being a Domme. Whereas for Amy, it was the simple pleasure of topping a sub. That was the point. The motive was different for *all* of them. Some natural, some benignly dysfunctional, but all healthy as long as it was consensual and no one was hurt in the wrong kind of way.

So reasonable and logical. During those weeks Athena had been managing her worries, she'd considered that she might be "making too much of it," just as Dale had suggested. That rationalization had brought her here tonight, with her insulated bubble of unchallenged ideas.

There'd been no physical violence. Sheila hadn't even raised her voice, not really, yet the bubble had burst, and those ideas had disintegrated in the air of reality. Athena felt shredded inside. Now that she'd revealed her true nature, she was hit by shame and misery. They thought she was a liar and a fake, so how could she feel validated as a submissive? Even knowing she was being irrational, the feelings only expanded as she left the building, like a thick black smoke obscuring everything else.

Yes, Dale had seen what she was, and when he looked at her, she felt she'd embraced her true self. For heaven's sake, she'd admitted she loved him. But she hadn't said it to him, had she? And here she was, her confidence in who and what she was shattered in a matter of minutes. If that sense of herself was that fragile, had she just been kidding herself all along, on all of it? Had she been right in the beginning, that she should have kept her request to Dale limited to physical sessions?

No. There was no way he would have ever accepted that. He'd said so at the beginning. So she'd stepped into his world, telling herself it would be a nice fantasy. Then he'd swept her away and it became so much more than that. *He'd* become so much more than that. But she couldn't back away from this and keep him. It was too much a part of what he was. She could never ask him to give it up.

She tried to ignore the fact that giving up being his submissive, for her own self, felt like a raw wound in her chest. That didn't matter. Maybe it was time to end all of it, go back to the identity she knew best. Athena Summers, businesswoman, philanthropist, a person who liked to read and garden on her days off. She'd handled losing a husband she'd loved for over two decades. She could handle . . . whatever else she had to give up.

As she headed for her car, she felt like a tired and downtrodden middle-aged woman, wanting a cup of tea and to go to bed early.

She was pulling in her driveway when the cell phone rang. She saw it was him, but she didn't answer. She listened to his message, though, her heart aching at the sound of his warm voice and children in the background. "Hey, girl. Hope you had a good day. I'll be coming back tomorrow. Want to do dinner and a movie? I'd suggest my place, but my crappy DVD player is a poor substitute for your home theater. I told Gayle's boys about it and they said if they had their own movie theater, they'd camp out in there every night, make it their bedroom. Sounds pretty good, right? Anyhow, gotta go. I'll see you soon. I'm thinking about you."

She sent him a text about thirty minutes later.

Will be busy next couple days, but maybe we can get together this weekend. I'll call you later. Gone to bed early. Headache. Glad you're having a good time.

Then she turned off her phone.

Hey, girl. Hey, girl . . . When she crawled into bed, taking two over-the-counter sleep aids, she dreamed of the two of them saying it. Dale's sensual tease, Sheila's scornful mockery. The sleep aids didn't work. She kept waking up, tossing and turning, and finally moved to her reading nook.

They'd put Roy's hospital bed in the solarium during his final days. He'd wanted to see the gardens, feel the sunlight. Since she didn't want to sleep in their bed without him, she'd slept here, because it was close by and she could hear him call out. After his death, she'd spent a lot of nights in this chair for the same reasons. She didn't want to be in their bed alone. From here, she could see the little garden she'd made around his marker. The bronze of the golf statue gleamed in the moonlight. Nearby was the corner she and Dale had redesigned. She averted her eyes from it.

This room was her place, her sanctuary. Her place to hide from the world, to be just Athena, the girl inside the woman, the one who had thought about being a ballerina, a famous writer, an equestrian rider, a tennis player. As that girl grew into a woman, those dreams had been released like balloons in a park, and she'd embraced happiness in ways not anticipated. She'd found a wonderful man who'd loved her.

Reality and romantic dreams didn't necessary mesh, but that was okay, because the day-to-day exercise of loving someone could exceed both. But what could she be with Dale? She loved being his sub intensely. Loved him, period. However, the Master and sub was an undeniably important, vital part of their relationship. Not because it was too weak to stand without it, but because it was who they were, that definition an integral part of each of their personalities. They'd woven that reality together, and there was no way to retreat from that. Not together. Dale would never be less than a Master, a pure sexual Dominant who would need that part of himself accepted in a permanent, committed relationship. Whereas she knew how to function as a submissive without actively being one, didn't she? She knew how to fake anything.

She swallowed the jagged ache in her throat and wrapped her arms around herself. She hated that a few cruel words had destroyed her confidence so easily, but what did it say, that they had? She was glad she'd managed to keep her composure, leave the club with dignity, but it didn't eradicate the sense of shame. She wanted Dale here, yet she didn't as well. She didn't want anything right now.

Except for the night to last forever, so she didn't have to face what came tomorrow.

On her most painful days of grieving, she'd understood why some widows said they wished they'd died with their spouses. It had been a while since she'd grappled with that feeling, but it was there, tangled with the mess of other emotions she couldn't overcome any longer. She put her head down and tried to make it all go away. She prayed for the oblivion of sleep.

On the third day, she still hadn't spoken to Dale. She'd done what was needed for work, and when she wasn't there, she worked in the garden or read. She felt Lynn's gaze on her as she moved through the house, Hector watching her as she weeded and pruned. She knew she was acting the way she had when she first started feeling the reality of Roy's death. Everything was on autopilot.

On the second day, she'd lost the energy to try and analyze why one incident in the club had unlocked all of this inside her. On top of that, those feelings had wrapped themselves up like barbed wire around her feelings with Dale, so that everything hurt so badly. All she could do to mitigate the pain was shut down. She couldn't examine a wound that raw, and though she knew she was in trouble, she couldn't make herself care. Not as long as she kept taking care of everything expected of her, and she was.

On day three, Lynn brought the house phone out to the garden. "It's Mr. Rousseau," she said clearly. Since the housekeeper wasn't covering the mouthpiece, Athena knew it was pointless to offer the silent gestures to indicate she wasn't available, but she tried anyway. In response, the housekeeper simply handed her the phone. "He said he knows you're here and"—she cleared her throat—"he says you damn well will talk to him. Apologies, ma'am." Then she fled.

Well, she shouldn't be surprised that Dale could intimidate

someone even over the phone. She put the receiver up to her ear. "That was direct enough," she said coldly.

"It was intended to be. What's going on, Athena?"

"Nothing. I just . . ." Hearing his voice, angry and rough, made her heart start to throb. If she opened up the locked box of her feelings, she was pretty sure it would explode. "I need some time, Dale. As I said in my message, I'll call you when I'm ready. Please respect that." She cut the connection, set the phone aside.

She went back to her weeding. When the first drop fell on her forearm, she thought it was starting to rain. Glancing up, she noticed a sunny sky, and felt the tears running down her face. Damn it. She bent to her task again, ignoring them, even as they continued to fall into the soil she was disturbing. Hopefully it wouldn't be enough salt water to harm the plants.

Stop crying, stop crying, stop *crying.*

She didn't even notice when Lynn retrieved the phone, until she became aware she was just standing there, watching Athena with worried eyes.

"Ma'am . . . can I bring you a sandwich? It's well past lunch."

Athena shook her head, keeping her face averted toward her task. "No. I'm fine, thank you. I'll fix myself something later. Why don't you and the other staff take the rest of the day off?"

"Well, I was going to do the curtains . . ."

"I'm sure they can wait." Athena stared down at the weeds. "In fact, tell everyone they have the week off with pay. Don't come back until Monday."

"Mrs. Summers—"

"*Lynn.*" She'd never snapped at her housekeeper. She curled her fingers inside her gloves, took a deep breath, and pasted a smile on her face, softening the admonition with a chuckle that came out sounding real and warm. A miracle. When she turned her face toward the housekeeper, she'd done a quick swipe, taking away the evidence of the tears. "I mean it. You all work too hard. Take the week. I'll be fine. Please."

If there was a touch of desperation in her voice on that last note, there was nothing she could do to help that. Lynn studied her face, gave her a nod. "I'll be just a phone call away if you need anything, though."

"Okay. I appreciate that."

She turned back to ripping up plants. A few moments later, she was alone. Sometimes a woman just needed solitude to figure out what and who she was. Not today, though. She'd think about weeds instead, pulling out what didn't belong and restoring order to her flower beds.

SEVENTEEN

She woke in her reading chair, her senses tuned to a sharp point. A glance at the wall clock told her it was past midnight. Someone was in the house.

The security alarm wasn't going off, but she couldn't remember if she'd set it. She slid out of the chair, moving silently toward the main library. Yes, she could have slipped out the back into the gardens, but she was isolated out here, and had no car keys to manage an escape in a vehicle. Plus, this was her home and Roy's. She wasn't going to permit it to be violated by a burglar. There was a phone in the library, but more importantly, there was a gun.

She had both in hand, was backed up in the corner, listening, when the footsteps drew closer. Then she recognized the tread. She cut off the phone before she pressed the final 911 digit.

His silhouette appeared in the doorway of the library, then he hit the light switch, which turned on a lamp on the desk. Beyond the illumination it provided there, it mostly threw shadows around the rest of the room. His gaze went right to the corner where she was standing, making it clear he'd tracked her here. She supposed she shouldn't be surprised he found her so quickly, despite the time of night. He'd likely followed enemies through much more difficult terrain.

His cool blue-green eyes slid to the weapon, back to her pale face.

"Going to use that on me?"

"I might have. If I hadn't recognized your gait."

"One thing having a fake leg is good for." He studied her. She was the one who finally broke the silence.

"I don't want you here. I want you to go." But she stood there, staring at him, wishing and longing. Wanting everything to be the way it was. Wanting to break out of whatever this was. He was right there, but a giant chasm was open between them. She'd messed up, on every level. Handled all of it wrong, and she didn't know how to make it better. She was so tired of trying to make it better.

He nodded. Then he extended his hand. "Come here, girl. Come to your Master."

She dropped both phone and gun on the desk, and ran to him.

He caught her, holding her close as she practically burrowed into him, hoping that his arms would keep her from shattering. Merely seeing him, and all those cruel bands clamped around her insides loosened, letting her draw a deep breath. She couldn't speak, just clung to him as he stroked her hair. She hadn't brushed it today, and she hadn't changed out of her pajamas, hadn't donned makeup. It was not her best look, which probably made the dim light a good thing.

She was shaking, and was bemused to find herself dizzy, such that when he eased her grip on his neck, pushed her far enough away from him to look at her, she was wobbling on her feet. He registered it, and other things, too. "Athena, when was the last time you ate anything? Drank?"

"I don't drink," she said. "Just wine occasionally."

"Water. Fluids."

"Oh. I . . ." She couldn't remember. Lynn had offered to make her a sandwich, and she'd grazed in the kitchen since then, here and there. Had that been two days ago?

"I need to go brush my hair," she said. "I look a sight."

"You need to come with me," he responded. Then he bent and lifted her in his arms.

"I can walk."

"I'm not sure you can. Adrenaline got you to the library, and that's why you're shaky now." He strode through the house, headed for the kitchen. Once there he deposited her in a chair and poured her a glass of water from the pitcher in the fridge, put it in front of her. "Start sipping on that while I put you together a meal."

She didn't want him waiting on her. "I can do it. You shouldn't—"

"Don't tell me what I should and shouldn't do, Athena." He was angry with her. He let her see it, such that she fell silent, though she nursed a little resentment of her own.

"You didn't ring the bell."

"No, I didn't. You gave me the entry code. You weren't talking to me." He dropped an armload of sandwich fixings on the counter, then nudged the water at her. "If you don't start drinking that, I'm putting you in the truck and taking you to the emergency room. Do it."

She gave him a sullen look but picked it up, took a sip or two. He kept glancing at her, the force of that look prompting her to drink more. In between swallows, she sat silently, holding the glass with both hands. She'd liked having his arms around her. She wanted to go up to the bedroom and sleep with him curled around her like that. Forever.

He set aside the bread knife, began to put deli slices on the thick wheat slab. "I figured it out," he said. "Not from you, obviously. I thought about the things that could make you shut down like this, and the way you like to make things easier for everyone. You went to the club, tried to give them an early heads-up, a trial run to see how they took it. And they slapped you down for it. Hard."

His face was set, cold. She didn't think she could take his scorn, but then she remembered how he'd held her. He was making her a sandwich now. "How did you . . ."

"After Jimmy figured out who your new Master was—and that I was willing to reach across the bar and squeeze the truth out through his testicles—he gave me enough info to put two and two together. I filed the complaint against Mistress Sheila you should have."

"She was just telling the truth."

He stopped what he was doing, and now his eyes went from ice cold to laser fury. "Whose truth, Athena? Is the way she sees you how you think of yourself? Have you let everyone else be your mirror for so long you don't know your own image? Who you really are?"

"No. I was . . . who I am. With you."

He came around the counter, turned her to face him. "You're talking in past tense, Athena. And that's not going to happen. What were you doing, when you went to the club? The thing I've tried to hammer in your head since day one of this relationship, goddamn it?"

His words hit her like rocks. As she flinched, he muttered an oath, cupped her face and held her briefly to his chest before pushing her back, gripping her shoulders like he might shake her until her teeth rattled. Instead, he released her to push the sandwich and water at her. "Eat and hydrate. I'm not going to fight with you when a good breeze could blow you down."

Since her hands were clumsy and slow, he picked up the sandwich and made her take a bite from it that way. Then he lifted the glass to her lips, getting her to wash it down her dry throat with a swallow of water. He kept that routine going until her hands steadied. During it, he took a seat on the stool in front of her, his right foot planted like a barricade, as if he intended to thwart an escape attempt.

The food and water did help. Except for functional comments, he remained silent until she began to feel less wobbly. She didn't know why he was angry with *her*. She'd gone there to announce who and what she was, so it wouldn't be such a shock the first time she and Dale came. She was trying to make it easier for them both. She'd wanted to handle it so he . . .

She closed her eyes. Why was that one thing so hard for her, such a stumbling block?

He was grumbling about it, even as he took care of her. "I'm starting to think I need to put you over my knee and beat your ass every morning to remind you that you don't have to handle things alone. You don't have to pave the way to make things easier for everyone else. Especially me." He stabbed the counter with his finger to make the point. "We should have done this together. We will do it together."

Her gaze snapped up at that, and she shook her head. "No. I don't want to go back there."

"Tough. Do you belong to me, girl?" He touched the necklace on her throat. She hadn't taken it off once, not even after the club. "Do you want to give this back?"

She immediately closed her hand on the choker, as if she thought he might take it away then and there. The hard look on his face eased somewhat. "Good answer. We're going to the club. Soon, and the right way. But now we deal with this." He ran his fingers through her limp hair. She tried to pull away, not wanting him to do that when it was dirty, but he made a quelling noise that stilled her. "What happened, Athena? Why'd you withdraw this way?"

Over the past several days, it had drifted through her mind, a thought she'd at first refused to pin down and examine any more closely, but with nothing but time, the truth had come into focus. She wasn't proud of herself, but she couldn't hide from it, either, not under the weight of those blue-green eyes that demanded brutal honesty from her. "The minute I let go, that I chose to be what I want instead of who people expect me to be . . . that happened. And it felt like, by letting go of those reins, that I'd let go of a rope."

"Hmm. You fell down into an abyss, didn't you?"

It was such an accurate description of the black hole feeling of the past few days it startled her, made her lift her gaze to his face again. He pushed the chips he'd found for her closer to encourage her to keep eating, and took one himself. "Did you do grief counseling, after Roy died?"

She shook her head. "It always seemed kind of silly to me."

"Yeah, me, too. Unfortunately, a couple times in my career it was mandatory. Though I only did the bare minimum required, I did learn something that helped me as well as men under my command. When it comes to losing a person close to you, the shrink warned me that sometimes people experience a second wave. You get through the first couple years, life is moving on, you're moving on, and then suddenly something happens. It can be something small or large, but it's like suddenly you've been stabbed and you're bleeding out. Instead of grieving the person you lost, you're grieving for someone else. Yourself, because who you were when that person was alive died, too. That can be an even tougher mourning process, because it ties up with the first, like a double whammy."

He fed her another chip, stroked a lock of her hair behind her ear and held it there, his fingers caressing her jaw.

"Once I was in that abyss . . . I didn't have to be anything." She whispered the words, feeling the sting of shame again. "It was wrong, but . . . I didn't want to leave."

A tear gathered in the corner of her eye but he absorbed it with the pad of his thumb, pressed gently there. "The first time you and I talked about where you wanted to go with this," he said quietly, "we talked about your fear of it becoming something with expectations, a role you were required to play. I think you do want to break out of that, but because it's what you've known for so long, it's a secure place for you as well. That's why you keep ending up in there, and the bitch of it is, it seems to creep up on you and take you down when things are going the right way."

His fingers tightened on her face, his countenance taking on that stern cast that always riveted her attention. It tightened up everything, even in a fragile moment like this where the reaction felt painful. "If you're in that cell, you're not living, Athena. Yeah, you've always been what people expected, and you did it well. That took courage, patience, a generous heart. But you know what else takes courage? Being who you are. Accepting the difference between bad behavior that you need to change, and people needing to mind their own damn business. When people strike out at you for being who you are, most times it's because of something about themselves, not about you. They liked having you meeting all their expectations. It keeps their world comfortable, doesn't it?"

"I'm not angry with anyone. I don't blame them for that."

"I'm not saying you have to. You're a submissive, Athena, the kind that likes to make other people comfortable and happy. But there's a line." His gaze sharpened on her. "When you decided to be who you really are with me, that meant you could no longer be what some other people want you to be. Unfortunately, Sheila has a narrow paradigm and some issues, and she struck out at you when you hit that rocky territory. That's her problem, not yours. Understand?"

She nodded. She wanted to do more than hear the words. She wanted to feel them, believe them. It was easier with Dale here, but the past three days had bogged her down in a swamp of reactions not easily overcome, even by his formidable presence. She remembered how easily it had come apart without his presence. It was hard to believe in a reality that fragile.

Dale touched her chin, drawing her attention again. "This relationship works for you and me because you're being who you want to be, and I *always* want you to be that. That's why I'm so tough on you when you start handling things. I love everything I know about you thus far, but you know what? There are going to be things I don't like. Beyond your fondness for *Stealth*. Maybe you have a hidden passion for reality TV or you'll want the toilet roll turned a different way from how I want it."

She almost managed a small smile at that, but his expression stayed serious. "And that's going to be okay. But what will *never* be okay, what I'll *never* accept, is you denying your heart just to please me. Because all I want is to love you and care for you. No, don't you start crying again."

Pulling her off the stool, he stood her between his knees and held her, cupping her skull with one hand and keeping his other arm tight around her. "The rest is just icing or chaff, girl, and we work through it. I'm sure you don't like everything about me, but you're still with me, right?"

She sniffled, drawing back enough to give him a teary smile. "You are kind of overbearing sometimes."

His lips curved in response. "Yeah, I've heard that before. Sorry. Retired Master Chief is listed as 'overbearing SOB' in the dictionary."

She reached out with trembling fingers, put them on his somber face. "I'm so sorry."

"The apology you need to make is to yourself, girl. You're a kickass, smart woman. I've seen you work a room of over five hundred people, understand who and what each one of them is with just a brief conversation. So why'd you let a couple catty women and one emotionally constipated bartender rip you to shreds like this?"

She shook her head. "I don't know. I'm really not sure. Maybe I thought . . . I went to them as myself, no shields, and so I wasn't ready for what that felt like, being hit without any protection in place."

"Yeah. Which is why I should have been with you." He gave her a sharp pinch on the ass that made her jump, but he held her in place. "Our relationship, your being a sub; you thought it was all a glass house because you couldn't handle it by yourself, didn't you? You are a formidable woman, Mrs. Summers. But on those very rare occasions when you aren't invincible, that's where you rely on your Master."

She could swear the man read minds. But since it was exactly what she'd thought, his answer brought relief, tears, and a hope that just maybe, he was right. He took a firmer grip on her.

"When you first learned how to drive, did you do it all by yourself?" When she shook her head, he gave her another one of those admonishing pinches. "No, you didn't. You were probably a little scared, too. It's something, being behind the wheel of a car for the first time, knowing if you do something wrong you could kill yourself or someone else. Try learning how to handle explosives."

She did smile at that, though her eyes were still dewy. He kissed both her eyelids, letting out a quiet oath. "When your eyes are full of tears, you break my heart, girl. I forbid you to cry ever again."

She snuffled at that, her face now pressed to his neck. "My point being," he continued with mock sternness that wasn't entirely teasing, "When you embrace something entirely new, you accept guidance, a teacher. Help. This is no different."

He tipped up her chin, stared at her. "It's time for you to trust me, once and for all, girl. No, don't you start thinking you failed me. Or yourself. This isn't like that. It's learning to do the three-point turn and the parallel parking. You're reaching for new skills, expanding who you are, who you're meant to be." He touched her cheek. "To trust me, you have to trust *yourself*. Give yourself that gift, Athena. Give us both that gift."

She rolled that thought around her tired mind, feeling that tiny spark of hope expanding inside her. It was so simple, really. So hard and so simple at once.

He sighed. "Christ, I missed you. I was trying to give you space, and then I just decided, fuck it, I'm going over there."

"I'm glad you did. Though I really need a bath. I look—"

"Don't." He stopped her. "Let's get you fed, then we'll worry about the rest. I'm here, and we're going to talk this out some more, figure it out, make it better. All right?"

She nodded. Trust him, trust herself. It was a leap of faith, and it started now. Maybe, as he said, she merely needed constant reminding to stay on the right track. Then she thought about how he'd said he'd do that, and that spark flickered with the possibility of a much different kind of heat.

He insisted she finish the entire sandwich and glass of water before they left the kitchen. If she managed it, he also promised she could have a shower. Though she had to accomplish it at a slow pace, he was patient. He also kept the conversation to easy things, random topics. Apparently his intent that they discuss what had happened further wasn't going to be pressed any more tonight, to her relief. As they went up the stairs to her bedroom, he kept his arm around her waist, steadying her as they went. He also brought a napkin of Lynn's oatmeal raisin cookies and an additional bottle of water, which he sat on her nightstand. "Take off your pajamas, Athena," he told her. "I'll sit with you while you take a shower."

She obeyed, but avoided looking at herself in the closet mirror until he came and stood behind her, pressing his clothed body against her bare one. She'd been so detached from everything these few days, his touch against her bare skin was startling, but in a welcome way. He captured her hands in his.

"Look at yourself, Athena. That's an order."

Limp hair, tired eyes, no makeup. His collar on her throat. Her posture reflected her weariness.

"You look like you've been through hell," he murmured against her ear. "But you're still the most beautiful woman I've ever seen. You get that, right?"

She closed her eyes as he slid her hair to the side and kissed her neck, lips nuzzling the collar. He slid his touch from her hips to her breasts, holding them in his large hands. Her lashes lifted, because she wanted to see how that looked. Her nipples started to respond to his touch immediately.

When she drew in a breath, she realized she hadn't been able to draw in deep like that for three days. In her self-imposed prison, Dale had been a vital element she'd denied herself, such that it seemed her lungs hadn't been able to work at full capacity.

"Why didn't you call me, Athena?" he asked, mouth still against her flesh.

"Because . . . I'd done something wrong. I messed it up. I was ashamed. I didn't feel like . . . I deserved to reach out to you to make it better."

He lifted his head, his grip on her increasing so she was leaning back against him. He stroked her breasts, making that quiet sound in his throat when her body wanted to move restlessly against his touch. He wanted her to be still, so she tried. But Lord, the man had magic in those long fingers. Then he spoke, and that velvet timbre subdued her.

"You remember why you said you wanted to help me take care of my leg? You said it honors your submission to be able to care for your Master. That my willingness to look to you for that would emphasize that you belong to me."

When she nodded, he put his thumbs under her nipples, slowly pressing upward so he tilted the sensitive tips, spearing sensation right down to her core. Her head dropped back on his shoulder and her throat arched, displaying her unconscious surrender to him as he increased the strength of that touch. "Masters have a similar need," he said in a husky voice, his eyes fixed on what he was doing to her. "You're a strong woman, Athena. When you turn to me for help, it's an honor I cherish. It tells me you trust me to be your Master, to step up when you need me. I should have been with you at the club, but after that happened, the first thing you should have done was call me. Next time something like this happens, I hope you'll do me the honor."

Normally he insisted, demanded, ordered. Did he realize what a devastating tactic it was to put it like that, taking them back to the critical and emotional first step of a Master-sub relationship? No matter how much a submissive belonged to her Master, she had to first give consent to that ownership. She had to give him her trust.

She wrapped her mind around that. "So if you trust me to care for your leg for the right reasons, and I trust you to help me when I can't figure things out, then ultimately we start having more faith in one another?"

"Yeah, something like that. Good way to shine that mirror on me, too." He gave her a fond pinch. "Are you sure you want to do a shower? I'm a little concerned about you being on your feet."

"It's easier to wash my hair that way." She looked up at him, dared to lift a hand and graze his jaw. "But if you're worried, you could come in the shower with me."

He chuckled. "I should have known you'd figure out how to manipulate that 'asking for my help' in your favor."

"You did say I was a smart woman."

Such simple things—seeing his smile, hearing his laugh—made things exponentially better. He was right. She should have called him.

He glanced down at himself. "If I do that, I can't put my leg back on until morning. Bathing changes the shape and size of the stump."

"Like trying to put on rings after you get out of the shower," she surmised. Since he'd dropped his touch back to her hips, she turned in his arms. "I don't have a problem with that. I do have a gun, Master. I can protect you."

A devastating and brilliant smile crossed his face. "I am capable of protecting myself—and you—with only one leg, Mrs. Summers. But it's nice to know I have backup. When did you learn to shoot?"

"I've always known. My father taught me, and of course Roy has a range on the property for his own target shooting. He liked skeet as well. It's a nice range. You're welcome to use it. As well as any of your friends."

"There she goes again, trying to get Lawrence and Neil back over here," he teased.

She pushed at him and he caught her hands. Sobering, he studied her face, bent to press his forehead briefly against hers. "You really should have called me, Athena. I wish you'd trusted me."

He spoke to her now simply as her lover, and his disappointment stabbed her more deeply than his anger or his fierce insistence as her Master. She wanted to tell him it would never happen again, but she couldn't. Hard as it was when she wanted to soothe that pain, she made herself tell the truth.

"I know. It will take me time, Dale."

"Yeah, it will. I'm proud of you for trusting me enough to tell me that, not trying to reassure me with bullshit. I don't need that, Athena. I just need your honesty." His eyes became more focused and intent then, back to being a Dom's direct expression. "In fact, I pretty much require it."

His hand slipped to her nape, and he drew her to him, kissed her forehead. It was a chaste blessing, but a reassuring one. "Let's get into the shower."

She remembered the first time they'd showered together here. When she'd seen the shower stool at his place and realized he needed it to bathe comfortably and safely, she'd made a point of directing his attention to a similar accommodation she already had in place at her own home. As Roy had become sicker, they'd had a shower bench installed in the master bath, one that swung outside the stall so he could sit down to take off his clothes. Athena could then help him maneuver himself and the bench into the large shower area and adjust the multiple spray heads appropriately.

The fact she hadn't had the feature removed made shared showers with Dale possible, a blissful experience. There were advantages to the set-up for two healthy people that Dale had quickly made clear to her, and re-emphasized now. Once he divested himself of his clothes and the prosthesis, he drew her closer to him, making her straddle his thighs as he ran his hands over her now bare body, laying soft kisses on her breasts, familiarizing himself with every inch of her once again, until she was trembling with emotion and physical response both.

He nudged her into the shower, following her using the bench and leaning back against the wall as she adjusted the water temperature. When she noticed gooseflesh on his skin, she turned it up even higher and made sure the jets covered him equally. She liked her showers hot, and had been pleased to find that worked for him as well.

As she closed her eyes, tilted her head back under the spray, his hands closed around her waist, brought her to him again. His palms bracketed her breasts once more, bringing her down on his lap to fondle them with simple pleasure before he ran his fingers through her hair, helping her get it wet.

Retrieving the soap, he lathered up his hands. As he began to work the fragrant foam into her neck and shoulders, her breasts, the sound that came from her was a cat's purr. She caught his smile, but she couldn't stop herself from doing it. At his nudge, she turned around on his lap so he could work his way around her body. He was hard, of course, but she wasn't sure he could be pushed in that direction. Truth, she still felt a little fragile, so it was nice to stay this way, a low hum of arousal between them. But that hum was pretty deep and intense, something she felt vibrate deep inside her, wanting fulfillment. Wanting the joining that would make everything right again.

When she came back to face him again, she held on to his forearms, then moved her touch to his biceps, pleased with their flex beneath her fingertips. "I haven't ever seen you work out," she realized. "When do you do that? And if you were lying to me earlier and you don't really work out, I will shoot you. I'm sorry, but it will have to be done."

He grinned. "Usually at night, before my evening shower. I go to a gym not far from my place. Sometimes I do the outdoor fitness course at the park, hook up with a buddy of mine there. Max works out early mornings, but he'll do a second workout or adjust his schedule and meet me there so we can push one another. He's younger than me, of course, so he gets to harass me about being an old man and I get to prove him wrong. Even if I pay for it with a bottle of aspirin the day after."

She ran her own soapy hands over his chest, sliding her fingers through the chest hair, across the flat nipples. "I love your body," she said sincerely. Fervently. Then she put her mouth on his. She leaned full into him, feeling every inch of that body against hers. She might still be a bit woozy, but any lightheadedness now came from this, how he put his arms around her, held her close, hand dropping to palm her ass, hold her more firmly against his growing erection.

"Finish your shower," he growled at her, pushing her back and confirming her earlier thought with his next words. "You're not going to get me to have sex with you when you were nearly fainting an hour ago. Consider it your punishment. Since it's punishing me as well, you can expect some more payback for that. Don't give me the pouty look, girl. You know exactly what that makes me want to do with your mouth."

She wanted that, too. She could well imagine him forcing her to her knees in the shower, her lips sliding down his hard length, tasting him on her tongue. But he was right. She wanted something her body wasn't quite up to doing. He was protecting her. Caring for her, even as he threatened retribution. It was a lovely and frustrating combination.

She didn't want to be alone in that, so when he gave her the soap to finish up, maybe she did slide it over her skin with more sensual intent than she would if she was alone. Her fingers slipped between her legs to rub and massage. She arched her back more significantly to clean between her buttocks, along her thighs, so the tips of her breasts jutted out toward him. He'd shifted to a cross-armed stance, looking like a palace guard watching the queen. Even in a seated position, he was daunting, his molten gaze promising dire consequences for being teased this way. Which only made her tease him more, until the corners of his lips were quivering.

There was another reason she did it, though. He could be a cruel, exacting Master when pushed over that line. She wanted that side of him, wanted to purge the past several days of helpless, self-imposed misery from her mind, drive it all away. She shivered in delicious longing at the thought, and tried not to pout. Somewhat.

They slept naked together. Despite their shared arousal in the shower, once she was lying down in his arms, lassitude took over. He made her drink the bottle of water, eat a couple of the cookies. After that, she was folded in his arms, head on his chest, while he stroked the wisps along her brow with his long fingers. She'd braided her damp hair, deciding she'd deal with it in the morning.

"Better?"

She nodded. When her eyes filled with an unexpected flood of tears, she resigned herself to irrational emotional responses until she'd had a good night's sleep. She pressed her face harder against the hair-roughened expanse of his chest.

"Thank you, Dale. For caring about me enough to come looking for me."

"I already told you"—his mouth brushed her temple—"Caring for you is part of the job."

"What job?" she asked, her heart beating high in her chest at his pause. *Being her Master?*

"Loving you, girl."

It really meant the same thing, didn't it? She closed her eyes and slept.

EIGHTEEN

The sunshine through the sheers was bright, telling her she'd slept long past her normal hour. Lifting her head, she saw it was eight o'clock. She rarely slept past six or seven, but she expected being in Dale's arms was responsible. Just as the fact he was no longer there was probably why she was waking up. He'd left the covers pulled around her, though, leaving her like a nested bird. The thought made her smile.

Lifting her head, she found him. He was sitting in the wing-backed chair, watching her. He was fully dressed, clean-shaven. He was reading her morning paper but, seeing her wake, he set it aside. As her gaze coursed up to his face, everything stilled. The expression he wore wasn't a lazy morning smile, a lover about to ask her if she wanted pancakes. It was that of a stern Master.

He'd called her an independent, strong woman, and she was that. She was capable, self-sufficient. Yet that expression awoke deeper, far more primal responses, bringing the submissive in her to full alert, uneasy and anticipating at once, though it was a little more weighted on the uneasy side, given his forbidding countenance.

"That thing I said, about teaching you every day not to handle the things that aren't your job to handle?" His eyes glinted. "I'm a man of my word. Bring me your hairbrush. No robe. You stay naked until I give you permission to wear clothes."

She slid from the bed, shivering a little in the morning air as she moved to the bathroom. The tile was cold under her bare feet. She picked up the wooden brush. It had the carving of a hummingbird on the back, surrounded by petunias. She'd bought it at one of NOLA's craft fairs, the brush carved by a local artisan. She brought it to Dale, lowering her eyes as she stood between the span of his boots.

"Am I your friend right now, Athena? Your equal?"

She shook her head.

"Then how should you be addressing me, girl?" he snapped, making her jump.

"Master. Sir."

He latched onto her wrist and pulled her forward. He directed her down over his knees, such that her breasts were pressing into his calves, her legs sprawled ignominiously over his other leg, spread by his knee there. He put a hand on her ass, holding her in the precarious position. "Put your palms on the floor."

It required her to shift forward, perching her ass at the highest point, centered between his legs. Her knees were bent, toes barely holding on to the floor, only his hold on her backside keeping her stable. Then he changed that anchor point, putting his hand between her legs and clamping it around her pussy, his thumb pushed against her rim. "You keep your legs spread. You don't worry about balance. That's up to me. Why are you being punished, Athena? Why will I punish you every day like this until I'm satisfied you've learned the lesson?"

Every day? Did that mean he'd be here every morning? Her pussy dampened at the thought, even as her pulse increased in trepidation. As tender as she knew he could be, he was equally capable of this, silencing every voice in her head but the one that told her she better follow his every order to the letter.

"For . . . for trying to handle things that I shouldn't. For trying to handle my Master."

"And?"

"I—I don't know, sir."

The brush came down on her left buttock, stinging and sharp, making her jump. "For not caring for your Master's property. *You are my property.* You understand, girl?"

"Yes sir." She bit back a yelp as he struck her again. "Yes, Master."

"I'm going to give you a pretty severe spanking this morning. Enough that by the end of it you're going to be trying to get away. But I'm just going to hold you down and keep going until I'm sure you understand. Because words alone won't do it."

"I'm sorry, Master," she said, trying to hold on to the floor as he shifted.

"Not as sorry as you need to be, girl." And then he made good on his word.

She was sure he was holding back, because he looked powerful enough to put someone through a wall, but it sure as hell didn't feel like it. She tried to be still and quiet, accept her punishment, but he'd predicted that correctly as well. Before he was done, she'd lost track of the count and was squirming, screaming, trying to get away. He proved without a doubt then that he was far stronger than she was, holding her in that position with one arm, bringing the brush down again and again until she was jerking at every blow, sobbing, clinging to his pants leg. Then he made her let go of him and put her palms back on the floor as he'd commanded, before giving her five more strong whacks. She squeezed her eyes shut and pressed her face into his leg, shuddering with the pain.

Her relief at seeing him place the brush on the side table was overwhelming. She was panting, her heart thundering. He eased her to the floor between his feet, positioning her so she was facing away from him. He wasn't in a mood to be tender yet, though. "On your ass, girl. Don't you try to avoid it. Draw your knees up to your chest, link your arms over them."

She winced as the position stretched the skin over the most abused portions of her throbbing buttocks, but she clenched her fingers together over her knees, rocking forward. His hands were on her hair, undoing the braid. As her sobs slowed to little hiccups, she wondered at his silence, wondered what he was thinking or planning next. He stroked his fingers through the wavy strands, loosening them. Then he picked up the brush and began to use it on her hair.

Deep, massaging pulls, the bristles scratching her scalp in a soothing way. She sniffled, shook, rocked against his touch. When he reached forward to pull a loose strand away from her face, she brushed her mouth against his fingers. As he stopped, holding his hand there, she turned her face into his palm fully. She cried, even as she nuzzled him, touched her tongue to the creases between his fingers.

She was a wreck, but that hard shell she'd formed around herself these past few days had literally been beaten to pieces. What was left beneath was raw and vulnerable, but not broken. If anything, she felt as if she was kneeling over her own soul, retrieving it from that shell, seeing it free at last.

He took his hand away and began brushing once more. She closed her eyes, letting the tears run freely, her ass hurting, every part of her shaking. At some point, she realized he was humming, a quiet, soothing sound as he followed each stroke of the brush with a stroke of his hand through her hair.

She wasn't sure how long he did it, but it was the most memorable aftercare she'd ever experienced *or* witnessed. The clock ticked on the wall, the only noise beyond the tiny adjustments normal to the house, the faint sound of birds outside. She was glad she'd given the staff off until next week. She liked it like this, just the two of them.

The simple stasis became something else as the tears died back. She thought of what she'd wanted last night. That had been the lust, the desire for emotional and physical release, but this had a different need entangled with it.

"Master?" Her voice was rusty with tears.

He paused. "Yes, girl?"

"May I . . . thank you?"

His hands resumed their movement along her hair. "Do you think you deserve that?"

"No sir. But I want to give you pleasure. Please."

He stopped again. She heard him shift, sit back. Eagerness flooded her as she heard the metal of his belt being unbuckled, his jeans being unzipped, the adjustment of clothing.

"Turn around and get on your knees. Arms boxed behind your back, hands holding your forearms."

He wasn't going to allow her to touch him except with her mouth. While that disappointed her, another part of it took it as an extension of the same punishment. She'd overstepped her authority with her Master. If she put it in Dale's terminology, he was sure as fuck going to make sure she didn't do it again.

As another side effect of his punishment, she realized she'd let go of what had happened with Sheila. It still felt raw, painful, but when her mind turned to it, there was no cringing embarrassment or sense of failure. At least right now. If she even considered those negative feelings, the punishment he'd just given her overrode it. It was a deliberate form of conditioning. God help her, he'd implied he'd be dishing it out to her regularly, but, perverse as it seemed, that made her feel better. He was in control. The punishment reminded her that any attempt to hold control broke his rules. And he was right. That reminder had brought relief. Pain had accompanied it, but as a result, there'd been no room for shame or regret. Paying the consequences of her actions took care of that.

He put his hands on her upper arms and shifted her forward on the carpet, bringing her mouth within range of his cock, jutting up hard from the nest of testicles. He'd merely opened the jeans, freed his shaft from them and the boxers beneath. He wasn't going to give her a tempting view of his ass or upper thighs. She was servicing her Master, pure and simple, and it made everything in her tighten up and contract, every nerve ending rippling with eager, excruciating need.

He gathered her brushed hair into a tail, holding it in his fist. With the pressure of his closed hand against her scalp, he brought her down to him. Because her arms were boxed behind her, she had to depend on his hold, the hand he had on her shoulder to control her descent and direction. Then she had her mouth on his cock.

She made a hungry noise as she enclosed it, slid down to the root. He grunted, hand tightening in her hair, and he began to control all the movements, up and down, making it clear her mouth was at his disposal, to use as he desired. Arousal from her pussy made her calves slick, but even before that she'd been wet, from the spanking of all things. Through the punishment, her nipples had stayed hard, her heart thumping erratically with arousal as well as pain-induced adrenaline.

She'd accepted she was a submissive, but discovering how much his harshest punishments could turn her on was still new at times. The moment she'd opened her eyes in the bed and Dale had given her that look, telling her he was going to be cruel with her, she'd started to respond. She didn't think she was a hardcore masochist, but she was realizing the punishment helped her put her mind in the right place. He had figured it out well ahead of her. Which was why he did it, of course. That, and because he purely enjoyed it, in a way that inexplicably thrilled her.

She focused on his taste, his scent, the heat and weight of him. It was more than his cock. She loved the sheer solidity and dense strength he possessed. His toughness was more than a surface thing. He was just as strong inside, a man who'd proven he was capable of handling a great deal, for himself and others.

So often he'd had to fish the words out of her, but during this pure service, she felt everything they'd discussed last night. She saw the difference between handling things she incorrectly felt like she couldn't rely upon him or shouldn't ask him to do, and wanting to do things for him purely out of love. She wanted to make things easier for him because he was her Master, and he loved her. He gave her a sense of safety and well-being that made her want to do the same for him.

It was amazing, what one spanking could do. If he delivered on his daily threat, she might solve all the world's problems in a week. Maybe they should have Dale hand out spankings to Congress. With a really, really big paddle.

But for now, she had one focus, and she gladly surrendered her undivided attention to it. She sucked on his cock, accommodating him by relaxing her throat muscles as he pushed her down to the root, then brought her back up again. She worked with him, bobbing up and down, flicking her tongue over him with mad, hungry delight, making matching noises in her throat as she increased the suction, nipping at him here and there.

"Fuck . . ." His oath was music to her. She kept at it, directed by his closed fist on her hair, the strength of his arm pushing down, drawing her up. *Please come for me, Master.* He could take her to a mindless state where she had only one sharp wish. To serve him, to feel his release and know she'd cared for him as she should.

His thighs shifted beneath her gaze, his breath increased. His fingers convulsed in her hair, the grip on her shoulder bruising. Her own fingers, gripping her forearms in the boxed position along her back, were damp from the effort she was putting into this. Then that effort was rewarded.

His cock jerked, convulsed in her mouth. She prepared herself, reveling in it when his seed spurted into the back of her throat, so violently she had to struggle to hold on to it, sealing her lips hard around him as he continued to shove her down upon him. She swallowed, coughed, swallowed, and took him down, using her tongue to lash at him, gather it all up, swallow some more.

He slowed with a shudder, a long, satisfied male sigh. She was worked up, highly aroused, but she wanted to stay that way. She wanted him to fuck her, but she also wanted to be like this, too, in a state of constant eager readiness for him. In some vague part of her mind, she realized she was hovering on the edge of a different type of subspace, everything gone except this, and she hadn't even climaxed. He'd taken her there another way, with the extreme punishment, followed by the demand of servicing him, two things she hadn't even realized how much she wanted and needed until she did them.

"Bring me a warm washcloth."

She rose on shaking legs, went into the bathroom and ran the water. She glanced up at the mirror as she waited on it, and saw two things. Her face, alive and vibrant, enraptured. His expression in the background, watching her with a possessive . . . contentment. She'd sated him physically for the moment, so what she was seeing was his satisfaction at knowing his sub belonged fully to him. It matched her fierce need to be possessed by him and him alone.

She came back to him, knelt. He took the cloth from her and cleaned himself as she watched with desire beating in her chest, pulsing between her legs.

He rose, tucked himself back into his clothes, rethreaded his belt and touched her head. "Get dressed and meet me downstairs."

He bent, tipping up her chin to give her lips a quick brush, and then he was moving away down the hall. She listened to his footsteps, the sound of him in her house, and felt . . . balanced.

Dressing was a little difficult since she was having some coordination problems, but by the time she managed to put on jeans and a suitable shirt, clean up her face, she was at least not fumbling her moisturizer. She clipped her hair back on her neck with a silver barrette, sure he wasn't in the mood to wait for her to style it. He'd said she was beautiful to him, and she was going to believe it. Though she did add a touch of concealer and eye makeup.

She followed her nose to the kitchen, where he was scrambling eggs and working on toast. "I would have made you breakfast," she said.

"Did I tell you to make me breakfast, Athena?"

"No sir." She thought of the formal contract that some Masters and subs wrote to clarify rules and structure. He simply led, guiding her with questions and insight, and ferreted out her desires through her responses, crafting that contract between them as they went along. She expected it was a skill from his training, thinking on his feet, mapping out a strategy, and she liked it very much. As nebulous and unspecific as she'd been about what she was seeking from the beginning, it was actually what worked best for her.

Perhaps it was part of what had drawn her to him, seeing those qualities demonstrated in his interactions with Willow or Sally. She thought about their volatile discussion over his continuing to take subs, and the warm memory of how that had been resolved. He was committed to her, and her to him. "May I help in any way?"

"Set the table. And you can wash out the frying pan. Not my favorite thing."

She suppressed a smile at that, and caught the twinkle in his eye when he saw it. She set the table and scrubbed the pan as he transferred their breakfast to plates and brought them to the table. He held her chair for her, scooting her up to her plate before he took the seat next to her.

Companionable silence reigned for a while as they ate. He commented about the hedge garden they could see out the window, asked about whether her wooden birdfeeders had been custom made. He liked carpentry, working with his hands, and that led to her asking him about his projects. She found out that, before Eddie's, he'd lived in one of NOLA's rougher neighborhoods, and had made flower boxes for the families there. He'd also helped with community beautification projects, like setting up a playground on an empty lot.

Impulsively, she reached out, closing her fingers around his resting on the table. He lifted her hand to his mouth, kissed it, squeezed. "Better today?" he asked, gaze searching her face.

"Much."

"No embarrassment." It was a mandate, not a question, and she smiled a little at that.

"Surprisingly, a lot less than I expected."

"Good." He gave her an appraising look. "Go to the living room. I have a bag there, on the coffee table. There's a bottle in it. Bring it back to me."

Curious, she obeyed. It appeared to be some type of ointment, handmade, because there was no labeling on it. When she put it in his hand, he gestured. "Turn away from me, drop your jeans and panties to your knees."

He was direct and calm about such orders, whereas they sent things careening in a hundred different directions inside her, like the thrill of a sudden jump of the car over a hump in the road. As she complied, she heard him unscrew the top, then squirt some of the liquid onto his hands. He must have rubbed it into his palms before he began to massage it into her tender flesh, because it was warm when it touched her.

"You'll put this on twice a day, morning and evening, as long as I decide to give you your daily punishment. Remember, I expect my submissive to care for herself. I like touching her soft skin."

Since she liked that, too, it seemed a mutually beneficial task. "It also keeps the nerve endings sensitive," he added. "I want you to feel that punishment, Athena, until I'm sure you've learned the lesson."

She thought of that spanking, shuddered inside at the idea of going through it a countless number of times before he was satisfied. She knew there'd be nothing she could consciously do to convince him; he would be guided by that damnable intuition of his to know when it finally clicked, and she couldn't really argue with it. It was hard to undo over twenty years of behavior, and she'd already proven, several times now, that it could ambush her, push her back into that cell, as he called it. He intended to seal off that room, and his punishment would be the mortar that did it.

A behavior modification proposal like that brought a dichotomy of anxiety and relief. She was also highly aware of his hands, kneading her buttocks, slipping intimately between them to finger her rim. Then he slid his touch lower and his other arm banded around her waist, bringing her down into a sitting position on his lap. The position allowed him to push his fingers between her labia, his thumb sliding over her clit.

"Whose pussy is this?"

"Yours, Master."

"Are you going to play with it when I'm not around?"

"Only if you tell me to."

He chuckled against her ear, a dangerous sound. "Wishful thinking, girl. Denying you makes you work harder to please me. When I finally tell you to come, you gush against my cock and mouth harder than when you aren't denied. Don't you?"

"Yes, Master. Ahh . . ." She moaned as he pushed his fingers in deeper, rubbed his thumb over her.

"Push your jeans and panties off and spread your legs wider, drape them over my knees. Lay your head back on my shoulder so your spine's arched."

He withdrew his hand to let her remove the clothes but kept his strong arm around her waist, seeming to enjoy the wriggling it took her to obey the command. She dropped her head back on his shoulder, looking at the play of sunlight across her ceiling, filtered through the window. Her legs were spread wide, her knees hooked over his thighs, and she cried out as he pushed his hand between her ass and his groin, coming up between her legs to bury his fingers inside her cunt once more. They were hooked at just the right angle to drive her crazy. She was moaning in no time, rocking against his touch, bouncing a little, as much as the position permitted.

"There she is, my hot and shameless girl. Push up your shirt and bra so I can see your nipples, how tight they are."

She fumbled to obey, tugging on the underwire cups to get them over her breasts. When the garment was resting above them, beneath her chin, the restrictive feel of the band made her think of the breast bondage he'd done on her. His hot breath caressed the right breast because of where he had his jaw resting on her shoulder. The nipple beaded further, winning an approving hum from him. It was indescribably erotic, sprawled on his knees like this, her lower half naked, him masturbating her in front of her west-side gardens, in her kitchen.

"Master . . . I'm so close . . . please."

"Beg me pretty, and I might let you."

"Please, Master. I'll do anything. Please let me come. I'm yours . . . I'll do anything for you . . . I want you to own all of me, every moment . . . every day . . ."

Maybe he hadn't intended her to go that far, but once she started, she couldn't stop the flood of words. His arrival last night, refusing to let her hide anymore, then the shower and curling around her while she slept. Even the spanking and this torment now, it summoned the words from her, gushing forth the same way the orgasm bearing down on her now would. Irrefutable, undeniable.

"I'm yours . . . please, Master."

"Music to my ears," he growled. "Your cunt is sucking on my hand. You are my sweet slave, Athena. Aren't you?"

"Yes, Master. I'm your slave. Always." In this moment she truly was, everything emotional and physical surrendered to his will.

"Then come for me. Show me your obedience."

She came so hard she almost blacked out, her vocal chords straining in one long yearning shriek. His fingers worked her throughout, his arm banded around her waist holding fast, no matter her involuntary struggles. She didn't come down until spots were scattered across her vision like a Dalmatian's coat, and she was clinging to his arm, panting.

"There you are, dear girl. There you are. Shh . . ." He was rocking her like a baby, and she turned her face into his, pressing against his temple. She loved him. Yes, she'd been through too much, had loved another man too long, to be ready to say it aloud yet, but with her body, her clutch of her hands, she knew she was telling him. She loved him.

He held her until the world evened out again, then he shifted her, held her steady while she stepped back into her jeans and underwear. He adjusted her bra and shirt himself, indulging the typical male desire to fondle her thoroughly first. He made her kneel between his feet, her hands placed on his knees.

"So here's the deal," he said. "This week, I'm going to see you once a day. You wear a skirt every day, no panties. You keep the brush with you, because you won't know when or where I'll show up. When I do, I'll take us to a private place of my choosing. Once we're there, you'll lift your skirt and bend over. I'll give you your punishment. Each night, I'm going to call you at bedtime. I've left that butterfly vibrator I gave you in your nightstand drawer. You'll use it from the time I call you until I hang up, but you will not come. After five days of that, we're going to go to Release together. You will be going as my sub. My slave. On that day, I'll tell you what I want you to wear, how to prepare yourself. Understand?"

"I won't . . . see you otherwise before then?" She couldn't keep the disappointment from her voice, even as the rest of her quaked at the itinerary he'd laid out. He touched her face.

"We'll see. I want your mind in a certain place, Athena. This will get it there."

"But I'll miss you."

"And I'll miss you." He gave her a disparaging look. "A slave's punishment can sometimes be just as hard on the Master, remember? So don't pull this shit again."

He sobered then, putting his hands over hers. "I think that therapist was right, and what happened at Release unlocked the things you've kept tamped down since Roy's passing. With your staff not due back until Monday, if I hadn't come to find you, you might have passed out from dehydration, fallen down the stairs; really hurt yourself."

Color rose in her face. With her head much clearer, the logic was impossible to deny. She'd been irresponsible. What if something terrible like that had happened, and Lynn or Beth had been the one to find her on Monday? How could she do that to them? Or to Dale?

He tightened his hands on hers. "Hey," he said quietly. "It's done. Don't beat yourself up about it. That's my job."

The wry curl to his mouth made her feel a little better, but when she gave him a helpless look of apology, he shook his head, touched her face. "You feel things much deeper than you realize. You've held so much inside for so long, when you let it out, it can take you by surprise like that. You scared me, Athena," he admitted. "It pissed me off, how pale and shaky you were. I wanted to say to hell with it, bundle you up and make you live at my place where I can watch you all the time. It's the good and bad thing about the kind of Master I am. You're right. I *am* overbearing and overprotective. I'm not going to let up on this until I'm sure you won't put yourself back there again. That you'll trust me enough to turn to me when you need me."

She understood that, but . . . "I liked waking up with you." She didn't want to be deprived of that for five whole days.

"It was pretty great for me, too." He ran his knuckle over her cheek, tapped her chin once with it. "Trust that I know what I'm doing, all right?"

She wanted to trust him for always. It was just never as easy as it sounded. She was already feeling nauseous about going back to Release on Friday.

She'd fantasized about being under a Master's full control, but as a practical woman, she realized such a thing was likely best left as a fantasy, the demands of her life being what they were. Over the next five days, Dale proved he was capable of coming pretty damn close to the fantasy, making it her reality in a way that had her mind going in lots of different directions.

She was self-conscious about wearing no panties to the office that first day. It made her feel naked, particularly wearing a skirt. For the first two hours of the morning, she had to force herself to focus, since she found herself listening for his voice every five minutes. At nine-thirty, she gave herself a firm chastising and then redoubled her efforts on the presentation she was preparing, moving from that to a review of their CEO's progress report for the latest quarter. At ten o'clock her phone vibrated on her desk. Picking it up, she saw his text.

> Meet me in the basement, maintenance corridor. You'll be gone ten minutes.

She shouldn't be surprised he already knew the layout of her building. Had he anticipated his SEAL training coming in handy for something like this? She suppressed a nervous snicker at the thought. He'd chosen a specific time block that wouldn't interfere with her ten thirty meeting, but it was close enough to it that when she faced her board she'd likely still be throbbing in multiple ways. Her Master was thoughtful *and* diabolical.

She picked up her purse, since it contained the brush, and left the office at the quick march in her heels. As she breezed past Ellen's desk, she told her she had a short errand to run and she'd be right back. Her admin's bemused reaction wasn't surprising, since Athena was probably flushed as a fall apple.

At this time of morning, the maintenance crew was dispersed through the building, only the dispatcher on the underground level, and his office was at the end of the hall. Dale was waiting at the entrance to the hallway. He nodded to her, unsmiling. At his gesture, she preceded him, quivering a little when he put his hand to her lower back. He stopped her at the fourth door on the hallway and opened it with his other hand, keeping her in the shelter of his body. It was one of the generator rooms, soundproof so the rumbling noise wouldn't impact other activities in the maintenance offices. He let go of her arm and locked the door behind them, sliding a device over the lock that appeared as if it would keep a key from turning the latch from the outside. Then he turned to face her and gave her a silent, expectant look. No greeting, nothing but that uncompromising stare and the crossed arms over his broad chest.

Putting the purse on top of a piece of humming equipment, she removed the brush, handed it to him. Her gaze lowered as he took it from her fingers, her breath shortening as she unzipped the skirt. She let it slide down to her ankles. He guided her to a steel pole, made her grasp it with both hands. Sliding his arm around her, he pressed his palm to her abdomen, and pulled her out further, so she was bent over, holding on to the pole, her hip pressed into his upper thigh and hip bone.

"Open up."

She spread her legs before she realized he was talking about the yellow rubber ball he was holding, the one he'd taken from her desk that first time he'd visited. She turned rosy at her mistake, but before she could close her legs, he cupped her there. Her pussy was already so wet, two of his fingertips slid into her quivering tissues.

"Good girl. My slave should always make herself accessible to her Master's cock, wherever he wants to put it. Now, open your mouth."

The ball gag was put in place, stretching her lips as before, and then he proceeded. He gave her every bit as fierce a spanking with the brush as he had before, such that she was soon squealing against the gag, her fingers biting into the pipe. When he was done and she was breathless, blinking back the tears, he nudged her to an upright position. While he had her continue to hold the pole, he made her step back into her skirt and aligned it properly on her hips, zipping the side zipper. After he straightened her blouse over it, he curved that arm around her waist, pressing her back against him. Leaning into his strength, she watched as he produced a wet wipe packet from his pocket. He cleaned the dirt from the pole off each of her hands, his touch as gentle and careful as it had been brutal.

He pressed his lips to her temple. "Day one, girl. I'll call you tonight. You sit as much as possible. I want you to suffer. Bad as you scared me, consider yourself lucky I didn't send you one of those wooden school chairs to sit on all week, instead of that cushy office chair you put your pretty ass into each day."

He opened the door and checked the corridor before escorting her back to the entrance of the hallway. He left her there with a nod, a press of her arm beneath his firm hand. Clutching her purse, she stared after him, striding across her lobby. The scattering of women all gave him a second look. Though most of the men passing through her lobby wore suits and ties, Dale didn't need any such fabrication of power. It emanated off the fit man in his dark jeans and T-shirt and commanded attention, likely inspiring all sorts of female fantasies. She tried not to begrudge them that, since he was actually part of her reality. But good heavens, the man had an arm.

Back in her office and sitting in her "cushy chair," she found herself wondering how much worse the wood would have been, given her ass felt as if it had been pummeled. He'd be doing this every day this week. The same thought that evoked trepidation also kept her pussy soaked, such that she had to go into her private restroom several times to dry herself. The sensitive petals screamed for her to rub them, to bring her some relief, but she restrained herself, remembering her Master's orders.

Denial just made the desire worse, which he'd made clear was his intent. She'd wear skirts with liners the rest of the week, and keep the box of tissues at her desk so she could put some between her legs while in her office by herself, to staunch the near-constant flow of arousal.

After making that prudent mental note, she gathered up her files and headed for her meeting. She felt like a fish floundering against a heavy, sensual current, threatening to sweep her away.

That night, the phone rang at ten, twelve hours after the spanking. Would he be that prompt every night? She expected not. He'd scramble the times to keep her off balance. Like he wasn't already excelling at that. When she answered, touching her hands-free piece at her ear, her mind was already locked into the place he wanted her to be.

"Yes, Master."

"Are you in your bedroom?"

"Yes sir."

"Take off everything, put the vibrator on yourself and lie spread eagle on the bed, legs out as wide as they can go."

Spreading her legs pressed the clit stimulator even more firmly against her. The first hum of it made her jerk.

"So tell me about your day, Athena. Not just your meeting. Everything you did from the time you got up until I called you just now. In detail."

She worked her way through her schedule, but of course he wouldn't leave it there. He asked her questions, making her think through her impressions of people, how she felt about those scenarios, the dynamics involved. All things she might volunteer herself, if she wasn't losing her mind a thousand brain cells at a time, like lemmings jumping a cliff.

She stumbled and stuttered, gasped, and he patiently kept her on track, sharpening his tone when needed. It became all about pleasing him, and somewhere along the way, she completely let go of herself, immersed in arousal and his voice, answering his demands.

"I'm . . . I'm close, Master. I don't think I can . . . stop."

"Stop the vibration."

She did, with shaky, uncoordinated fingers, and returned her hands to the rails of her headboard, where she'd been clinging, trying to resist the overwhelming desire to come.

"Good girl. We're done for tonight. You remember to keep your hands away from what's mine."

"Yes sir." She wanted him to keep talking to her, needed something from him, but she didn't know what. What he gave her helped.

"I love you, Athena. Sweet dreams."

The simple, straightforward way he said it made her cry for some reason. Being so fiercely aroused made a woman emotional, for sure, but it was also because she now knew how deeply he meant it. Dale was a man of commitment. He didn't make promises he didn't keep, and he knew *I love you* was the biggest promise a man could offer a woman.

I hope you get to feel what you've given me. Had this been what Roy meant? If so, the love of the husband departed and the lover present were enough to overwhelm her. She almost didn't get out of bed the next day. She was still aroused, yes, but other emotions were churning inside her as well. She wasn't due at the office, so she worked in the garden and prepared herself for a tea with several women from the Junior League, another planning meeting for the spring festival.

She was glad Dale had persuaded her to call Lynn and ask her to come back to work before Monday. Okay, well, he'd ordered her to do it, stating he wanted someone around the house with her during the day until he was sure she was solidly on her feet again. She was, enough to resent being treated like a child, but understanding his worry enough to capitulate with grace to the overbearing request . . . this time.

Now, though, she found herself grateful for the companionable chatter with her housekeeper as they set the table in the gazebo and she arranged cut flowers in a vase. Her mind slid to her first meet with Dale there. The way she'd gone to her knees beside him right where Lynn was standing. She'd taken food from his hand.

He'd said he loved her.

Intense BDSM practices like the spanking were so incredibly physical it could leave a woman's soul feeling a wistful twinge, a craving for the emotional. By cleaning her hands after the spanking, by leaving her with a statement of his love last night on the phone, he weighted the scale firmly back on the side of her heart. With each punishment, he was also helping her reconcile what had happened at the club, tipping the scales away from her fixation on that and instead on what they could have together. At least she sincerely hoped that was what was happening. Trust and faith. That's what he'd asked of her, and she was trying, day by day.

After the tea with the ladies, she did her workout, a hundred laps in her pool. Usually she donned her functional one-piece for that. But teetering all day on a sharp edge of arousal, trying to predict when Dale would next appear, she was a creature of pure sensuality. It didn't matter if he arrived now or three hours from now. She wanted to dress as if her Master might come to her at any moment, and when he did, she wanted to give him a reason to linger. Maybe test his control a little bit. The idea gave her a spurt of wicked mischief.

The bikini was a sea green color that picked up the green in her eyes. The first time she'd worn it, Roy had reacted like a randy teenage boy, a gratifying and memorable response. The straps crisscrossed over the sternum so her breasts were lifted and pressed together, the deep cleavage drawing the male eye. The bottoms were a Brazilian cut with several horizontal strands of beads dangling low over the crotch. When she looked at herself from multiple angles in the mirror in the pool house, she saw the bottoms hitched high enough to display the faint bruising of her buttocks from her Master's punishment. She wanted to show them off like a brand of ownership, and she guessed that was what they were.

She started her laps. On the twenty-fifth, she noticed the light on her phone. She came to the edge, looked.

I'll be at your place in fifteen minutes. Be ready.

He'd texted that eight minutes ago. She responded:

I'm in the pool house, Master.

Then she called the kitchen to let Lynn know he'd be arriving but wouldn't need an escort. He knew where the pool house was.

She did five more laps to burn off the nervous energy, then left the pool and padded over to her towel. She started, seeing him leaning in the doorway, thumbs hooked in his jeans pockets, his gaze sliding over her like his hands. Firm, proprietary. She stopped in the act of reaching for the towel because he shook his head, crooked his finger at her.

She picked up the brush off the lounge chair and came toward him. The blue-green eyes became even more vibrant, watching her walk, the jut of her nipples through the thin suit. When wet, it clung to her pussy and breasts in a way that was pretty much indecent. He put out his hand for the brush, then motioned to her to turn, show him the back. She heard him let out a breath that made her glow. Then quake, because of his next words.

"Going to be extra hard on you today, girl. You're purposefully tempting your Master, and you're too damn good at it."

Her toes curled. He took her arm, guided her into the private changing room, closed the door and took a seat on the bench, reaching out to manacle her wrist with his strong fingers. "Everyone's in the house," he said, his tone dark and dangerous. "No one to hear you scream, especially after I gag you with this."

Instead of the ball gag, today he had a ring gag. There was only one reason a man would put a ring gag on his sub, and that was because he wanted her jaw locked open wide and her tongue pressed down so she was helpless to do anything but take the thrust of his cock.

He gave her a look. "Going to make it interesting, girl? Fight me?"

She thought about the pain of that brush coming down on her haunches. As if following her train of thought, he let his gaze slide that way. "Your ass is nice and wet. It hurts more that way, you know."

He increased pressure on her wrist and their gazes locked. In an instant, she understood what he wanted, the intense play he wanted to give them both. The pressure of the past two days obliged, her mind willing to play rabbit to his wolf. She twisted, broke the grip, bolted for the door. He caught her, moving much faster than she would have expected. The man was so unbelievably strong, catching her about the waist and swinging her toward the bench as she thrashed and fought him, trying to get away.

That strength also kept her from hurting herself, because though he was relentless, he put her down on her stomach on the bench as if she were an egg. Her knees pressed against the outdoor carpet as he straddled her, gripping her wet hair to bring up her head. She tried to worm away from him as he forced the ring into her mouth, strapped it on. Her struggles earned her a sharp slap on her thigh that quieted her, made her surrender. He cinched the gag around her head, then stepped back.

"Take your bottoms down to your knees. Your thumbs stay hooked into either side of them to keep those hands there."

Her stomach was on the bench, her breasts on the other side, and as she complied, he circled her, squatting before her to lift her chin.

He gazed at her face, her mouth stretched wide with the ring gag, her fevered eyes upon him. His touch dropped so he could play in the cleavage the suit presented, then moved over the wet fabric clinging to her nipples. She whimpered, her fingers tightening in her swimsuit bottoms as he pinched her.

"You're a wet dream, girl," he said. "Looking at the way that suit pushes your breasts together, I'm getting some good ideas about the next time I tell you to put it on. I'll put my fingers in your pussy, collect some of your honey and lube up this sweet cleft"—his fingers stroked the channel between her breasts—"then I'll put my cock between them and fuck your tits until I come."

She swallowed, her gaze now pleading. He was making her insane. His next words suggested the feeling might be mutual.

"When you look at me that way, you rip my heart right out of my chest."

He rose. Moving behind her, he started on day two of her punishment. He was right. Wet flesh made the slap of the brush even more severe, such that she was screaming against the gag in no time.

After it was over, he laid the brush next to her, came back to her front and lifted her onto her knees with a firm grip on her hair and a steadying hand pressed against her chest. As she swayed there, waiting on his pleasure, he opened his jeans, revealing an enormous erection. He stroked it for a few agonizing moments, denying her as her tongue worked against the steel ring, wanting his taste, wanting to do that for him. Her hands were still bound by her swimsuit bottoms, fingers pressed against her thighs.

Finally, he moved forward, taking hold of her hair again and pressing his knees against the bench, his cock to her spread lips. Bound by his will, her mouth controlled by the gag and her hands by his imposed restraints, she could only close her eyes and savor the way it felt, being used by him in whatever manner drove his pleasure, which in turn heightened hers to an almost drug-induced euphoria.

He came quickly, reminding her of what he'd said, about a punishment for the slave testing the Master. She did her best to swallow all of his seed, though of course some escaped, along with the profuse saliva caused by the gag. He didn't seem to find it unsightly, though. After he tucked himself back in his jeans, he removed the gag and wiped her chin with his fingers, letting her suck on them before he cleaned her face up with another wipe. She stayed as he'd bade her, shaking like a leaf, while he put the gag and wipes back into a small bag he'd brought with him.

"Day two, girl. I'll call you tonight. Don't you go back into that pool. You've finished your workout for today."

And so it went. She dreaded and longed for the spanking each day, applied the lotion per his direction, grateful for it, and looked forward to his nightly call, despite the fact he'd leave her trembling on the peak of an orgasm. After the second night, she had an ice pack on standby at the end of the call. She'd hold it between her thighs until the throbbing subsided. That way she had half a chance of keeping her erotic dreams from making her come in her sleep.

She remembered how, at the beginning of the week of punishment, she'd felt like her mind was going in all directions. What amazed her was how those vacillating emotions started to spin into one braided rope as the week went on. As if, when all was said and done, all roads led to him. Her daily schedule became easier as she let go of worry about when he would appear, what he would require of her. She trusted him, she anticipated him, she longed for him. She wanted to fulfill her punishment so he could be her Master in other ways. She would never do anything to force his hand like this again. Of course when she told him that, he gave her an amused look.

Don't make promises you can't keep, girl. You have a stubborn streak and your own way of doing things. I like that about you. I liked it when you fought me. His eyes acquired that lazy, dangerous look that never failed to make her wet. *I'll have to teach you some other maneuvers so we can do a little sparring.*

She'd just arrived at her office that morning when the phone buzzed. Her body prickled with heat. Had Dale decided to come and see her this early? He was going to kill her. She had a demanding day ahead. Pulling the phone out of her purse, she read the text.

Day five, girl. No jewelry tonight, just your collar.

She nearly dropped the phone. Sometime over the past few days, a miracle had happened. She'd completely forgotten about the significance of the fifth day. Her mind had become so fixated on all he was doing to her, how she could comply with his demands.

Wear a sexy dress and heels, one of those tiny panty/bra combinations that make me want to fuck you in public so every guy knows you're mine. Tonight, I'll be doing just that.

Heat prickled over her skin. Everything about him she'd gleaned from Jimmy suggested he'd always kept it to oral or manual, not actual penetration with his partners. So if he did that, he would be making a statement. She wasn't just his sub of the evening. She was his sub, period. Sheila's sneering derision and Amy's look of dismissal crossed her mind again, as well as Jimmy's . . . lack of support. She didn't know exactly how to classify his reaction, except that it hadn't been positive.

She wished Dale would take her to another club, where their focus could simply be on each other. It had been too much to hope the worry would disappear entirely. As she tried to breathe through the mini–panic attack, she thought about how much calmer she might be if her Master would permit her One. Bloody. Orgasm.

She put it away to deal with her day. A phone conference, emails, a meeting at one of the plantations that would be hosting an upcoming event for the company. When she came home late afternoon, she decided to take a second shower, additional preparation for tonight. It wasn't until she'd stepped out of the spacious stall and was standing before her closet she realized she'd put herself into a numb mode most of the day, and that wasn't where Dale would want her to be for this. It wasn't where or how she wanted to experience it, either. He had made it clear he wanted her to embrace her own desires, that that was what pleased him the most.

Well, if that was the case, she really didn't *desire* to go to this club.

She sighed, knowing that wasn't what he'd meant. She was fingering a dress but waffling over whether or not to wear it. She'd bought it a couple of weeks ago, thinking Dale would really like it, but now she was worried the garment would forever be tainted by what happened tonight, if it went as catastrophically as before.

Why was she letting them define her, have so much power? When Roy was alive, his approval and love had been enough. She had a justifiable pride in her accomplishments, of course, but there was a confidence underlying any victory *or* failure, fueled by her knowledge his love was truly unconditional. No matter what happened, he would support and help guide her when she needed counsel. As a result, she'd wanted to succeed, not just for her own satisfaction but as a reflection upon him. True love made a person want to be even better for their significant other. Wasn't that what tonight was about as well?

She was going as her Master's possession, his cherished sub. Her actions would reflect upon him, and yet, at the same time, by following his lead, she was showing her trust in him. The wall she felt about going to the club needed to be broken down. The best way to do it was face it. Only this time she wasn't facing it alone.

You never should have done it alone.

Remembering Dale's words, she resolutely pulled the dress off the rack, and started thinking about her hair, her makeup.

t was eight o'clock. She was on the second-floor landing, about to come down, when he punched in the key code, entered. She held on to the rail to balance her shaky legs, but she made an effort to put an extra sway in her step, knowing that the low cut of the dress would draw the eye to the movement of her breasts as she descended. The black lace edging of her bra was a tempting garnish along the neckline. The various slits of the above-the-knee skirt made it swirl around her legs like feathers. The bottom portion of the dress was sheer enough a man could see the outline of her hips and legs beneath it, the hint of the black thong she wore. Her black heels had thin ankle straps.

When she reached the bottom step, he was there to take her hand. He studied her as a Master would, no hint of warmth or affection yet. She could use a hug before doing this. Several in fact, but that expression kept her quiet, her eyes lowered before his intent gaze. Everything inside her coiled tight, waiting for his approval.

"I told you your punishment is for five days. Today is day five."

She thought about enduring the sting of that brush one more time, and she didn't think she could bear it. "You don't have your brush with you," he said in a mildly accusing tone. "Turn around, lift your skirt. Let me see how cruel I was to you."

She knew there was mild bruising, reddish abrasions, but not as much as she'd expected for how excruciating it had felt. Apparently that part of the body could sustain a lot of impact without reflecting the results. But she still quivered as he traced the marks on her buttocks, visible from the scrap of thong. "What does my girl think? Does she need one more spanking to help her understand the lesson?"

She imagined herself kneeling on the stairs, fingers digging into the carpet as he administered her punishment. She wanted to say *no* vehemently. But her body quivered, anticipating.

"That's for my Master to decide."

He was silent, then his arm slid around her waist. He stood on the floor level and she was still on the bottom step, so his jaw brushed the juncture of throat and neck, his lips finding the latter. She melted into the first openly sensual and affectionate gesture he'd given her all week. She hoped she had permission to touch him, because her fingers curled into his forearm, never wanting to let him go. Her sore buttocks pressed against his hard body, dressed in the club wear he'd worn the first time she saw him. Black dress jeans, heavy-weight black T-shirt, and his belt with the silver buckle. He wore the silver-tipped boots. "Good answer, girl. I think we're done with that part of things, for now."

Chuckling at her relieved sigh, he turned her in his arms, cradling her face in one hand as he held on to her with the other. "You look pretty enough to eat. I plan to do that tonight, too. I've missed tasting your pussy."

But he started with her lips, putting his mouth over hers. She would have expected the wild animal he'd kept stoked all week within her to come to life, tear him to shreds in the attempt to crawl all over him, crawl inside him, but instead everything went completely still. The knife edge of her arousal was so intense, it was paralyzing, locked with an equally strong emotional response.

She made a little noise, her arms limp at her sides, her body leaning into him as he framed her face, plundered her mouth, teased her tongue and lips. Her hands ended up on his hips, thumbs hooked in his belt, and when he lifted his head at last, he held her full weight against him. With a faint smile, he tightened his arm and brought her to the floor so she was looking up at him. He fingered her collar, sliding his finger underneath the Trident pendant. "You're wearing it."

"I've only taken it off for the shower. But I . . ." It was new to her, to ask for new structure, new rules, rather than just letting him set them, but she hoped that was part of what he wanted her to explore as well.

"I know I'll need to wear other jewelry at times, for different things. But I'd prefer it if . . . when I did, I had to ask your permission to remove it."

His gaze heated, his body rippling against her as he tightened his grip on her waist, fingers sliding over her tender ass to stroke with devastating gentleness.

"Agreed. You definitely don't have my permission to remove it tonight, Athena. You belong to me utterly. The moment we walk out this door, until we come back through it tonight, we're one hundred percent in scene. You understand?"

It meant every word he uttered was a command, that she asked permission if she wished to speak, and that she was completely his. Tonight was graduation for all the lessons of the week, to see if her trust had reached the level needed to handle tonight's . . . obstacle. She pushed the word away, not wanting to think of it that way, and that in itself was a heartening change. She was going somewhere her Master wished to take her. That was the beginning and end of it. The rest didn't matter.

NINETEEN

As they pulled up to Release, Athena's belly quaked. There were nearly forty cars in the parking lot. Maybe they were having a demo tonight, like the rope bondage. If so, that could be a good thing, because if the members' focus was elsewhere, it wouldn't be directed solely on the two of them.

Dale put the truck in park, cut the engine and then turned on the seat to look at her. She couldn't meet his gaze. Her hands were tight in her lap, her back straight, her breathing shallow. She stared at the doors and thought there was nowhere in the world she wanted to be less. Her resolve at the house had drained away with every mile.

"It's more than just Sheila and Amy, isn't it?"

He was so good at that, though in all fairness, anyone who knew anything about her would know this reaction had to be more than that. "It's not you. I don't want you to think—"

"Stop." The quiet command drew her attention to him. Dale closed his hand over the two of hers. "My ego doesn't need stroking. This moment is all about you, nothing else. You're not Roy's wife, his widow, Lady Mistress or name-your-mask. You walk in there as who you want to be, claiming something for yourself, a gift for *you*. There's nothing harder for a woman like you to do. That's what's scaring you so badly. Isn't it?"

As always, he waited her out, let her think it through. She nodded and felt a wave of sheer misery. "What if I can't do it? What if it feels wrong to me?"

"Then you make that choice." He stretched his arm along the back of the seat and played with her hair. He nodded toward the street. "There's a great Cantonese place a few streets over. We'll go get dinner, maybe—"

"You'd be okay with that?"

His body language seemed to answer that question, since he was relaxed, no censure in his tone. All this preparation, yet at this moment, he saw it as no more than a change of plans. "This isn't about me, Athena," he reminded her.

"Yes, it is. We're . . . together. You have needs as well. And I . . . part of who I am, what I want, has to do with your happiness. Truly."

"I get that. I know making the person you love happy will always be a significant part of what brings you joy. That's not just the sign of a natural submissive, but a generous and loving human being." He gave her a smile then, and they weren't Master and sub, just Dale and Athena. "But when I say something, I mean it. As long as I believe that what you want, what you *truly* want, is not to go into that club, but to explore what we need from each other in other ways, ways like we've been doing, I have no problem with that. I want you to be yourself. That's my desire."

He took both her hands again, rubbing her cold fingers inside the grip of his warm ones. "Whenever I master you, you open up and show me that deep, beautiful submission that's so much a part of who you are. I feel like a kid at Christmas, given every present he ever wanted. Yes, I want to walk through that door. I'm enough of a guy that I want to show off this gorgeous, smart woman who trusts me enough to let me be her Master. But more than that, I want *your* happiness. I want you to value that as much as you value my needs. I want you to realize, once and for all, they're the same thing. Those two things feed off one another, and become even more than either of us ever realizes." He moved one hand to her shoulder, tightened there. "Okay?"

"Okay." She looked back at the doorway again. He'd given her an image she liked. She imagined walking in there as his possession, with him as her Master. She thought of how often she'd brought Roy here, and the way he'd looked at her. There was another misconception about male subs, that the Domme was "the man" in the relationship, that it was a role reversal, but she'd never felt that. She'd always felt safe with him, physically.

Yes, at times she'd felt a little alone with her emotions. Roy was the kite she sent flying. She held on to the string, controlled his direction, yet it was him soaring in the clouds. But the way Dale described it, when each was playing the role they truly desired, it was more like two birds, chasing one another through the clouds, twisting and playing. Soaring together. Tonight he was giving her the chance to experience it.

"Master?" She turned, met his blue-green eyes.

"Yes, Athena?"

"Please . . . I'd like to go inside. Will you take me?"

"Yes, I will." He unbuckled her seatbelt, fingers caressing her hip. "I'm very proud of you."

As a wave of warmth suffused her at the praise, he curved his hand around the side of her neck, bringing her to his mouth. She let out a pleased hum as he made it hot, demanding, teasing lips and tongue, giving her a sharp nip that made her gasp. When he lifted his head, that mildness was gone. She looked into the face of her Master and was deliciously lost. His hand dropped and her legs parted for him. She made a tiny noise of need as he cupped her sex beneath the feathers of the skirt, making idle circles with his thumb as she held his gaze, jerked in aroused reaction to the intimate fondling.

"You trust me?"

"With everything."

"Any fear?"

"A little," she admitted. "But other things . . ." She bit her lip as he pressed on her clit. "Seem to be outweighing it."

A feral grin crossed his expression then, making her heart lighter, even as her body was heavier, needier. "Stay there," he ordered.

He stepped out of the truck, pulled a duffel from the back, then came around to her side, opening the door and handing her out of the vehicle. She'd seen Masters who made their subs walk behind them as they entered, snapping a leash on them once inside, since blatant displays of BDSM practice weren't allowed in the parking lot, but Dale wasn't one of those. He took her to the door with a hand on the small of her back, low enough it rested the upper curve of her ass, a titillating tease. He opened the door for her, a Southern gentleman, and once inside, pressed against her side.

"You keep your eyes lowered unless I tell you to lift them, Athena. You rely on me to guide you, and you don't speak unless I give you permission to do so or ask you a direct question. All right?"

She nodded. He pinched her and she jumped, clearing her throat. "Yes, Master."

Keeping her gaze lowered was like being partially blindfolded. She expected he'd realized that. It relieved her of the need to confront expressions. When he stopped at the desk to check them in, she felt Susan's eyes on her, heard the tone of surprise as she responded to Dale. The hostess did the obligatory check of their membership cards, which Dale had secured from Athena at the house.

"Have a good time," Susan said. "Both of you." There was a question in her voice, as if she wanted Athena to respond, to confirm her unexpected role.

"You may respond to the hostess, Athena."

Athena lifted her gaze then, more ready to do that than she'd expected herself to be. She met Susan's gaze fully with a faint smile on her face. "Thank you. I intend to."

"Would you like to sign the guest registry?" Susan's well-manicured hand pushed the book more squarely beneath her view. Dale's touch on her back told her it was okay. Picking up the pen,

Athena made a slash mark and wrote her name next to his. *MC / athena.*

She was one of the lowercases now, as Jimmy said. *No.* She'd always been, just as Dale had known.

He took her past the bar, through the main room. She heard the voices, tried not to pay attention to any modulation of the conversation that suggested they were being stared at. Dale took her to the suspension room, like he'd taken Willow, only his destination wasn't one of the large frames. Instead, he took her to the stockade. It was an upright T-shaped steel device. A sub's collar and cuffs could be attached to the horizontal piece and then the vertical part of the T would be lowered or lifted to the angle the Master desired. A different interpretation of the stocks of historic times.

Putting his bag down next to it, Dale grasped her hand with all the ceremony of a man taking a woman's hand to dance at a Victorian soiree. He'd brought cuffs for her, as well as a stiff strap collar. After he buckled the cuffs around her wrists and the collar around her throat, a looser fit to allow her Trident to rest beneath it without harm, he secured all three restraints to the horizontal bar. He attached the cuffs to the clips that stretched out her arms so they were level with her shoulders, the collar secured to the center of the bar. He stroked her loose hair away from her neck so it spilled along the right side of the bar.

She'd seen Masters and Mistresses lower the vertical bar to the point that the sub's head was hanging down, but Dale wasn't interested in such an extreme angle. He lowered the horizontal bar so her upper body was at a ten o'clock angle from her hips. Then he guided her feet onto the foot pads and strapped them down, her legs shoulder-width apart.

She kept her eyes on the floor, but she was aware of people coming closer to watch. They were bound to attract attention. It wouldn't be just her identity, but because Dale's skill in conducting a session routinely drew interest. He wasn't wearing a mask tonight. Maybe he'd worn it that night with Willow because the idea of an anonymous Master particularly aroused her.

Was Sheila or Amy part of the crowd? Were they staring at her with derision, or simply prurient curiosity? The thought gave her a wave of uneasy feeling, reminding her she was the center of attention, so vulnerable. Thinking of her dream, she had an unpleasant thought about what an accused witch might have felt, dragged from the safety of her home, strapped in a wooden stock with no defense against the ugly fear of her neighbors, their censure.

Dale's boots were in front of her, his denim-clad legs. He stroked her hair, her face. He traced her lips with his thumbs, making them part. "Such soft, pretty lips," he murmured. "All the things I want to do to those lips."

She thought of all the things he'd already done with them, and a small shiver of anticipation went through her.

"There's my girl. Dressed up so sexy for me, taunting her Master with her charms."

He moved behind her then, hands sliding over her hips in the filmy dress. He pressed his body up against her, letting her feel his solid strength, his thighs against the back of hers, the heat of his groin against her core in the perfect position for fucking. If he'd meant his text, and she had no reason to think he didn't, he planned to do that to her tonight, here in front of them all.

"When I'm ready for a break, I'm going to shift you over there." He nodded to the forced orgasm frame next to them. It consisted of one upright pole, against which the sub was firmly bound. It had foot pads like the stockade, to lock the feet in place. A short, adjustable rod in front of the main pole was designed to hold a vibrator of the Master's choice. The rod could be angled so the vibrator could be pressed against a pussy or pushed up inside it—or into a slave's ass, if they were bound facing the pole. Then the Dom could force an orgasm as often as desired, while he or she watched.

"I like to take a coffee break, midsession. I'll enjoy a cup and watch you come a couple times. Would my slave like that?"

The idea terrified her. And her thong was soaked. "Yes, Master."

"Good answer." He tugged on her hair. "We should get one of those for our bedroom." He put his hand on the horizontal part of the T, between where her neck and wrist were restrained. She wished she could reach his hand with her mouth, but she was held fast. "We could put a stock like this out in the garden, and when you need a reminder of who your Master is, I'd make you stay in it for thirty minutes or so while I'm helping you out there. I know you'll need that reminder, Athena. You get too lost in your own head, in others' expectations of you. Whose expectations matter?"

"Yours, Master." She took a deep, shuddering breath, let it out. "I want to please you, sir."

He tsked, gave her a swat. "Talking out of turn." But he sounded pleased. "We'll have to take care of that."

He slid his hands under the skirt, heated hands making contact with her bare thighs. With her legs locked in that spread position, she was open to him, and he took full advantage of it, pressing harder against her ass as he reached over her thigh, fingered her pussy through the tiny thong. All the unspent arousal of the week was gathering in her stomach, such that she made a guttural sound of pleasure when he barely brushed her.

"Such a hot and needy little pussy. I'll bet you'll come in less than a minute."

He kept stroking her, pinching her engorged clit. His other hand slid up to reach inside the low-cut neckline, scoop her breast from the bra cup, fondle it, tweak the nipple. "I'm going to do breast bondage on you tonight, before I put you on that forced orgasm tower. You'll be an unforgettable picture. Fuck, I'm hard as a rock, girl, thinking of everything I can do to you here."

She was getting lost in his ideas as well. Initially, she'd been distracted by the murmurs around them, trying to decipher if the tone was derogatory or voyeuristic in an unpleasantly personal way, but he was spinning a web around her that was making all of that far less important. In fact, the idea of them watching her was starting to be unexpectedly titillating. Her Master was here, doing as he desired to his sub, his slave, because that was his right. He was the wall between her and those others, her protection. He was the only thing that mattered.

He untied the dress and released her left wrist to guide her arm back, slide the dress off it. Then he remanacled the wrist, did the same to the other, leaving her only in bra and panties, her collar and the functional restraints. He caught his thumb under the stiff collar. "Look at me. Only me."

When she lifted her head, she could have come from the look on his face alone. Everything that had drawn her to him that first night was there in full spectrum. It was as if she was captured at the bottom of his soul, staring up with reverent devotion at her Master, while he stared down at his most treasured possession, so treasured he put her deep in the center of himself.

"Master," she whispered, staring into his face. "I love you."

His hand gentled on her face. His blue-green eyes dominated her vision, showing her how much the words meant to him, the first time she'd ever said them aloud. Leaning forward, he touched his forehead to hers, and she closed her eyes. "I love you, too, girl." Then he drew back, gave her a wicked look. "But it's not going to save your gorgeous ass tonight."

She knew her own gaze sparked in reaction. Showing anticipation, dread, as well as a whole lot of desire, because that response was reflected in his own.

"Eyes down again." Shifting behind her, he trailed his hand down her back, down to the thong. He hooked his thumb in the strap between her buttocks, tugging it against her swollen and wet pussy. "Raise that ass for me, girl. Let me see those marks I've put on it. See if I've missed a spot."

She arched her back, lifting to him, and moaned as he gave her exposed pussy a hard rub through the silk. "Yeah, there's a spot." He dropped to one knee out of her sight, and she jumped as he bit her ass cheek hard, making nerve endings scream in pleasure and pain both. Then he'd moved aside the thong and was licking her cunt.

A gasp escaped her lips, that contact shooting her up to the cliff edge. She was trying not to be too loud, given that they were in a public place, but the attempt to restrain her cries made it all the more intense.

"It's time to give those spread legs some different marks." He pulled back, leaving her vibrating like a humming engine. She heard him open his duffel, and now a switch slid along her thighs. "You were embarrassed the other day when you opened your legs instead of your mouth. I'm going to remind you there's no shame in showing me that beautiful pussy of yours. Ever."

He used a lighter hand with the switch than he had her brush, but it didn't take much for a switch to deliver a wealth of sensation. Her bleats became yelps of pain, but her mind was doing that odd thing, wanting the pain to stop, yet not wanting him to stop, all at the same time.

Still, she was making pleading noises for mercy when he finally granted it. But apparently this was only the warm-up. As he ran his fingers over the marks, he leaned over her, speaking softly in her ear. "You're trembling, sweet girl. Time to make you mindless. I want your only thoughts to be about what your Master desires. That's all there is."

She didn't know everything he'd brought with him, but over the next timeless eternity, he must have used them all. A flogger on her back, then a plug he slid into her anus, holding it there as he worked his fingers over her clit and the slick inner lips of her labia.

When he took his touch and the plug away, she was so close to coming she cried out in protest, winning herself another punishment. Then he switched to nipple clamps, ones that he tightened gradually until she was squirming, almost whining with the discomfort. As he removed them, the rush of blood made her moan. For that she earned a rubber ball gag he cinched around her head, making her feel the bite of the straps against the corners of her mouth. Pushing down her bra cups again, he started suckling her nipples, soothing the pain and making her empty pussy ache.

She was a shuddering, sobbing, mindless slave in truth when he at last opened his jeans behind her, nudged her pussy with the head of his cock. She was almost too disoriented to register that he was at last going to fuck her, but that realization centered her. When he slid that bar of thick steel into her, she moaned in intense relief. The act of penetration fulfilled a need so great it was as fierce a release as an orgasm. He felt it, pressing his body fully against hers, curving his hands over hers on the bar as he worked himself slow and deep into her. "There she is," he murmured. "Am I being too cruel, sweet girl?"

She shook her head vehemently, wanting, needing to be everything he wanted, because that was what she wanted as well. She couldn't explain it even to herself, how she could dread the torture and yet embrace it like this, finding a euphoria inside its embrace that let go of everything she'd ever worried about. She gave him every iota of control and received bliss in return.

She lifted her hips to him, so he slid in deeper. She clutched him with those internal muscles, her own challenge, earning a perilous chuckle in her ear. "So be it. You're a brave girl, provoking your Master."

He put his hands back on her hips, began to work himself in her, hard, powerful thrusts that let her feel the purely selfish pleasure he was taking from fucking her while she was restrained. He knew that was part of the rush as well. Meeting one's own expectations, giving oneself a gift, was a gift to both.

She tried to warn him, but with the gag she couldn't ask permission to come. She couldn't tell him when she was going over that cliff. He knew, though, but this time he pushed her off himself, taking her there with those pumping thrusts into her pussy. Denied the climax for over five days, and for the entire session, it hit her like an asteroid taking out the earth. Everything exploded.

She spasmed over him, screamed against the ball so hard it stripped her vocal cords. The hot shot of semen inside her only made it more intense, the weight of his body against hers, his teeth biting into her shoulder, marking her there. She was going to be a mass of bruises and bite marks . . . and she'd love every one of them. Her Master's marks.

As he slowed, her aftershocks were like a seizure, jerking her body in short waves of involuntary movement against her restraints. He kissed his way down her spine and then back up. Slow. So sweet and slow. He ran his hands down her quivering sides, gently cradling her breasts in his hands as he eased out of her. He readjusted her thong, putting it back into the crevice of her buttocks, smoothing it over her swollen cunt.

She was in a fog as he removed the gag, uncuffed her and unbuckled the collar. He had her by the waist, turned her so she was holding on to his shoulders. With a little hitch, he lifted her, one hand under her ass, the other around her waist, carrying her over to the forced orgasm tower.

"No," she whimpered against his shoulder. "I don't think I can."

He brought her to the device and stood before it, rocking her with a swaying movement. When he at last let her feet down beside it, he stroked her hair, kissed her temple and just held her some more. In the end, it was she who turned toward it, steadied by his hand as she put herself in position to be strapped into it. She lifted her lashes, daring more punishment so she could lock herself inside the blessed prison of his gaze. Anything for him. Her quivering body wanted more, as crazy as that sounded.

He bound her hands behind her, around the tower pole that followed the line of her spine. Now at last he removed the thong, setting it aside before he added straps at the waist and thighs, her shoulders and forehead, holding her fast. Retrieving a Hitachi Magic Wand from his bag, he fitted it into the shorter rod. He adjusted its angle so the bulbous head of the vibrator was locked against her sex, the wand's stem pressed against the seam of her thighs.

After he was done, he stroked her hair some more and then turned the wand onto a medium setting, his fingers sliding over her sensitive skin. A rasping plea came from her lips. He brushed his mouth over hers, and she could tell he was absorbed in her every reaction, in how she was completely his, no will of her own. Even if she was surrounded by a whole stadium of judgmental faces and angry voices, she wouldn't hear, see or know anything but him.

"Time for my coffee break, sweet slave," he murmured.

If there was such a term as diabolical selflessness, she thought it would apply to him. He asked someone to bring him a coffee, refusing to be more than a few feet away from her. He put the gag back in her mouth and cinched the straps tightly around her head once again. Pulling up a stool and balancing his coffee, taking an occasional swallow from it, he studied her. The twisting of her expression, the twitching of her body like she was being shocked as the wand worked against her clit, making the overstimulated tissues scream in protest at first. Eventually, though, her body reset. Everything started to get tight and needy again, ramping her up and then locking her into a stasis of hard arousal, unable to go forward or back, something that was frustrating as hell as well as impossible to resist.

After a time he rose, unhooked the back fastener of her bra and reached beneath the loosened cups to grip one of her breasts, tease it as she stared at him with pleading eyes, her mouth filled with that gag. He'd wrapped it in a cloth to absorb the saliva, but he traced her stretched lips with a finger. Taking his attention back to her breasts, he clasped the left one and spilled several drops of the hot coffee on it.

She squealed against the gag, undulating against her bonds. He did it again, then did it to the other one. "I should cover your tits in wax one night," he observed. "They'd be gorgeous, vanilla-scented wax melted over them. Then I'd come over them, over your stomach, your pretty pussy. I'd clean you up myself. Look at those gorgeous, pleading eyes of yours. You want mercy but you don't want it, too, don't you, sweet slave?"

She nodded, spoke the words even if they weren't intelligible. He would understand them, would require them. "Yes, Master. Ohhh. . . ."

He turned the vibrator to a stronger setting, and now her head thrashed this way and that, her throat raw from crying out in frustrated pleasure. He unhooked the bra straps, removed the garment entirely. Standing back, he watched the way her breasts quivered, the nipples jutting out. He took another sip of his coffee.

He hadn't told her she had to look down again, so in this position, staring hungrily at him, she had an impression of what was behind him. Lots of people, gathered and watching. But it was so vague, no specific features. She was trapped in a painting, detached from her audience, a wavering shield behind Dale, the only thing she cared to have in focus.

He stepped forward and turned the wand on the low setting, thank God. Squatting, he withdrew several coils of nylon rope from his bag. She sensed the stirring of the crowd. They liked watching him do this, and who could blame them? Being the subject of it was mesmerizing.

Whereas the switching, the wand, all of that had been high powered, volatile, what he did now slowed everything else, even as things inside her curled up in a concentrated constant arousal.

He wrapped her upper body, her shoulders. Crisscrossing over her sternum, he slowly constricted her breasts in the hold of the half-inch nylon. Her nipples began to tingle, that sense of hampered circulation. That feeling spread throughout the curves and slid lower, like syrup over the edge of a pancake, pooling in her loins. Her hips moved in slight motions against the vibrator now, her head tipped back against the pole. Her lips pressed against the gag as she swallowed. To have her body be tied up in such an excruciatingly incremental way, to watch his hands move over her skin, to see the intent focus of his eyes on what he was doing . . . she wanted to do those demonstrations with him. She wouldn't care who his audience was, because to her, there was just him, his hands, the way he was making her feel.

"Beautiful." He stepped back, and directed her gaze to the mirrored wall across from her. He'd wrapped her breasts tightly enough that the swelling was noticeable, the nipples and areolae distended and dark. When he brushed his knuckles over a curve, the nerves responded like chimes touched by a breeze. He didn't stop there. He did a diamond pattern down her abdomen and tied it off before commencing a leg wrap. He started at her ankles and wrapped her to her upper thighs, rendering her almost completely immobile. Now only her pussy wasn't covered by rope, still exposed to his whim on that vibrator.

She was making little noises, her tongue taking kitten licks at the gag, her eyes following his every movement. She wailed against the gag when he reached between her legs and turned the wand back onto high.

Forced orgasm was an apt term for it. He'd noticed her slight, flirty movements against the vibrator and had taken away that ability with the ropes. Now she experienced what it was like to be driven to a climax with no ability to move, no mercy from the pummeling of the vibration. It was excruciating and unforgettable. She shrieked and shrieked against the gag, knowing she couldn't take any more.

She begged, pleaded, asked for mercy once more, and at the same time was forever lost in the avid pleasure in his steady gaze, the tension of his powerful body, the impressive erection she wanted back inside her.

As the climax ebbed, it was an Inquisition torture, having that rapid vibration against her spasming clit. Proving he wasn't a complete sadist, he turned it off, and she sagged against her bonds in relief.

Thank you, Master. Thank you.

She was mumbling it against the gag. From his tender look, he understood. He removed her gag and must have read her needy expression, for he immediately put his mouth over hers. He licked her dry lips, teasing her tongue, giving her his own saliva before he offered her the bottle of water. He held it to her lips, cupping the back of her neck.

"How are you, sweet girl?"

"I want . . . I need . . . please fuck me, Master. Please. I feel . . . empty."

She was exhausted physically, but never had an emotional need felt so large, so imperative inside her. She absolutely had to have him inside her or her heart might shatter.

He nodded. Unwrapping her legs, he freed her from the pole. He left the breast harness in place and swung her up in his arms, because she literally had no strength. He took her to the last piece of equipment in this section of the room. It was an I-frame bolted to the floor. It already had cuffs and a functional collar so he put her on hands and knees and cuffed her wrists, knees and ankles to the frame. An upright pole at one intersect of the I-frame held the collar. He wrapped it around her throat, keeping her head up and her facing forward.

She'd seen Masters and Mistresses put their subs here and then pull over the fucking machine to pump a dildo into their submissives while others watched, but Dale didn't do that. He gave her what she fervently needed. Kneeling behind her, he once more opened his jeans. The erection he pushed against her soaking wet cunt was even larger than before, telling her how her reactions had affected him. Her climaxes had also made her tight as a virgin, such that she made a soft noise of distress as he stretched her. But he took his time, sliding his knuckles down her spine, caressing her hips with his big hands. Then he stopped, only halfway lodged inside her.

"Beg me again, girl."

"Please, Master." Tears were in her eyes. "Please. I love you. Please."

She could barely form the words, but that was all he needed. He slid in slow and deep, easy. She felt the stretch, the demand, but she felt the power of his gentleness as well. He pulled back, pushed back in. From his size, she expected the easy rhythm he set was an effort to maintain, but he'd made it clear, hadn't he? His first priority was always caring for her, and she knew that was what he was doing, aware of how sensitive everything was at this point.

She didn't care about climaxing; this wasn't about that. She just needed to know her connection to him was there, unbreakable. He was inside her, in all ways. She wanted others to notice he was inside her without a condom, proving the bond between them.

The man's control was phenomenal, as always. He took a while to come, drawing it out, making the experience so deeply pleasurable to her that she was moaning with every stroke, far beyond the base physical response of a climax. This was the pleasuring of her heart and soul. She would have gripped him tighter if she had any strength left, but she didn't. He'd attached a padded upright bar to the middle of the I and adjusted it beneath her lower abdomen and hips to support her. That, the pole holding her head up, and the sure grip of his hands, were the only things keeping her upright.

When he started moving faster at last, he still kept the pace even, steady. She heard the rasp of his breath, wished he'd put her at an angle she could see him in one of the mirrors. Maybe later . . .

at home. She wanted him on top of her, all that strength caging her, his hands tender on her face, fingers digging into her hair. Her legs would be spread by his body lying between them, and his cock would be sunk deep into her. She wanted to hold him like that all night, let him lie upon her, as unrealistic as that was. The man was two hundred pounds of muscle. But she felt the need to be crushed, held, surrounded, fused together in such a way.

As he climaxed at last, she let out a blissful cry, lifting her hips to take all of him, to show her desire and willingness to be taken by her Master, no matter her soreness or exhaustion. He'd gripped her hair there at the end in the way she loved, tugging on her scalp as he worked himself against her, pelvis striking her abused flesh. Tonight he would lie her down on their bed, massage her with his wonderful hands. He would care for her, punish her, need her, love her.

She now understood to the very depths of her being why it had been wrong for her to come here alone, to try and explain it to the others. She couldn't define or explain such a thing, any more than she could have made them understand why she'd embraced being Roy's Mistress with joy. They thought she wasn't being true to her nature, but she'd been as true to it then as she was tonight.

Love was like that.

TWENTY

He retrieved her bra from their small stack of items. After he removed the rope harness, he put it back on her, adjusting her breasts in the cups, then he released her from the frame. He dressed her himself, threading her hands into the sleeve holes of her dress and straightening the seams. He guided her to step back into the thong with gentle hands, caressing and stroking her like a cherished possession, one that had pleased him greatly. She basked in that glow, even as she didn't think she had the energy to do anything else. When he picked up their bag of belongings, he took her out to the lounge area with a secure arm around her waist. She leaned against him drunkenly, and he encouraged her to do so.

"You're still in the zone, girl. Don't worry about anything. I'll take care of you."

Two different sides of the same wonderful coin. Harsh and demanding, punishing and strong, matched with cosseting and protective, spinning a cocoon around her. He took a seat on one of the sofas and started to guide her down next to him on the cushions. He would put her under the shelter of his arm, let her lean against him.

Here at last, she wanted something different, though she didn't think it was different from what he wanted. Instead of following the pressure of his hand, she sank to her knees on the floor. She wanted to sit at her Master's feet, lean against his knee. It was the prosthesis side, and she put her head on his knee where the socket and flesh met, pressing her lips there.

"Stubborn girl." But his voice was thick. She'd moved him. He made her adjust so he could put a cushion under her and a blanket around her shoulders, but he let her stay where she was. There she rested, his hand stroking her hair as she simply floated.

People came and went, people who knew him, complimenting him on the scene, asking questions. Master Craftsman, the name they'd given him. He was a master of his craft. Her Master. She thought again about doing those demonstrations with him. She liked the idea of becoming known as his sub, the only one associated with him.

A pair of boots stopped in front of him, a pair she recognized, since she'd admired them the first time Sheila had worn them at the club. She didn't feel anything other than mild interest in that. None of her earlier trepidation remained. In this setting, in this state, she belonged to Dale utterly. Only his approval or disapproval mattered.

"Master D."

The Domme had used his actual honorific, rather than the nickname he'd accepted so good-naturedly. It suggested she intended to address him formally, not the appropriate moment for "MC." Dale said nothing, and from the shift of his boots, the thrum of tension she felt through his leg, Athena knew exactly what kind of look Sheila was getting.

Or maybe not.

When she peeked at him beneath her lashes, she saw his gaze was more than forbidding. It was cold, almost dangerous. While she knew he wouldn't harm Sheila, she wasn't sure if his demeanor would convince anyone of that.

Sheila cleared her throat. "I wanted to apologize. I acted inappropriately toward your submissive, and insulted both you and her."

"Yes, you did. You hurt her deeply. She considered you a friend."

That was her SEAL, not beating around the bush, stating what others, even herself, might imply with the roundabout etiquette of Southern courtesy. But by doing so, he took away any of the bullshit associated with such awkward conversations and cut to the chase. Athena knew she wasn't supposed to speak, yet his fingers tightened on her hair, anticipating her automatic compulsion to smooth things over. It was a clear message that she didn't have his permission to talk. He was her Master, and this was his matter to handle.

"I'm sorry about that, Athena. I—" Sheila stopped. "I'd like to tell her that directly, Master D, if you'll allow me to make amends to you both."

There was a weighted pause, then Dale's grip eased, giving Athena a reassuring caress. "I think she'd like that. Athena, you may speak to Mistress Sheila."

Athena lifted her head as Sheila squatted before her so they were eye to eye. A Mistress clad in impressive regalia of soft leather, a single tail coiled in her gloved hand, and a dazed sub in thin dress and blanket.

"I am sorry, Athena. I didn't get it. Not until I saw you tonight, and then it made so much sense, thinking about the way you were a Mistress to Roy. Amy said it that night, didn't she? Granted, in kind of an obnoxious manner, and I expect she's going to apologize to you, too, but I guess neither one of us was paying attention to the right things. I saw the connections tonight. It was the same language, in a different way. I admit that I don't get that side of the language"—a smile touched her mouth—"but it was really, horribly wrong of me to treat you that way. I hope you'll forgive me for being such a total bitch."

There was a vulnerability to her expression now, one that Athena couldn't help but answer. She reached out without thought, closed her hand on Sheila's.

"I love those boots even more, seeing them at this level."

The words came out throaty and rough. She was pretty sure she was going to have no voice tomorrow, and imagined having to tell Ellen and her staff she had laryngitis. "All's forgiven. Thank you for apologizing to my Master."

Sheila touched her face in answer, then she rose. She gave Dale a nod and moved on, the matter settled. The relationship between them would be different now. It had been in Sheila's light touch on her face, the glance at Dale to ensure it was okay. The way she looked down at Athena as she rose showed she now saw her as a submissive. It would give things between them a different shape, but it was an okay change.

"I didn't give you permission to touch the Mistress, Athena," Dale reminded her.

"No Master. I'm sorry."

He grunted. "If you get a future urge to touch another woman, I want you to let me know immediately. And in great detail."

She smiled against his leg, tightening her fingers on the socket. "Yes, Master."

Jimmy brought Dale two drinks and, at his nod, he also squatted, offering hers. "The soda's full octane tonight, not diet," he said. "Your Master says you need the sugar. After that session, I agree."

Whereas Sheila's apology had been a simple balm for the wound created, the acceptance on Jimmy's face stung Athena's eyes with tears. The good kind. She took the drink, though her hand was still shaking. Jimmy wrapped his around it, steadying her, and gave it a squeeze. "I'm sorry, too," he said. "I should have been a better friend that night. Guess I always kind of harbored hopes that we might have a session together. I forgot the most important deal of a place like this is accepting one another as we are. Even if the face of that changes, the heart of it doesn't."

When he was hailed from the bar, he gave her another nod and smile, then returned to his post. She was thirsty, but she realized she couldn't bring the cup to her lips. Her hand was trembling too badly. She needn't have worried. Her Master leaned forward, his large hand ensconcing hers, guiding the cup to her mouth. "There you go. Easy sips."

"He touched me, I didn't touch him," she mumbled, in case he was going to chastise her for that. Those blue-green eyes twinkled at her.

"Yes, I noticed that. I'll have to have a talk with Jimmy. I'm particular about men touching my sub. Especially a man who has such an obvious interest in her."

"Jimmy? He . . ." At Dale's ironic look, she realized there might be some truth to it. In the end, Dale had been right. All of their reactions had had more to do with them, rather than a reflection on herself. It didn't matter now. Everything was clearer, even if she was so tired she wasn't sure she could stand. But she did have the energy to do one thing. She looked up into his face. "Master, may I touch you?"

At his nod, she put her hand on his face, staring at him. She knew subspace could make one loopy and overly emotional like this, but this whole scenario had confirmed a lot of things she hadn't known for certain about the two of them. She was so glad Dale had insisted on doing this, and that she'd had the courage to follow through. It gave her quiet pride, and utter faith in their future. She traced his cheekbone, the firm lips, his hard jaw. When he captured her wrist, kissed her palm, she closed her eyes.

"Will you stay with me tonight?" She wanted to be sure.

"Try to keep me away."

He didn't take her right home, though. He took her to a quiet place on the riverfront, bundling her up in a car coat he had so she'd be warm on the bench where they sat, watching the lights reflect in the lapping water. He also brought a cushion from the truck and made her sit on that, a kindness she appreciated.

"When we get home, I'm going to give you a full massage and put that balm on every sore spot," he promised, kissing her brow. She laid her head on his shoulder.

"So they'll heal up and you can give me new spots."

"Absolutely." His lips curved against her. "You were magnificent tonight. It was watching you get so lost in it that changed their minds."

"You took me there. I've never felt so . . . unencumbered. There was nothing in my mind but you, and this feeling of crazy peace, as odd as that sounds. Even in the midst of the pain."

"You gave me everything, held on to nothing. You trusted me fully, Athena. You let go."

She automatically started to put her hand on his chest, but then stopped herself. He caught her fingers and pressed her palm to his heated flesh, a heat she could feel even through his shirt. "You can touch me how you like, girl. Say whatever you want. I like hearing your voice. Especially when it's raspy because of how much you screamed for me tonight."

She decided to let the smug male satisfaction pass, since it was obviously well deserved. "I have a place in the Keys," she said. "I thought I might go there in the next few weeks. It has a private stretch of beach. I go there to read, take walks, get away from work. Would you be able to go with me?"

"Yeah. Let me know the dates, and I'll get a couple guys to cover for me with the dogs. Remember what I said, though." He brushed a kiss along her temple. "No matter how much real estate you have, I'm not becoming your kept man, Mrs. Summers."

"What about when you're old and doddering and need someone to care for you?"

"That won't be your problem. You'll have kicked me to the curb well before then."

Her brow creased. His tone said he was teasing her, but as he'd said, she read people well. That intuition made her sit up, close both her hands on his. "If we get old and doddering together—and I truly hope we will—you *will* let me take care of you, Dale Rousseau."

His eyes narrowed, and she recognized the set of the jaw,

countered it by slipping her fingers over it. "Not just because I'm a submissive and it's my nature to care for others. I love you. It doesn't matter if I'm a Domme, sub or a vanilla person. When it comes to that, love looks the same. We care for the ones we love. We hold on to them as long as God allows and gives them the joy of life. And when life has no more joy, we walk with them all the way to the water's edge, and hope for the day when we'll get on that boat, too, and see them again."

His gaze held hers, undecided, but this was something she knew deep down, with enough certainty for them both. "You've taught me about letting go, about not handling the things I shouldn't. That was my blind spot. This is yours."

She laid her hand on his knee, deliberately drawing his attention to his prosthesis. "You are a strong, stubborn and proud man, and you wanted to make sure you took care of every aspect of this yourself. But you really didn't, did you? You even said so. Having the support of SEALs like Neil and Lawrence helped you deal with it emotionally, physically. Your doctors helped you refit the socket until it worked correctly, and you still see them periodically to ensure it's doing what it should. You may view that like maintenance checks on your car, I get that, but it's a reminder that none of us gets through this life entirely alone, without help. There are connections that make us stronger, not weak. Do you consider me weak because I surrendered myself to you?"

His change of expression to that was instant and gratifying. "No," he said decisively. "And if you think—"

She put her hand on his mouth, not surprised when he closed his over her wrist, took it away, but it gave her the moment to speak. "I don't. You taught me that. I've told you I love you. It's a different love from what I had with Roy, but I can already tell, as we move forward, it will be as deep, possibly even more intense. It would be an honor to that love to allow me to care for you if ever you need it. Whether it's if you have a sore on your leg," she glanced down at it, then back up at him, a smile in her eyes now, "a head cold that makes you irritable and grumpy, or something that might take you from me."

She sobered then, placing her hand on his heart. "You know more about honor than any man I know. Giving the one you love the honor of caring for you, when it's necessary, that's everything. You could crush me by not giving me that privilege, Dale. It's a privilege you give to no other. That's why it's in the marriage vows, you know. Better or worse, in sickness or health."

"Are you proposing to me, Mrs. Summers?" He'd recovered enough to tease her again, but there was a thoughtful look to his eyes, a tightness to his jaw that said, while she hadn't completely convinced him, she'd given him something new to think about. As he'd said, they were both stubborn, independent people. It would take time for them both to think differently about certain things.

"I believe that would be my Master's job, when and if the time is right." She knew that it wasn't, not now, but her heart tripped a little faster, just thinking what it would be like to belong to him in every way. "For now, I'd settle for him being a little less rock headed."

He snorted at that, but as she laid her head back down on his shoulder, the silence drew out, both of them mulling. She had her hand on his opposite thigh, idly tracing circles, her ear pressed to his heart, listening to the steady beat. His fingers slid up and down her upper arm outside the thick coat. She wanted his touch on her skin, but at least she felt the pressure of his grip, his attention.

"I want to take you home, Athena. I want to make love to you."

She nodded, touching her lips to his chest. "That's what I want, too."

A s she lay in bed, waiting on him, she lifted her hand, studying it against the shadows. She and Roy had done that some-times, trying to make discernible shapes, but often they were just content playing finger games, tracing the digits, caressing one another.

Dale had let her help him take the prosthesis off, showed her how he examined it for abrasions. Then he'd put them both in the shower, bathed her, not letting her do anything but stand compliant under his thorough soaping of all her crevices. He explored her body both for pleasure and to ensure he hadn't done her any type of harm that required more care. She was too exhausted to reach the same high level of arousal she had before, but as he touched her so intimately and she thought of his intention to make love to her before they slept, it made a nice, promising swirl in her lower belly.

His cock wasn't fully erect as he focused on her care, but it was interested, enough to encourage her to steal a few strokes of his length, despite his mock sternness at her for the transgression. He'd punish her for it later, of course.

After the shower, he'd laid her down on her love seat and done all he'd promised with the massage and the lotions, though she was sure he was tired as well. But she didn't protest. She understood this was part of his responsibilities as Master, which he not only took very seriously, but wanted to do, if his attentive caresses were any indication. By the time he tucked her into bed and bade her stay there while he disappeared into the bathroom, her body was on a slow, pleasant simmer, anticipating, yearning for the touch of his.

He was moving around with the aid of the gift she'd given him several weeks ago. After taking surreptitious measurements of his crutches, she'd presented him a pair of carved wooden ones, made by a local craftsman. She intended them as a convenience, so he didn't have to remember to bring his own when he spent the night here. When she gave them to him, he'd given her a weighted glance, such that she wasn't sure if her initiative had been welcome. But then he'd examined the bald eagle carving on the cross pieces, the semblance of sailor's knots along the shafts, the anchor shapes burned into the wood. The curve of his lips suggested he approved the use of naval symbols. Eventually he'd grunted, brushed a kiss over her cheek and given her a pinch. That night, he'd used them for the first time, and he'd used them quite a bit since, pleasing her.

Now he emerged from the bathroom, putting them beside the bed before he stretched out on the mattress. "Come here," he said, low, and she closed the distance between them, making a soft sound of pleasure as his arms slid around her, his hand gripping her ass, holding her fast to push a now-fully-recovered arousal more firmly against her. She thought he might want her to straddle him, but instead, he rolled her to her back, putting himself on top of her. Just as she'd imagined and hoped.

As his gaze held hers, he parted her legs with his knee. They willingly spread to accommodate him. He slid into her without preamble or foreplay. None was needed, her tissues slick and ready to take her Master.

He propped his elbows on either side of her face, giving her most but not all of his weight. Enough to offer her that delicious pinned-down feeling as she ran her hands along his broad back, down to his hips, over the muscular buttocks. Her nails dug into them and he adjusted deeper, eyes glinting as her lips parted.

"Didn't I wear you out?" he complained. "I see there'll be no rest for your poor Master."

"Neil and Lawrence told me that SEALs have unlimited stamina. No matter how far a normal man runs, they can run farther. Lawrence was very clear that extended to other superhuman qualities."

"Remind me to bash that little bastard's head into a wall." But Dale smiled at her, his eyes getting more serious as his thumbs slid along her cheeks. "God, you're beautiful."

Her hands slid up to his waist, the small of his back as her legs curved over his thighs. "You are too, Master. As beautiful as a book that makes the day disappear, or the first flowers coming out in spring. I look at you, and there's no sadness in my heart."

His eyes darkened. The way her heart leaped, proving the point, was a feeling that spread to loins and throat, all the way from head to toes. "My librarian," he murmured. "My girl, at last."

Then he put his mouth on hers, and no further words were necessary. That overwhelming sense of give-and-take, Master and sub, and the individual souls beneath, took over. They were locked together in their wants and needs, their love for one another. It was beyond definition.

Indescribable but understood, by the two hearts that felt it.

Keep reading for an excerpt from

NAUGHTY BITS

Available now from Berkley Books

A compact UPS package the size and weight of a cinder block was propped against the back door when she arrived at the shop. As she lugged it inside, Madison wondered what item would have that poundage *and* belong in a lingerie store, but then again, Naughty Bits was far more than a lingerie store. In the BDSM section, there were plenty of things that should be in a medieval dungeon. Maybe it was a ball and chain, complete with engraving. A special-order gift for the Master who had everything.

A special order gift fit, since it appeared to have been delivered this morning, but the store had been closed for weeks. She hefted it through the stockroom and took it up front, since it'd be easier to have it sitting behind the counter, ready for whomever had to be contacted to pick it up.

She left it there as she went to unlock the front door. Not because she was open or expected any customers this early in the morning, but because she'd never liked the feeling of being locked in. She turned back toward the display counter, and saw the envelope.

All curiosity about the package vanished.

To MadGirl was written on the outside. Unlike the package, it looked as if it had been placed in its current location weeks ago. It bore a light layer of dust, same as the glass of the display counter beneath it.

Leave it to Alice to think of doing something like this. Taking a breath, Madison fished out a letter opener from the drawer beneath the cash register and slit the envelope open. Bracing her elbows on the counter, she ran tense fingers over her face, a reassuring hard stroke, then unfolded the pages.

Sell *doesn't have to be a four-letter word. You used to know that.*

Madison blinked. Now, of all times, her sister would choose to be snide? Through a letter sent from the other side of the grave? She had to give her credit for a great hook line, though. Alice always did that with her letters. She never started one with the traditional "Dear Madison." Her handwritten script had flourishes as if she thought she were Thomas Jefferson. She'd done cursive that way since the eighth grade.

Nearly every day for the past two months, Madison had broken down and cried over some little quirk about Alice. Today it was going to be her sister's damn handwriting. She blinked through her tears and kept reading.

I'm not being snide. Sell *connects to two other really important four-letter words.* Want. Need. *But I think the word that best describes it is* provide. *Did you ever look that one up in the Encarta dictionary? The legal term means to require something in advance as a condition or as part of a contract. The nonlegal term is to supply somebody with something, or be a source of something wanted or needed by somebody. Sets off a whole lot of feelings deep in the gut, doesn't it?*

Madison swallowed. "Stop it, Alice," she muttered. "Just stop it."

Fuck *is another four-letter word, one I think gets a bad rap.* Cock, cunt, come . . . *somebody was on a roll with those. Do you think God and the Devil were playing a word game*

*that day? See how many naughty words can start with C,
and whoever wins gets to oversee everything connected to sex.
Go! You know the Devil won that one, hands down. God's
still pissed about it. Probably why He started the rumor that
sex was a sin.*

Madison choked on a laugh, tasting the salt of her tears on her
lips.

*Okay, starting to get tired, so have to cut to the chase. Here's
the thing, MadGirl. Great selling isn't about tricking
someone into buying crap. It's about helping them get
something they truly need that adds value to their lives. The
salesperson who does that is the one who really deserves the
Maserati. I think angels are the master salespeople of the
universe.*

"Okay, now you're just loopy on the drugs." The ache in her
throat increased as her voice echoed in the waiting silence of the
store. Waiting for a mistress who would never return, who'd known
how to turn a lingerie store into an adult Disneyland, complete with
the enchantment, promise of princes and happily-ever-afters. She'd
told Alice that once, with derision dripping off every word. Now
she thought it simply as it was. Truth.

*Yeah, you're thinking they overdid the morphine today, and
you may be right. But it doesn't mean I'm wrong. So,
exercising the right of the dying, I'm going to play angel. I'm
leaving you my store. You knew that, but what you're going to
find out from my executor when you call him about this letter
is that I set aside enough money for you to live on and run it
for the next several years. If you don't want to keep the store*

*after a year, sell the inventory and return to the life you were
living, or seek another path. But promise me you'll give it a
year. I'm thinking the fates will align to make that possible.*

They had. Which was as remarkable a coincidence as reading
the words now. She moved to the last paragraph.

*I wanted to "provide" you with this. I loved you more than
anyone, MadGirl. Given how many cool, amazing people I
met in my absurdly short life, that's saying quite a lot. You
always did underestimate what kind of gem you are. Maybe
you'll get a chance to shine here and see what I always saw
in you.*

Okay, *goddamn* her. Madison put the letter down on the counter
and slid down the wall behind it, giving in to the hard sobs.

Her sister hadn't let her in on any of it. Madison had been up in
Boston, selling stocks and bonds, managing people's investments.
Alice had called once a week, despite Madison being passive aggressive at best during most of the conversations. Because that had been
the state of their relationship for the past few years, Madison hadn't
caught the vital clues, the allergy attacks that came more frequently,
the colds and flu bugs. Her sister had been getting weaker and sicker.

Then, a couple months ago, Alice had called on a Thursday, not
their usual day. In her matter-of-fact way, she'd said if Madison
could come home that weekend, she'd really like to give her a quick
last hug. She also wanted Madison to go through her collection of
high-end, well-sterilized sex toys to see if she wanted any of them
before they had to be boxed up and dumped. Incredibly enough,
the Senior Citizens' Auxiliary at the hospital wouldn't accept them
as donations for their thrift shop. *You'd think they'd realize there's nothing better for cardiovascular health than a good daily orgasm . . .*

Her lips twitched at Alice's acid observation now. During that call, she'd simply been stunned. To the point she'd said absurd things like, "Okay, let me check my schedule, I have this meeting, but I know I can get out of that . . ."

Alice had always known her so well, no matter how much Madison hated that. She'd merely listened. "No worries, little sis. Come if you can."

Of course, once off the phone, Madison's brain had cleared. She'd called her boss, told Barbara what was happening, and that she had to go. With her typical sensitivity, Barbara had said she had to at least come in Friday and handle her scheduled client meetings, because Barbara had a tee time with board members. Madison refused. Barbara told her it could cost her the job, and Madison retorted that if she was that replaceable, Barbara could keep the damn job. They'd find the files that would cover anything needed for those meetings sitting neatly in the center of her desk. Hell, her assistant could run two portfolio reviews.

Just like that, she walked away from a job at which she'd excelled for five years. Crazy, right? But it was like she'd been treading water in a pool, blinded to the fact dry land was as close as the nearest ladder. Until Alice arranged a wake-up call in the form of a simple death bed request.

Come give me a quick hug, little sis.

If the memory had theme music, it would be something sad, wistful. Instead, the overtly erotic strains of *Boléro* injected Dudley Moore and a running Bo Derek into Madison's brain, jarring her fully into the present.

She'd forgotten music played when someone came into the store. Alice not only had the classics like *Boléro*, "Somewhere in Time" and *Claire de Lune* on the playlist, but sultry Latin numbers by Enrique Inglesias and pure fuck-me-now Barry White and Boyz II Men songs. Madison remembered she'd also thrown Rod Stewart's "Do Ya Think I'm Sexy" and "Tonight's the Night" into the mix because, well, why not?

Once the door triggered the music, it would play the whole song, unless someone else came in. Each time the door opened or closed, it switched to a new song, a way for Alice to know she had a customer arriving or departing. If there were no new customers, after a song played in its entirety, there would be silence. She'd asked Alice once why she didn't set it up so the music played constantly, and her sister said there was value in silence as well.

Honest to God, Alice's choices gave the store a personality all its own. Madison wouldn't be surprised if she could hear the store breathing during those quiet periods.

She yanked her attention back to the more important issue. She wasn't alone, and she was hiding behind the register counter. She shouldn't have unlocked the door yet, but she hadn't expected lingerie shopping to be popular at seven a.m. Jesus, she hadn't even flipped the OPEN sign over or turned on lights, not that people paid attention to those things. Having worked sales before, she knew customers were as bad as kindergarteners when it came to noticing details.

She should just pop up from behind the counter like some kind of macabre cartoon. *"Yes, how may I help you?"* Instead, she wiped her eyes and rose into view in a way that made it look like she'd been bending below the counter to get something out of the cabinet, rather than pushing herself up the wall as if her weight had tripled since she'd landed there. "I'm sorry, we're not open yet."

The words were spoken before she took a look at her first customer. A good thing, since she might have stammered. He wasn't what she was expecting. Not just because he was a *he*, though she'd assumed men weren't the store's target demographic. Of course, it had been a long, long time since she'd been in a lingerie store herself, and Alice had possessed an eclectic clientele.

This guy was in his early to mid-twenties, and looked like he'd escaped from the cover shoot for a romance novel. His stone-washed jeans belted at his lean waist, the style defining a superior tight ass, noticeable because he was turned away from her, examining the merchandise on the rounder closest to him. The sleeves of his denim shirt were rolled up at the cuffs, exposing tanned forearms. He had good shoulders—wide enough for his age. As he grew older and his muscle weight thickened, they'd probably get even nicer. She expected beneath those clothes his body was well-sculpted by the gym. Guys who worked out hard moved like wild animals, with easy grace and strength.

His sandy brown hair brushed his collar and brow, and when he glanced toward her beneath an attractive scattering of strands, his blue eyes reminded her of the sky. "Hi. I'm Troy. I work next door."

"Oh." Not a customer then, even though he'd been perusing a rack of bras, fingering a lacy D-cup with speculative interest and no self-consciousness. Cross-dresser? A lifetime ago, before their falling out, she'd spent time in Alice's world, brushing shoulders with everything from transgender to cross-dressers to dungeon masters. She'd learned enough about the various cultures to pick up the basics.

Because of that, she didn't think he fit the type. He wore his clothes without any excessive fashion sense. Simple, basic guy clothes: blues and denims, work shoes. Though a cross-dressing straight guy was possible, his gaze marked her with automatic hetero interest. Interest in what she looked like out of her clothes, not how she wore them.

"Nice to meet you." She regretted her listless tone, but he didn't seem fazed by it, approaching the counter to extend his hand. She suppressed the urge to take another swipe at her face, make sure her nose wasn't running. Yeah, that would be nice. Wipe her nose, then offer her hand to shake.

In Boston, her client list included exacting millionaires and powerful corporate businessmen. She could handle an employee from . . . what was next door? A hardware store, that was right. In this artsy downtown area of Matthews, a quaint municipality on the outskirts of the much bigger city of Charlotte, all the stores were kitschy boutique-type ventures. The hardware store, the brief glimpse she'd had of it, was a historic leftover from eighty years ago, maintaining the original brick façade in front. It was still run like one of the old-timey general stores, advertising horse feed and strawberries in season, for heaven's sake, as well as small engine repair.

Alice had relocated here from a Charlotte strip mall location a few years ago. In those previous visits, before their two-year estrangement, Madison hadn't had a chance to meet her new neighbors.

"When we heard you knocking around, Mr. Scott told me to come over and see if you need anything."

She realized he still had his hand out, and she was staring at him as if he'd sprung out of the walls. With a jerk, she lifted her hand to clasp his. Instead of doing the functional shake, he closed his fingers over hers, just held them. He had a rough palm, a strong, warm grip, and those eyes never left her face. "We're so sorry about Alice. She was an incredible person, and she loved you so much."

Wow. He just zeroed right in on the personal, leaving her nowhere to hide. Madison blinked, hard, and unconsciously squeezed his hand, to find her own squeezed right back. She'd been dealing with lawyers, city clerks, real estate people . . . all of whom talked about Alice in distant niceties. This man was just as much a stranger as they were, but his obvious personal connection to Alice, physical and emotional, made her hungry to maintain the contact. She didn't want to make a fool of herself, but Troy saved her from that. He covered her hand with his other one, holding hers sandwiched between them and giving her an appropriate excuse to keep it in that position.

"She left me this place," Madison heard herself say. "I'm not sure how to run it. I mean, I know how to run it, I've been in sales, but . . ."

Good grief, Madison. She shrugged to get him to let her go and put both hands on the counter, pressing her palms against the cool glass. Beneath it was an array of jeweled nipple clamps and clit jewelry, displayed as elegantly as any offering in New York's Diamond District. She was pretty sure some of them had actual diamonds, since one had a $2,000 price tag. For nipple jewelry? In contrast, on top of the counter, Alice had a basket of plastic hopping penises, breasts and bright red lips. There was a cheerful yellow bow on the basket to draw attention to it.

Alice. God, I'm going to miss you.

Troy hesitated, then picked up one of the toys, wound it up, let it hop across the counter, making them both smile. "She was crazy," he said. "Crazy, wonderful, beautiful, sexy."

She glanced up at him. Had they been lovers? Somehow she didn't think so. Yet his tone was intimate. He lifted his dark lashes to meet her gaze. It was impossible not to focus on his mouth, those eyes. When she saw him recognize that she was staring, she flushed. He straightened to his six-foot height.

"Sorry. Mr. Scott says I need to be careful about doing that. I tend to be distracting." He said it without ego, giving her a half smile. "He says there's nothing wrong with looking the way I do, as long as I give as much pleasure as I take. But since I love giving it, it gets kind of confusing, because that's a form of taking, you know?"

Fortunately, he didn't seem to expect an answer to such a complex question. "Anyhow," he continued, "I'd better get back. Come by later if you want to check out our store. You're always welcome. Mr. Scott wanted to give you time to settle in, but remember to call if you need us. We're here for you."

With a nod, he moved back to the front door. Bolero was in its final strains. As he opened the door again, another song started. It was "Twinkle, Twinkle, Little Star," done in a poignant ballad piano style. Alice used to sing it to her, call her Little Star.

Christ, how was she going to do this?

She locked the door and worked in the back on inventory for a couple hours, but eventually she came back to the cash register, pulled out her handheld and started making a list. Okay, if she really was going to do this, she needed to plan an ad in the local paper, announce a grand reopening under new management.

When her palm settled on the folded letter she'd left on the counter, she saw she'd missed a postscript on the back of the last page. Unfolding the thin paper, she lifted it up to catch the dim light, since she still hadn't turned on the overheads and the sun was high enough that she wasn't getting as much of its light through the east-facing front window.

> *P.S. You can trust Logan with anything, MadGirl. Don't forget that, no matter what. You can trust him like you trust me, like family. No, even more. Like a soul mate. He took care of me until you came.*

Alice had died three days after she arrived. There was already a nurse in place, helping with bathing, medications and the like, but Madison's understanding was she'd only been called in full-time right before Madison arrived. Because of everything else going on, she hadn't thought about the day-to-day primary caregiving, and Alice hadn't brought it up. Nor had the nurse discussed someone else. Had Alice instructed her not to say anything? Who the hell was Logan?

Alice had never mentioned him in her letters or emails, not ever. Yet Madison could supposedly trust him more than she trusted her sister, the only person she'd ever trusted?

With a sigh, she set the paper down. She shifted and bumped that heavy package, a reminder that it was still there. When she squatted to take a closer look, she let out a mildly irritated oath. It wasn't her package. It was supposed to go next door, to *A Different Time Hardware*. Damn it, she'd had Troy right here.

Well, she could use the break. The quiet of the place was getting to her. It was like Alice was standing there, waiting, watching, yet separated from her by a veil that couldn't be penetrated. It was making her head hurt.

She also hadn't brought a soda, and she'd bet they had some over there. With the times-gone-by theme, maybe even an orange cream one, something she rarely indulged but today seemed to call for it. Maybe that and a Mallo cup. She'd pass out from sugar shock and discover this was all a bad, crazy dream, her sister gone, leaving Madison to run Naughty Bits.

When the store was in its planning stages, about a decade ago, Madison had been the first to call it that, teasing her sister: "A career selling naughty bits . . ." Next thing she knew, Naughty Bits had its Christmas grand opening, with the catch phrase "Where naughty *is* nice . . ." She'd helped Alice decorate a tree with everything from filmy, sparkly thong panties to crystal snowflakes and tiny bullet vibrators in gleaming colors of blue and silver. They'd put a porcelain angel at the top dressed as a dominatrix, complete with wings that looked like two fanned-out floggers, tipped with gold.

She picked up the package, the weight on the label indicating it was a little over twenty pounds. The clanking she'd mistaken for chain was probably nails or some kind of fastener. Exiting the front door of her store and locking it behind her, she walked down the sidewalk. It was about ten o'clock, so the other stores, mostly bistros and clothing boutiques, were starting to open. According to the hours printed on the hardware store window, they opened at seven a.m., Tuesday through Saturday, which explained why Troy had been able to show up in her store at about that time.

The humid air suggested it was building toward a hot June day, but enough of a breeze stirred the crepe myrtles planted along the sidewalk to keep things pleasant. Around the entrance to the hardware store, hanging baskets spilled out lush falls of petunias, tempting pedestrians to buy.

The door was already propped open with an iron boot brush. A chalkboard sandwich sign had been placed beside it with the day's specials: *tomato plants, $3; all garden implements 20% off; fresh baked apple pie and coffee, $1.50.*

Heated apple pie was one of her favorite breakfast foods, and she smelled it the second she stepped into the shop. Given that the next thing to hit her senses was Troy, it wasn't a bad combination.

She had a direct view down the aisle to where Troy was stocking. He'd donned a work apron, which didn't diminish the view a bit, given it didn't cover anything in the back. The shirt stretched over his shoulders as he reached toward the higher shelves. Since he was on a ladder, his ass had a nice taut lift. Maybe it was because she'd spent her morning immersed in articles of erotic fantasy, but her mind was flooded with an image of him sprawled facedown across a bed. He'd be sleeping, wearing nothing but a very artfully arranged sheet. She'd see a hint of pale buttocks just above it, the lengths of firm thighs exposed below. His fine toes would be curled against the cotton. One sandy lock of hair draped in his eyes, his lips parted, inviting a lover to press her lips to his, tease his tongue, wake him in all ways.

"He's beautiful, isn't he? I've seen women's hands curl at their sides and them not even realize it, as if they're restraining an overwhelming need to touch him."

She jumped, not only because she had company, but because her private thoughts had been intruded upon so accurately. When she turned, she discovered something even more unsettling.

Her tongue had tangled at the sight of Troy. What she was looking at now stole all words and left only incoherent need, strong enough to close her throat entirely, take her breath.

Yes, Troy was beautiful. Everything a virile young man should be. What was standing behind her was what such a young man could aspire to be, even though she expected few achieved it. It wasn't just this man's looks. It was everything beneath, the inside creating the outside.

Like Troy, he was six feet tall or better, with shoulders like what she'd imagined Troy's rounding out to with maturity. He wore jeans and workboots as well. The cotton shirt unbuttoned at his throat gave her a glimpse of curling chest hair. She saw Anglo-Saxon in the strong bones of his face, a large man with large hands, a commanding presence. The warm brown eyes that focused on her face held so many things . . . Standing inside that gaze, it would be impossible to feel anything bad, no heartache daring to intrude while she was under its spell. He was near, and that was all that was needed.

Okay, rein back the crazy and return to reality. He was close to forty, with gleaming, thick brown hair brushed back from that masculine face. It was long enough he had it tied back. She couldn't see how far it fell down his back, but the fact that he had it tied back suggested it went past his shoulders. She mocked men who wore long hair after they left their teens. It was pretentious and ridiculous, an attempt to hold on to vanishing youth. On him it looked right, a natural part of his persona, the way it would on a man born into a time period where long hair was the fashion. Vikings, seventeenth-century Scotland . . . It only enhanced his masculinity, the way it did a pirate or desert sheikh. She'd told Alice she loved that look in men—just not many men could pull it off.

He did.

For the second time today, she found herself caught simply staring, not responding like an articulate adult. She took an extra moment, struggling to recall his remarkable statement about Troy's beauty. Not the usual thing for a straight male to point out. "Are you two . . . together?"

The word trailed off as his gaze sharpened on her. Christ, even if Matthews was an annex of the urban Charlotte area, she was still technically in a small Southern town, not Boston. "I'm sorry. That was rude."

"Not where you're from, obviously." The trace of amusement in his brown eyes relaxed her, on that point at least. He crossed his arms and hooked his thumbs under his armpits, giving her a thorough perusal. "Down here, it's still like congratulating a woman on her pregnancy. If you're right and she is pregnant, all's good; if you're wrong, you're telling her she's fat."

He had a voice that could narrate books. Whether they were romances with quiet whispers in the dark, seafaring adventures that called for commanding roars or English mysteries needing a sexy, cultured tone with the right pauses for emphasis, his voice would hold attention, ears straining to catch every intonation.

He shrugged. "No, we're not together. And not just because you're my preference. I'm training him for someone else, in exchange for blatant exploitation. Home Depot has fifty thousand square feet, but I have Troy. The local ladies turned out in record numbers for my spring gardening sale. I even lured a healthy percentage of gay men away from the Depot's home décor offerings." He winked.

"Do you offer to let everyone touch him?" she asked.

"I wasn't offering that. Just observing how tempting it is to do so."

"Sounds like entrapment."

The brown eyes got warmer. "Spoken like a woman who knows the rules and rarely breaks them." He glanced at the box in her arms. "Is that for us?"

"Oh. Yeah, here."

"Since we share an address, deliveries sometimes get left at the wrong door. Sorry, I should have had you put this down right off. It's like a pile of bricks." He'd taken it from her as he spoke, moving behind the counter. She tried to keep her focus on his face, rather than the way the shirt strained over his broad shoulders. The temptation to reach out and touch the curls of coarse hair at his throat was making her fingertips tingle.

She cleared her throat. "I figured someone had sent you a cinder block."

Those attractive lips curved as he fished a box cutter out of a drawer and slit the box open. "Lead. We have customers who pour their own bullets for hunting, self-defense and historical reenactments, so I keep a supply, along with primers, powder and the like. But there should be something else in here." His expression brightened. "Right here on top."

He freed the item from the packaging with remarkable gentleness, revealing a set of antique gold metal hinges. "The supply house for bullet lead also does metal work?" she asked.

"They're an eclectic enterprise. A mom-and-pop place in Missouri. They even have a blacksmith who shoes horses and makes swords for Renaissance faires. I've been out there and visited. Almost bought an Excalibur replica, but decided on a good wood lathe. The lathe was cheaper."

She studied the engraved design on the hinges. It looked like barbed wire, but on closer inspection she assumed it was a vine of thorns, interspersed with tiny leaves and loops. "You don't usually see thorns without a rose."

"No, you don't. The potential of the thorns is often overlooked." He extended a hand. "Let me show you."

She curled her fingers together, uncertain, though she knew she was being foolish. She *was* intrigued, and she was in a public place. Still, she hedged at the physical contact. This guy was doing weird things to her. She needed to get back to her store. "Hand holding? We haven't even been introduced officially."

His gaze met hers. "I'm Logan Scott."

Trust Logan. Like you'd trust me. Or a soul mate.

This was the man who'd cared for her sister, all except those last three days. While she couldn't fathom why her sister had made sure they wouldn't meet until after she was gone, the knowledge of who he was now gave Madison the confidence to comply with his request. She put her hand in his.

His fingers closed around hers. She'd never thought of a man's touch as unforgettable, but she drew in a breath at the way it felt. Reassuring. Firm and strong. Something that would become a permanent craving if taken away.

"At last," he murmured. "We meet."